Praise for BLOOD ROSE

"Page's *Blood Rose* has scorching love scenes to make you sweat and an intriguing plot to hold it all together."

—*New York Times* best-selling author Hannah Howell, *Highland Savage*

"*Blood Rose* is an action-packed, sexy paranormal overflowing with suspense, horror, and romance. Sharon Page is a master of the menage—prepare to be seduced!"

—*USA Today* best-selling author Kathryn Smith

"Buffy the Vampire Slayer meets Regency England! Two sexy, to-die-for heroes, a courageous heroine, and a luscious ménage make *Blood Rose* a sinful treat."

—USA Today best-selling author Jennifer Ashley, *The Mad, Bad Duke*

BLOOD RED

"Wickedly sensual and exquisitely drawn. Historical erotic romance doesn't get any better than this."

—Kate Douglas, best-selling author of the Wolf Tales series

"A blazing path into forbidden dreams . . ."

—*Romantic Times*

"Sharon Page blends history, emotion, and hot, hot, hot sex within an amazing love story. Blazing erotica!"

—Kathryn Smith, *USA Today* best-selling author

"An erotic and suspenseful tale . . . puts you on a sexual roller coaster and doesn't let you off . . . if you're a lover of vampire romance, curl up on a cold winter night with *Blood Red* to warm your heart!"

—*Just Erotic Romance Reviews*

"Sinfully delicious. Sharon Pag

—Sunny, *New York Tim*

Over the Moon (anthol g

SIN

"How do you have an orgasm without sex? Read *Sin* by Sharon Page! Thoroughly wicked, totally wild, utterly wanton, and very witty, *Sin* is the ultimate indulgence."

—*Just Erotic Romance Reviews*

"Strong, character-driven romance . . . extremely sensual and erotic."

—*Romantic Times*

"Wonderful characterizations . . . and sultry, sexy love scenes will have you begging for more!"

—*Fallen Angels Reviews*

"*Sin* delivers sizzling sex and engaging characters in an erotic romp through Regency England. Irresistible temptation."

—Patricia Grasso, best-selling author

WILD NIGHTS

"*Wild Nights* delivers . . . wickedly hot sex, action, dominant males, and feisty heroines."

—*Coffee Time Romance*

"Page's story is sensual and sensitive."

—*Romantic Times* on *Wild Nights* anthology

A GENTLEMAN SEDUCED

"Sharon Page is a lady to watch out for. . . . Sharp, sexy, and will seduce you from the very first page."

—*Just Erotic Romance Reviews*

"Wicked, witty, and wonderful . . ."

—*Romantic Times*

BLOOD ROSE

SHARON PAGE

APHRODISIA

KENSINGTON PUBLISHING CORP.
http://www.kensingtonbooks.com

APHRODISIA BOOKS are published by

Kensington Publishing Corp.
850 Third Avenue
New York, NY 10022

All Kensington Titles, Imprints, and Distributed Lines are available at special quantity discounts for bulk purchases for sales promotions, premiums, fund-raising, and educational or institutional use.

Special book excerpts or customized printings can also be created to fit specific needs. For details, write or phone the office of the Kensington special sales manager: Kensington Publishing Corp., 850 Third Avenue, New York, NY 10022, attn. Special Sales Department, Phone: 1-800-221-2647.

ISBN-13: 978-0-7582-1544-4
ISBN-10: 0-7582-1544-4

First Trade Paperback Printing: August 2007

10 9 8 7 6 5 4 3 2 1

Printed in the United States of America

With many thanks to my wonderful critique group
(you know who you are)!

1

The Hunters

London, October 18th, 1818

Sex. She wanted sex. But she wanted this anticipation, too. Serena Lark stirred sensually on the bed, enjoying the feel of silky sheets beneath her bare skin.

A candle lit the room—it could only be one, for the light was weak and the candle must be close to guttering. Golden light wavered on the wall and danced with the reflections of silvery-blue moonlight.

Serena's hands skimmed her tummy and touched—boldly stroked—her cunny, which ached in delightful agony.

Shadows swept over her. She saw the sudden darkness cross her belly, and she looked up. Her heart hammered but she smiled a greeting at the two masked men who strolled arrogantly into her bedchamber. Lord Sommersby and Drake Swift—the Royal Society's two most famous and daring vampire hunters. Both men were dressed for the hunt, though masked, and they swept off their greatcoats as they crossed her threshold.

A gold mask framed Swift's glittering green eyes, and a deep royal purple mask clung to Lord Sommersby's face. Swift threw his hat aside, revealing his unfashionably long white-blond hair. He dropped a crossbow on the floor, followed by a sharpened wooden stake. He lifted a heavy silver cross from around his neck, let the chain pool on the floor and the cross fall with a clunk.

As dark as Swift was fair, his lordship gave a courtly bow and doffed his hat. Thick, glossy, and dark brown, his hair tumbled over his brow. Her breath caught at the heat in his eyes—the deep, delicious color of chocolate.

Serena crooked her finger and both men came to her, tugging their cravats loose as they prowled to her bed. They tore at their waistcoats, their shirts, and stripped to the waist. She could barely breathe as she drank in the sight of two wide chests. Swift's skin was bronzed to a scandalous shade, which brought the gold curls on his sculpted muscles into stark relief. The earl was massive, possessing a barrel chest and biceps as big as her thighs. He looked like a giant, one with a body honed by battle with the strongest creatures on earth.

She was dreaming. Even lost in it, she knew somehow. And in this dream, Serena had no idea what to say—what did one say when two men came to one's bed for the first time? Words seemed inane. She was most terribly shy. And as a governess, she'd been well trained to be a silent servant. But she gave a welcoming moan—the prettiest, most feminine one she could muster.

Tension ratcheted in her. Desire flared as the men approached. They would touch her. Her heart tightened with each long, slow step they took. *Yes. Yes!*

Laudanum. Even here, in her dream, she remembered the laudanum. A few swallows in her cup of tea because she couldn't sleep.

Mr. Swift paused to yank off his trousers, and he flung them aside as he stalked toward her, his ridged abdomen rippling. He wore no small clothes. His magnificent legs were formed of powerful muscle, lean and hard.

And his cock. Serena couldn't look away. It curved toward his navel, thick and erect and surrounded by white-blond curls. She knew it would fill her completely, stretch her impossibly, and she knew it would be perfect inside.

Mr. Swift reached the bed first. He smiled, his teeth a white gleam in the darkened room. His hand reached—she followed the arc of his fingers with breath held—and he touched her bare leg. *Oh!*

"Miss Lark." He dropped to one knee. "Let us dispense with the pleasantries and begin with the delights." And with that he parted her thighs and dove to her wet cunny.

Candlelight played over his broad, tanned shoulders and the large muscles of his arms. His tongue snaked out, slicked over her, and Serena arched her head back to scream to the ceiling.

So good!

Boot soles sharply rapped on the floor. Leather-clad knuckles gently brushed her cheek. Lord Sommersby. She flicked her eyelids open as Mr. Swift splayed his hands over her bottom, lifted her to his face, and slid his tongue as he tasted her intimate honey.

Lord Sommersby looked so serious, but he never smiled. He required encouragement so she held out her hand to him, but her smile vanished in a cry of shock and delight as Mr. Swift nudged her thighs wider, until her muscles tugged, and feasted on her. His lips touched her clit, the lightest brush, and pleasure arced through her. She tore the sheets with her fisted hands, heard silken seams rip.

Then squealed in frustration as Lord Sommersby lay his

strong hand on his partner's shoulder and wrenched Drake Swift from his work.

"She is a woman beyond your ken, Swift. A woman to be both pleasured and treasured."

Pleasured and treasured. Serena could not believe she'd heard those words from the cool, autocratic Earl of Sommersby's lips. He thoroughly disapproved of everything about her, didn't he?

And then the earl was gloriously nude. The hair on his chest was lush and dark, and the curls arrowed down his stomach into a thick, black nest between his thighs. His cock was straight and hard and remarkably fat, and it pointed downward, as though too heavy to stand upright.

A sweep of his lordship's arm and his rich purple mask flew aside, revealing dark brown eyes, narrowed with lust, and a predatory determination in his expression that made his fine features harsh. "Out of my way, Swift."

"I think the lady wants *me* to finish, Sommersby." With an insolent grin, Swift rolled back onto his lean stomach and lowered to her sex once more. She lost all her breath in a whoosh.

To have two such beautiful, naked men argue over which would lick her to ecstasy . . .

It was almost too much to bear.

Lord Sommersby bent and licked her nipples. Of course this was a dream, for she lifted her breasts saucily to the earl and spread her legs wider for Mr. Swift. His lordship sucked her nipple at the exact instant devilish Mr. Swift slid fingers in her cunny and—dear heaven—her rump.

Her heart pounded; her nerves were as taut as a harp's strings. "I will let you bed me," she gasped, "if you let me hunt with you."

Drake Swift laughed, and thrust *two* fingers in her quim and ass. "You were made for this, lass. For naughty fucking. Not for hunting vampires."

How illicit and wonderful it was to be filled, to feel invaded with each thrust of his fingers. Serena looked to Lord Sommersby.

"I would never risk your life," he said.

"But you know it is what I want most of all," she whispered.

"Is it?" Drake gave a roguish wink that set her heart spiraling in her chest.

In the blink of her dreaming imagination, both men were kneeling on the bed at her sides, looking down on her, their smiles hot and wild.

Mr. Swift's cock approached her mouth from the right, his lordship's from the left. The two huge, engorged heads met in the middle, touching right over her mouth.

Serena had never seen anything so erotic—so wildly arousing that she forgot about decorum, about bargaining, about hunting vampires.

What would if feel like to run her tongue around and between the two heads?

Their fluid was leaking together, making them deliciously wet and shiny—

What on earth was she doing? This was scandalous!

Her mouth opened to protest.

They moved to push their cocks in, parrying for position. Serena lost herself to the moment, shut her eyes, and stuck out her tongue—

Something sharp pricked her tongue. She pulled back, shocked by the pain, as thick liquid spilled into her mouth. Hot, with a strange yet impossibly familiar metallic taste.

Blood.

Icy horror snaked through her veins, and she forced her eyes open.

The men were gone. They'd vanished and a young girl sat on the bed in front of her. A child dressed in a fragile white nightdress with loose, tangled, golden hair.

Anne Bridgewater. Little Anne, who had died young—she

remembered holding Anne's cold hand, laying her face to the girl's quiet chest . . .

As though floating over the scene, she saw herself twine the blond hair around her wrist to expose Anne's slim neck. Anne cocked her head, and her sweet scent of youthful skin flooded Serena's senses. Pain lanced her jaw and fangs shot out.

She was a vampire! Serena tried to resist, tried to fight, but she saw herself press her pointed canines to the girl's fresh, clean skin. The pulse thrummed beneath, fervent and strong, and the rushing blood sang in her ears.

Against her will, she bent to the young girl's neck . . . but everything tilted and a sudden light poured into her room. Havershire Manor. She was in her old bedchamber, and Mrs. Thornton was tossing her half-packed case out the window while Mr. Thornton paced in front of the fire. Neither seemed to care that she wasn't wearing a stitch of clothing, and she desperately tried to cover her body with her long black hair.

"You are in love with her!" Mrs. Thornton screamed at her husband.

Serena fought to protest, but she could not force the words out. She had done nothing wrong . . . nothing but read poetry with Mr. Thornton, and walk with him, and fall in love with him . . . and let him kiss her once—but nothing more.

Mr. Thornton raked his hands through his hair. "The wretched girl bewitched me."

His wife wheeled around and pointed at Serena. Her triumphant laugh rang out around her. "You'll starve in a week, you little fool."

She woke on a scream. Serena found herself bolt upright, sheets tangled around her legs, sweat pouring between her breasts. She pressed the flannel to her skin to soak up the rivulets as she gulped down air.

Not again! So much for dosing herself with laudanum—it

hadn't helped at all. Foolishly, she ran her tongue over her teeth. No sharp points, of course. No fangs. And she had never, ever hurt Anne Bridgewater.

Serena kicked back the covers and jumped down from her bed. She rubbed at her eyes, scratchy with sleep. She hadn't slept properly for two months. Not since coming to London, meeting Althea—Lady Brookshire—and joining the Royal Society.

She flung open the velvet drapes. Her bedroom in Brookshire House overlooked Hyde Park. Beyond the line of trees, pink touched the sky, promising dawn. How could she look upon the rising sun if she were a vampire? How could she stand in the sunlight?

But the erotic dreams of the magnificent Lord Sommersby and that enticing rogue Drake Swift—didn't they prove she was not a normal, proper Englishwoman?

She leaned against the window, staring out at the shadowy green park. She had promised she would not give in to her baser nature this time. Twice she had fallen in love and she'd ended up in disaster. She thought she'd loved William Bridgewater, Anne's older brother. He'd come to her bedroom, kissed her senseless, and she wanted him. Wanted him with the same urgent fiery need she felt in these dreams. And that need had got her banished from the house. Then there had been Mr. Thornton, and his poetry, his brooding pain as they walked together, his stories of his wife's madness and rejection. She, the simple governess, had fallen deeply, impossibly in love—

She was never going to do that again. She could never do that again.

With the daylight spilling over her, Serena folded her arms beneath her breasts and paced to her bedside table. She slid open the drawer and drew out the small stack of folded pages. The edges were torn and curled and smudged by tearstains.

My dearest A,

I am writing to express my fears in regard to the behavior of S.L. She shows an unhealthy interest in men; she is brazen and wanton and disobedient. Often she slips out of her room at night, and returns only at dawn. One afternoon, a fortnight prior to my writing here, S.L. pricked her finger on a rose's thorn. She put the wound to her mouth and suckled—not of great concern perhaps—but I saw her return to the same place in the garden the next afternoon, deliberately wound her finger, and delight in suckling the blood from her flesh—

I greatly fear that your concerns are quite accurate estimations of the truth. You do see, do you not, why I beseech you to bring her to London, to keep her under your watchful eye? Dear Anne is devoted to her and the child is fragile and impressionable. I am not at all certain how to proceed—I have raised S.L. as a daughter, but she is not normal. Subhuman, in my opinion, and I fear, a danger to us all—

I must fervently await your reply,

Yours in devotion and admiration unsurpassed,
Mrs. Ariadne Bridgewater.

Every instinct inside her yearned to rip the words to shreds. But she couldn't do that—she needed these copies she'd made. There'd been so many of these letters, written to *dearest A.* She'd found them last week, neatly filed away in chronological order, in one of the bookcases in the Society's vast library. Letters written by Mrs. Bridgewater, the woman who gave her food, shelter, the woman who had raised her—the only "mother" she had ever known. A "mother" who thought her subhuman.

Who thought her a vampire.

Serena tipped her face to the weak strands of daylight, closed her eyes. Still hazy from the opiate, she struggled with the questions that plagued her day after day. "Dearest A" was the elderly Earl of Ashcroft—the most powerful man of the Royal Society for the Investigation of Mysterious Phenomena.

To think she'd believed every word of Lord Ashcroft's story when he'd brought her to London two months ago. To think she'd believed he would teach her to slay vampires. *A tragic secret has been hidden from you, Miss Lark . . . the truth is that vampires killed your parents . . . but I will help you learn the truth, if you serve the Society.*

Lies. All lies. She'd been so thrilled to come to London, to stay with Lord and Lady Brookshire, to join the Royal Society. Ashcroft must have known she had been tossed out of the Thorntons' home without a reference and had no place to go.

Worse, her parents hadn't been killed by vampires. The letters had made it clear. Serena's throat closed. She shuffled through the copies she had made but didn't look down at the words. She didn't need to; she'd cried over them so often the words were burned in her head. *I suppose this is exactly the kind of behavior we should expect,* Mrs. Bridgewater had written, *from the daughter born of a vampire and a mortal.*

Serena shoved the letters back into the drawer and shut it tight.

What did Lord Ashcroft want with her? Why had he kept her alive?

Was he waiting—waiting to see if she changed?

Would she? For all the books in the library she'd pored over, she didn't know. She didn't know if she could start out as a mortal and become a vampire without being bitten.

Serena stalked back to the window and pulled the curtains shut, filled with a sense of purpose. She was not going to wait; she would not be meek and docile and simmer in fear. If she wanted the truth she would have to bargain for it. And the journal of Vlad Dracul would be a temptation Lord Ashcroft wouldn't be able to resist. Once she had it, she would trade it for the truth about her parents, the truth about herself. And her life, God willing.

All she had to do was break into the brothel to find the journal. It was a deadly risk, but worth it. She had to find out the truth.

Was she the child of a vampire or not?

2

Bound

"I do love a woman in stockings and garters."

Serena smiled dreamily as the seductive male voice, strangely accented, murmured teasingly close to her ear. Large hands skimmed up her calves, brushing over silky stockings, reaching her ruched garters . . .

Hands? Her garters?

Serena's eyes snapped open. This was no naughty dream, and this was certainly not her bedchamber. *Where was she?*

The hands moved away. Dark—fathomless dark—surrounded her, and though she could not see, she knew the man—a real man, not a fantasy—still stood somewhere beside her. She felt the stirring of air across her skin, across everywhere—arms, thighs, belly, even breasts. She *was* naked! Except for her lower legs. The silkiness of her stockings touched her calves, and her garters bit into her legs. Her slippers were still on her feet.

Her head felt groggy, as though sheep's wool stuffed it full, and a faint, sickly sweet scent teased her nose.

"Indeed," agreed a different male voice. "A woman in stockings and garters and not a stitch else."

A second man! Serena bit back a cry. He was somewhere in the dark, and he spoke with the sensual tones of the Italian tongue.

Goosebumps raced over her skin. She became aware of the tug in her muscles, the awkward position of her limbs, the sensation of being stretched apart.

Panic knifed through her. She was spread-eagled on a hard surface, her wrists and ankles firmly secured by—she shifted, slightly, felt the cool bite of metal against her skin—shackles.

She was captured.

The brothel. With a jolt of fear, Serena remembered the ornate doors facing Jermyn Street and the face that had leered out at her through the iron grill. A beefy footman with a thick neck and a scowl. He had taken a long look down her low bodice before ushering her inside. Laughter, smoke, heavy perfume—and a rich, ripe aroma she knew was the smell of sex. Lovely, seductive women had boldly flirted with many handsome, dangerous vampires. Gentlemen, to all outward appearances, but with one look she'd known they were Nosferatu.

Serena pulled again at her bonds as her blood ran ice cold. She was bound. Naked. In the dark. With vampires.

They had to know she was no courtesan, even though she'd been disguised as one. They had her clothes. In the sleeves of her scarlet gown, she'd tucked stakes. Down her bodice, she'd slipped a slim dagger and a vial of holy water. In the cavernous pocket of her skirt, she'd hidden a clever folding crossbow.

She had no weapons now. No mask. Nothing but her wits.

Why had they not killed her already?

"She is exquisite, is she not? And now, she is awake." Deep, silky, the first vampire's baritone voice compelled her to listen. Heat coursed through her blood at the sound of his voice. She knew, if he chose to, the vampire could incite carnal desire with just the whisper of his voice.

"Good evening, beautiful one," the Italian male's voice called cheerfully.

"What the . . . the hell do you think you are doing?" Serena cried out. She winced at the warble in her words. She had to sound fearless—like the most arrogant of the male slayers of the Royal Society—the commanding, autocratic Earl of Sommersby. Or like Drake Swift, all piss and vinegar and deadly confidence. "Let me go, damn you!"

Boot soles scraped across wood. Even in the dark, the vampires could see her every movement. Her expressions. Her nakedness.

If only she could conjure Mr. Swift or Lord Sommersby to her side now as easily as she did in her dreams.

"Don't come near me!" She tried to wrench back. It was impossible. Clanks and rattles answered her frantic motions as the chains slapped the surface.

A third male spoke. "Light a candle. *Mon dieu,* the lady is at a disadvantage."

And in response, yet more men laughed.

Her heart stopped for dizzying moments. How many could there be?

Fury and frustration and fear rushed through her. All she'd wanted was to find Dracul's journal—she'd believed it had been worth risking her life for.

What a fool she'd been.

She fought rising panic—otherwise she had no hope of escape. Vampires behaved like a wolf pack. They would obey their leader. She'd been a governess, she'd dealt with undisciplined boys. She must pretend these dangerous demons were merely naughty schoolboys.

One of the vampires was still at her side, she realized. Even though he stood motionless, silent, she knew he was there. She knew his hands were above her face. There was no light, not even a hint of it at a draped window, and her eyes had not become accustomed. The room was hot, completely black, and that cloying, pungent scent filled her head . . .

She would have guessed the smell was solange . . .

When the oil of the solange flower was burned, the fumes would capture a vampire in a trancelike state. The undead would not burn solange. It was too dangerous for them. This must be a drug, an Eastern drug.

Or had they burned it because they sensed she was a vampire?

Even as the horrifying thought gripped her, Serena pushed it away. Why would they risk destroying themselves to subdue her?

The floor creaked, cloth whispered, and she turned toward the sound, staring into blackness. Air brushed her face. He was going to touch her!

"My name is Roman." It was the owner of the first voice, the darkly sensual baritone. A sharp fingernail rasped along her lower lip, and she froze. Her lip tingled at the touch, the sensation horrifyingly erotic. Desperate to escape it, she turned her head, but his hand followed. The nail gently punctured, and she gasped at the shock of pain. Warm wetness touched her lip. A droplet of blood. She flicked it away with her tongue. Quickly. Hopelessly.

The taste exploded upon her tongue, coppery and tart.

Delight flooded her at the taste. No! It was disgusting.

. . . deliberately wound her finger, and delight in suckling the blood from her flesh . . . Mrs. Bridgewater's damning words floated into her head. Surely she hadn't done that. She didn't remember doing that.

The nail brushed again, and Serena held herself rigid, afraid he would deeply slice her lip this time. Yet she wanted to lift her face to him. She wanted the prick of pain. Wanted more of the taste of her blood—

Roman's clawlike nails traced her skin again, and a jolt of pleasure and pain arced through her. Was he compelling her to want this or did hot need race through her blood because she was a vampire?

"Stop, Roman." It was the Italian. "She belongs to the master."

All her breath left her chest as Roman did lift his hands away. She heard his hiss of anger. She had a reprieve, but for how long? Minutes? Hours? Roman served a master—only a powerful demon could control a pack of vampires. A master's disciples would not dare disobey him.

Deep and mocking, Roman's voice vibrated through the dark. "Just a caress, Leonardo. A taste of perfection. Lukos would not condemn me for a touch."

Lukos? She now knew the name of his master. Lukos, the Greek word for wolf.

Fear sliced through her.

A spot of light flared, then flamed high. The scent of burning wax overwhelmed the drifting odor of the drug. Tallow. Strong. The candle sputtered, the glow radiated.

She blinked until her eyes stopped watering. Her lashes were wet, glued together by tears. The first things she saw were Roman's hands, resting on a band of polished wood. She lay on green fabric. Something clicked over in her mind.

She was chained to a billiard table.

A soft male voice seemed to whisper in her mind, a charming Irish voice. "Such a lovely lass—her skin is the color of pale champagne."

Serena jerked toward the voice. She saw the others in the light now. Candle glow touched the pale, austere faces of two men sprawled on a sofa and two who lounged in club chairs. White shirts and cravats gleamed, and the light sparkled at the tips of long, sharp fangs. Their eyes—their dark, soulless, eyes—were shadowed and hidden to her.

She was the captive of six vampires.

"You are wondering why we haven't drunk from you, aren't you?" Roman asked, his voice so compelling she couldn't help but turn to him.

He was shirtless, his chest as pale as marble even in the golden light. Dark hair dusted smooth, powerful muscle. His hair fell in long, thick, black waves. She looked up higher, caught her breath. He was smirking down at her, impudent, confident, but the innocence in his face shocked her. He looked barely twenty years of age and beautiful, with a full-lipped, lush mouth, high cheekbones, straight white teeth, large mirror-like eyes of silvery blue. But he was not innocent.

"Unlock me!" she demanded. "You have fallen into a trap."

"A trap, my dear?" Roman crossed his arms across his chest. His biceps bulged, solid and enormous.

Never once had she successfully bluffed her charges as a governess, but she couldn't give in now. She watched Roman stalk along the length of the table toward her bound feet. She knew her eyes were wide, dilated, like those of mesmerized prey, but she replied, "Of course," with the lazy disdain the male vampire hunters used.

Low, throaty, damning, Roman's laugh washed over her.

He touched the chain securing her right foot, running his fingertips along the taut links. The cuff vibrated against her ankle. *I know you are here alone, my dear.* His voice resonated inside her mind.

She should try to block out his voice in her head—but she had to listen, had to know what he planned to do. So she could outthink him.

She saw the swift movement of Roman's hand, the blur of it in the corner of her eye. He cupped her right ankle just above the cuff. His caress was gentle against the frail silk of her stocking. Serena swallowed a cry of surprise so abruptly she almost choked.

Wrenching her leg, she tried to pull away from his hand, but the chains restrained her. Her skin tingled beneath the web of silk as he traced his finger over her ankle and up along her calf.

"Roman, release her."

The command came from the second vampire—the one named Leonardo. He prowled toward her. She stared helplessly at his tousled dark curls, almond shaped eyes of deep black, and cupid's bow lips. He possessed the beautiful, symmetrical features of an Old Master's portrait, but she knew he was a ruthless predator. A cape shrouded him; the black collar points grazed the deep hollows beneath high cheekbones.

A hazy memory returned. She remembered looking into that face in the brothel—he had stepped out of a doorway and grabbed her as she'd reached the hallway that took her to the basement staircase. His triumphant laugh echoed in her memories. There'd been a sharp pain in her neck, then blackness—had one of them bitten her to make her faint?

Such beautiful legs, Roman murmured. *I would love to have your ankles wrapped around my neck.*

"Don't touch me!"

But Roman ignored both her and Leonardo with a mocking laugh. Her heart pounded so loud it was like a drumbeat by her ear, but at the sound of his enthralling voice, her quim throbbed like a pulse.

I know what you are, Serena Lark, Roman said in her thoughts.

How could he know her name?

Because we have watched you for a long time now, Serena. Waited for you to be alone, away from the slayers.

Somehow she had pushed her thoughts into his mind. It froze her as much as his words in response. But she must continue to speak with him this way, despite the danger—if she allowed him into her thoughts, he could gain control of her mind. *W-why? What do you want?*

"Come on, gentlemen," Roman urged aloud, and he squeezed her calf possessively before moving his hand away. "Introduce yourselves."

Leonardo flashed a glare at Roman, his narrow eyes glittering in the candlelight. But he sketched a bow over her shackled hand and murmured his name.

The other men stood and took bows in turn.

"Liam," announced the lilting Irish voice.

"Brittan."

"Aristide."

"Guillaime." The French voice she had heard before.

Roman flashed a cocky grin at Leonardo, even as he spoke in her head. *They are dutiful servants, here to fetch you for Lukos. They are slaves—slaves when they were mortal, slaves now.* Disdain dripped from Roman's voice in her thoughts. His eyes grew brighter, as though a flame burned behind them. *They have no idea what you are. How valuable you are.*

Roman intended to betray his master. She could not believe it—a disciple always obeyed his master. Could she use this to escape?

Roman flicked out his tongue, his long, pointy tongue. Bending, he licked the inside of her leg. She pulled away hard. The chains rattled, but she could only move an inch. And with a low chuckle, he followed and licked again. Slowly, sensuously, he laved his way up to her garter. *I know how very special you are, Miss Lark. The child of a vampire. And if you wish to survive, you will do as I say. Can you still smell the solange, Serena? Obey me or I will drain your sweet blood and rip out your throat.*

Her head roared as Roman's lips neared her bare skin—

He was jerked away, and he sailed backward. He slammed into the wall, cracking the plaster. Serena held her breath as he lurched forward. Snarling, he flashed his fangs at Leonardo, who shrugged and adjusted his cuffs with the grace of a London dandy. "If you disobey Lukos, you will be destroyed."

With infinite grace, Leonardo paced to her side. His look of reverent obedience turned her stomach. "You will delight in your submission to the master, Miss Lark. He only wishes you to know pleasure, to know the joy of serving at his side."

"Unlock me." she cried. "I cannot know pleasure like this. How could you fear me? All of you against a m-mortal woman?"

"It is the master's command that you be bound," the French vampire, Guilliame, called from his chair.

"You have no minds of your own?" she goaded.

Roman swaggered back to the end of the table. "My dear, I could make you beg me to do anything I wish to you. And I will prove it." His gaze swept over her—it felt as though ants crawled over her.

"Do not touch her," Leonardo warned.

It was working. She had managed to pit them against each other. Vampires were . . . beasts. All she had to do was prod them enough to make them fight. Serena took a deep breath and called out, "Are you too cowardly to take a risk?"

Roman shoved Leonardo back. He reached to the cuff at her wrist. Victory! It was not locked, only had a closed hasp, and this he flicked open with his thumb. He freed both hands, then her feet.

Desperately she rubbed her wrists and squeezed her hands tight to bring feeling back. She rotated her feet but had no idea if they moved. She was free but still trapped, still shockingly nude.

It was a struggle, but she managed to sit up, and she covered her naked breasts with her tingling hands.

Roman reached for her leg—she lashed out with her foot, and he caught it and kissed the lacy trim on the top of her stocking. She clawed at his back, as his tongue slid from silk stocking to bare flesh. That touch—that warm, wet tongue against her skin—

Sensation screamed through her.

Her anguished cry electrified the room. The heightened sexual arousal of the vampires hit her like a wave of water.

You have incited them too much, my dear, Roman warned.

Her fingernails gouged into his shoulders, but she couldn't push him away. The four vampires stood from the sofa and advanced. Serena saw their chests rise and fall with their deep, heavy breaths. A generous splash of holy water might drive them back, but her vial was gone.

They surrounded her—Roman and Leonardo at each side, two at the top of the billiard table, and two stopped at her feet.

Roman lifted his head from her thigh. "Go to the brothel!" he shouted. "Amuse yourselves there. I will attend to Miss Lark."

But the two vampires at her feet stripped off coats, waistcoats. Both were blond—one had dirty wheat-blond hair captured in many long braids; the other's mane of gold was waist length and loose. The golden blond opened his shirt, threw it aside. The sudden violence of the motion stopped Serena's heart for dizzying moments.

She had to think—think of a way out! Knowledge was her only hope. "W-when is your master to come for me?" she stuttered. "Tonight?"

"He sails." The curt words had come from Roman.

From the continent. On a ship of innocents. No doubt they would all arrive dead, the poor helpless souls.

Roman crossed his arms over his chest. Of all of them, he had the most powerful chest, the broadest shoulders, the biggest biceps. Power and menace. Veins snaked up his huge forearms. Had he been a soldier, turned in battle? The most brutal warriors of the past made the wildest, most uncivilized vampires.

"You are aroused and you need to feed," he shouted at the others. "Go to the whorehouse and find your pleasures there. No one is allowed to touch her."

Cursing, the other vampires nodded in obedience, and Serena felt a surge of relief. Left alone with Roman, surely she could escape—

But he turned to her and leered. *You have never been bitten, have you?* He opened his trousers.

Held in thrall by his gleaming eyes, she crawled back along the table—

The door exploded into the room. The thick slab of wood hit the wall with the crack of a gunshot. Deafening. Paralyzing. Light flooded in, silhouetting two men in the doorway.

The sharp, crisp twang of crossbow fire sliced the sudden silence. Horrified shrieks rang in her head as Brittan and Aristide fell. Roman spun toward the door, his mouth open in fury, his jaw wrenched wide. His fangs flashed. Before her eyes, he arched back, his head snapping with a crack. Blood launched from his chest. A silver arrow, tipped in blood and gore, tore out of his chest. *Below* his heart.

Roman screamed in rage, and she flinched as he jumped up on the table. His powerful legs straddled her. Tangled and wild, his hair hung around him. Blood poured down his bare chest, dripped onto his hard, clublike cock, which swayed above her. A demonic red fire burned in his eyes. *Come with me, Serena. Come to me.*

He reached down.

Like hell. Serena kicked upward, aiming for his ballocks. She missed. Her heel harmlessly smacked against his thigh and skidded away. Roman launched forward, in a kind of sailing flip, and he hit the wall feet first. Impossibly, the wall gave way, a panel opening for him like a door, and, in midair, Roman vanished. His trousers and boots dropped empty to the floor. A huge black bat soared into the black opening and disappeared. Roman had shifted shape.

The Irish vampire, Liam, leapt on the table, his auburn hair flapping.

She kicked at him, but Liam lashed out at her with his foot. His boot struck her hand, enough to jar her shoulder and send agony screaming through her arm. Damn him. Instinct made her grab. Her damp, aching fingers held fast to smooth leather as she clung to his boot. He could shift shape and fly away, but she held on.

Another man jumped up on the table—he grabbed Liam by the hair and hauled him back. One hard thrust of the slayer's arm and he drove a stake through the vampire's heart from the back. A toss and Liam tumbled to the ground. Slain.

Her savior caught her gaze and grinned. His blond hair—startling white-blond hair—swung free and wild around his face. His green eyes flashed with excitement. And then he glanced lower and winked.

Drake Swift. Drake Swift and Lord Sommersby had come to her rescue.

A silk robe flew at her.

Swift caught it.

"Cover her!" The command could only have come from his lordship. Humiliation, frustration, and fear burned through her. Mr. Swift and Lord Sommersby had laughed at her determination to become a vampire hunter. She'd planned so carefully, yet she'd made a mistake and proved them right.

And if they knew that she was a vampire, they would stake her. Kill her.

It was too late to even pretend she was in control. She was shaking. Mr. Swift was sweating from the fight, his platinum hair damp with it, his handsome features gleaming. Towering above her, he looked like an avenging angel. He dropped the robe over her. But he was distracted for the moment, and out of the shadows, Guillaime lunged, fangs bared.

The scream died in Serena's throat as Guillaime plunged his teeth into Drake Swift's neck.

3

Destined

Serena rolled down the billiard table, toward Guillaime's outstretched legs. Toward his dangling ballocks. This time she wouldn't miss. She slammed her foot up and connected, driving her heel hard into his most sensitive place.

The vampire jerked, flinched, but his hands clamped tightly on Mr. Swift's broad shoulders.

Mr. Swift snapped his head to the side. "Christ Jesus! Thank you, sweetheart, but he's plunged deeper!"

Blood rolled down Mr. Swift's neck. Rivulets of it, racing over his tanned-bronze skin, soaking into his pristine white collar, into his cravat and coat. He flicked his arm and a sharpened stake slid into his hand.

Serena kicked again to divert the vampire's attention as Mr. Swift gripped the stake. It worked—Guillaime kicked out at her. His foot slammed into her ribs before she could roll. The wind flew from her lungs. She couldn't breathe. Whimpering against her will, Serena tensed for the next blow.

"Stay down, Miss Lark," Sommersby commanded. He trained a crossbow on Guilliame. Her heart pounded furiously, in panic for Swift, while his lordship adjusted his aim, his movements calm and controlled. With a flick of his hand, he fired, and the bolt raced toward them. Instinctively she shut her eyes. She heard Guillaime's shriek as the bolt drove through his heart. He fell away from Mr. Swift's neck, crumpled to the table. She had enough breath to push herself away as his body dropped. For a brief moment she was in free fall. Then the floor greeted her with a smack. Her teeth rattled. Her head seemed to separate from her neck and then snap back with a shattering pain.

She craned her neck, though it hurt like the devil to do it. Aristide and Brittan sprawled, slain, on the floor. Liam and Guilliame were destroyed. Roman was gone. Where was Leonardo?

"Bastard!" Mr. Swift shouted. "Two escaped. Damn them to hell! I've never lost a bloody vampire before."

She didn't care that they weren't destroyed. She was safe.

Or was she? Why were the hunters here? What did they *know* about her?

"Miss Lark?"

Elegant black-clad fingers brushed her tangled hair back. A face came into view—one surrounded by tousled hair the color of coffee. Lord Sommersby bent over her, and she gazed up into compelling and worried dark brown eyes, fringed by the longest lashes she'd ever seen.

"My—my lord." She must have clutched the robe as she fell off the table. It had landed with her, and now she was wrapped in it, so she was covered at least.

"God—" Sommersby abruptly drew back. His mouth became a grim line—he had a beautiful mouth, wide, firm. Quite unlike Mr. Swift's, which was pouting, boyish, and heartwrenchingly sensual. "You almost got yourself killed, you little fool."

"I am *not* a little fool." Defying the throbbing pain in her skull, Serena sat up. She held the silk robe to her chest, and though she fumed at his arrogant tone, she prayed Lord Sommersby's only thought was—*how could this silly little governess imagine herself to be a vampire slayer?* She prayed he didn't know the truth.

She cast a horrified look to Mr. Swift. He stood on the table, his hand at the wound on his neck.

He grinned down at her. "A flea bite, love. I've had worse. I'll live."

Sommersby's hand shot out, and his fingers wrapped around her wrist. His touch was gentle as he traced the red marks there. "What did they do to you?"

The soft stroke of his lordship's thumb sent a warm tingle through her. She intended to tell him, but she knew she had to lie, and her lips trembled as she met his astute, penetrating gaze.

Fool! She could not cry—and she knew how to fight tears. All her years as an unwanted ward and then a dutiful servant had taught her that. How odd that curbing emotion to be a gray and invisible governess had been the perfect education for a vampire huntress.

She pulled her hand away.

"There's a passageway on the other side of the wall and stairs leading underground to a tunnel." The table creaked and groaned, and then Mr. Swift jumped down. "I can't believe demons escaped me."

Mr. Swift dropped into a crouch at her side as Sommersby stood. His thighs bunched, solid and powerful. Serena looked up into green eyes—darkly lashed green eyes. The lashes dipped. She saw pained concern. She had never seen Mr. Swift look worried—she had never seen him without his cocky confidence.

"Why did you come to this place?" The growl was Lord Sommersby, now pacing, as he raked his fingers through his hair.

She couldn't tell his lordship she feared she was the first child of a vampire. That Lord Ashcroft—his commander—had lied to her. That she needed the Vlad Dracul journal to *black-*

mail the arrogant lord who controlled the Royal Society and force him to give her the truth about her past.

Lord Sommersby turned on his heel. "You haven't answered my question, Miss Lark."

"Leave her alone, *milord.*" Mr. Swift snarled the title. "The little lark has had a bad fright. She doesn't need your questions."

Little lark? Yet the name sent warmth to her heart. Mr. Swift moved his arms around her and leaned gently against her from behind. The satin of his waistcoat brushed her back. Smooth leather—the gloves covering his palms—skimmed down her arms. He was cradling her! "There's nothing to fear now."

"Thank you, Mr. Swift, but I am able to withstand his lordship's examination." She hoped. She knew she should draw away from Swift's touch, but she couldn't. Straining, she kept her voice even and cool. "I came to find vampires, my lord. I am training to be a vampire slayer, after all."

"You did not have permission to come here. You are not yet a vampire slayer." Sommersby crossed his arms over his chest, frowning. The earl stood six and a half feet tall—with enormous shoulders, massive arms, a huge chest.

Serena tipped up her chin in answer to his glare, aware she was cradled close to Drake Swift. "I did not require your permission."

"Yes, you do, Miss Lark. You are an apprentice member of the Royal Society."

"You can give me any punishment you wish, my lord, but I'd do it again. I am not a servant any longer."

Swift's low, dangerous laugh rumbled from behind her. "You are always a servant, love," he said. "In the Royal Society, everyone is a servant to some master."

Sommersby shot him a dark look before returning his disapproval to her. "You risk all hunters by such a foolish mission, Miss Lark," he said.

"I do know what to do. I came very well armed."

"And a lot of good it did you. You have read books. It is an entirely different matter to hunt a vampire."

"What I would like to know is where I am now," she said. "And I would like to know where my clothes are."

But Sommersby ignored her question. He dropped to one knee before her and caught hold of her wrist again. In a throaty growl, he urged, "Tell me what they did to you. Why did they not bite you?"

Sommersby began to stroke her sensitive wrist. Mr. Swift was caressing the bare skin of her shoulders with the familiarity of a lover. Serena gulped, her throat tight. She was reliving every dream she'd ever had about these two hunters. She was so dangerously aware. Aware of the weight of their hands on her skin, aware of the tang of male sweat, the sharpness of their breathing.

How could she explain why the vampires hadn't bitten her, the way they would any victim?

"You do not have to answer his questions," Swift urged.

"I can." She tightened her grip on the robe, knowing her cheeks were pink. "They chained me to the table. They said they were saving me for their master, whom they called Lukos. That is why they didn't bite me, or . . . or attack me. He is supposed to be sailing to England."

"You are very brave," Mr. Swift murmured. "Now you should put that robe on properly. I fear it might fall down at any moment. No more blasted questions, Sommersby."

His lordship glowered, but he inclined his head, let go of her wrist, and stood up. "For the moment," he agreed. "Put the robe on, Miss Lark."

She cast a nervous glance at the door. "We are in a vampires' brothel. Others must have heard the attack—"

"We aren't in the brothel. You have enough time to dress." Mr. Swift assured. "We'll give you privacy, my dear." He bent closer. His warm breath danced over her neck. She was chilled—trembling. The heat in his breath felt so good.

"Then where are we—?" she broke off. For one mad moment, she felt Mr. Swift was leaning in to kiss. She'd been kissed on her neck before—it was a touch that made her wanton. That sweet, intoxicating drug still filled her senses, made her feel sensual. Her nipples were erect, and the brush of silk against them made her dizzy.

Her wantoness frightened her. *Vampires* had uncontrollable sexual cravings.

"How did you escape the chains, love?" Mr. Swift's voice was gentle and reassuring.

Serena twisted around to meet his brilliant green eyes. "I convinced them to release me."

"Convinced them? Bravo." With that, Mr. Swift moved back. The heat of his chest left her, and goosebumps rushed over her shoulders, down her arms.

He straightened in a smooth, graceful movement, turned his back, and prowled toward the one burning candle. Serena tried to stand, but her legs felt like mist. Lord Sommersby reached down and caught her hand—his gloved hands were larger than any man's hands she'd ever seen. His lordship helped her up without a word, then turned his back.

Serena held the robe against her, vainly searching for the sleeves to slide her arms in. Finally, with a sigh, she grasped it by the neckline, let it drop, and then swept it around her body. But both men behaved as gentleman, not even taking a peek—Sommersby was closing the door, Drake Swift searching the room.

The silk enveloped her—the robe was enormous. It smelled clean—freshly laundered. She was so relieved at that.

But she'd failed. She'd be hauled out of here—wherever here was—naked beneath a borrowed robe.

Swift strolled over toward her. "No sign of your clothes, love." His gaze swept over her—over the swell of her breasts, the belt at her waist, her hips swathed in sapphire silk—and flame touched her skin in its wake.

"Miss Lark?" Lord Sommersby gently jostled her arm. He'd returned to her side.

"I want to know exactly where I am!" She turned from Swift to Sommersby. "Not in the brothel, you said."

"No—in an empty house beside." His dark eyes narrowed. "You don't remember, do you?"

Her cheeks burned. "Fine! I'll admit it. I barely remember anything after being let into the brothel. I have no idea what went wrong." She tried to jerk her arm from the Earl of Sommersby's grasp, but he held firm. "But you, of course, were able to infiltrate the brothel, then find me, without any trouble at all, I suppose. And how did you do that?"

"Skill and experience." Sommersby replied, and condescension hung in the room like smoke.

She gritted her teeth. "And how did you even know to come here?"

"Mortimer. He mentioned you had been researching this brothel."

She had pleaded with the Society's librarian for his discretion—he'd obviously ignored her. It was infuriating that her wishes had been discounted, though it had saved her life.

"You were engaged to assist in research, Miss Lark," Sommersby said. "Not to steal stakes and crossbows and plant yourself in a brothel surrounded by aroused vampires."

"Let her alone," Mr. Swift growled.

But she was too angry to cower. "I was engaged to do nothing more than return books to shelves!"

The earl shook her arm. "What is it you want here? What did you come for?"

She glanced from his lordship's intense dark eyes to Swift's emerald ones. She must convince them to help her—without revealing exactly what she wanted. "I discovered there are journals kept here—kept in a hidden library beneath the brothel. The writings of vampires—writings that detail everything about their existence. And I am not leaving without searching for it."

Sommersby frowned. "You should have told the Society about this discovery."

"And have them take all those books and lock them away from me? The precious Society will not allow a mere woman to read their most important works."

"You want to know who killed your parents."

"Of course! Wouldn't you, if you were in my shoes?" Serena's heart thundered. She had to ensure his lordship and Mr. Swift continued to believe Lord Ashcroft's lie about her parents' death. "The gossip is that you still search for the vampire who killed your fiancée, my lord. That you are driven by vengeance."

"Don't listen to gossip," he snapped.

"Guilt, my dear." Drake Swift laughed. "Guilt keeps him in his laboratory all day and hunting all night."

"Vengeance is a waste of a life." Lord Sommersby grasped her elbow. His fingers wrapped firmly around her arm, promising power.

"I am *not* leaving without finding the library," she repeated.

Drake Swift gave a wild grin. "You want moldy old books, I want to destroy vampires." He winked. "You do want to return to the brothel, don't you, my dear?"

His hand cupping Miss Lark's delicate elbow, Jonathon Lyon, Earl of Sommersby, shot a glare at his partner. "We cannot just walk through a brothel to chase vampires. And we cannot bring her."

"I hate to let a demon get away clean. Spoils the record,"

Swift complained as he sauntered toward the fallen vampires by the billiard table.

Swift's perfect kill record. Tonight would be the first night in years that a vampire escaped him. Of course they'd had the distraction of a very naked, very lovely damsel in distress—

"The library," Miss Lark insisted as she tried once again to tear free of his grip. "I am not leaving without trying to find it."

Jonathon's patience was at its end, but he let her elbow go. He was squeezing too hard; he'd left faint bruises. Goddamn his unwieldy hands. "We aren't searching every room of a bawdyhouse to find a library that may not exist."

"It does exist. After all, I am skilled at *research.* I pieced together a plan of this brothel—"

The word *brothel* on Serena Lark's full lips shot a bolt of forbidden desire through Jonathon. The memory of her curvaceous naked body on the billiard table made him hard. He wasn't a gentleman who sought perverted diversions, but that sudden forbidden image had him aching.

He moved to stand between her and her view of Drake Swift, who was dealing with the fallen vampires.

Gritting his teeth, he snapped, "Forget the books, Miss Lark. I intend to get you to safety." But he couldn't stop himself from lifting Miss Lark's bare hand. He touched his mouth to the red mark on her wrist, to the bruising there. A trace of rose scent from her silken skin fought with the smell of vampires' drugs.

He released her hand. The taste of her skin made him yearn to taste more—her lips, her throat, and lower . . . to the sweet curves of her breasts, belly, and her hot, honey-drenched quim.

Hell, Jonathon knew exactly why he desired her so much. Why his need for her bordered on madness. He wanted her because Serena Lark was a vampire's child, destined to transform into a vampiress on her twenty-fifth birthday—on All Hallow's Eve. She already possessed a succubus's magic allure that drew men to her—and she had no idea what she was.

Damn Ashcroft for assigning him to this mission.

Her beseechingly innocent eyes widened with desperation. "I can't forget the books. I need to see them. *You* should understand, my lord. I need to know who—what—killed my parents."

You should understand. The familiar coldness touched his heart. The hell of it was that he couldn't summon a memory of Lilianne's face. He wanted vengeance for her death because it had become a mission to him, but his anger, his hatred, the pain of lost love had long since died. All he had left was cold guilt.

"I do know what it feels like," he said. "And that's the very reason, my dear, I can't let you wander around a vampires' brothel."

"How can you walk away from a treasure trove of vampires' books?" Miss Lark asked. "I know you've spent a lifetime studying the creatures, my lord. The entire history of vampires will be in those books. You are a man of science—how can you resist finding the truth?"

Jonathon held back an ironic laugh. Serena Lark thought she could appeal to the noble scientist in him. She had no idea, the poor sweet.

He took a deep breath, inhaled more of the drugs the demons had used—they had been burned earlier in another room and allowed to seep in through holes made in the wall. They must have left Serena alone with it. Solange and another drug—one he hadn't recognized, though he could guess at its purpose. It must be an aphrodisiac. How much Miss Lark had inhaled, or how long it would affect her, he couldn't speculate.

Having finished the job of decapitating the destroyed vampires, stuffing the mouths with garlic, and stowing the remains out of sight, Drake Swift stepped behind her. Jonathon saw her become immediately aware of Swift. He gritted his teeth as he saw her stiffen in tension—in appreciative tension, not fear. Her pretty tongue licked her lower lip, her fingers played against the silk of the robe. Miss Lark kept flicking glances at Swift beneath demurely lowered lashes. Lashes that tempted Jonathon to touch with his lips—to catch her by surprise with a kiss.

Of course Drake Swift was definitely aware of her. Swift let his fingers lightly graze her tumbled hair. Jonathon noted Swift's breathing was quicker, his trousers tenting in an obvious display of his notorious sexual appetite.

"We should hunt down the vampires—find out from them about this master." Swift glanced up at him. "And let Miss Lark find her books."

The one advantage of large hands is they would fit easily around Swift's bloody neck.

"Surely you want to see that library, Lord Sommersby," Miss Lark insisted. "Every answer you've ever sought could be in those books."

Jonathon grimaced. She was holding out the juicy apple of knowledge—begging him to take a bite.

Swift nodded, encouraging her. "It's easy enough to infiltrate the place. Grab a couple of masks and pose as clients to our lovely Miss Lark. The tunnels likely lead two ways—next door and to safety."

"We have to go through the brothel," Miss Lark added. "We can only get to the tunnel that leads to the library through it." She crossed her arms over her chest, which made the silk gape and gave a view of shadowed cleavage.

"Then you, Miss Lark, are going to have to pose as a jade." Swift gave a wink. "You must convincingly convey that you intend to share your bed with both of us."

"Shut it, Swift," he warned. "It's utter bloody madness to waltz through a vampires' brothel." He scrubbed a hand over his chin. "How do you know about these tunnels, Miss Lark?" he asked sharply. "Have you been in them?"

Spots of color came to her cheeks. "Not yet—I merely did

research! These tunnels connect to the underground rivers. The ones covered over by the city—the Fleet and the Tyburn."

"Research? How is it no other hunters have unearthed this knowledge?" His hair prickled at the back of his neck. Was Ashcroft wrong—did Serena Lark know of her destiny? Was she leading them into a trap?

"Because no other hunters are assigned to dust library shelves, my lord," she snapped. "And no, the information is not obvious—I had to piece it together from dozens of volumes."

"And you really believe vampires have a library beneath London?"

"There are underground rivers, my lord. The tunnels carry the sewage to the Thames. Is it so impossible to believe that there would be more catacombs? That vampires would use them?"

Jonathon had to concede that point. It was, in fact, very likely.

If she was right, it would be the most amazing discovery made on vampires in centuries.

He looked into her hopeful eyes and wanted to agree to this mad scheme. "Is there any other way to get in there?"

Swift groaned. He was sliding a stake back up the sleeve of his coat. "Christ, Sommersby, we don't have time for blasted dithering. We have vampires to hunt."

Miss Lark frowned again. "We can only get into those tunnels from the brothel. Unless you wish to travel up the Fleet River to do it—and the only way of getting in there is at its end, at the Thames, and that's below water."

"The brothel, then." Jonathon nodded to Swift. "Swift, bring the disguises in." They'd left their capes and masks in the hallway—hindrances during battle.

"I don't fetch," Swift snarled, but he turned on his heel and stalked out to the empty hallway.

Miss Lark touched Jonathon's arm. Her silvery-gray eyes flashed. "But aren't all the gentlemen here vampires? Won't it be obvious that you aren't?"

"How long will it take us to access the tunnels?"

She smiled, obviously pleased to be the one holding the information. "We have to pass through the brothel, but it shouldn't take more than minutes."

"Then we should be able to remain unnoticed for a few minutes."

Swift strolled back in wearing his mask and domino—a voluminous black silk cloak, the traditional masquerade of Venice. Silver moons and stars glittered on the ornate purple mask that covered Swift's face from hairline to lip. True to his word, his partner had bought only his own disguise in from the corridor, where they'd discarded cloaks and masks to attack. Jonathon would have to retrieve his own.

He took one last look into Serena Lark's eyes before leaving her side. She met his gaze with an open expression that spoke of hope. She didn't look afraid.

Unease rode Jonathon as he left the room and found his own mask and cloak. Had Miss Lark really pieced together information in plain sight in the Society's books and discovered a secret no one else knew? Or was she leading them into a trap?

He tied on his mask, knotting the cords. Swift was right—they needed to hunt down information on this master. Jonathon knew how valuable Serena Lark was. She was the first known vampire child. If this vampire Lukos knew . . .

Hell.

Jonathon swung his cloak around his shoulders, pausing on the threshold of the room. Drake Swift held Serena Lark's hand, and she was smiling up into his partner's eyes.

Jonathon's heart felt like ice. Since he'd first set eyes on her—on her glossy black hair, seductive gray eyes, sweet heart-shaped face—he'd been obsessed with Serena Lark. Even before Ashcroft told him to watch her. He was obsessed with her in his dreams. When he bathed. When he rode. When he toiled in his bloody laboratory. Damn, even when he hunted. Especially when he hunted. While he stalked the fog-laden London streets, he dreamed of being in Miss Lark's bed, making love to her, and hearing her cry his name—

Ashcroft wanted to let her change, wanted Jonathon to study the transformation of mortal to vampire. She was to change on her twenty-fifth birthday—All Hallow's Eve. It was her destiny, Ashcroft insisted, and they would learn how to save vampires if they studied Serena Lark. Jonathon had to admit that was true. He hated letting her change, but he didn't know how to stop it.

He knew exactly what service the Society would require of him when they decided Miss Lark was no longer of value. Once she transformed and gained her power, she would be too dangerous.

He would have to stake her.

4

Enslaved

Serena reached the bottom of the stone steps and held her candle up to illuminate the dark tunnel. It stank. There would be rats. A cold drop splattered on her neck, and she gave a smothered cry.

In front of her, Mr. Swift turned. His mask hid most of his face, shadows hid his eyes, but his lush lips cranked down in a grimace. "Smells like piss."

Before she could agree, he caught hold of her waist and lifted her. "The floor is mud, Miss Lark." He juggled her with ease so he was carrying her in his arms, one solid arm beneath the crooks of her knees, the other around her waist. His gloved hand splayed over her bottom.

He grinned, revealing a dimple in his right cheek—she could see the shadow of it, half-hidden by the exotic mask.

"Are you truly so concerned about saving my slippers, Mr. Swift?" she asked.

"Of course, Miss Lark. Don't ask me to put you down—I won't. I'm enjoying this too much."

She had to laugh at that. Just a small giggle that only he could hear before the blackness swallowed it up. She held out a candle, but it did little to fight the dark. Lord Sommersby strode ahead—she could see his light a few feet ahead of them, hear the reassuring slap of his boots in the mud. The walls of the tunnel were too dirty, too covered in sludge to reflect much light. They were curved and gave the strangest sense of enveloping, like demonic arms.

The light played on the arched stone ceiling above them. At once Serena saw her research had been correct—the tunnel ended a few yards to the left, narrowing and closing to a wall of dirt and stone. It stretched into blackness in the other direction, and there was no sound but their breathing and the splatter of drips on mud.

Mr. Swift gave her bottom a squeeze, but he lifted her also, as though he'd only intended to improve his grip. She should protest, but she liked the pressure of his hand there. She hooked one hand around his neck. Even carrying her, Mr. Swift strode confidently into the dark.

Daringly, she let her bare fingertips brush his hair. So soft. So remarkably pale blond. He caught her gaze, his green eyes glittered in the faint light, and she saw wicked desire there.

Lord Sommersby stopped abruptly, his candle held in front. "Ahead," he whispered. "I see the outline of the door." His light twinkled on the gold painted stars on his rich midnight-blue mask. Serena glanced from his masked face to Mr. Swift's. Both the Venetian masks sported strange long noses—noses with a downward curve at the end, like vicious beaks. They looked like creatures of fantasy, masked and swathed in black silk capes.

Twisting in Mr. Swift's arms, Serena saw nothing but shadow, until the glow of Lord Sommersby's candle touched a padlock, open and hanging off the hasp.

Serena's heart leapt—there was nothing to stop them getting into the brothel.

"Remember, little lark—" The nose of Drake Swift's mask

bumped her lips. His voice held dangerous promise, as he set her on her feet. "You are our courtesan—our lover. You must play the part to keep us alive."

Around her, dozens of people—vampires, courtesans, gentlemen—were having sex. Serena tried not to stare. She truly did. But the groans made her legs ache, and each time a woman cried out, it was as though a bolt of lightning struck her quim.

She remembered her confident answer to Mr. Swift. *Yes, I can play the part.*

Now, she wasn't so certain.

Her hand on Lord Sommersby's arm, Serena gaped at one vampire, his trousers down around his ankles, his tight, muscular derriere exposed. A woman's bare white legs were hooked around the vampire's waist and he held her up against a wall. He was thrusting into her so hard he shook the wall.

"I die!" the woman cried.

Goodness, they had to save the poor creature! But the woman screamed in pleasure and ripped at the vampire's clothed back with fingers curved like claws.

The woman was enjoying herself. Her life wasn't in danger—yet.

"Hell and perdition."

She heard Sommersby mutter the curse. "My dear, you really don't belong here."

It was true. She'd steeled herself to expect audacious sex acts and lewd couplings—she'd seen many such illustrations in the Society's hidden texts—but she knew he was right. She was not a virgin, and she truly liked sex, as illicit and unladylike as that was, but she was shocked by this. By women who willingly gave themselves to demons, who exposed their breasts to catch male attention, and who were willing to sink to their knees and kiss a man's privy member at his command.

Many jades cast glances at Lord Sommersby and Mr. Swift—

below the bizarre masks, both men's beautiful lips and strong jaws were visible. She guessed the women knew the masks covered handsome faces, that the cloaks shrouded muscular, beautiful bodies.

The three of them kept to the shadows—though in this crowded corridor it was almost impossible. Serena noticed the care Lord Sommersby and Mr. Swift took to disguise the fact they had no fangs.

She was masked, too—in harem style, with a subtle strip of white cloth hiding her face. Mr. Swift had torn fabric from his cravat to fashion it for her. He'd chosen the part that wasn't bloody from his wound, a wound that he cavalierly disregarded.

A woman with wild henna-red curls leapt in front of Drake Swift. A quick tug of her hands and her low-cut bodice popped beneath her breasts. She jumped giddily so those breasts wobbled up and down, like jelly aspic on a platter. The woman's hand snaked out and clamped onto Mr. Swift's crotch.

Drake Swift gave a hearty laugh. "Not now, wicked wench. I promised to stuff the arse of this one with my companion. But those luscious tits of yours look like a meal for two."

Sensual need forked through her at his crude words, and she almost stumbled in shock. The woman gave a playful pout of scarlet-painted lips, then raced off, and leapt into a vampire's arms. This gentleman was most definitely a vampire—his fangs lapped his lower lip. He possessed white hair; a grizzled face; a strong, lean body. He pulled out his cock and the woman toyed with it. It was incredibly long, curved like a scythe, and soon many women's hands teased it while the vampire moaned his pleasure.

Serena looked away. These women must be fools. This vampire would drink from them. He would hurt them. The books described the vampire's bite as the most intense pleasure, but Serena didn't believe it.

"Are you all right, little lark?"

It was Drake Swift, murmuring by her ear, setting her skin tingling with the warmth of his breath.

Serena nodded. She was. Her heart beat a wild rhythm as they passed men—the dozens who prowled the hallways or who suckled women's breasts or who rutted wildly against the wall-papered walls. What would happen if she walked into Roman? Or Leonardo? But she did not recognize any of the handsome faces with their glittering, reflective eyes, their long, curving fangs.

Every vampire she saw was attractive and wore clothes that spoke of great wealth. Many smiled at her. With just a glance, a vampire could make a lady lust and need so much she willingly offered her neck, but the heat these demons ignited—which she fought—was nothing compared to the sparks that scorched her each time she brushed against her hunters' bodies. She walked between the two men, Mr. Swift on her left, Lord Sommersby on her right. She no longer knew which man's hand rested on her waist, her shoulder, or gently grazed her arm.

"Which way, sweet?" Mr. Swift whispered.

"The ballroom," Serena said.

Suspicion glittered in the earl's dark eyes. "The most crowded place here? No other way?"

She swallowed hard, and whispered, "There's a gallery that overlooks—and stairs on both sides. We could pass through there, go down the stairs, and then down to the tunnels."

"And all this you learned from books?" Sommersby asked.

"Yes, all this I learned from books." This brothel had existed for decades—she had traced its ownership back hundreds of years, to the original Tudor building that had been on the site.

A gong sounded—it was subdued, but it must act as a summons, because people began to flow in the opposite direction to the gallery. Some vanished into bedrooms on the way. But Serena could see that no one was looking in their direction as they reached the draped entrance to the gallery.

His lordship went in first, simply vanishing behind the curtain. She was alone with Drake Swift. It was eerie to gaze at his mask, to have no idea of his expression. He moved in front of her, to trap her back against the wall, shielding her from the eyes of a couple of women who passed.

He bent as though biting her neck but did not touch her. His words were soft. "Do you want my touch, Miss Lark?"

His voice was deep, roughly accented—Serena knew he'd grown up around Covent Garden—but his brazen words only made his low baritone more sensual.

Serena felt his warm breath on her skin and grew indecently wet. She felt dizzy still—from the drug, she assumed. From shock, too, no doubt, but she couldn't give in to that. "Yes," she said simply. She touched Mr. Swift's cheek, below his mask, and didn't care. She pulled him closer, drew him until his hot mouth ignited against her neck. "I do want your touch."

"You're a brave woman, Miss Lark," Mr. Swift murmured as his lips skimmed around her throat, down to the hollow at the front. Heat flared in her blood.

Was she brave? She was nervous. Were brave people nervous? She knew that Drake Swift was wildly courageous. He'd told her that once in the Society's library—*I'm addicted to the hunt, love. It is almost as fun as making love.* She hadn't blushed for him then, which she had suspected was his goal—to embarrass the prim former governess.

His teeth brushed her neck, and the pressure sent a bolt of pleasure rocketing through her. Warmth. Wetness. A delicious tickle. He was running his tongue over her neck! Her quim ached with the contact. Even the brush of the mask's long nose along her neck made her legs wobble.

She pushed on Mr. Swift's shoulders to force him away. He conceded, lifting his mouth from her neck. "Did I frighten you?"

Serena tipped her head back to look into his eyes, dazzling

green behind the mask. "Of course not! But I'm so close now—I can't be sidetracked."

He laughed at that, leaning back against the wall, his eyes bright behind his mask. "Do you really think books are more important than hunting? More important than passion?"

"Tonight, yes," she answered, trying to banter.

"Do you really believe that words, not stakes, can destroy vampires?"

She hadn't expected such a question from Drake Swift, the man known as the Mad Slayer. Strangely, having him forsake his devil-may-care persona and show a glimpse of his soul made her heart thump against her ribs. She moved closer to the drapery. "Words have great power. And I have no choice but to bury myself in words—the Society will not let me hunt."

"But tonight you defied them. Are books worth risking your life?"

He was questioning her motives, and she couldn't have that. "Are you offering, now, to let me hunt with you?" she asked. "To take me on as an apprentice?"

He looked more startled than if she had lifted her robe and jumped on him. Of course he would never consider hunting with a mere woman by choice.

"Hurry—" It was Lord Sommersby, holding open the drapery.

Mr. Swift gallantly offered his arm, but she ignored it to dart up the stairs, holding up the trailing hem of the oversized robe.

The gallery was empty, shadowed. The dangling chandelier that should illuminate the salon below was unlit, but the crystal caught golden light from wall sconces below and dazzled. Urbane laughter welled up, as did the strains of cultured music and feminine giggles.

She'd expected wildness, rowdy sounds, mayhem—like an uproar in a theatre pit.

"The exit must be there—shielded by those curtains," Lord

Sommersby directed. His domino cloak flapped around him as he strode across to where the railing reached the wall, beside crimson curtains. His long legs crossed the space in seconds.

"Wait." Mr. Swift kept his voice low as he prowled to the gallery's edge. "We should see if we can spot Miss Lark's captors in that crowd."

"Even if we do, we aren't attacking here," Sommersby warned.

Her library—and Dracul's journal—were so close. Serena moved to the gallery's edge to look down on the ballroom. She wanted a glimpse into the vampires' world. If she was truly a vampire, she wanted to know . . .

How could she be a vampire yet not drink blood? Not be undead? She didn't understand—and she was determined to make Ashcroft tell her.

The brass rail around the gallery was smooth, cool beneath her touch—her hands were still bare. She needed a moment to plan. How was she going to retrieve the Vlad Dracul book without Lord Sommersby discovering what it was? He'd take it from her, likely by force. He might be known for heroism, but it was known that if he wanted something, he took it.

How could she find it and hide it?

She heard the click of boot heels behind her, Sommersby approaching her. Drake Swift was scanning the crowd below. Blinking, Serena looked down on the scene. Everywhere she saw women. Courtesans, high-flyers, jades, lightskirts—but all were voluptuous, lovely, fascinating. Many were young, with long silky hair that reached their bared bottoms, but they were of all ages, all coloring, all sizes and shapes, and most wore the same costume. They wore corsets of black with scarlet strings, dyed black stockings, and heeled shoes.

It was scandalous, but it also seemed so freeing to be unafraid to parade around in such clothes—certainly wearing just a robe made her feel both courageous and nerve-wracked.

There were men below, of course, dozens of men. In the

center of the salon was a raised dais, a large one, like a stage. It was empty. Around it, many of the men strolled. Men in evening dress, in capes, in robes. So many men on the move it was almost impossible to search them for her vampire captors. All were surrounded by women—women fawning on them, touching them, whispering to them.

It still startled Serena to see the lusty smiles on the women's faces—women who should be terrified. It was like watching rabbits leap into foxes' jaws.

Serena glanced up. On her left, Drake Swift was slowly scanning the crowd. On her other side, Lord Sommersby did the same.

Did she see Roman? No. To Serena's astonishment, one dark-haired man, wearing a cape, tossed a blond woman onto the stage. The woman giggled, and her expression was a blend of lust, excitement, and playfulness. She was delighted to be a vampire's plaything. The man pushed her back, and she flopped back on the stage, arms outstretched. Her breasts were exposed, her waist cinched impossibly small by the corset, her nether hair exposed. The man shoved her legs apart—wider, wider, until the woman let her head fall back. He dropped to his knees and pressed his face to the woman's quim.

Applause and cheers abounded.

Serena knew what that act felt like. William Bridgewater had done it to her—she had been shocked and enthralled. At the time, her heart had been as excited as her body. She had believed it an expression of love. She had been quite wrong.

She could not look away from the moaning woman as the vampire feasted on her cunny. He pulled the jade's hips to his mouth, the way an uncouth man would lift a soup plate. The woman's eyes shut tight, her hands fisted. She banged those fists against the polished floor of the dais.

"Oooh!" The vampire's plaything cried out in pleasure. Her limbs went slack, her head lolled. The vampire slid his hands up to her waist. He stood, lifting the woman, his face still in her quim as—

"What do you see, little lark?"

Serena blinked at Drake Swift's voice. Startled, she saw Mr. Swift stood behind her. He had approached her and she hadn't noticed. His black-gloved hands rested beside hers on the rail.

"I do not see any of them—any of the vampires who captured me." She tried to be as nonchalant as he, but her face flushed. At least her mask disguised some of the red heat on her cheeks. She wanted to appear unmoved by what she saw. She didn't want to appear to be just a "delicate" woman.

"We should go and find the library," she urged.

"You are a remarkable woman. Tougher than any I've met."

She wondered at that—he had grown up in Covent Garden. Women there were tough.

"Have you ever wondered why we really kill vampires?" he asked.

Serena frowned and shivered—because vampires killed mortals. Why else? But she knew he was teasing. She was aroused. Burning. But also terrified—what would he do if he knew she might be a vampire?

"Because they have all the fun." Mr. Swift's voice held naughty wickedness.

He wanted her to step unwisely into sexual banter. The drug was still in her head, still making it hard to think. She was watching sensual acts and beautiful lovers, and each time she moved the silk of the robe skimmed her nipples, brushed her nether curls, and maddened her.

"Do you really believe that?" Serena challenged, because naughty boys required a firm hand.

Drake Swift laughed. "Sometimes, my dear, I am tempted to get bitten."

She recoiled at that, remembering the horrifying sight of Guilliame biting him. Was that why he discounted the bite?

Anger flared—how easy for him to joke. Mr. Swift did not fear he was truly a demon.

Then she saw him—Roman. Flitting through the crowd, his long dark hair flapping with his hurried steps. He now wore a robe. A tall woman emerged from the throng and grasped his arm. A woman strong enough to stop Roman in his tracks.

Serena pointed. "Look, there is one of the vampires who captured me. The one with the long hair, with that woman in the topaz gown—"

She felt the excitement ignite in Drake Swift. "Wait, little lark. Watch awhile. We will see what he does." He stepped behind her and braced his arms on either side of her. "Learn about your foe before attack."

"You don't do that," she protested. "I've heard that you race in madly, and by a miracle, somehow you survive."

"Didn't Sommersby warn you not to listen to everything you hear, my dear?" Mr. Swift bent close. "Does it frighten you to watch him?"

"No—yes," Serena admitted. She could feel the bite of the manacles on her wrist and ankles again and felt the fear of being vulnerable. And a deeper fear—that she was vampire, too.

"Fight it, angel. If you want to hunt, you have to learn to fight your fear."

Serena found Roman again, in the crowd. The tall woman had left him, and he stood watching the stage, his arms crossed over his chest. She was afraid to look too long. Roman would sense her.

She glanced up and saw Lord Sommersby a few yards away, walking slowly alongside the gallery railing, watching the scene below.

She should call out to him. Tell him where Roman was. But she knew once she did that protective Lord Sommersby would ensure she had no part in pursuing him. He would get her out of here, and she'd have no chance to find the library.

Horror rushed like ice water through her veins—if Sommersby and Swift captured Roman, Roman would tell them what she was.

The madam—the tall woman with the shimmering topaz gown, the pile of raven black curls, the magnificent diamonds—clapped her hands.

At the sharp clap, many of the corset-clad girls scurried to the center of the room. Giggling, the girls began to kiss. The madam spanked one on her bottom with harsh slaps of her open palm, and the girl turned, presenting her now-rosy derriere. She still lushly kissed the other girl, mouths wide open. Grunts and murmurs of male appreciation filled the room, especially when the madam picked up a black leather switch. The girl held her cheeks apart, and the madam thwacked the girl's rear thoroughly with the leather straps. After the girl's buttocks were flushed red, the madam lifted a device from a table, a long rod of black with a tail of peacock feathers and two gold chains attached. Graceful fingers dipped the rod into a tall brass container and withdrew it. Clear, viscous liquid dripped from the tip.

"What is she doing?" Without thinking, Serena asked the question of Drake Swift.

She immediately regretted letting the words slip out.

"Penetrating her arse."

A quiver of heat and agony shot through Serena.

The madam pushed with hearty force until the rod disappeared deep into the girl's bottom. The girl was rocking and panting with each thrust, her loose auburn hair tumbling over her back.

Once the rod was within to the hilt, the woman—the madam—looped two chains around the girl's bare thighs. She attached two to the girl's corset. The girl giggled with delight, waggled her bum, and began to spin and dance around the room. Peacock feathers swirled and spun with her wild motions.

Mr. Swift breathed heavily. Serena felt the warmth of those deep breaths against her ear.

"Does that not hurt?" she asked. Her own bottom tingled.

"It pleasures her," he insisted. "She will perhaps reach orgasm many times. Eventually she will wish to remove it, for it is large and is spreading her wide. After several hours, she will yearn to stop. That is when she will be selected by a vampire as his companion and he will heighten her pleasure."

Serena could not understand why the thought of such a bizarre thing made her own body weak and shivery.

The madam continued to slap the girls on their bottoms and continued to slide large rods into their derrieres. She chained each one in place. A larger and larger rod was used on each girl. For the last, a beauty with chestnut ringlets, two other girls held her to support her as the madam worked the enormous black pole inside.

The first girl was already straddling a man's lap, crying out in pleasure as she bounced upon him. The chains were taut, straining to keep her filled. Two other girls lay upon a divan and began to kiss each other's privy curls. One banged her bottom roughly against the divan. The other spread her thighs wide and wriggled. Did that provide stimulation?

Men—vampires—sprawled on the various chairs, watching the display, exuding raw sensual power. All were cast in shadow, so they looked mysterious and dangerous. Some crooked their fingers—summoning a girl to dance before them.

The girls would play with their nipples or hold open their nether lips, then spring around to display their bottoms. One girl with enormous breasts was able to reach her nipple with her tongue, eliciting a cheer from the bright-eyed man watching her. Another man dragged the girl toward him, until she crawled on her knees on their chaise. He pulled her hips to his face so her quim was at his mouth. With his large, gloved hands, he began withdrawing the rod and thrusting it in her, the chains attempting to resist.

Serena realized his tongue was licking the girl's privy parts, tasting the moisture there, and the vampire made hungry, growling sounds. Another girl crawled between his thighs and began to undo the placket of his trousers.

Serena's face was aflame, her throat dry and tight.

Mr. Swift leaned forward—heavens, she felt his erection push against her backside. He was aroused. She wanted to push back against him. But she tried to stay completely still.

"Is this the sort of thing you do?" she croaked the question at him. She should disapprove. But she found watching so arousing, so irresistible.

"Is it the sort of thing you would want to do, little lark? Wouldn't you wish to perform for him, to entice him beyond all control?"

She had no answer, swallowed hard. "But those women are enticing vampires. The vampires will feed from them, hurt them."

"But you know vampires do not always kill—and the only ones allowed here are those with control over their feeding urges. And the girls are well treated, in a way. They have warm beds and beautiful clothing, and are very well fed. They have every comfort they could imagine. These are not girls trapped and abused by a brutal madam."

"They are free to leave?"

"Yes, but they don't leave."

"Why not—if they have freedom, why would they not take it?"

Swift leaned closer. "Because they need to offer their blood. They cannot exist any longer without joining with a vampire and surrendering their blood."

"Slaves? Or worse—food!"

"In all relationships, one partner feeds on what the other offers. In different ways. The vampires are as much their slaves."

"I don't believe that." She glanced up and caught Lord Sommersby's gaze. She saw the way his lips parted, the tense way he held them. Shadows shielded his eyes, but something in his expression knocked all the air from her chest.

Slowly, like a prowling beast, Lord Sommersby walked toward her. Instinctively, she wet her lips in anticipation of his touch, his kiss. She was living her dream. She moved back from the rail, which pressed her derriere against Drake Swift's rigid erection. She was aware of her heat, her scent, her wetness, and the power of the two men who had vowed to protect her.

Serena gasped as Drake Swift kissed the back of her neck. As he suckled. A burst leaped from there like a tiny firework. It raced through her, furiously fast, and exploded between her legs in a flood of wetness.

Ecstasy. Pleasure. Goodness, at just that touch—that hot, lovely touch—she'd climaxed!

She cried out.

5

Addicted

Jonathon heard Miss Lark's little cry of pleasure and almost came on the spot. A bolt of sensual agony crippled his legs, and he had to stop walking.

Miss Lark's head arched back, her cheeks flushed pink, and she breathed frantically. She'd climaxed at just the touch of Swift's mouth to her neck. Of course she would. She was a born vampiress.

Swift groaned, "Yes, sweeting," and reached for her plump breasts.

Jonathon clamped his hand on Swift's shoulder and shoved his partner. Swift took a step back, a dangerous gleam in his eyes.

This wasn't the first time Swift had pleasured a woman Jonathon had wanted . . .

"This isn't a game, and Miss Lark is a respectable lady." Jonathon kept his voice low, but his temple throbbed and he felt the beat of his pulse in his skull. Damn, he was hard and aching for Serena Lark. He hadn't sought sexual release in a year. Frustration kept him sharp on the hunt. And what woman would want to be the mistress of a man who spent his nights slaying demons and his days locked in a laboratory, slicing the brains of vampire cadavers with a scalpel?

He couldn't let himself desire Miss Lark. And he had to ensure his blasted partner did not learn her secret.

"Out of my league, you mean." Swift's hands fisted at his side.

"I—I fear it was the drug," Miss Lark said, and she touched her cheeks, wincing as though she'd burned her palms.

Swift, who thought she was an innocent miss, was taking advantage of her shock and confusion. Jonathon lifted his fists.

"Gentlemen, stop!" Miss Lark managed to make a whisper into a shout. She wagged her finger like a disapproving governess. "Roman—the vampire who captured me—is leaving. He was speaking with the madam once more and is going into the crowd. We should go now to the library."

Miss Lark set his head spinning. Beneath her veil, her cheeks were still flushed from her ecstasy. Her words were rushed as though she still hadn't caught her breath. She'd just witnessed the lewdest acts he'd ever seen. But she was fixated on the bloody library.

What did she want there? Did she really not know she was a vampire? Did she believe Ashcroft's lie about her parents' deaths by vampire attack? Had she really come here to find a book that might tell her about her parents? She was such a mix of innocence and determination, vulnerability and strength, he couldn't tell if she was lying to him.

He saw Swift move to her side. "We should follow the vampires."

Jonathon had the privilege of rank, and he gripped the brass rail to spend some of his tension. "Too dangerous to combat a half-dozen vampires in their own den." He looked to Miss Lark and tried not to remember her climaxing for Drake Swift. "You said the vampire was speaking to the madam?"

With bright pink cheeks, she nodded, and her raven-black curls danced against her back.

"Then Madame Roi is who we want to speak to. The vampire Roman will be subordinate to her. She had a great deal of power. She rules the vampires of London."

Miss Lark frowned. "That is something I have never understood. If you know she is a vampiress, why do you let her live?"

Swift grinned. "Because she has the protection of powerful men."

"Which powerful men?"

Jonathon sensed she had already guessed the answer, but he gave it to her. "The Earl of Ashcroft. His Grace, the Duke of Russex. Lord Williams."

Miss Lark looked perplexed. "But why would the three most important men of the Royal Society protect a vampire madam?"

With lordly arrogance he waved the question aside. "Miss Lark, why don't you tell me how to find the library?"

Her gray eyes narrowed. "Only if you bring me with you."

"No. Too dangerous."

"Then I won't tell you. Instead, I will come back and find it."

Swift grinned. "She will probably come back . . . alone."

Good Christ. "All right, you can come, Miss Lark," Jonathon conceded. "But you will do everything we say."

"Indeed." Swift grinned.

Jonathon let a seething growl escape. Sexual banter had not been his intention.

"I'll go first," Swift added in his irritating devil-may-care tone. "Check for trouble."

Jonathon had never been happier to watch his partner leave.

Serena saw Drake Swift vanish behind the heavy crimson

drapery. She was alone with the earl, and the instant the curtain stilled, Lord Sommersby grasped her arm and drew her close to his side. Within the narrow slits of his mask, surrounded by the deep violet paint, his eyes were molten, reflecting golden candlelight. "What book is it you want, Miss Lark? What exactly are you searching for?"

The man had instincts too well honed for her good. "I don't know," she lied. "I wanted to search the library and see if I found any—"

She broke off at the sound of a coarse female voice. "I want ye to fuck me from behind over the gallery rail, milord. Won't ye please?"

Astonished, Serena watched as the curtain opened and a blond courtesan sashayed in. The woman wore one of the black corsets, with the gold chains attached, and one of the wands was buried up her bottom. Her companion, a man who stood almost as tall as Sommersby, also wore the domino and a mask of black silk.

Why hadn't Mr. Swift warned them the couple was coming?

"Oh!" The blond jade saw them and gasped in surprise.

Before Serena could think, Lord Sommersby's broad shoulders and wide chest filled her view. He bent, until his mouth hovered just an inch over hers. It was part of the disguise. He would not kiss her—or if he did he would not mean it.

Had he known she had climaxed? She had foolishly cried out—and had been mortified. It had been so unexpected, so astonishing. She'd prayed both men had no idea what had happened to her.

Lord Sommersby's lips grazed her cheek, through the veil. How sensual his mouth was. The firm brush set her skin tingling, made her gasp. "You must know how much I desire you."

His hand cupped her chin and turned her lips to his. "No, my lord. I had no idea."

A smile. His lips quirked up in a smile. A brief one that vanished quickly.

Out of the corner of her eye she saw the dark-haired vampire bend the blonde over the railing. His legs spread, and he thrust his hips forward. A frantic womanly squeal followed—obviously he'd penetrated. The man began to grunt, hoarse, fierce grunts. And the woman cried, "Yes! Yes!" and "Deeper! Deeper!"

Serena swayed—Sommersby settled his hands on her hips. Held her steady. "Start moving back, my dear. We'll slip away without them noticing."

"No kiss?"

"No. Now take a step back."

For one mad moment, Serena wanted to press forward, push her lips to the earl's, but she obeyed him. She let him guide her backward until the velvet drape brushed against her back. She thought of Mr. Swift, and fear began to throb around her heart. Where was he?

Christ Jesus, his hands were shaking.

Drake Swift looked down and dispassionately watched his fingers tremble. The signs always began this way. First, he'd slowly lose control of his limbs. Then his speech. Blackness would creep in on the edge of his vision.

Bloody solange was killing him.

Drake reached into the slim pocket sewn in his coat lining. One vial left. He needed more—this would be enough for tonight. A few minutes away from Miss Lark and Sommersby was all the time he needed. He'd ducked into this unused room, while Miss Lark and his partner waited on the gallery.

Hell, hiding in a brothel's bedroom to drink a potion that would kill him. Christ. He'd fought hard to be better than this.

Beneath the pad of Drake's thumb, the glass was smooth. Fragile. His thumb toyed with the stopper, easing it up.

As much as he hated leaving Miss Lark with his partner, he didn't think for an instant Sommersby would take advantage of his time alone. Miss Lark was a beauty, but Sommersby wouldn't try to seduce her. Sommersby seemed to like to punish himself by denying himself sex.

Hell. Women were like drink. Like solange. Guilt, regrets, fear, anger—all vanished when you had a woman's heels hooked around your neck and you were pounding your cock deep in her wet, welcoming pussy. A mind-shattering climax was a good as a drunk any day.

There was something about Miss Lark that commanded Drake to stay near her.

All it had taken was the touch of his mouth to her satin-soft neck and she'd climaxed . . . he knew female ecstasy when he saw it. And she was a deliciously noisy woman when she came. Inside the studious governess there lurked a seductive woman.

Bloody stopper was stuck. With a snap of his thumb, Drake flicked the rubber wedge so savagely he snapped off the top of the vial. It tinkled as it struck the floor.

He knew the warnings about solange. He'd heard the other hunters speak of it. None touched the drug. All knew it destroyed faster than opium.

Drake didn't have a choice anymore. He tipped up the vial.

It would make him forget. Forget Mary, the lost babe, his past—it would obliterate the memories and nightmares.

The vile taste hit his tongue. He grimaced, his stomach rebelled, but he swallowed fast. Christ, he hated this stuff. It rushed through him, and within moments he had a cockstand as rigid as iron. One thing about solange—it made a man hunger to fuck.

Drake tossed away the vial. The glass struck the ground, rolled beneath the fireplace fender. The faint glimmer from the moonlight touched the room with blue. Warmth spiraled through him, warmth that fought the cold in his heart, his limbs, his head. Within seconds, the shaking stopped.

"Where is Mr. Swift?"

Drake could hear Serena Lark's voice. The room seemed to light up for him. Hell, he didn't care if she and Sommersby found him in here. He soared now.

The solange changed his face, he knew it did. He'd seen his eyes in his ex-mistress's mirror after taking solange. The pupils became mere dots in green irises. He'd looked mad but he'd felt like a king. He'd dragged his mistress—what had her name been?—back into bed, had thrust into her for hours. Until she'd been so slick they'd lost the friction and so weak from her orgasms she'd pleaded with him to stop.

Tonight, the mask hid his face and shadowed his eyes enough that Sommersby, or Serena Lark, wouldn't notice the change.

As he strolled back into the hallway, he saw Miss Lark turn at the sound of his boots on the wood floor. Behind the gauzy veil of her mask, she glowed as she saw him. Relief. Happiness. Hell, it appeared the lady cared whether he lived or died.

She stood waiting for him. Her black hair curled over her shoulders, tendrils fell into the valley between her generous round breasts. Her cry of pleasure still rang in Drake's head. He wanted nothing more than to sweep her into a bedroom and—

"Where the bloody hell were you?" Sommersby growled, but Drake ignored him.

Miss Lark glanced up and down the now-quiet hallway. "We must get to the servants' stair at the end of the hallway—it leads down to the tunnels."

Sommersby took the lead, striding down the hall, but Drake waited. He caught hold of Miss Lark's wrist to keep her at his side. The drug was hot in his blood. He wanted to fill his senses with her.

He took her hand, and she moved to him—he knew she expected him to lead her down the hall. Instead, he cupped the neat indent of her waist and brought her into his embrace. He wanted to hear her quickened breaths. He wanted to smell her skin, her intimate honey.

In front of them a door creaked. A woman's throaty laugh washed over Drake—the lush sound of a woman well pleasured. His cock responded; blood surged there, making him painfully hard.

He glanced up. A red-haired prostitute lounged in the doorway, stroking the jaws of two dark-haired vampires. She wore a robe of rose silk—loosely belted. Her enormous tits were exposed, her rouged nipples hard and jutting. Her neck was punctured, and blood smeared her pale skin.

Against his chest, Miss Lark gasped and Drake pulled her hard against him. He nuzzled her neck. "A bit of playacting, sweet," he warned.

He traced the arch of her neck with his tongue and caught sight of the grins of approval from the pair of vampires who kneaded the courtesan's breasts. Their caresses were rough but the woman tipped her head back in pleasure—most women enjoyed rough play. The vampire cocked his head—looked a question. He wanted to be invited to taste Miss Lark's neck, too.

Drake gave a rueful shake of his head, staying in the character of the sexually driven vampire. Christ Jesus, it was no stretch of his acting skills—his cock throbbed against Miss Lark's silk-clad belly. He forced himself not to reach down and fill his palms with her voluptuous arse as he suckled her neck.

The vampires' courtesan was a beauty, with magnificent breasts that bounced as the vampires played, but she was no match for Miss Lark.

Hell, he was no gentleman, and Drake admitted it freely. When he'd burst into the billiard room where Miss Lark was a prisoner, he taken a long look at her naked form while battling her captors, and he'd savored the sight.

Miss Lark's pulse fluttered in her throat, and Drake angled to get a better view of the scene before them. The vampires bent to their lover's breasts, and two tongues flicked the hard nipples. Miss Lark gave a startled cry, then a moan—a husky moan that spoke to Drake's soul.

He cradled her breasts, knowing he'd gone too far. Her sweet nipples rose at once at the scrape of his fingertip. Drake's voice was a rasp from his dry throat. "Do you desire me as much as I want you, little lark?"

Serena knew she must stop. Lord Sommersby must have noticed they hadn't followed—he would return any moment. She had to regain control of herself. Vlad Dracul's journal—she needed the journal. And this was not a dream! What was to happen tomorrow, in daylight, after she'd let these two hunters touch her?

She had to concentrate on her goal—but Drake Swift's body, lean and powerful and solid, pressed against her. She should push his hands from her breasts. But she couldn't. She wanted them there. It thrilled to look down, to see him cupping and fondling.

"Of course, I desire you—" His thumbs strummed her nipples through silk, and she lost her voice. She struggled to speak. "Don't all women?"

He chuckled. "Putting me in my place, little lark?"

She couldn't answer his question. To her shock, she saw the vampires part the courtesan's robe. Their hands disappeared inside, and the woman's moan was pleading, agonized. Serena could imagine the way his fingers—in black gloves—would look as they played within glistening pink lips—

"The vampires want to perform for us," Mr. Swift murmured. "If we leave, they might grow suspicious." His voice sounded like Lucifer, urging the innocent to offer their souls. As dangerously seductive as a drug. She knew now why the other hunters called Drake Swift a madman.

He squeezed her bosom, his tongue slid up to her earlobe, and her legs became melted butter. "But Lord Somm—"

"Do not think about Lord Sommersby, sweeting. Think about me."

Both vampires played between the woman's full, nude thighs—so many fingers. The woman moaned at the invasion, and as they withdrew, Serena could smell the woman's desire. Their gloves would be soaked and sticky with the woman's juices.

"I would like to touch you that way, Serena."

Her Christian name. Spoken with a softness, a vulnerability, in his voice that Serena had never heard before. "Mr—"

"You can't shock me by enjoying my touches. It pleases me to know you do. Life is short—a shame to endure it in frustrated piety."

"Yes, touch me," she invited, and wondered if she'd plunged into madness.

The nose of Mr. Swift's mask ran teasingly along her neck. Shivers tumbled. Her cunny throbbed. "Do you know what the nose of the mask is used for, love?" Swift asked.

Had she thrown herself off the cliff into wanton insanity? She knew, she knew, she could never tame a rogue like Drake Swift.

She gave one brief shake of her head.

"The nose of the mask would tease your clit while I licked your sweet quim. Do you know about your clit, Miss Lark? How touches there can make you explode?"

She froze. Yes, she knew about pleasure, about a man's touch between her thighs, but she had never revealed her sin to anyone.

It had been a mistake. A foolish mistake. Too often girls made mistakes, and she'd been a very foolhardy girl, with a foolhardy heart.

"I could slide the nose inside you, filling you, while my tongue circles around your bum—"

Serena moaned. Pleasure, demanding and intense, built in her. Her hips began to sway. Her nether curls were soaked.

Footsteps sounded behind them—the click of boot heels on wood in an impatient stride. In an instant, Lord Sommersby was at her side.

"What the hell are you doing, Swift?" he snapped. He pushed Swift's hand away from her breast. But his settled on her stomach, on the belt of her robe. For just a heartbeat and then left.

Drake Swift merely laughed—his low, dangerous laugh. "Claiming my prize. Actually I'm avoiding suspicion."

The words *claiming* and *prize* hit like Serena a douse of cold water. Was that how he saw her—a woman to seduce because he'd rescued her? Was she just a reward of battle?

She stepped away from them both. And caught her breath.

Over Lord Sommersby's shoulder, Serena could see one of the vampires open the falls of his breeches and pull out his cock. It was dusky brown, the engorged head purplish and thick. One violent thrust, and he was inside, and the woman was weeping in pleasure as he banged his hips mercilessly against hers.

The other vampire held the woman up from behind—with his palms beneath her breasts, cupping them. He grinned at Serena, and she felt her cheeks catch fire.

"Care to join us? An orgy would be a fine diversion." He spoke affably but lust burned in his reflective eyes.

Lord Sommersby's lips were grim, his brown eyes almost black. She sensed his rage. Drake Swift stepped around her and shook his head. "Not tonight, my friend. Another perhaps." Swift turned to her. In the same jovial voice, he asked, "And where is your room, maid? I've had enough teasing for one night."

The perfect exit line. Her voice faltered on hers. "This—this way, sir."

By the time they'd reached the stairway door, the vampires and their lady had vanished into a room. A groaning bed could be heard. And each frantic moan they made pricked Serena's legs like an arrow.

Sommersby turned the door handle, revealing steep steps descending into complete blackness. But before they could step inside, a door opened directly across from them. A vampire stood in the doorway.

Before Serena could think, Lord Sommersby wrapped an arm around her waist and pulled her against him. Drake Swift's erection nudged her bottom—she realized they'd cuddled up to her to hide the open door. She could barely breathe. Lord Sommersby's gorgeous face lowered—his wide, hard lips came down over hers. It wasn't like the fierce open-mouthed kisses she saw from the gallery. This was a slow kiss, and his lips slanted over hers with unhurried desire. Hot, wet, and so commanding. Stubble brushed, his tongue teased, his breath joined with hers, and everything fell away from her, leaving her clinging to a kiss.

Her legs splayed, her body instinctively pushing against Sommersby's erection, the long, unyielding ridge of it. Mr. Swift pressed against her, his lips on her neck. She was book-ended by their massive erections!

Time stopped, and when his lordship drew away, when Drake stepped back, they left her spellbound.

The door closed with a click and reality roared in. The vampire had returned to his lover. They were alone again. Serena's lips yearned for another kiss. She ached everywhere—mouth, nipples, quim. Her thighs were slick with her juices, her nipples taut.

But her goal was so close. "Downstairs," she insisted.

Mr. Swift went first. She heard the creak of the stair treads. Taking a deep breath, she followed, and the narrow stairway seemed to close in on her as she descended. Only the faintest glimmer of light showed at the very top—a touch of moonlight that turned Mr. Swift's hair to silver and shimmered along the folds of his black cape.

"Is this library worth the risk, Miss Lark?" Lord Sommersby growled. He filled the stairwell behind her. She was trapped between the two of them—cocky scoundrel Mr. Swift ahead and the dangerous, guarded, taciturn Earl of Sommersby behind.

Her slippers trod on the worn stairs, but she felt the warmth of his lordship's breath. She felt the brush of his hand against hers on the wall as they descended. "Knowing the truth is worth any risk, my lord."

"Is revenge worth so much risk?" His voice was low, authoritative.

Serena shivered—she was going to have a devil of a time sneaking Vlad Dracul's journal from under the nose of this perceptive man.

"I need to know. I *have* to know." She couldn't tell him the truth, but she wanted to make him understand. "I want to know how my parents died. I want to know who killed them. I—" Her voice faltered. "I barely know anything about them." That much was the truth. She knew nothing about who her parents really were. All she knew were Ashcroft's lies.

"How could you not know? Who raised you?"

Madness, but she wanted to confide in him. She had to be careful. "I was raised in a noble house—but turned out at sixteen. The lady of the house, Mrs. Bridgewater, she did not like me." An understatement! "I became a governess, and then Lord Ashcroft communicated with me, and brought me to London."

A light was struck—it flared. Then the spherical glow of a candle filled the space. It meant Drake Swift was at the bottom of the stairs. Swift leaned in the narrow doorway, the candlelight lit the silver stars on the glossy paint of his mask. "All clear."

But Lord Sommersby touched her elbow lightly, and her step faltered.

"And the master or mistress of this house told you nothing?" Sommersby asked.

"They told me a story, a lie. I didn't know vampires killed my parents until Lord Ashcroft told me. Mrs. Bridgewater died of illness two years after I'd left; her husband perished in a carriage accident soon after. And Lord Ashcroft refuses to answer my questions."

"He felt it was better that you did not know."

"And that is not his decision to make," she retorted. She lifted the trailing hem of her robe and darted down the last steps. She didn't want to answer any more questions. Her slipper touched wet, dank ground. She'd reached the bottom. The entrance to the tunnels was arched and low—she had to duck, and she held the stone wall to support herself. The cold wrapped around her, and a shiver raced down her spine. Drake Swift's candle lit the tunnels—there was no other light, of course. Vampires did not need light. The space opened up both ways. "To the right," she said.

Drake Swift grinned in the light that spilled from the candle—it threw flickering shadows on the arched stone walls, the dirt and flag floor.

"What's that?" She grabbed Mr. Swift's arm. It sounded as though a wave was bearing down upon them. Could it be a change in the level of the Thames—could the tunnels flood?

"You can hear the river," Lord Sommersby said. "The sound of it will travel through the tunnels and will be distorted. There's nothing to fear." The coolness of his voice did not relieve her any, but Serena was determined not to show any fear. She waited as Lord Sommersby lit a small torch from Drake Swift's candle. Unfortunately the light was a warning to vampires. It made them targets, but there was nothing they could do. They needed light.

"To the right, you said." Swift flicked his arm, drew out a stake. His wicked chuckle sent another shiver down Serena's spine.

"Don't take mad risks," she warned.

"Of course not, little lark. I intend to return for you." And with an audacious wink, Drake Swift strode ahead.

6

Discovery

Serena found herself alone again with Lord Sommersby, dark and lethal and radiating impatient anger behind his dark blue mask. He appeared more likely to throttle her now than sweep her into a kiss. She couldn't help but smile—Sommersby was obviously not pleased she had forced him to bring her down here.

His lordship lifted the torch, and Serena heard the scurry of rats as the light drove them back into the shadows. She fought the senseless urge to scream. Then Lord Sommersby caught hold of her hand, sliding his fingers between hers.

Warmth flooded through her body at the touch—innocent, reassuring, but so intimate it seared her soul.

A touch like this had led to heartbreak. To a lost child. Guiltily, she remembered holding hands this way with William Bridgewater—when he was leading her to bed, or a blanket, or a stone wall, or oak tree—wherever he planned to make love to her. She'd been a fool, imagining that this gesture expressed deep love.

She was not going to be a fool again. And the library was so close—she was so close. She let go of his lordship's fingers to run ahead.

"Have a care, Miss Lark," Sommersby snapped. With his long strides, he outdistanced her, putting himself in front, and he took hold of her wrist. Serena rolled her eyes behind his broad back, but she followed, because in a few yards he would be waiting on her word.

As she'd known he would, his lordship slowed his pace as he reached Mr. Swift, who held his candle up to throw light on the fork in the tunnel.

"We take the one on the right," she whispered with confidence. "We must go about fifty yards—we will pass three other tunnels. There is a fourth—it is so small it will not appear to be a tunnel. Not a proper one."

Neither man spoke, but they followed her directions. Drake Swift approached the other three tunnels to take a glance down, but they passed them quickly and found the next one. It was right beside a larger offshoot, and Serena imagined that was planned for confusion.

She pointed to the opening that was barely three feet wide and about waist height off the ground. "That one."

Mr. Swift drew down his mask and twisted it around his neck so it dangled down his back by the ties and revealed his grimace. "We're going to have to crawl."

The thought revolted her, but she knew she couldn't turn back. She nodded. She had to admit she was impressed as Swift hoisted himself in the tiny opening without hesitation. How could he be so fearless?

As Lord Sommersby lifted her by the waist, she bit back a laugh. There was no way she could go from his arms to that tunnel in a ladylike way. "Will you fit in there?" she asked. She did wonder.

"I must—and pray I don't get stuck." She saw his lordship's

firm lips crank into a small smile. What a bizarre man—the two things to make him laugh were kissing her and the threat of being stuck in a tunnel in a sewer.

Serena tentatively put her knee forward. There was no other way to get through but to hike up her robe and scramble on bare knees. Candlelight glowed from ahead. "I've reached the end," Drake Swift called back. "It opens into a larger room. A vaulted room."

The dirt and grit bit into Serena bare knees as she crawled, and Lord Sommersby's powerful arms bumped her rear end since he could move much faster than she. His lordship's apologies made her ache to laugh. Finally Draft Swift reached for her arms, locked his strong hands on hers, and helped her forward. With a reassuring wink, he set her to her feet. Foolish to feel such triumph over conquering a tunnel, over Swift's approval of her courage.

Mr. Swift's candle threw light on the circular space surrounding them, revealing stone blocks, oozing muck, and several shadowy doorways. Swift immediately went to the nearest arched wooden door set into the stone wall. "How do I open the lock, sweetheart?"

"Miss Lark," Sommersby corrected through gritted teeth.

They were facing danger and arguing over endearments. "It is a special type of lock, gentlemen. It contains a barrel-type device, with numbers that must be lined up to a pin for the pin to slide free."

"Let me, Swift." Sommersby handed Serena the candle and moved to take his partner's place.

"I can line up a few numbers, Sommersby," Swift snapped. "What are they, Miss Lark?"

"1, 3, 7, and 9, sir," she said. At least, those were the numbers recorded in a vampire hunter's journal.

Swift's fingers turned the numbers slowly. From the side,

she saw him struggle with the old lock. Her heart sank as he tried to pull the lock apart. "It doesn't work," she breathed.

"A moment, Miss Lark." He pulled again, harder. With a reluctant creak, the lock opened. She'd been correct! She'd solved an ancient puzzle and found something no other vampire hunter had done.

Swift peered around the door. "There's another door, Miss Lark. With a padlock."

"There can't be!" She hoisted her robe and ran around to look. But it was—a padlock that required a key. Her shoulders sagged in despair. She hadn't read anything in any of the Society's books about a second door or about a key. Perhaps the lock wasn't truly locked. She prayed that was so, but Swift tried it and it would not open. Serena seethed in frustration.

Lord Sommersby drew out a slim piece of metal and pushed Drake Swift aside. "Lock pick" was all he said, and he slid it into the keyhole. He jiggled it and then she heard a "click."

Suddenly Serena felt panic. She must get in there before Sommersby told her she could not. She raced up to Drake Swift and put her hand on his hip. His hip was solid, lean, and a flame seemed to race through her blood at the touch. Swift glanced down at her, and she caught her breath at the desire in his eyes. A sudden battle waged behind his heated eyes. Would he grab her or send her back? Then he caught hold of her wrist and pulled her along with him.

The room was unlit, though Swift's candle gave a circle of light. The anteroom they'd been in was an ill-fashioned domed space. Serena pulled away from Swift and spun in a circle, drinking in the room. Excitement surged. This room was rectangular—a large, carefully crafted vault below ground. It was fashioned of finished stone, and shelves lined the walls. There was a true floor of stone, each slab perfectly interlocked with the others. A simple table and chairs sat in the middle of the room. There was dust, though; fine brown silt seemed to cover everything. Serena supposed that modern vampires found little use for the journals of the past.

"So you were correct, little lark."

Before she could answer Swift, Lord Sommersby ducked to cross the threshold. He let out his breath in a low whistle.

Now she had to be clever. She crossed to the shelves at the farthest corner of the room. The system used to arrange the books was obscure. It had taken her a long time to decode it from notes. And it had been hard to keep the gentlemen of the Society distracted while she was trying to do it. They always had such meaningless tasks and errands for her.

Hesitantly Serena reached out and touched the leather binding of a book, but Sommersby moved immediately to her side. His torch threw light on the shelf. He bent, as though to study a volume in front of her, and he murmured by her ear, "You know how these are arranged? You're a clever woman."

"I am." Agreeing seemed the best option. She drew out the book, bound in red leather and untitled. She lifted the cover. The ink had faded, the script was ornate, difficult to read, and the date was 1582. She slipped it back in and drew out the next. Writings on Elizabeth Bathory from 1700.

It confirmed what she'd expected. She put the Elizabeth Bathory book back into place and scanned the rest of the shelf.

"I was right." She couldn't help but let triumph creep in. "They aren't organized by date or by author. They are organized by each vampire who tends the library—it is always men—in a system unique to him. Each librarian had a section. This book came in during the end of the last century, when the library was brought here."

She knew exactly where she had to look, but Sommersby watched her every move. "You could look at the other shelves, my lord," she suggested.

"But I have the light, Miss Lark. We should work together."

Blast. Serena moved to the shelf she wanted, her heart pounding. Could she distract him in some way when she found the book? Or grab the one beside it and then slip out the one she really wanted?

"I'm going out for a moment." It was Swift's voice. Going out? Where? But she couldn't worry about that now.

Serena counted back six books. It should be . . . it wasn't. Her fingers trembled over the two books and the slight gap between them. A book was missing. Vlad Dracul's journal was gone!

She slid out the nearest work—a sheath of linen held with a slim ribbon. The paper had yellowed, the ink faded, but the Latin script was painstakingly beautiful. She would guess it to be a piece of a monastery manuscript—perhaps six centuries old. She held ancient history in her hand.

But it was not Vlad Dracul's journal. It might be a phenomenally valuable book, but it was worthless to her. Had the journal merely been misplaced? Heart pounding, she pulled out book after book.

"Looking for a particular book?"

The book she held fell from her hand.

Lord Sommersby's leather-clad knuckles stroked her cheek. "Easy, my dear."

She wasn't crying, but her breath was fast, almost beyond her control. Without Dracul's journal, what could she use to coerce Ashcroft to give her the truth? How could it not be here? It was forbidden amongst vampires to take from this collection—

Really, what was she thinking? Vampires preyed on humans. They fought constantly for supremacy. As if they would obey the rules of the library!

"What book did you want, Miss Lark? Tell me." Sommersby's voice was soft, soothing.

What was she to do now? Here, in one of these books, could

be information about her vampire father. But did she have the time to look at all the books? And she had no idea what to look for or where to start.

Serena drew away from Lord Sommersby's touch and forced herself to sound calm. "I want to find the books from the time of my parents' deaths," she lied.

"Miss Lark." He cupped her chin. She obeyed the command of his long, elegant fingers and met his gaze. His lips were just a hairbreadth from hers. Warm, promising safety, promising escape from failure and from the damned constant fight to learn who she was.

Serena arched up on her toes, seeking him. Her lips touched his. Heat. Sparks. Pleasure. His mouth opened and hers followed. His tongue teased—coaxing hers into play. She dueled with his tongue as he plunged it deliciously into her mouth, a promise of so much more . . . Her fingers closed around the earl's strong arms. All she wanted to do was kiss him. His mouth on hers was so erotic. Her heart beat in her throat.

She'd failed, she'd almost lost her life on this gamble, and all she wanted to do was kiss his lordship. She wanted to melt into Sommersby's powerful embrace, lay her hands on his massive chest, and kiss him until she forgot everything.

What was wrong with her? How could she be so wanton?

His lordship's hands encircled her waist . . . but his mouth eased back, breaking the contact—

"Vampires!" Drake Swift leaned into the doorway, his silver-blond hair wild around his face.

Serena almost fell back against the books as Sommersby pulled away from her.

She grabbed at the shelf—a few volumes tumbled to the floor around her feet. She glanced down—one book had fallen open over her slipper. On the cover was one embossed word. *Lukos.*

She bent and grabbed it.

"Hell." Sommersby scooped his arm around her waist and hauled her up. He lifted her over the fallen books.

Struggling, she tried to break free of his grip. "I can't go. Not yet! There might be something here."

But Sommersby carried her back to the anteroom—their only way out.

A vampire was climbing out of the small tunnel. Serena saw the vampire's face, the mouth open wide, fangs pale white. The vampire and Drake Swift met in a crash—Swift's arm plunged as the vampire's teeth latched to his already-wounded neck. With an unearthly shriek, the black-clad vampire dropped to the ground.

"There's more coming," Swift yelled. "And we've got no way out of here."

"There is a way," Serena cried. "The first door leads to the tunnel, but it goes to the Thames—"

Swift raced to the door. "Blast! Forgot there's numbers." But the lock opened in his hand as he dragged his fingers away. "It's unlocked."

Unlocked? Someone had gone through before them, but Serena raced headlong after Mr. Swift into the room, not caring what she found. Lord Sommersby, on her heels, grasped her shoulder. "Stay at my side, Miss Lark." As he propelled her forward, she held tight to the book in her hand, her fingernails driving into the leather cover. Mr. Swift ran out ahead, his candle throwing a glow on the masonry walls, on the damp floor. "Where do we go from here?" he called back. "The Thames?"

Serena's lungs dragged in air as they ran. Her feet slapped painfully on the wet, rough floor. "T-there's no other way."

"Is there any fork in the tunnels at all? Even a dead end?"

Serena managed an astonished stare at Lord Sommersby. "There might be. . . . There is a church above with . . . with some catacombs." She panted the words out. If it weren't for Sommersby's grip on her arm she would have fallen into the muck. Her knees ached from the crawl. Her slippers slid sloppily on her feet as she tried to keep running.

"Can you find the catacombs?" his lordship demanded.

"But then what?"

"We double back, Miss Lark," he answered. "And go back through the brothel."

7

Duty

How could they outrun creatures that could fly? And who was ahead of them—more vampires?

Even as the thoughts tumbled through her mind, Serena felt the brush of air, the fierce flap of wings through the dark.

Mr. Swift stopped abruptly. "Goddamn."

In a maelstrom of wind that drew water and dirt from the floor, a vampire materialized before them. Lord Sommersby held her at his side; his torch threw out light on Roman's powerful naked body, his long dark hair, his face.

His nakedness startled.

"Come with me, Serena Lark," Roman crooned.

She felt the power of his voice—she stared into his reflective eyes, mesmerized, trying to will herself to look away. Sommersby shook her and she jerked free of the spell, just as Drake Swift charged forward, a stake raised. She screamed—expecting Roman to launch at Swift. But Roman turned and fled down the tunnel, his hair a long stream behind him. Swift laughed, the laugh of a man enjoying himself, and followed.

"No!" she cried. "It must be a trap."

"I have to go after the bloody fool, and I'm not leaving you alone." The earl grasped her hand and pulled her along.

"He must be—be leading Mr. Swift into disaster." She gasped the words. Lord Sommersby's hold on her arm again kept her from falling into the muck. Her slippers skidded as she ran.

Mr. Swift vanished into the dark ahead.

"You—God—Aieeee!"

Someone screamed. The worst scream of unholy pain.

"Christ Jesus!"

Her legs wobbled in relief beneath her at the sound of Drake Swift's voice. He was alive, thank heaven, and while his voice betrayed astonishment and surprise, he didn't sound weak or in pain. Serena forced her feet to keep moving forward.

Then a great force of air rushed over them, and the edge of the torchlight illuminated wide, black wings. Roman had transformed into a bat and flew back toward the brothel.

The earl stopped first. Under the light of his torch, Serena saw Drake Swift in a crouch. Had he been hit?

With a cry, she pushed around Sommersby and stumbled forward, just as Mr. Swift straightened. "I bloody missed him. He dove at me, clawed me, and I staked him—got him below the heart again." Swift stared right into her eyes. "Miss Lark, angel, don't look so distressed. I'm not hurt."

The earl held up his hand. "Listen."

She strained to hear—and suddenly her mind was filled with the splatter of drips, the distant rush of the water in the tunnel.

"I don't hear wings or footsteps," Sommersby murmured. He drew out his pocket watch, and for the second time, he gave a slight smile. "A quarter of seven. Daylight."

Mr. Swift winked. "Saved by dawn, little lark. We can go back through the brothel—it will be empty now."

"The library," Serena whispered. "We must return to the library."

His lordship shook his head. "No, Miss Lark. You have had a traumatic night—you will be returning to Lady Brookshire's house. With me. The Society will take care of the library today."

"My lord—no!" She reached for his arm.

"Yes, Miss Lark."

Seething in frustration, she looked to Mr. Swift, but he nodded in agreement. "Little lark, we must get you to safety."

Without the book, how could she find out the truth? Panic gripped as the earl turned and swept her up into his arms. No, she had to go back—

"She gave you a right shiner."

Jonathon touched the swollen corner of his right eye, but he would be damned if he'd give Swift the satisfaction of wincing at the shot of pain. Serena Lark had indeed pasted him right in the eye as she'd struggled in his arms. He should take it as proof she was a vampiress—she had incredible strength for a female.

He scrubbed his jaw. She'd been after a particular book, one that was missing. He would have to discover which one. Since Ashcroft's story about two vampires raiding her parents' home was a lie, what book could she have found?

Swift poured more coffee into his cup and leaned back in the chair, holding the cup, then insolently propped his booted feet on the breakfast table. He drained the steaming brew in one gulp. "Miss Lark was damned angry at you for taking her away from those books. I suspect you won't be kissing her again anytime soon—not without getting a slap for your trouble."

"Leave her alone," Jonathon snarled at his partner. "I behaved like a bloody cad last night. As did you."

"We risk death, *brother*—the rules of polite society needn't matter to men who risk death every night."

"We face death by choice, Swift." Jonathon refused to show any reaction to Swift's use of the word *brother.* They weren't brothers, not by blood, but he knew their relationship was stronger, more intertwined, more damned infuriating than the one between real brothers. "It's no excuse not to behave as gentlemen."

"Then it's fortunate I'm not a gentleman." Swift swung down his feet and stood. "I'm off to bed. Regrettably alone. Are you going to lock yourself in that bloody laboratory again?"

Jonathon grunted. That was exactly where he was going. He swallowed his coffee without tasting it and poured another brimming cup as Swift sauntered out. Damn, he was exhausted, but he had to fight it, and the coffee helped invigorate him. Forgoing cream or sugar, he gulped down the second scalding cup and set it rattling on the saucer before striding out of the room.

Rumpole, his elderly butler, stood in the hall, looking as morose as ever. "Lord Ashcroft, my lord. Waiting in the laboratory."

Jonathon gave a brief nod and hurried down the corridor. He passed the many unused rooms of his home—the curtains drawn, the furniture swathed in Holland covers, fires unlit. The coolness of fall was beginning to settle into the house.

He thought of his father's words of warning as he passed by dark room after dark room. *A vampire hunter's life is a solitary existence. You're better to be alone, because you'll fear the risk to someone you love.* It was the truth. He possessed a house that was no longer a home, populated with a few aging, trusted servants. He never attended parties or balls. Never gamed, never drank to excess, never spent the night in a mistress's arms. His house was devoid of the sparkle of a woman's touch, a woman's laughter . . . a woman's soul.

That thought spurred Jonathon to race up the stairs, to jog toward the dark, tomblike east wing that housed the laboratory.

After last night, he knew he could no longer obey Lord Ashcroft or the Royal Society. He couldn't let Serena transform into a vampire, and he knew he couldn't destroy her.

If he wanted to try to save Serena Lark's soul, he had to get to work.

* * *

The door to the study adjoining his laboratory stood open. Inside the study, Ashcroft cradled the jawbone of a vampire in his hand, holding it up to examine it under the sunlight that drizzled in the windows. His mentor—the man who had been more of a father than his own—turned at the sound of his step and touched the long upper fangs. "Fascinating."

Jonathon gazed on the face of the man who had always encouraged him—who had often acted as peacemaker between he and his father—and realized, with shock, how cadaverous Ashcroft looked. The tall, lean body stooped, the back rounded, the shoulders slumped. Deep lines etched Ashcroft's face, and his few remaining strands of hair were chalk white. His cheeks were sunken, his eyes shadowed.

Jonathon frowned. "Are you ill, sir?"

The older man gave a thin smile. "Blunt as always, Sommersby."

His words had been ill mannered, but he didn't have time for niceties. "The truth, sir. What ails you?"

"I take it I don't look at my best." Ashcroft looked amused. "It's the loss of sleep, my boy. And old age."

Jonathon got to the point. "Who the hell is Lukos? And why does he wants Miss Lark? Could he know what she is?"

"I've no idea who Lukos is." Ashcroft eased himself into the club chair closest to the low fire. "There's no mention of such a vampire in any of the literature possessed by the Society. We have only begun to remove that treasure trove of books you found beneath the brothel."

Jonathon raked his hand through his already disordered hair. "Miss Lark found that."

"A clever woman." Ashcroft leaned his head back, shut his eyes for the moment. Jonathon moved to the brandy decanter. He poured two drinks. Given the odd hours he kept, he took brandy whenever it was convenient. Ashcroft did the same.

Ashcroft accepted the glass.

Jonathon cradled his between his palms. "You told me that Serena Lark has not yet transformed—that she is still mortal. She still has a soul; she doesn't yet have the characteristics of a vampire. I want to try to stop her change into vampire."

"Impossible." Brandy spilled from Ashcroft's glass as the earl pounded his fist into the leather chair arm. "Her transformation on All Hallow's Eve cannot be stopped—and it will be the Society's first chance to witness the actual moment of change."

"My father believed there was a way to stop it."

Shock registered on Ashcroft's shadowed face. "You found your father's journals? Where?"

"Not the journals, just notes and a letter. Unfinished and hidden underneath a secret panel in his desk."

"A letter? Written to who?"

"To me." His father had started it the day before his death of a heart seizure.

"And what did it tell you?" Ashcroft barked. He perched on the edge of the seat now, pale blue eyes burning with intensity.

"Only that my father kept records of Serena Lark—meticulous records of her life. From records kept by the people who raised her—apparently from Mr. Bridgewater, who died shortly after she left their care—when she returned looking for answers."

His mentor's face jerked up. "From Bridgewater? But why—" Ashcroft broke off and passed a gloved hand over his jaw. "I had no idea your father and he corresponded. It was dashed unfortunate that Bridgewater and his wife died."

"I believe my father was keeping these records for you, sir. He was planning to unveil his discovery—the way to stop the creation of a vampire."

Ashcroft was trembling. "I never saw his journals, Jonathon. He never showed them to me."

Jonathon put his untouched brandy on the desk. Frustration surged in him. "I'm still searching for the journals. I've tried every blasted property belonging to the estate—and I'm back here, none the wiser. In that unfinished letter he was gloating over the grand discovery. Why would he hide it from me?" He could understand his father's care in hiding the books, but not why his father would have left no clues for him. "I've been trying to work from the laboratory books prior to those that are missing—to see if I can replicate what he found."

"But you don't know that this discovery is in any way related to Miss Lark."

"It was, sir. In the journal I did find, my father specifically says that he believed he had a better use for Miss Lark than waiting for her to transform, then cutting her open—" Jonathon's stomach lurched as he remembered what his father had planned to do. In the name of protecting humanity, his father had dispassionately listed the procedures he would perform on Serena Lark's corpse.

"And that use would be?"

"Proving, with her as example, that he could prevent the loss of soul. That he could reverse the transformation."

"Impossible!" Ashcroft shouted. "We must observe what happens—Sommersby, we will never have this chance again."

"She's a living, breathing human being, not an experiment."

Wheezing, Ashcroft shook his head. "She is a vampire, Sommersby. This is her destiny. Imagine how many others could be saved."

Jonathon clenched his fists at his sides. He remembered Lilianne's eyes—that moment of trust, of hope. "I cannot sacrifice Miss Lark."

"You will have no choice. You do not have your father's notes. You can't replicate his discovery, can you?"

Jonathon gave a curt shake of his head. No. No, he had no idea what his father had done. "His journals are somewhere. I will find them."

With a groan and a pained grimace, Ashcroft lifted from the chair. "Sommersby, your duty is to the Society, to England. To mankind."

Jonathon closed his eyes. Remembering the mantra—think of the innocent lives a vampire will claim. One life sacrificed to save many.

He heard Ashcroft's rasping voice. "I have watched her grow from infancy, Sommersby. A vampire who would live as a mortal until the prime of her life, then transform into a being more powerful than any we have ever known. Since her birth, I have kept her under control . . . waiting for this . . . waiting for the moment of change. I had to take great care—she was my precious secret."

"But you told my father."

"Of course. I could trust your father." Ashcroft clapped a weak hand on his shoulder. "Lady Brookshire informed me that Miss Lark is determined to hunt Lukos. She wants to destroy him before he goes after her. Sommersby, we cannot take the risk of letting Miss Lark get near Lukos. Your mission is to protect her—to keep her away from Lukos."

"Lady Brookshire is a vampiress," Jonathon pointed out. "A good one. She has never killed." He thought of Lilianne again. His pretty fiancée had not been a "good" vampire. He had lost her to one of the most brutal of vampires—one who created true soulless drones. She had become a monster.

And when he'd staked that vampire—that nameless, inhuman beast—he'd found that getting vengeance hadn't given him peace.

Lord Ashcroft shook his head. "Lady Brookshire lusts for blood and she has the power to kill. Even though she helps the Royal Society, we cannot forget that. I have kept it hidden from Serena Lark that her ladyship is a vampiress—you must not reveal the truth." Ashcroft's face was grim. "A vampire can never be trusted. How can we allow them to flourish? They are stronger than we are—we are mere prey to them. Serena Lark is the key to saving human souls, Jonathon."

Jonathon's heart tightened. He was running out of time.

"I'm going to need the time in the laboratory, sir—to try to save her. And I want to hunt Lukos."

Ashcroft shook his head. "I'm afraid that won't do, Sommersby. I have assigned other hunters to destroy Lukos. I want you to let Miss Lark hunt with you—"

"And how the bloody hell will that keep her safe?"

Ashcroft held up a quelling hand. His eyes gleamed. "You will make her believe she is helping you pursue Lukos, but you will keep her away from Lukos. You will keep her under your protection. In ten days she will turn . . . and we will learn how a vampire is made. We will be able to study her power." Then, his mentor flashed the autocratic look of a father. "This is your duty, Sommersby. I expect you to carry it out."

Moonlight filtered through the trees, casting puddles of blue-silver light on the path ahead of her. She was running, her chest heaving, her heart pumping hard enough to burst. Her hair flew out behind her; her skirts flapped around her, trapping her legs.

Serena tripped over a root and fell to her knees. Sharp rocks bit through the wool of her skirts. The stake ripped against her bare palm, tearing her skin, releasing blood, and she heard the howls behind her as her scent was carried back on the wind.

Two large hands gripped her shoulders, lifting her. Sheer horror tore through her. Lukos. It must be Lukos—she jerked her head up to see . . . Lord Sommersby. He towered over her, dressed to perfection, a cloak swirling around him.

"I know what you are," he said, "and I desire you in a way that is completely unholy. You have bewitched me."

His mouth lowered and she lifted hers, breathless—how long did they have before the vampires caught them? Minutes? Or mere seconds? Sommersby pressed her back against a tree; the rough bark bit into her. His mouth, hot and demanding, claimed hers. He cast a spell on her again, and she hauled up her skirt, tangling her tongue with his.

His fingers filled her cunny, thrusting into her, and she sobbed with need and pleasure into his mouth. She was going to die this way.

Another man. She sensed him at her side. Out of the corner of her eye, Serena glimpsed pale silver-blond hair. Drake Swift.

His hand slid up her exposed inner thigh, brushed Sommersby's, and found her derriere. Delicately, his finger toyed at her anus, touching until she began to melt with pleasure.

The need to orgasm took her. She began rocking on their fingers. Sommersby freed her mouth, and she panted with hunger and fierce desire. Yes, yes, more. She didn't care about death. Didn't care about anything but coming, now, here, on the thick, skilled fingers of the men she desired—

Oh yes! The orgasm slammed into her and she screamed with it. The vampires would hear her, they would come—

She looked helplessly to Drake Swift as she shuddered and shook in ecstasy. He grinned and bent close, his breath heating the tingling rim of her ear. "We are going to make love to you together, little lark."

And before she could gasp, she felt the delicious pressure of Lord Sommersby's enormous cock against her drenched cunny—

Fangs. She felt fangs explode from her mouth.

She heard Sommersby's horrified shout, Drake Swift's cry of shock. Swift's hands gripped her shoulders. Sommersby held a stake. The stake arced toward her heart—

She bolted upright, chest heaving. Sweat drenched her nightdress, her forehead.

A rap came at the door. From behind it, Althea, Lady Brookshire, called out, "Serena?"

8

Ménage

"And so, you saved their lives, of course, you clever girl!"

Serena couldn't help but smile at the enthusiasm in Althea's declaration. Trust Althea to make her whole disastrous night at the brothel sound like a triumphant adventure.

"Of course," Serena replied, trying for modesty. With the blankets and sheets drawn up to her waist, she hugged her knees closer in a vain attempt to soothe her still-trembling body.

Althea rested her hands on her round belly, a lush curve beneath her ivory silk peignoir. "I've been up all night. I'll summon tea—and biscuits, I think. Sugar biscuits. A little something to take the edge off before I have my breakfast, then go to sleep."

Serena did laugh and felt much better for it. Had she ever once thought her best friend—her only friend—would be a countess? Althea de Wynter, the Countess of Brookshire. Of course, enceinte Althea, with her auburn curls; twinkling, fey green eyes; scandalous sense of humor; and penchant for vampire hunting, made a very unusual countess.

After she sent a maid to fetch tea, Althea continued, conspiratorially, "I'm sure those two daring vampire slayers couldn't believe a mere woman could do all that you did! You found an absolute treasure—and by using dusty books that they think are insignificant!" Poised on the edge of the water-blue silk chaise, Althea gave her soft, lovely, infectious laugh.

Serena knew Althea was deliberately not speaking of Lukos yet, trying to make her forget about fear, about threat. She fought the urge to forgo stoicism and crumble into tears. She'd been captured by vampires, she'd discovered a demonic "master" was pursuing her, she couldn't find Vlad Dracul's journal, and she'd lost all the other books to pompous, lying Lord Ashcroft. And, on top of that, she was most likely a vampire.

Dimly, she realized Althea was still speaking. "We women can do remarkable things with books," Althea declared. "We women do the most remarkable things in every way."

She stroked her tummy and Serena's heart gave a sharp pang.

Althea sat down next to her on the bed. "But in all seriousness, Serena, what of this Lukos demon?"

"I don't know anything about him—other than what I told you. He is sailing to England, and he knows who I am." Serena held back the reason Lukos knew who she was—that he knew she was a vampire. Nor had she told Althea about Roman's intent to claim her.

"And he had a pack of six vampires as disciples!" Althea gave a shiver.

Serena nodded. It was not unusual—vampires were driven to create other vampires; increasing their numbers gave them protection. Lukos was building his own private army.

Althea frowned and tapped her chin. "When I woke at dusk, I read through that book that you brought back, after Yannick and Bastien went out to hunt." Althea sighed. "I'm not allowed to join them anymore, due to my condition. Really, I shall have the fortitude to give birth to this child in a few months—I'm certain that being a vampire hunter will not be as exhausting as that."

Serena could hardly imagine thinking of handsome, aristocratic Lord Brookshire as Yannick and his devastatingly gorgeous twin as simply Bastien. Both men were completely devoted to Althea—and Bastien was shockingly seductive with his brother's wife, though Serena had never seen Brookshire show jealousy.

Serena reached out and touched the ancient book sitting on her bedside table. The binding was old and cracking, the stitching worn, the linen sheet tearing at the edges. There were smears of dirt on the pages. It was written in one of the runic alphabets, and these she was studying but did not completely understand. "I tried to read it, but I'd taken the laudanum then, and I couldn't stay awake."

"They are written in Orkhon runes," Althea clarified. "I saw examples that had been discovered in the Orkhon river valley of Mongolia." Althea stood, shaking out the skirt of her peignoir. "I believe the book tells a tale of a creature known as Lukos—a creature who could become wolf or man and who served Lucifer, taking lives at his command."

The maid knocked, then brought in the tea tray including a plate heaped with cakes and biscuits. Althea licked her lips and Serena smiled.

"So Lucifer wishes me and has sent Lukos to fetch me?" Serena reached for the teacup after Althea poured. She looked down at her wrist—she still felt the horrifying bite of the shackles.

"I don't know, but this is very serious."

"A demon knows my name and tried to capture me? Of course I know this is serious!"

"I'm surprised you aren't hysterical."

"Being a governess taught me to be neither emotional nor hysterical. Really, a good governess can't have any human weaknesses at all." Serena tossed the comment off with ironic humor, but it had been all too true.

Vanilla and lavender surrounded her as she felt the warmth of Althea's arms.

"You've been very brave, Serena. But you must trust us to help you."

She'd never had hug from a friend—she'd never even had a friend. Althea did not know she was a vampire—what huntress would allow a vampire into her home? But she was so confused. Why would Lord Ashcroft put enceinte Lady Brookshire at risk by having her bring a vampire into her home?

"I had your stockings from last night burned," Althea said. "They smelled of a smoke—a smoke that reminded me of solange. Though it couldn't be. Why would vampires burn solange?"

Because they know I am a vampire. But she couldn't say that to Althea.

"What were you searching for in the library, Serena?"

She took a deep breath and straightened. "Lord Ashcroft knows about my past, about my parents, but he won't tell me. I thought the library would give me a way to coerce him to tell me. There was supposed to be a special book there—a journal written by Vlad Dracul."

"And you wanted to trade that for the truth about your parents?"

She nodded. "But now I have nothing."

Althea drew back. She toyed with the smooth silk at the lapels of her wrapper. "The past needn't matter so much. You can't change it—you can only move forward."

Serena bit back a bitter laugh. What did she have to look forward to? And she couldn't forget the past. Everything haunted her. The venom behind Mrs. Bridgewater's smiles. The hopeless and pitiful way she'd thought William Bridgewater had loved her when he came to her bed. But how could she explain this to Althea? How could she talk of that horrible night when she'd told William she lost the baby and he'd whooped with joyful relief?

"I need to know," she said, softly. "Do you know you are the only friend I've ever had, Althea? I've never belonged anywhere. I need to find out who I am."

"I never had friends either." Althea hugged her again. "I followed my father on his expeditions. I understand what you are feeling, but you can't risk your life to find out what happened. It's not worth that."

"It is to me."

Althea slid off the bed, her hand on her lower back. "You should speak with Sommersby. His father kept journals—he had done very extensive studies on vampires. I know that he knew about you. I believe he was the one who encouraged Lord Ashcroft to extend help to you."

"You mean that the previous Lord Sommersby has records about my past?"

"I don't know that for certain, Serena. I have never seen his books." Althea stood by the door, a frown on her pretty freckled face.

Serena stood up. She had to see those books. Could the present Lord Sommersby know what she was? But why hadn't he killed her? Perhaps he had the books but hadn't read them yet. She must get to them before he did.

Desperate to dress, to race to his house, she slipped out of bed.

"Serena—please wait!"

She turned, startled by the sharpness in Althea's tone.

"Sommersby might not have anything. I had heard that he was not able to find all his father's records when he returned to

England. And there are six estates—the papers could be hidden anywhere. Please, don't . . ."

"Don't what?" He might not have read them—thank heavens. Serena fumbled with her nightgown buttons.

"Don't pin all your hopes on this. The past doesn't matter. It doesn't make you who you are."

She undid the ties at the throat of the gown. "It does, Althea. I know that it does."

"Serena, what are you going to do?"

"Go to Lord Sommersby's house." The earl would be out hunting vampires. And if she didn't find the books before he did, she would pay with her life.

Why had she done that?

In her boudoir, Althea stroked her rounded belly—she couldn't resist giving a little poke. She giggled when the baby kicked back. And shivered. The sight of a little bulge crossing her stomach, a little bump completely independent of her, still seemed both miraculous and a little frightening—and she was a vampire!

Althea studied her reflection in the cheval mirror. Heavy, full breasts. A rounded tummy with taut skin—how could she grow any larger? But she still had so many months to go, and at the end, she would be enormous.

"It's almost dawn, sweetheart."

The deep, loving, seductive voice sent a tingle of love and pleasure through her. Althea smiled into the mirror at Bastien's reflection. Naked, gorgeous, and scratching his ballocks without a touch of self-consciousness. This was what married life resulted in, she thought, and saw her lips curve in a tender, wry smile.

Bastien leaned against the doorframe, his long, lean legs crossed at his ankles. His blond hair, as golden as candlelight, hung loose, the waves brushing his broad, bare shoulders. "Time to sleep. Sleep is good for the babe, and for you."

He looked so deliciously sexy any thoughts of sleep vanished. Althea's gaze lingered on the reflection of his green-blue eyes, his inexplicably dark lashes, the play of his tongue along his full lower lip. Even the veins on his naked forearms made her hot and aroused, and she loved how he groaned when she traced those with her tongue.

Bastien grinned, pushed away from the doorframe, and swaggered toward her. "I recognize that smile, my love."

Not a minute went by that she didn't have lusty thoughts for Bastien, or Yannick, or both. But when a lady had two husbands—two vampire husbands with powerful sexual drives—she barely had time for activities that didn't involve the bedroom.

Bastien cupped her nude bottom, and he kissed the top of her head with heat in his eyes. "You are so beautiful, Althea. So lush. So abundant."

"So big?" Althea couldn't help a rueful quirk of her lips as she cradled her heavy, hard tummy with both hands. "You are finding very ingenious ways to avoid the truth, Bastien. I can't share a coffin anymore."

He bent to her neck. "Not to worry, sweetheart, I've commissioned a larger one."

"Where is Yannick?"

"Not home. We're alone, darling wife." And then the rogue licked her cheek with a long, languorous sweep of his tongue. Althea pushed him away with a palm on his handsome forehead.

"Yannick has been very annoyed that you ensure you are always here when he is not." She spoke teasingly, for it was all in good humor. Though sometimes she did have to tread a fine line between her two alpha males.

She saw the vulnerability beneath Bastien's rakish wink. "I

am merely ensuring I keep my dear wife satisfied." He reached up and tapped the undersides of her full, round breasts. He groaned as he watched them bounce, her nipples hardening. He tweaked them, and she cried out.

"I don't like staying here, Althea," he murmured. "We should sail soon—you don't have to do anything the Society demands."

"It's for Serena." Even as shots of pleasure raced from her nipples to her cunny, Althea tried to concentrate. "That's what I was speaking about." He tugged on her oh-so-sensitive nipples. She had to tip her head back and shut her eyes. "Oh, Bastien, I did something impulsive. Something I know I should not have done."

"Confide, Althea. I suspect you're fretting over nothing."

A guilty blush touched her cheeks, hot and sudden. "I told Serena that the late Earl of Sommersby kept journals—I hinted that she might find answers about her past there." Althea turned in his arms. "Serena is so alone. She told me how happy she is that she has me, that it was so much nicer than being completely alone. I feel so horrid, keeping the truth from her."

Bastien gave a kiss to her shoulder, then dropped to his knees in front of her. Althea saw support and caring in his gorgeous blue-green eyes.

"Then tell her the truth," he said.

Althea shook her head. "It isn't so simple."

"Is it loyalty to the Society—?"

"No! It's because I'm afraid for her. Lord Ashcroft has told me that Serena is the first child ever born of a vampire and a mortal, a feat they believed impossible. Her mother was incredibly powerful, and Serena will inherit that power. And I'm worried what will happen when she knows—"

Bastien kissed her—just below the curve of her belly, above

her red pubic curls. "Althea, love, don't worry. It's not good for you or the baby."

"I know you don't approve of my relationship with the Royal Society."

"I understand it, love, but I still believe it's damned unholy for a vampire to be involved with those who want to destroy us." The wretch tickled her now-protruding navel.

Her giggle bubbled up, relaxing her tense shoulders. "I know. But we are the only ones who can stop truly evil demons."

Though she knew how frightened the Society must be of her coming child.

Bastien bent, brushed a soft kiss to her bare nether curls. "We have to sail, love. Before your pregnancy has advanced much further. You can't sail when you are too close to your confinement."

"I know," she said again.

"The truth is, my angel, I believe you don't trust the Royal Society. You should tell Serena the truth. If anyone can help her cope with that discovery, my sweet, it's you. Now, let's play for a while—before dawn, before Yannick returns."

Bastien stroked her thighs as his tongue slicked down through her curls to her clit, and she arched her head back on a cry of pleasure.

"You are always trying to steal lovemaking on your brother, aren't you?"

"Of course, dear love. Because I love you so much." His large fingers toyed with her wet and sticky nether lips. "And I know that being enceinte has made you very aroused. I have some very naughty games in mind."

She reached down and stroked his silky hair, but the rogue fooled her—he whipped her clit with such vehemence that her legs became jelly and only his hands on her hips kept her from falling. "Bastien!"

* * *

Bound to the chair, Bastien watched Althea approach.

She dropped her robe and turned her back to him, displaying her voluptuous derriere—plump, rounded cheeks caressed by warm candlelight. His naked cock jolted up a notch higher.

She swayed her hips back and forth, the gesture tempting and hypnotic.

Bastien prayed she planned to sit astride him and not just torture him. God, he loved her—he could not believe how he had deserved a woman like Althea—loving, clever, and so wantonly inventive she left him astonished.

He also could not believe he shared her with his brother, and how she had opened his eyes to the beauty of a love shared between three.

Ropes bit into his wrists and ankles. He loved this game. He loved putting her in charge—because he was still in control. A few naughtily whispered suggestions and he could coerce Althea to do what he wished and send them both into explosive ecstasy. "Well, your ladyship," he teased, "what do you plan to do to me now that you have me tied up?"

"I think I shall sit quite daintily, Mr. de Wynter, and have my tea."

God, yes.

Her bottom lowered until the tip of his cock brushed a plush cheek. She reached down and held him steady, swallowing him in the valley of her bottom.

Bastien's prick pushed against the tight, hot entrance. He tried to lift his hips but was too tightly restrained.

Althea rubbed him against her, wetting herself with him. Gripping him tight, she sat down on him, taking him slightly inside. The tight pressure enthralled.

She pumped up and down slowly, taking him in inch by delightful inch. She let go of him and sank right down to his hips. He felt his cock invade her and push her fire-hot walls apart.

Althea lifted on him, then dropped back down, her body clamping around him. Being inside her bottom was the most illicit pleasure.

She let only the softest sighs escape. Each time she almost moaned, she bit the sound back. Playing the dominant, she wanted to disguise how much he pleasured her, and how she loved to be filled with his cock.

Bastien watched as she arranged herself to sit like a lady on him. He wanted her to pump on him like a wanton; instead she sat with demure grace, not moving at all. And rang the bellpull.

The stretch of her arm shifted her around his cock, and he let a howl of pleasure ring to the rococo ceiling.

"What are you doing?" He laughed.

"Summoning tea."

"You plan to have a servant come in here?" The chair scraped the floor as he jerked in surprise.

"If you are silent, he will never be the wiser."

"And how—" Even seated on his cock, she held up her hand imperiously. He shut his mouth, intrigued.

A blindfolded footman brought the tea tray and followed her directions to place it on the table before her. Bastien cast him a brief glance and worked to lift his hips, thrusting lightly into Althea's derriere. He bit back a lusty laugh, as he heard her soft gasp, as he saw her breasts—and her larger, darker, longer nipples—bounce with each jiggle.

How had he ever deserved such an inventive and luscious woman?

The muscular footman bowed and withdrew.

Althea leaned forward, changing the glorious pressure surrounding his cock as she set about making tea.

How he wished he wasn't bound. He'd soon put an end to her game. His fingers on her nipples and between her legs would quickly have her desperately working to an orgasm.

She began shifting her hips slightly on him, teasing him.

Then she opened herself even more with her muscles and swallowed him deeper.

Squeezing the muscles of her lush bottom, she jiggled up and down on him. Calmly, she lifted her cup and sipped tea.

"Come on, my lady, give me a good hard fucking." Bastien kept his voice a harsh rasp, full of male need, male hunger—and heard her splutter her tea. "Fuck me hard with your sweet rump. I deserve it, don't I? And you—" He made this a brash and confident statement. "You want it."

"You might remember, my devilish husband, that you are bound and now serve me at *my* pleasure." There was laughter, lust, delighted agony in Althea's voice. Then she cried, "Oh, I can't bear it anymore—!"

She began bouncing on him. Her saucer fell to the carpet. Her tea sloshed out of the cup. She rode him like wild, and their chair tipped dangerously. But he didn't care. He was almost ripping the legs off it, trying to pull against his bonds to pump into her.

He was close—too damn close—he had to make her come first.

The door opened. The footman strode in, still blindfolded, but he moved with the assurance of a man who could see. Hell and damnation! But the footman yanked the blindfold away and tossed off his white wig.

Christ! Yannick!

"You little wanton witch," Bastien groaned against Althea's ear. She laughed—and then cried out as she ground her bottom hard into his crotch and took him impossibly deep. Yannick gave an austere glare. "You cannot steal my wife so easily, brother."

"*Our* wife!" Bastien shouted it, gnashed his teeth, fighting not to explode. He almost yelled in relief as Yannick dropped to his knees and buried his face into Althea's quim. A few flicks of his brother's tongue and Althea climaxed. She ripped at Yannick's shoulders, mercilessly pounded his cock, and screamed.

Bastien's orgasm tore through him like fire through a dry forest. It consumed him, flared into a massive, brilliant flame, and scorched him.

The chair broke with an explosive "crack." He fell hard in the jumble of wooden legs and twisted seat. Althea fell with him, but his cock fell out, and Yannick collapsed too.

"Athlea, love, are you all right?"

She giggled—the sweet, naughty giggle that he knew so well—and began to untie him. As soon as he was released, Bastien fell back, sated, massaging his numb hands. He cracked open his eyes to see Althea present her rear to Yannick and his excited brother plunge into her sweet pussy from behind, and from his view, Bastien could watch her luscious tits bounce.

God, he loved married life.

Yannick de Wynter, Lord Brookshire, bent and brushed a kiss to Althea's cheek as she slept. Her nightgown was a satin tangle around shapely silken legs. The bodice had slid down, giving a tempting hint of her breasts. It was true—enceinte women did glow—she seemed to shimmer like a star. Althea had always possessed a special magic that had captured his heart. He couldn't let her put herself in danger, not even to save a girl who had no one else to champion her.

As Yannick joined Bastien for one last swallow of brandy before dawn, he met his twin's wary and concerned gaze.

Bastien handed him a glass, half-filled with French brandy. "We have to get Althea out of England—away from the reach of the Society."

Yannick could hear the vicious edge to his brother's words. Bastien was afraid.

As the eldest twin, he'd always been the cool, rational one of the two. But where Althea was concerned, emotion ruled him, too. He had to force himself to plan carefully. "I agree, brother. But we aren't going to the Carpathians."

"What in hell are you talking about? We have to leave—those blasted vampire slayers are not going to allow a vampire child to survive." Bastien stalked around his open coffin, ran his hand through his tangled hair, and tossed back his glass of brandy like water. "I fear they want to destroy our child—and Althea. I think this Serena Lark is a tool of the Society. The bastards are using her to get to Althea, to make her vulnerable."

Yannick shook his head. "They might be using Miss Lark, but I don't believe she's a willing participant. I hadn't told you yet, but I've purchased a villa in Italy—very discreetly. We will make it appear that we have gone to the castle as we had planned, but instead we will travel to the villa and stay there."

Bastien's face set in a restrained fury. "You suspect they'd pursue?"

Grimly, Yannick nodded. "As you said yourself, our child is a great threat to the Society. For once, brother, we are in total agreement. We need to do anything to protect Althea."

Bastien set down his empty glass and strode back to his coffin. He leaned on it, arms braced, obviously warring with his emotions. "Althea had her heart set on returning to the Carpathians to see her father again."

Yannick finished his brandy. He hated lying to Althea. Hated hurting her. Their unusual marriage—between he, his brother, and Althea—had been forged by honesty. It was only when he and Bastien could be honest with each other, honest about their pasts, that they had captured Althea's love. What would it do to their marriage to lie to her? "We have to protect her," Yannick vowed, "even if it means breaking her heart. Even if she hates us for it."

* * *

The slim blade caught the reflection of light and sent it shimmering through the gloom. Jonathon adjusted the metal platter in front of him. He glanced up at the clock, and with his left hand he scrawled a note. *Dissection of the brain taken from Miss Abigail Litchford, vampire, commenced at 1:30 p.m.*

With his right hand, he aligned the blade, even before he'd finished the sentence. He could carry out tasks with both hands at once. He could even write with both hands at once—forward and backward. His father had been both delighted and unnerved by his skill, but he'd followed his father's advice and ensured no one else learned about it.

His father had been correct. The world feared those who were different.

Jonathon steadied the tray—the soft, gray brain was fixed in place by taut wire attached to thumbscrews. The blade sliced through cleanly. He had his father's journals of meticulous detailings of the vampire brain. Pictures. Weights. Notations of similarities, differences—in color, in structure, in unusual construction or markings.

None of it had given any answers.

Damn, he hated this work, hated the smell of it, the very act of it. He tried to be dispassionate. What was a body, after all, when the soul had left?

A clue, his father had said. *The most valuable clue we possess to understand the vampire.*

But after four decades of study, his father had been no closer to understanding the vampire. How could he hope to do it before All Hallow's Eve? He had nine days to save Serena Lark's life.

He needed those bloody books of his father's. Repeating these experiments would get him nowhere. He had to hunt down those books—

The sharp knock surprised him. Enough to slip a fraction of an inch, to slice where he hadn't intended. Damn and blast!

Cursing, he strode to the door. Abruptly opening it, he found Rumpole behind it with a note on the salver. Jonathon flicked it open and scanned Ashcroft's summons.

His mission as guardian to the tempting Miss Lark was about to begin.

9

Tempted

"Good evenin', Mr. Swift."

Drake flinched at Ma Bellamy's loud, coarse voice. The madam scurried through her dimly lit parlor to reach his side. She put out her hand, lightly resting her gloved fingers on his arm, and leered into his face. Ma Bellamy was a bloody revolting sight, her face marred by burn scars, pockmarks, and a knife wound that had cost her an eye, but that was why he came here. No gentlemen did, so Ma Bellamy appreciated his money. She kept her mouth shut and was clever enough not to be tempted by blackmail.

"What be yer fancy tonight?" she cooed, and candlelight sparkled on the diamonds at her throat, her ears, and on her bejeweled eye patch.

"Solange is my fancy, tonight, Mrs. Bellamy." Drake threaded a gold sovereign through his fingers.

She shook her head, her greasy hennaed curls waving. "The apothecary bloke 'asn't been tonight, sir."

Goddamn. The apothecary knew he would pay any price; why deny him the supply?

Drake flicked Ma Bellamy's clutching fingers from his arm and turned to leave.

She grabbed his wrist. "But the twins are 'ere, sir, if you've a fancy for fine tits. And I'll send Crenshaw round to that apothecary. Ma will take care of ye, sir, just ye leave it to her. The twins are pining for ye, Mr. Swift."

The "twins" were no more twins than he and Bellamy were. But Kitty and Emma possessed large breasts, a boundless enthusiasm for cock sucking, and surprisingly sunny smiles for hard-working jades.

Drake felt his arm begin to tremble. His eyelids were starting to twitch. Two whores in a bed would take the edge off the need, but it was not what he wanted anymore. He wrenched his shaking arm free of Ma's grip. "Not tonight, Mrs. Bellamy."

Serena had thought he would never leave.

Fog rolled over the circular drive and swathed Lord Sommersby's waiting carriage in an eerie mantle of silvery white. Clad entirely in black—her raven hair an advantage now—Serena waited in the shadow of an oak, hidden behind its large trunk.

She had waited here since dusk, armed with two vital tools—a lock pick and a description of the location of his laboratory. Serena prayed Mr. Bastien de Wynter had remembered its location correctly—he'd admitted to only being inside it once, while the late earl was alive. He hadn't shown any suspicion as she'd idly asked him questions.

Boot soles crunched on the gravel. The lamp glow touched the tall, massive, dark figure as he crossed to the open carriage door. It must be Sommersby. No other man was quite so large. The earl vanished into the carriage, the door closed with a decisive snap, and the traces jingled as the four grays began to walk.

Serena gave a triumphant smile in the dark. The arrogant man had sent a note to Althea insisting she be locked in her room for her own protection. At least Althea had crumpled his presumptuous missive and had tossed it in the fire.

Now it was time for her to get to work. The moon lit up the night, but clouds soon slid past. With her hood up, Serena crossed the gravel path toward the kitchen entrance. The door would be unlocked—there would be scraps and waste going out, along with used washing water and such. At least here, in Sommersby's mansion, she would not have to worry about being captured by six vampires.

As for being captured, it . . . rankled. The humiliation of it was worse than the fear.

Serena darted across dew-damp grass and slipped around the rear corner of the house. Other houses along the street blazed with light, even at this time of year, and carriages filled the street. But Sommersby's house was silent. Large and dark—like its master.

Squaring her shoulders, she moved along the rear façade, her shoulder brushing the stone. The door to the kitchen opened and an elderly woman sauntered out, balancing a basket on her hip. Plastered back against the wall, Serena held her breath—this had to be the cook. Sommersby kept only a handful of servants. Taking a deep breath, Serena sprinted in through the door, into his lordship's house.

The strangest smell wafted at her through the door. Serena glanced once more down the shadowed hallway and stayed motionless, listening.

In a distant room, windowpanes rattled as a gust of October wind struck them. A clock ticked beyond the locked door at which she was crouching. No other sound reached her ears—no footsteps, no voices, no clink of a servant's keys. It appeared no servants ventured in this part of the house with the master out.

Moonlight glinted through an undraped window, striking

the lock in front of her. Serena eased the long, slim end of the lock pick into the keyhole, just as Mr. de Wynter had taught her. There had been something quite naughty about "getting the feel" for the insertion and engaging the lock with the gorgeous gentleman leaning over the back of her neck.

Click! The lock sprang open, and Serena turned the knob carefully. Soundlessly the door swung wide, revealing a large well of blackness, with only slivers of bluish light giving a hint of what might be inside. Was it the laboratory? Widening her eyes, she fought to focus on the gloom. There was a wardrobe beside the door, and a candleholder sat upon it—with a stub of a candle, but a flint at least. She could suddenly see surprisingly well in the faint silvery glow cast by the moon, but she doubted she could read without a lit candle.

This part of the mansion overlooked the high stone wall that surrounded the property. The light would not be seen from another part of the earl's house. She struck the flint, and the spark took to the wick. It flared as the wax fed it, and the light grew. But that new light blinded her for the moment, and she held the candle ahead of her, blinking.

A skull grinned at her.

Serena bit down on her lip, holding in a scream. Her hand moved, sending light glancing off another skull, and another. A row of them sat on a set of shelves. Her stomach whirled in horror—half of the skulls were tiny. Children.

The flickering light gleamed on bones of every description—the long bones of legs, the tibia and fibula of arms, rib bones, even wide, intact pelvic bones. They were all stacked on the shelves, and tags hung from them, tags with numbers, place names, dates.

Jars sat on the other shelves, beside curious pieces of scientific equipment. She recognized a set of scales and burning apparatuses, but the others she did not know. She held the candlelight close to the jars—she had no idea what the parts were, but she guessed they must be organs. Human? Or vampire?

Serena swallowed hard, her mouth filled with a horrid taste—it was as though she could imagine the taste of the organs in the jars. She could certainly smell an acrid, sharp scent. Was it the liquid in which they floated?

Books. What she wanted was his lordship's books. But even as she turned away from the jars, she shuddered. What did she fear—that the intact hand she had seen in the jar would reach for her shoulder?

But what did Lord Sommersby do with these macabre keepsakes? She knew that physicians—training surgeons—used the bodies of the dead for practice. Sommersby must be carrying out some kind of experiments. But what kind? Did he hope to find a way to change vampires back to human?

Concentrate on the journals! Her half boots shuffled over the floor; she was afraid of what she might step on. A discarded corpse? Body parts stacked on the floor?

Serena rounded one of the large tables in the center of the room. Her hip hit a shelf and sent the jars pinging against one another. Oh no!

Now she saw that the rows of shelves reached from floor to ceiling and that they ran along the width of the room and stretched for half the length. The rest of the space was used for the massive wooden tables. She tried the other end of the room, which led her far from the door—to more shelves with more jars. Two shelves held displays of jawbones, dozens of them, all mounted on boards with pins. They sported fangs of every imaginable size.

Books covered the last row of shelves, and these stretched around the walls. Serena held up her candle and stared at row upon row of leather-bound books. There were hundreds. She slid out the one directly in front of her.

A shiver tumbled down her spine. Lord Sommersby must

have read his father's books. If the truth of her past was in any of these books, Lord Sommersby must know.

Hesitantly she walked the length of the shelves. At the row nearest the end, she found a space in the crowded shelves and a sheath of papers laying flat. Serena's heart almost ceased to beat as she read her own name in faded sepia ink on the top sheet.

Cut slices of her brain? Examine her heart? Serena's stomach roiled, and she let the journal fall back to the table. Lord Sommersby's father had believed she was going to change into a vampire and he'd planned to dissect her—while she was alive.

There were only three pages of text in this horrible book. Where were the other journals?

Footsteps! She leapt to her feet.

"Miss Lark, what the hell are you doing here?"

She almost sobbed in relief as she recognized Drake Swift's voice, but he stepped into the candlelight and the sense of security fled. Golden light caressed his hair, his fallen-angel face, his piercing green eyes—and revealed his open shirt, his bare chest . . . and his linens. He wore nothing on his lower parts except his small clothes. His muscular legs were bare.

And she most certainly knew what that bulge in his linens was.

Serena jumped back as Mr. Swift strode toward her. She bumped into the edge of the table behind her, winced as it bit into her hip. She skirted around it and darted to the other side, keeping the pocked wood surface and the strange glass contraption atop it between them.

"Miss Lark." His deep gravelly voice washed over her.

"I—I believe the late Lord Sommersby knew about my parents," she said.

"So you decided to break into his laboratory?" Mr. Swift crossed his arms in front of his bare chest. Such beautifully sculpted muscle. And his skin was so remarkably bronzed. His shirtsleeves were casually rolled up, like a laborers', revealing powerful muscles, the lines of long veins, the gleam of golden hairs reflecting the light.

Her mouth dried as she saw his abdomen—the solid planes of muscle, more soft golden hair, the enticing indent of his navel. Her gaze dropped to his small clothes, riding on his lean hips . . .

It was as though she had stepped into one of her scandalous dreams.

"Do you know what happens to housebreakers, Miss Lark? Sometimes they get transported." His voice was silky. "And, like me, sometimes they serve a sentence in prison—and learn about all the perversions of mankind." His eyes narrowed, hard and cold in the soft light. "You should be thankful that I found you. I don't know what Sommersby would have done if he had."

Serena knew she couldn't show fear. "And what will you do?" she asked.

He reached down and picked up the journal she'd been reading. She caught her breath—waiting to see his reaction. He threw it back to the table and grinned. Astonished, she felt her jaw drop. How could he smile at such monstrous thoughts?

"Meaningless scribble to me," he said.

"You—you mean you can't read?"

"I was born in a whorehouse, love, where women serviced rough men for pennies."

"But Lord Sommersby—the previous Lord Sommersby did not teach you? I thought he had taken you in as an apprentice."

He shrugged. "From your look of shock, I take it that to a governess a lack of education is sinful, indeed." Mr. Swift's deep voice lingered on *sinful,* and her quim dampened in response.

"I could teach you to read," she offered. Perhaps it was a

way to convince Mr. Swift not to have her arrested, to convince him to help her, but mostly she wanted to help him.

He had desired her in that brothel. He desired her now. She could read the heat, the male promise, in his beautiful green eyes, and it set her heart racing even faster.

"Why would you want to do that, love?" He paced to the table and leaned on it. Beneath his shirtsleeves, his muscles bunched, and she licked her lip nervously. Mr. Swift looked utterly unconcerned about being half-naked. But why should it startle her so? Vampires were often naked.

"You don't know much about me, do you?" he asked, his voice husky, with a gentleness that wrapped around her heart.

"No, Mr. Swift," she answered with equal softness. "I do not." She read vulnerability, poignancy in his emerald eyes.

"I would like to know about you, Miss Lark. You fascinate me. Why does your past matter so much to you? You can't bring your parents back, sweetheart."

"I know." She blinked away tears—tears at having to lie. "But my past has made me who I am—and I don't know anything about it."

"What do you really want, Miss Lark? Vengeance on the vampire who took your parents? Perhaps that vampire is already dead. Is that the most satisfying thing you can imagine, Miss Lark?"

"I—I don't know."

Mr. Swift walked away from her, to the shadows, and he picked a jar up off one of the shelves. "A vampire's brain." He lifted it. "What was it like to be a governess? Better or worse than slaying vampires?"

"I liked to teach." How weak that sounded. She had wanted to do so much more than that. Suddenly Serena wanted this man to know what she had tried to do. Why, when she had been tossed out of the Thornton household, she had left with the knowledge that the children had profited from their time together and that she had, in some small way, influenced their futures. Improved them. She wanted him to know that she was . . . human.

"I encouraged my charges to strive. To reach for a goal and grasp it. I believe every person should have value in the world."

"So Lord Sommersby meets your approval, since his goal is to destroy vampires?" Drake Swift had placed his jar back with a decided thump that rattled the other jars on the shelf. Even the candlelight seemed to scurry away from him. His brows lowered, and his eyes lit with a fire that forced her to try to take a step back. The table's edge gouged her bottom.

The candle flame straightened, and the glow touched the streaks of blond in his hair, igniting the sharp line of his cheekbone, caressing the full curve of his lower lip. A mocking smile touched his mouth.

The smile irritated her—not because he was laughing at her but because he insisted on laughing at himself. "You meet my approval," Serena pointed out. She took a determined step forward and planted her palms on the worn surface of the table in front of her.

The brains still bobbed and spiraled in their fluid prisons, like lily pads on a rippling pond. This was absurd. This room. This conversation. This heat she felt.

"Lass, I've never achieved anything in my life." Swift shifted with grace to perch on the corner of the table, his muscular legs splayed. His bare feet still touched the floor, and he leaned toward her.

She stared at his long, seductive, naked feet. "Your feet must be cold."

"I'm used to being barefoot, sweetheart. I grew up that way."

To respect propriety she should scuttle back, but Serena refused to retreat. "You have saved countless lives. You have faced death with courage to save lives."

"But not for noble motives, sweet lark."

"Then why?" Serena asked, her voice cool and patient, and

she knew at once that he resented the measured way she spoke to him.

Swift leaned closer. He'd just bathed. She'd never smelled a man right from his bath. So deliciously clean, yet underneath there was still the compelling raw scent of him.

"You asked me why the late Lord Sommersby never taught me to read. Do you really want the answer?"

"Of course."

"Why?"

"Because I find it criminal that he did not." But the truth sang through her thoughts. *Because I want to know more about you. I have since you touched me so intimately at the brothel. Since you kissed my neck. Since I had those shocking dreams! Even though I know that it is a mistake, I can't resist. I need to know.*

"I'm a killer, love. A killer doesn't need to know how to read. It's better to keep a killer ignorant."

"You are not a killer!"

"I am a killer. Soldiers are killers. Magistrates that sentence men to hang are killers."

"That is too simplistic."

"I killed before I came here, sweet. I'll kill after I leave."

"I am accustomed to the machinations of boys who want attention, Mr. Swift."

He laughed at that, head back. His sinfully beautiful baritone flooded the stale little laboratory. Drake Swift laughed all the time—how could a man who so enjoyed life, even the danger in it, be so angry?

"You are a clever young woman." he said. "I do want your attention. And I want to give you mine."

The double entendre made her gasp. It made her look down, to his linens, pulled tight across a long, thick bulge that snaked up from his crotch and cranked to the right.

"I'm rock hard, my dear. For you." His voice was soft, his eyes magnetic and compelling.

She'd been told such things by William Bridgewater. Were all men so unimaginative in the way they seduced women? But she couldn't deny she felt hot and molten inside at the thought of arousing Drake Swift, and she knew she was a fool. "You would be for any woman."

"Not like this, Miss Lark. I've never burned so fiercely before."

"That's not true, of course."

"I'm not lying to you, little lark." He reached out for her hand, gently held her fingers, and the caress made her burn inside. "I want you to understand what I am, Serena Lark. I am here because his lordship believed I would kill without question or compassion. His lordship believed that I, like an animal, didn't have a soul."

"Preposterous. Of course you do." Pain and anger made her snap the words. How could the late earl have treated this wounded man so harshly? Drake Swift couldn't even see himself as a hero.

"But I don't, little lark." Swift slid off the table's edge and dropped to his knees in front of her.

Serena's heart pounded like a frantic grouse in flight as he reached for the hem of her skirts. "If you believe you have no soul because you want to toss up my skirts and ravish me, Mr. Swift, then I must have no soul either—"

Her inner thighs were slick with her hot juices, her nipples hard and aching against her shift. Her cunny throbbed, and she wanted this man—she wanted to kiss him, to taste him, to hold him tight as he drove deep inside her—

She wanted him so much, so wantonly, because she was a vampire. And he would kill her if he knew.

10

Tasted

Drake knew he couldn't stop. He could still taste the bitter tang of solange on his tongue—the solange he'd finally bought from the apothecary—but it wasn't the drug firing him like this. It was Serena Lark's luscious scent.

She smelled of feminine juices; of rich, musky creaminess; and of the fragrances of a lady—roses, lavender, and soap. That trace of ladylike perfume reminded him that she should be untouchable for a rough man like him. But her husky voice sang in his mind, driving him on. *Then I have no soul either . . .*

She wanted him. Drake could smell her desire, see the heat of it in her radiant silvery-gray eyes. His fingers tangled in the soft eyelet lace of her petticoats, and he lifted the mass of her skirts up to her knees. *Oh yes.*

Her leather half boots followed the arch of her delicate feet and emphasized the slender grace of her ankles. The neat buttons marched up her pretty leg, drawing his gaze to silky white stockings, to rose-silk garters, and up higher . . . to the creamy skin of her thighs. He kissed the inside of her right leg, at the top of her boot, and her gasp rippled through the dark laboratory.

Against his mouth, her stocking was luxurious and gossamer thin. Her petticoats were fine and gauzy and beautifully embroidered. Lady Brookshire had ordered the finest for Serena Lark, and Miss Lark deserved nothing less.

He didn't deserve her—

Drake nuzzled his way up her leg, smiling at her cry of pleasure. Behind her knee was the place he sought. A flick of his tongue brought a gasp of surprise. Her soft moan sang in his ears, a promise of the little lark's pleasure.

He needed to pleasure her. Needed to listen to her scream in delight.

But not here—not in this place he'd never been allowed to enter. This gruesome place. This place meant for intelligent, privileged men, not gutter-bred killers.

He met her gaze, her eyes half-shrouded by her thick lashes yet as brilliantly pale as moonlight. "I want to take you to my bedchamber, love."

Miss Lark held back her coal-black curls as she gazed down at him. Her face was a white oval in the gloom, cheeks flushed pink. "I cannot go to your bed, Mr. Swift."

"But do you want to?"

Just a slight hesitation. A quick intake of breath. And her thick, dark lashes dropped seductively. "Yes. Yes, I do. But I can't . . . I . . . How could I hunt with you after that . . . ?"

Hunt with you. Ripe, lush, seductive, her aroma triggered his lust for a different hunt than vampire slaying—and his cock strained against his linens in response. Hunt with him. Suddenly, he wanted it—to partner her, take her into adventure and hunt at her side. "There is no reason you can't come to my bed . . . if you want to."

Shifting his hips to move his cock in his small clothes, Drake reached up and pressed his hand between Miss Lark's thighs. He groaned at the fiery heat of her against his palm, through her drawers.

"Oh!" Her head dropped back, her throat arched in a sensual curve.

"What's the harm, if we both want this?"

"You would no longer respect me. I am well aware of how a gentleman behaves toward a woman he has just bedded."

"You are, are you?" He bit back a laugh—after their night in the brothel he'd discovered her innate sexuality and he wanted to release it.

"And there is always the issue of children."

And her virtue. She didn't speak of it, but Drake knew, of course, how precious that was to a woman of her position. "But I want to give you pleasure, Miss Lark, and I can do it with my tongue. No loss of virtue, no children—only ecstasy. Here. Now."

Even as Drake Swift spoke the words, Serena thought her skin would catch fire from the heat with desire. *This man had saved her life. This man had charged into a den of vampires for her.*

He rose up, and her skirts caught on his shoulders. Her pelisse and dress and petticoats rose up with him to expose her legs. He pushed them to her waist, to expose the flare of her hips, the vee between her thighs, and the ivory satin of her drawers. She could smell her intimate scent, and she blushed.

But Mr. Swift gave a throaty chuckle. "Hold up your skirts," he directed, and she did. Serena understood what he intended, but she could not speak.

When she'd had her affair with Mr. Bridgewater—with William—she'd barely spoken to him. Things had happened with implicit understanding. She had liked them, but she'd been too confused, too shy, to speak of it. She'd spoken through sighs and silences. While making love, neither had spoken at all.

But she'd been naïve then, and innocent, and had used her silence to hide from her wanton nature. Now, for better or worse, she was a woman, and if she was truly to claim ownership of her life and destiny, she had best start here.

"I want you, Mr. Swift." There, she'd said it.

There was no lightning, no crack of thunder. No break in the earth to let the demons of hell come through. Only Mr. Swift's grin—a devilish curve of his lips that stole her breath.

He stroked her bare tummy. "Talk to me, little lark. Tell me what you feel."

"I—I—" She let her lashes drop. "I couldn't imagine how to express it."

His elegant fingers hooked in the lacy edges of her drawers and drew them down. Confronted with her own dark curls, dewy and wet, and a glimpse of her dangling pink lips, Serena felt her entire body flush.

"You're lovely, little lark." Mr. Swift drew his finger down from the ivory curve of her stomach to her dark curls. "And I love burying my face here. I love the smell of you. I know I will love your taste."

He glanced up, a naughty gleam danced in his green eyes. "Tell me exactly what you want, Miss Lark. Do you want me to taste you? To lick you?"

Helplessly, she nodded. The soft humor in Drake Swift's voice, the intimacy in it, spoke deeply to her. She had never met such a brazen man, one so determined to be ungentlemanly and rebellious. It made him irresistibly seductive.

Serena now knew why women offered their necks to vampires. Danger and the thought of complete surrender appealed to her soul. *Yes.*

"As you wish." He grinned—a flash of white teeth and cocky bravado. He bent forward, golden lashes lowered, and stuck out his tongue to lick her . . . belly.

She couldn't help but giggle. But his tongue dipped lower and lower, and she drove her fingernails into the hard wood of the table. This view was so unbearably erotic—to see his powerful body crouched between her thighs, his platinum hair loose, his shirt open, the sleeves rolled up so he could attend to his work.

Again a little laugh escaped.

"I am delighted to know I please you," he teased. And then he kissed her dark nether curls, and her laugh caught in her throat. He tugged them with his teeth, but the small prick of pain only made her moan in pleasure.

Oh God . . . his thumbs traced the insides of her wrists as he pulled on her curls, and the mix of intense pleasure and soft pain brought honey to her quim in a rush. She was soaked with her juices, and he must know. She heard him inhale deeply and groan.

His rough palms slid around her thighs, magic against her skin, and he clamped his hand hard onto her bare bottom. Dragging her forward, he drew her to his face. His tongue rasped that sensitive bud at the very top of her cunny lips.

"Mr. Swift—"

Somehow he chuckled while licking her, and her legs almost gave way. Stars exploded before Serena's eyes. She grabbed at his broad shoulders, and her fingers drove into linen and hard muscle. Oh, it was too much . . . he had to stop . . . she didn't think she couldn't take any—

But he pulled back and she cried out in frustration. "No!"

"Open your gown." His voice was a hoarse croak.

She saw him lick his lips and knew he could taste her there. Shakily, she attended to the sensible front buttons. When her bodice sagged, he urged, "Play with your nipples while I eat you, sweet lark."

"I couldn't possibly," she protested. But she wanted to. How delicious it would be to touch herself while he made love to her . . .

And he was waiting for her to do it. The rogue probably wouldn't lick her again unless she did. She tipped her nose in the air. "I might . . . but only if you . . . you . . ."

How embarrassing to lose her nerve.

But Swift laughed. "Only if I please you well enough. I damn well love a challenge, sweet."

He buried his face into her quim. Open wide, his mouth pressed to her, lips drawn taut and he rasped his tongue over her. Rough. Demanding.

Blast propriety. Blast secrets. Serena didn't care if he did discover she was a vampire. She ground herself against his face, pumping on him, racing toward release, and she pinched her nipples mercilessly through her shift.

The most erotic image came into her head—his cock sliding into her mouth so she could suckle him.

God, yes, he groaned, as though he could see the image too. *Yes, I'd love you to suck me.*

Roughly, he squeezed her buttocks. He pried her bum cheeks apart, and the tug on her anus was pure pleasure. He licked and tongue laved everywhere—over her clitoris, down to her passage to thrust deep, then back to her tingling, aching clit.

Despite his command, she let go of her breasts. She gripped his head, held him between her thighs, at just the right spot, so he was giving just the most perfect—

Serena! Her name. Her Christian name. She'd heard his voice although he hadn't spoken, but he gave one hard suck and her body shattered.

Oh God! Beyond her control, her hips slammed into his face. Her cunny pulsed hard, over and over. She'd never known . . . this. Her mouth stretched wide. A scream flew out into the dark. Tears wet her lashes. They raced down her cheeks as the last spasms of exquisite pleasure died away.

Drake Swift sat back, holding tight on her hips. She'd clutched the table—she now felt the pain of wooden splinters driven beneath her fingernails. She hadn't even felt that!

But the realization of what she'd done chilled her. She'd read his thoughts. Only *vampires* were capable of that.

And he had seen her naughty thoughts. Vampires had the power to place their thoughts in a human's mind—they used the magical skill to compel and control a victim. Thought projection. She had read a dozen modern texts on the subject, all written by educated men trying to rationalize a power they couldn't understand. But there was no way for an ordinary, mortal woman to put her thoughts into a man's head—

Swift straightened, and she had to tip her head back to look up at him. His blond hair grazed his shoulders—the shoulders she'd clung to for support. "I don't have to hunt for a while yet, tonight, sweet. Sommersby has gone to meet Ashcroft. Stay with me, sweetheart. Come to my bed."

Serena fought to find her voice. Her wrinkled skirts fell to the floor with a soft swish. Her thighs were sticky with the flood of her creamy juices. She couldn't go to his bed. At the base of her throat, her pulse fluttered wildly.

Sommersby had gone to meet with Ashcroft. The urge to flee overwhelmed and she quickly tried to take a step around Drake Swift. "No—no! I have to go! Now."

Somehow she had to escape.

But Swift's hand grasped her wrist. "Serena—Miss Lark. No. You must stay." Light fell across his eyes, and she could see them clearly. The green irises were enormous, and his pupils were tiny black dots. His words came slowly, a little slurred—he must have been drinking. That must be why he hadn't noticed she'd put her thoughts into his head—like a vampire. She had to escape before he remembered—

The journal was still out on the table. Serena's stomach churned as she looked at it.

She now knew exactly why Lord Ashcroft had kept her alive. She was an experiment—he had been keeping her so Lord Sommersby's father could cut her to pieces and study her. Sommersby knew of his father's plans, but Drake Swift obviously didn't know the truth. Why hadn't Sommersby shared it with his partner? Was he afraid Drake Swift would help her—or was he afraid Drake Swift would kill her?

"I have to go!" The panic in her voice rang out through the laboratory.

Swift jerked his head, as though snapping himself to his senses. He released her hand. "Sweeting, it's all right. I'm sorry, I've scared you. You're an innocent and I am a reprehensible fiend. I will take you home."

Serena's fingers were shaking as she reached for the journal on the desk. She had to put it back—she couldn't take it. Darting away from Swift, she returned it to the shelf and gave a longing look at the hundreds of books. The other journals might be there . . . but she couldn't search now.

She heard the padding of Swift's feet across the floor, and she spun around. She backed away from him. Against her rib cage, her heart hammered. "I don't need you to take me home. I can get a hackney—I came in one."

Gathering her skirts, she turned and ran for the door. Even though she ran terribly fast for a woman, she wasn't certain she could outrun Drake Swift. At least she'd taken him by surprise.

"Miss Lark—wait."

She stumbled down the hall and saw a faint square of moonlight on the carpet ahead. Panting, she sprinted into that room, the one with the open drapes. Light spilled through terrace doors. Perfect.

Was Drake following her? Serena heard her name called softly again as she fumbled with the catch on the doors. They swung open without a sound. She ran out onto the small balcony, out to the corner. The stone post was rough under her hand as she clambered on top of it. She took one look down—at scratchy-looking bushes. The fall wouldn't hurt her.

Ruefully, she realized that if she became a vampire, she could just transform into a bat and fly away.

Closing her eyes, Serena jumped.

* * *

If she ran, where was she going to go?

Serena stared in frustration at the small pile of coins on her bedspread. This would hardly support her—it might buy her coach fare out of London, but not much more. It was all she'd saved out of the allowance paid to her by the Society for her work.

A soft rap came at the door. "Serena?"

Althea.

"A moment," Serena called. She slid all the coins into her right hand, then flung them in her dresser drawer. As she hurried past the cheval mirror, she caught a glimpse of herself. Scratches on her face—almost healed, but they made strange, red lines. Leaves in her hair. As for her gown, it looked as though she'd been dragged behind horses.

She was tempted to jump out of her window but knew that would be foolish. And hopeless. She turned the lock.

Althea surged into the room, belly tipped forward. "Where have you been, Serena—?" Althea stopped and clapped her hand to her mouth. "Ashcroft and Sommersby are here. Don't tell me you were breaking into Sommersby's house while he was here waiting for you."

"All right, I won't tell you." Serena brushed at the leaves in her hair.

Althea giggled. "Did you—did you find anything?"

"Only Drake Swift," Serena said. And regretted it. Color rushed to her face. What had she been thinking to speak of that?

"I see." Althea stroked her belly, and a wicked smile curved her lips. "Well, this just arrived for you—from Sommersby House. My, you are a sought-after lady tonight." Althea held out a folded paper.

Guiltily, Serena went to Althea so her friend would not have to walk across the entire room. "But shouldn't I go downstairs?"

Althea gave a mischievous smile. "They've waited an hour—

there's no reason why they can't enjoy themselves with the brandy a little longer."

Serena tore the paper around the wax seal to open it. Inside, the writing was careful—a cramped hand with badly formed letters.

Miss Lark

Mr. Swift arsked me to write this to ye. He wants ye to hunt at his side tomorrow night. This 'ere Lokkus is to be on a ship. Mr. Swift will come for ye at eight.

Hetty Wilson

"He cannot read," Serena explained. "He must have asked the housekeeper to do it."

But why had he sent this? Was it because he wanted to help her . . . or hurt her? Or was it because they'd been intimate . . . and he wanted to see her alone?

Hot and sudden, the guilty flush hit her cheeks. Serena dipped her head away from Althea's curious gaze. "I suppose I'd best go down and face the Royal Society."

Fighting to appear calm, Serena dropped a curtsy to the noblemen she feared wanted to destroy her.

Sommersby bowed to her, large and dominant even in Lord Brookshire's lavish gold and scarlet drawing room. She sat on the edge of the sofa, and Sommersby settled back into the largest wing chair in the room. The solid piece of furniture looked in peril beneath his powerful body.

In contrast, Lord Ashcroft looked like a walking cadaver. He did not rise for her, but his gaze never left her face. "Miss Lark, I will come directly to the point. You wished to hunt vampires with Lord Sommersby and Mr. Swift—you wished to become their partner. They are, without question, the most successful hunters in the history of the Society."

Perplexed, Serena glanced at Sommersby. He sipped his brandy, watching her.

A response seemed required, so she said, "Yes, and they refused me the opportunity." How long ago that had seemed! Only two months. She'd been desperate to hunt—determined to learn from legendary Sommersby and rebellious yet heroic Drake Swift. And the blasted arrogant men of the Society had laughed at her.

Sitting on the sofa, trying to look like a docile female, Serena seethed inside. Ashcroft had fed her venomous lies—he'd made her believe a vampire had killed her parents; he had made her yearn for the chance to hunt that vampire and get revenge.

But it was all a fabrication. He'd played upon her desperate need to know about her parents.

"I know you will be determined to hunt Lukos, Miss Lark," Ashcroft continued, and Serena bit her tongue. "But it is too dangerous for you to do this alone. While I respect your intelligence and your remarkable skill with research, you have no idea of the power you will confront."

"So you have come to forbid it? Lord Sommersby wished to have me locked in my bedchamber for my own good." She had to continue to let Ashcroft think she believed his lies. If she played along with their game, she could learn the truth. But if she lost this gamble, she ended up cut open. "I'm capable of hunting Lukos. I've been well trained by the Society." Serena played her part. "I certainly proved my abilities at the brothel."

At the word *brothel,* Lord Sommersby's glass burst with a delicate pop, and brandy spilled on his hand and sleeve. He waved his hand, sending a shower of droplets to the scarlet carpet.

Jonathon met Miss Lark's startled gaze. He almost lost himself in her magnificent eyes—so large, so lovely, and now looking at him as though he were a dangerous giant from a fairy tale. "Things are not made for hands like mine."

He could not find the next words that he'd planned. What was it about Serena Lark that made his tongue thicken, made him want to retreat back to his laboratory? Was it that "governess glare" she was giving him? He didn't trust governesses—his first had strapped him with abandon. He'd been too big and too bloody clumsy his whole life. Getting strapped hadn't made his legs any shorter, his hands any smaller, his body any less beyond his control.

Miss Lark possessed two frustrating abilities—to make him feel clumsy and to make him hot, hard, and damnably aroused.

"You are to hunt with me, Miss Lark," he growled.

"Exactly," Ashcroft decreed. "I have decided it is the best way to keep you safe. And the most expedient way to draw out Lukos."

"It is not necessary, if his lordship's heart is not in it," Miss Lark declared. "Mr. Swift has already invited me to hunt with him."

Swift? Damnation, what in hell was going on? Jonathon was not about to let Swift hunt alone with Serena Lark. Either Swift would discover she was a vampire or Swift would seduce her. And he wasn't about to let either happen. "Miss Lark, if you wish to hunt with us, you will take your orders from me."

Sparks shot from Miss Lark's silvery-gray eyes. He groaned softly. Every time he opened his mouth around women, he tended to lodge his boot firmly in place. It was why he belonged in the lab—his father was correct there. And why he hunted vampires. Vampires didn't expect witty conversation before a slaying.

"I am going to be your partner, my lord," Miss Lark said, and her honeyed voice sent a bolt of arousal through Jonathon that made him want to howl. "Partners do not take orders."

"In this case, Miss Lark, they do."

"The ship was found floating along the chalk bluffs of Dover. The captain was lashed to the wheel, but he was a mere corpse."

Jonathon nodded at Lord Denby's words—it was what he'd expected. Of all the Society's hunters, Denby was the one he trusted most.

Jonathon hunched his shoulders against the patter of the rain—it soaked into his beaver hat and the thick tiers of his greatcoat. Denby's cane hit the rain-slick cobbles at they strode down the narrow dockside lane. Fog billowed up toward them, wreathing the other dark shapes hurrying up and down the dank-smelling street.

Denby remarked cheerfully, "Well, Sommersby, had the *Bonny Lass* not been found and boarded, she would have floundered or smashed on the rocks. But they were searching for her after receiving your message, lad. And they found her."

"But no sign of Lukos, a coffin, or any trunks or belongings of his," Jonathon bit out. Damnation, he'd been too late, of course. There'd been no way to catch Lukos—it had been a desperate bid to fire off a missive to the magistrate in Dover. Jonathon knew he was playing a dangerous game—Ashcroft believed he wasn't going to hunt Lukos, but Lukos was his best chance of saving Miss Lark, and Jonathon couldn't trust that mission to anyone else. Denby was a good man whom he could trust.

"We suspect he sent everything else ahead, by a different ship. He had no passage on this one—alas, the crew had no idea they had a demon on board with them."

"All dead."

"Aye. Each and all. Drained of their blood. Not all accounted for—assume that the first were buried at sea. Then, as it became evident they would all perish, they didn't bother with the dead." Fifty, grizzled, and silver-haired, the viscount appeared to make freetraders—smugglers—his quarry. Jonathon knew that wasn't entirely true. Vampires were spreading out from their apparent origins in the Carpathians; they had begun to cross to England's shores centuries ago, and Denby attempted to capture them before they landed.

"The captain's log?" Jonathon asked. His boots took heavy steps on the rough cobbles. Between them, he and Denby almost filled the lane, forcing others to skirt them. Dirty, rain-soaked buildings loomed around them. Laughter spilled out, and feminine screams—either mad laughter or pain, it was impossible to tell.

"Records the panic and the fear they felt," Denby said. "They thought it was a murderer amongst them—the captain slit the throat of one he suspected as his paranoia grew. And he shot the last one remaining but him in cold blood. Wrote it all down—a form of confession, I suppose."

"Catholic?"

"No, lad."

A man's religion was not relevant—the cross around the neck never stopped a vampire, at least not in his experience. He had slain dozens of vampires, but he still did not understand what a vampire really was.

The answer is in science, his father had insisted. *The answers can only be found in study, in faith in the work.*

How many brains had he sliced for his father's work? Hundreds. How many rancid corpses had he prodded, measured, dissected? An army's worth. And how many answers had he found? None. Each clue he grasped at with a combination of hopeful faith and rational logic brought him nowhere.

"Lukos left the ship before it reached land," Jonathon mused. "He could have taken that final step in many ways—he could have swam for it; his disciples might have met him with a small boat. Or he transformed shape and flew—which I suspect is the most likely. So we're a step behind him—finding his victims."

Denby clapped a hand on his shoulder. "Relax, lad. There's

information to be found here—the 'ghost ship' is the talk of the docks."

Jonathon groaned. Another night spent gathering wild tales, most of which would be outright lies. A dozen drunks would claim to have seen the demon with their own eyes. He brushed his damp brow.

At the last place on the lane, outside a narrow curved window of thick glass in black frames, Denby tapped on the glass. "This is it."

On the inside, men's backs pressed up against the grimy windows. Over their heads, Jonathon could see the glint of lamplight in glasses hanging over the bar. A narrow little public house—the wall behind the bar couldn't be more than a dozen feet from the window.

Denby yanked the door open, and Jonathon stepped into the heat, the loud belligerent conversation. The smells of fried potatoes, spiced meat, and male sweat hit his nose. All around him, tankards sloshed their contents over the floor, as men conducted merry arguments.

Was there really a trail to Lukos to be found here? Hell, he wished he could be with Miss Serena Lark tonight.

She was with Swift—and his heart was hammering, his teeth on edge, the hairs on his neck prickling. He wanted to see her, to reassure himself she was safe.

The drizzle, the fog, turned all around them into a blur. Serena held tight on the lapels of her pelisse and clutched her simple black umbrella. The cold seemed to run in her very blood. Whipping down the narrow lane, the wind blew the droplets right into her face. They dripped from her lips and lashes and ran down her nose, icy and irritating.

Drake Swift linked his arm in hers and laid his hand over her trembling fingers. She avoided his eyes. His conduct had left her adrift, unsure how to behave. He'd been a complete and utter gentleman, acting with such cool deference she might have thought she'd imagined their entire scandalous encounter.

In complete bewilderment, Serena had tried to open conversation about everything but their intimacy. About Lukos. About where they were going. About what he and Lord Sommersby had learned. Mr. Swift had charmingly avoided her every question. Finally he had leaned forward in the carriage—he'd sat across from her, his back to the direction of motion. His great, black-clad hands had clamped on the seat on either side of her knees. She'd caught her breath, parted her lips, expecting a kiss.

Instead, he'd turned his intense green eyes on to her. Serena had felt her chest tighten. "Do you trust me, Miss Lark?" he'd asked.

No, in truth she did not. But she knew that was not the answer she needed to give.

"Why does it concern you that I might not?" she'd parried.

"Your answer is 'no,' then," he'd said. Then he slumped back against the carriage seat and propped his boot on the velvet cushions. Stretching his arms along the back, he had flashed his devilish smile. He certainly looked every inch the gentleman in a three-tiered greatcoat, trousers that clung to lean legs, and the obligatory shining black boots.

And he looked so disappointed, she reassured, "I do trust you, Drake Swift."

Now, as they walked through the fog, Serena glanced at Mr. Swift—at the side of his face, the curl of his long lashes, the firm set of his lips, the high ridge of his cheekbone. She wished he would turn to her, yet, at the same time, she hoped he would not.

He pointed ahead, his face shadowed by the mist, the dark, and his tall beaver hat. "Here."

She eyed the blackened door warily. No light spilled out of the windows—black material shrouded them and hid all inside from prying eyes. The eyes of the law, no doubt.

"What is it? A tavern?"

"A brothel."

Her lips curled at that. There was a flash of light as the door across the lane opened, enough to illuminate his eyes. She saw no mischief, so he wasn't doing this merely to discomfit her.

"This is my world, love." Mr. Swift held out his hand for hers. "If there's one thing a vampire wants, it's a fetching young virgin to feed from. And Mrs. Bellamy knows every one that's used and abused in London."

Serena shuddered. "Doesn't that bother you?"

"Aye, it does." He rapped on the door and it swung open, revealing a gloomy foyer and a bulky servant. "Here, love." Mr. Swift grinned. "Come with me."

Serena squared her shoulders, shot him a glare, and passed by him to cross the threshold. After all, she had been to a *vampires'* brothel. How could one that serviced mortal men be any more scandalous?

11

Favorites

Serena saw at once that this was a different world than the vampires' elegant brothel. Only two wall sconces cut the gloom of the narrow front hall. A woman bustled forth, a woman in a dress that had once been vivid scarlet. The woman's hair was garishly red, and it fell in thick, untidy curls. The woman neared the lamp. God help her, but Serena recoiled at the sight.

Shame hit her at once. It was hardly the woman's fault she'd been disfigured. She'd had to survive, hadn't she? Who was she to judge a woman who'd had nothing but her wits, her body, and her determination to survive?

But the wide smile of recognition on the woman—the madam, obviously—set Serena's stomach churning. Drake Swift had been here before. Often, she'd guess.

For information on vampires? And, of course, for sex.

"And what do ye be wanting tonight, sir?" The madam's gaze swept to her, and the face changed. The one good eye narrowed. The woman's lips pursed, revealing deep, powdered lines. "Mr. Swift?"

"May I introduce my partner, Mrs. Bellamy?"

"Partner, sir?" Mrs. Bellamy curtsied, which set Mr. Swift chuckling. "And what be both your pleasures, sir?"

Shocked, Serena swung to face Mr. Swift and caught that mischievous glint in his eyes. The devil—what was he about?

"Miss Lark is a vampire huntress," Mr. Swift said. He dug his hand into his pocket and withdrew something—something crumpled in his fist—and he gave this to the madam. While Serena couldn't see the amount of the note, the woman didn't even glance down at it. Apparently, the madam expected a certain fee and Mr. Swift knew what it was.

"Have there been any men of means requesting virgins?"

"Every blooming day, Mr. Swift."

"You know the sort I mean, Mrs. Bellamy."

"There was a foreign gent. He had the twins—yer favorites. Wasn't particular about them being pure. Gave them the mark, though 'e left them living."

Twins? Favorites? The stifling air would not go into Serena's lungs. She took deep, desperate breaths, but it felt as though she were trying to breathe in flour. It was hot, so horribly hot—probably the body heat of all the rutting inhabitants. Moans and groans drifted down the shadowed staircase.

"What did this gent look like, my dear?" Swift asked.

The madam gave a careless shrug and trailed the note over her powdered, freckled cleavage. Mr. Swift handed her another and she cackled in delight. "He was a well-dressed bloke, but he kept in the shadows. He doffed his hat, so I saw that he 'ad black 'air streaked with white. 'Andsome sort—but very foreign. White teeth—no fangs, mind."

Serena gasped as Mr. Swift's hand clamped tight around her waist. He drew her to him, holding her up. Had her legs almost given out? She wanted to tear at the buttons of the tight pelisse. Rip her corset off, let her lungs expand—and breathe.

A breath, even a shallow one, steadied her nerves, gave her

time to summon her voice. "Do you know where he lives? Where did he go?"

Mrs. Bellamy kept her eyes on Drake Swift—he'd provided the money, after all, but Serena felt the heat of his gaze on her. In the indent of her waist, his fingers stroked. He stood slightly behind her, hips cocked forward to press into her derriere. The heavy fabric of his greatcoat seemed to fall forward, surrounding her. Giving her a sense of safety.

His favorites were twin courtesans!

The madam pursed her painted lips. "No, and after I found them, I was bloody irritated. Never took him for one of those types. As I said, 'e had no visible fangs."

"There are men who come here who do?" Serena asked, appalled.

Narrowing, those shrewd eyes locked on her face. "The bold ones do, the ones who thirst so strongly or who are so cocky they believe no one can stop them."

"But—" Serena felt the floor tip beneath her feet. How could this woman so calmly sell girls to demons? A quote from *The Nature of the Vampire,* a book by Jonathon's father, burst into her thoughts—*a vampire will take pleasure in the consummation of the hunt—the bite, the blood, the carnal pleasure that accompanies . . . but beauty and purity are a vampire's true prey . . .*

Drake Swift's drawl broke in. "Are they here? Kitty and Emma?"

"Of course, sir. They're at work."

He handed more money to the madam. "They're finished. Have them meet my partner and I in your best room."

Mrs. Bellamy withdrew a ring of keys. She pulled off one and handed it to Mr. Swift. "The room at the end of the hall."

Each stair groaned as they ascended, and the walls were dingy from the smoke of cheap candles. He came to places like this. But why? Was it the coarseness of this that he liked? There were no artistic scenes of erotica on the walls, no seductive elegance. Only sound—shrieks and guttural groans. And smells—tallow, urine, the earthy smells of sex.

Serena tried to ignore the cries that came from behind the doors, but one came with piercing clarity, and she looked.

The door was wide open, revealing the bedroom scene.

A naked man, from the back—well muscled. The shadows accentuated each bulge, each line. Trim buttocks, broad shoulders. Candlelight spilled across his flank, highlighting the curve. He moved his arm with a snap, and the end of a whip cracked against the board floor. Another man watched from the bed.

Her breath escaped in shock. The blond woman who stood in the center of the room—she was to be whipped?

With a light laugh, the courtesan pulled her shift over her head. White and gauzy, the delicate thing fluttered to the floor behind her. The woman turned, presenting her pale, round bottom. Parting her legs, she balanced on tiptoe—she leaned forward slightly, supporting herself by gripping dangling ropes.

No wonder the men, the customers, groaned at the view, Serena realized. The woman's bottom thrust back temptingly, the gap between her thighs displayed for their enticement. With a half-turn of her head, the girl gave a coquettish smile.

The customer raised his whip, and Serena braced for the blow. But he didn't strike the courtesan's bottom—he caressed it with the lash and then the handle. The plump cheeks quivered as the blunt end traced their shape.

Serena saw the second man then. He carried a bundle of black cords. She breathed deeply. Sandalwood. The scent of dampened wool and the erotic aroma of male skin. Mr. Swift was behind her, his hands on her shoulders. His cheek brushed hers, and she shivered at the rasp of whiskers.

"Inventive rope play."

How could his voice be so calm, so unaffected? Heat raced

over Serena's skin—her underarms prickled, her belly was damp, and she felt slick and hot between her thighs. Her nipples shoved against her shift and the confining gown. Her feet seemed to have dissolved into hot puddles, and she couldn't take a step.

Fiery, firm, Mr. Swift's lips pressed to the nape of her neck. Only a small strip of her skin showed between bonnet, pinned hair, and the collar of her pelisse. But he touched there with his soft lips, then dabbed with his wet tongue.

Oh goodness.

The men began trussing the courtesan's legs, entwining her with the cords. They worked slowly, deliberately, and the woman sighed her pleasure.

"They will take their time . . . to heighten her excitement."

Serena couldn't help but turn her head to look at Mr. Swift. Those green eyes flashed, his smile widened. "But we haven't time to watch."

She should be worried about finding Lukos—about protecting herself. About those poor jades who'd been attacked by the beast.

"If you'd like to try sometime . . ." Mr. Swift's fingertips trailed up the curve of her neck—he'd removed his glove and his nails scratched . . .

"We should find the room." Serena's gaze connected with his. She hadn't planned to look so deeply into his eyes. Drake Swift stared at her as though everything else around them had dissolved away, his breathing harsh and ragged.

"God, I—" He broke off.

Strangely, his breathing came at the same speed as hers. He breathed out at the same instant she did. As though their hearts beat in unison.

"Mr. Swift, the bedroom—" Serena broke off. Entirely the wrong thing to say, as the searing image of Drake Swift on a bed swept into her mind. Naked, on his back, a sheet tangled carelessly around his legs, and that naughtily inviting smile curving his lips.

Oh heavens—had she just planted that image in his thoughts?

Serena gasped as his hand curled around her bottom.

"You are right, my dear—the bedroom," Drake said. He realized he was groping Miss Lark in the middle of the hallway. Silvery and beautiful, her eyes captivated him. He couldn't tear his gaze from the flutter of her lush black lashes.

Lukos. Normally Drake itched to hunt and kill. Often he went into a hunt aroused—the sexual need drove him, angered him, make him wild and bold. But he'd taken solange tonight, and that was what drove him now—solange and his desire for luscious Miss Lark. Hard as granite, his cock throbbed in time with his heartbeat and his mouth hungered to feast on the lovely little lark again.

To tempt her. To pleasure her until she yanked up her skirts and begged him—

"The bedroom," Drake repeated. He twined his fingers in hers—hers were small, slim, reminding him how vulnerable she was. He led and she followed at his side. Twice, he looked at her, but she kept her gaze on the door in front of them.

What was she thinking of? Lukos? Or sex?

Gripping the doorknob, he felt it tilt in his hand. It was old, loose, worn—like everything in this place. He pushed open the door, revealing an empty bedroom. A fire burned low in the grate, casting light to see by and enough warmth that they wouldn't be chilled to their souls while waiting.

Miss Lark slipped her hand free of his and walked farther into the room. Bathed in soft gold, she was unspeakably beautiful. Her pelisse shimmered over her curvaceous derriere. Her hips swayed with melodic smoothness. Even in a brothel, she moved with her head high. Such pride—damn, that aroused him. Serena Lark walked like a lady, measured, graceful, restrained, and Drake hungered to reveal the wanton woman inside.

She paused by the bed. Holding her reticule at her waist, she stood, unmoving. "There's a whip on the bed," she observed. "And the sheets are rumpled. I assume the sheets are not changed between customers."

Miss Lark's voice was cool and condemning. To his surprise, Drake flinched. That calm note of disapproval was almost as effective as a strap across the hand—he'd never experienced such a timid punishment as a boy, but he knew men of Jonathon's class did. And they likely cried.

Hell, the things he'd endured without even a whimper.

She spied the ropes hanging from the bedposts and stared at them, her arms crossed over her chest. Strangely, her pinched lips only made her more sensually enticing. He fought the urge to yank off her bonnet, rip out her pins, drop to his knees, and make her come with his mouth.

"These girls are your favorites?"

Had Ma Bellamy said that? Drake hadn't noticed. Was that what had made Miss Lark look so bloody prim? "I pay them—but after I realized how much I adore you, I stopped rutting with them."

"Really?" Her voice gave no hint of how or if his declaration affected her. "It's no crime for a gentleman to be promiscuous."

"I'm not a gentleman, remember?"

"Have you ever whipped them?"

"Do you know what I want, Serena?" He saw her little jolt of surprise because he had again used her Christian name. He had sucked the delicious juices from her climaxing cunny, but what stunned her was the use of her first name. "I would want you to whip me."

"Why would you want me to inflict pain, Mr. Swift?"

The governess had returned—cool, composed, the perfect servant who would accept any bizarre, scandalous, ridiculous thing he said and carry on regardless.

"But you sorely want to, don't you, Serena? Don't you strap naughty boys who misbehave?"

She crossed her arms beneath her lush breasts. "I do not believe in corporal punishment."

"You've never spanked a charge? I find that hard to believe."

He grinned as a little smile came to her lips—a crack in her cool demeanor, a wry smile that changed her from perfect servant to human woman.

"It leads to escalation, Mr. Swift. What do ten lashes of the strap lead to? Twenty, I assure you. A child will push boundaries, and then what is a governess to do? Keep making worse and worse threats? And once a threat is issued, it must be acted upon. Children know at once when they have taken control."

"So you wouldn't spank me in punishment."

"You are a grown man, Mr. Swift."

"Would you spank me in fun?"

A blush. He'd expected her to blush, to be a little embarrassed. Instead, Serena walked calmly to the edge of the bed and picked up the whip. She curled her fingers around the grip, weighing it. "If I were to spank your bottom, Mr. Swift, I would be tempted to do it with the flat of my hand."

Now this was becoming damned enjoyable. Drake opened his mouth to answer—

The bloody door burst open.

Kitty and Emma tumbled in, both panting hard, as though they'd raced to the room as fast as possible. They wore their shifts, and their hair was loose, the curls a matted mess. Kitty flopped down into the nearby armchair, slouched as low as possible, and spread her legs wide.

He grinned—she probably thought she looked erotically inviting. She looked sloppy and half-drunk. Emma raced up to his side. She grasped his biceps and lifted herself to plant a kiss on his cheek. Emma greeted him like a friend, not a customer, likely since he paid far better than most.

"Ma Bellamy says ye're going to catch the vampire that bit our necks! And that ye planned to fuck us first."

Kitty gave a great yawn. "What do ye want us to do?" She licked her lips, fluttered her lashes. "Come over here, sirrah, and I'll suck yer big cock."

Drake cleared his throat. "Have a care, there is a lady present."

"Blimey!" Kitty's eyes widened as her gaze fastened past him. "And so there is. Oo's she? She yer mistress?"

"Miss Lark is a huntress—a member of the Royal Society."

Kitty lifted her legs, knees bent, so her legs opened wider and her thin, worn chemise rode up. "There, that's me curtsy then. So, Mr. Swift, 'ave you come planning to do something naughty?"

Drake strode to Kitty, grasped her chin, and tipped her head to arch her neck.

"'Ere now!" she protested. "It 'urts."

With his gloved index finger, he pushed in around the two small puncture wounds. The vampire had not bothered to heal them, to make them disappear. The surrounding skin had hardened, and a scab covered the wound—just as his had healed. Neat, clean, no tearing, no clumsiness.

"Tell me everything you can about the vampire, sweetheart. I will make it very worth your while." He held up a hand to warn Serena to stay silent, to wait.

Kitty bit her lip, twirled a blond curl around her finger. "'E was very tall—seven feet tall. A huge ox of a man—but beautiful. He spoke strangely. It seemed also as though he spoke inside my head! It was right creepy." Her blue eyes widened and looked startlingly innocent. She thrust her breasts forward, too.

Hell, he knew when he was being lied to.

"He didn't want to have sex at all," she went on. "And he wasn't rough—"

"How do you remember all this, Kitty?" Emma protested. "I can't remember anything."

Drake groaned and he heard Serena's soft gasp. As he'd suspected, Kitty was lying, and she turned beseeching eyes onto him. "I think this was what happened, sir. I do remember a bit—kind of dim, like. I *think* he was big. That's worth something, ain't it?"

Lukos had controlled their thoughts, so the jades couldn't remember what had happened. Damn.

"I remember 'is smell. This I do remember, sir."

"What? Did he smell of earth? Brimstone? What?"

"Oh no! He smelled . . . good. I breathed in his scent and wanted to fuck him."

With a crook of his finger, Drake summoned Emma to come to him. Though he knew it would give him nothing, he examined her neck. Her wound had almost healed. He dropped a few sovereigns into their outstretched hands and they scampered off, shutting the door behind them. For a fleeting moment, he felt an ache in his gut. Would they service another demon tonight and die surrendering their blood or just a rough customer with a taste for brutal sex?

He couldn't save Kitty and Emma. Over the months since he'd discovered Ma Bellamy's, he'd given the two tarts a fortune, but they didn't leave. They drank too much, they were too afraid, and they'd worked on their backs too long to think there might be a place for them anywhere else.

Miss Lark's boots tapped on the rough floor as she approached. Drake had his back to her, and he couldn't turn just then. Soft, cultured, controlled, her voice spilled over him. "You gave them quite a lot of money, considering they told us nothing."

He forced his mouth to form his normal cheeky grin and he faced her. "You disapprove?"

"No. You intrigue me, Mr. Swift."

All the signs of an aroused woman—Serena Lark sent them. Her eyes burned like molten silver, her lips softened, her movements grew seductive. She touched things—her curls, her cheek, the full curve of her hip.

He almost lost control as she tapped her finger—swathed in a blue silk glove—to her lips. "Those two women, they appear to be perfectly healthy now," she mused. "There are vampires who merely feed and then attack another victim. And those who return, who claim blood again and again, until the victim becomes near death, and then the vampire transforms their poor prey. Do you think Lukos plans to return and claim these women?"

"You've read the Society's books. How do you think Lukos will behave?"

Her brows drew together, and she pursed her lips as she considered. Sweet little lark, she could bewitch him with that expression. "I don't know," she admitted at length. "You hunt them—you have far more experience than me." She fiddled with her reticule, fingers caressing the clasp.

Nearing Serena, Drake breathed deeply, drawing in her feminine scent. "He murdered the crew of the ship that brought him, Serena, so I don't understand why he would spare two prostitutes' lives. This vampire might not be Lukos."

"But could we catch him here?"

Drake was amazed. Serena should have been quaking at his words. Instead she faced him with a level gaze and betrayed not a hint of terror. Beneath the soft, reddish-gold firelight, her skin looked dewy and satin soft. He couldn't resist brushing his knuckles along the curve of her cheek and touching heaven.

He took his time, trying to force his mind to think. "We should question other taverns, other brothels—"

Serena's lower lip was plump, glistening, so damned tempting. Gently, Drake pressed his thumb to the center. It was his duty to protect her.

His lips neared hers; she closed the distance by surging up on her toes. Her arms hooked around his neck, her mouth pressed on his—hot, open, inviting. But she drew back at once. "I shouldn't, Mr. Swift—"

"You should," he groaned.

He loved to hear countesses, duchesses—all those aristocratic women—call him Mr. Swift. Especially when they did so while wrapping their soft, long legs around his hips and tearing their nails down his naked back. He never invited women to be familiar with him.

But he wanted Serena to call him Drake. She pressed hard against him, breasts shoving against his chest, full thighs against his legs, belly cradling his rigid prick. She stroked along his neck, her fingers ran up through his hair. She knocked off his hat.

He wanted more—damn the dirty bed. Hell, he'd throw his greatcoat down on it and let her ride him. That's what a gentleman should do. He'd never been so unsure about caressing a woman before. He wanted Serena like he'd never wanted any woman—even Mary, whom he had adored—and that terrified him.

He kneaded her breasts through the layers of fabric. On a moan, she pushed her chest forward, forcing her full curves against his palms.

"Oh yes—"

Claiming her mouth, Drake drew his tongue back. Her tongue followed, twirling around his, exploring his mouth. Not a trace of innocence or shyness. Hell, she wanted this. She wanted him.

With swift flicks of his fingers, he opened his trousers. His knuckles stroked her stomach as he did, but she didn't pull away. Already his cock had dampened his linens, and he pulled it free of his clothes, wiping away the fluid with a swipe of his palm.

Filling his palms with her lush bottom, he pulled her close, kissed her lavishly, and clamped his cock between his abdomen and her dress. God, he could feel the heat pouring off her. His blood pounded in his head, surged down to his loins. Undoing her gown would take too long. He wanted her now.

Serena moaned as Mr. Swift eased back from the kiss. Why did he stop? She couldn't think—he took a step back, and the waning firelight spilled over him. Jutting forth, his cock compelled her to look. Long, rigid, curving toward his belly. He was completely dressed, except for his naked cock rising out from the open placket of his trousers.

"Not here. Not this place."

She was shaking with need for this man, and his words startled her. "What do you mean?"

"You're a well-bred woman. This can't happen here."

Did she dare take a step toward him? Could she be as bold and comfortable as the jades? If he learned the truth . . . learned what she was . . . he'd kill her. But he might anyway, and she wanted this. "Why not?" she asked softly. "It's here for this very purpose, isn't it?"

"You deserve better. This is . . . common. You deserve beauty."

"It doesn't matter to me, Mr. Swift." She reached up and touched his firm lower lip. "All I can see is you."

"Serena . . . tell me what you feel, Serena. What you really want."

She delighted in the sound of her name on his lips but could not call him Drake. He hadn't invited her to. She searched for words, fighting fears. "You . . . this . . . now."

Rich, vividly green, his eyes never left hers. After shaking off his greatcoat, Mr. Swift tossed it behind him, and it fell like a blanket over the rumpled bedsheets. He backed away from her, then lay back on his coat, legs slightly spread. One arm rested bent beneath his head. His other hand reached out for her.

"Come on top of me," he invited in his low, sensual growl. "Come straddle me."

The sight of him, the luscious smell of him, overwhelmed her senses. It was as though she could hear the steady, hard beat of his heart. He swallowed; she saw the movement in his throat. He tore at his cravat, wrenched the knot free, and exposed the hollow of his throat and his muscular neck.

Serena thought of the wounds on the women's white throats. A separate pulse seemed to beat in her quim. "On top?" she repeated.

"Straddle my waist, love. Or my hips."

Full of bold invitation, his smile stole her breath. Women did ride on top—the Society possessed scandalous books that displayed demonesses doing so to innocent male victims. But she couldn't. She couldn't make love to him.

Why not? Asked a willful, internal voice.

He would learn what she was. At the very least she would lose her heart . . . if not her life. He wanted nothing of her but sex.

And what did she want of him? She ached for him. Ached to feel his curving cock slide into her quim, pushing her walls apart, making her feel full. Stroking, stroking, stroking the wet, soft walls of her cunny until she thought she'd die.

The first button of her pelisse popped free, the neckline sagged. She'd opened it without even thinking. The next was straining—she opened it, too. And the rest. She dropped the coat to the floor.

Serena walked toward him, drawing up her skirts on the way. Really, she should be applying the strap to her own wrists, beating sense into her own head.

He would discover she was a vampire. He would destroy her.

She didn't care. Up, up went her frothing skirts. His green eyes were brilliant as he watched her walk to him. She revealed her fine ivory stockings, the blue garters at her knees. She reached the bed, and he helped her climb on top of him. With her skirts spilling over her arms, her drawers were the only barrier between her quim and his cock, and a lace-trimmed slit split those.

He knew it. His hand slid down, slipped into her drawers, and found her moist nether lips. She was wet, so lushly ready for sex. She wanted to see more of him—more of that tanned skin, the shape of his shoulders, his chest. Golden hair trailed down his belly to the thick curls around his cock and ballocks.

His fingers parted her lips, and she gasped. A flood of juices had just washed out over his hand. His grin told her he'd liked that.

She couldn't speak. What did one say to a partly naked man whose fingers were stroking in one's most intimate place? One crooked finger slid into her cunny, and her muscles greedily clamped around it.

Oh yes!

"Take it slow, love—there's a little bit of pain when you try to break your barrier." Mr. Swift tossed the comment out as though they couldn't possibly turn back.

And she couldn't. But her cheeks heated. Seated on his hips, Serena bent forward to hide her confession. She could make it, but she couldn't look in his eyes while she did.

Her lips touched his throat. She felt the bob of his Adam's apple as he swallowed. Such warm skin, so delicious—clean and salty and lightly musky. Her bottom was now in the air. Two fingers tangled in her nether curls—

"I have no barrier, Mr. Swift," she whispered against his throat. If that bothered him, he didn't show it. With a husky groan, he slid his two large, long fingers inside. She was drenched with fluid, and his fingers filled her instantly.

"Then there will be only pleasure for us," he promised. "Experienced women are a delight in bed—so receptive, so sensual, so desirable." He thrust his fingers slowly in and out. "I want this to be perfect for you."

Oh, it was even now. Worth dying for.

Breathing hard against his neck, Serena curled her fingers around his cock. His velvety shaft pulsed against her fingers. She could smell the earthy scent of his member, the tang of enticing sweat in his pubic hair.

He pushed his fist against his cock to hold it upright, and the heat brushed her wet drawers. "I want you inside," she murmured, pushing his hand so he had to withdraw his fingers. They glistened with her wetness.

He moved his hand to his mouth, put his wet fingers to his tongue, licked them clean. "Make love to me, sweetheart—and call me Drake while you do it."

12

Revealed

Firelight cast their shadows onto the wall. Serena saw the tumble of her wild, loose hair in soft shadow, magnified against the faded wallpaper. Also displayed larger than life—the curve of her breasts and her hard nipples. As for . . . for Drake, she saw the shadow of one bent knee, the long lean line of thigh and calf, and his cock standing enormous in silhouette, stiff and long.

Catching her breath, she lowered on him. She wanted him now. What did tomorrow matter?

Wet, slick, burning hot, her cunny took him inside. Oh, she loved the pressure as the taut head parted her walls. Drake's lids dipped, sending a sweep of thick, impossibly dark lashes over sparkling emerald eyes. Shadow rendered him dangerous, seductive. A haze of blond stubble obscured the boyish dimple in his right cheek. Freckles—she saw the dusting of freckles across his straight nose. Every bit as aristocratic as a gentleman's, his alluring face made her heart leap as he smiled.

Gloved, graceful, his fingers tickled her clit as she lowered herself on him, moaning with each wonderful, thick inch. She understood at once his experience—Drake knew how to tease, how to steal her every breath.

Serena bounced a little, gasping as his cock went deep, as it bumped her womb. She'd taken him to the hilt, her bottom flush on his firm thighs. Her skirts spread over his legs, his chest, and he gave her a wild, lusty grin. She shared it.

She was mad. Utterly. Yanking her skirts, she held them up and rose up, sliding up, up, up, rubbing him against her cunny walls.

Oh! It was so good. So deliciously good. Only the head of his cock was inside. With her skirts in her hands, she felt like a maid who'd grasped a stolen bit of heaven with a comely footman. She sank down. Heavens, he filled her so.

"So, you like it slow?" Drake asked.

He drew his fingers away from her clit, and she gave a cry of frustration. That had felt so good. "I don't know. I—what do you wish me to do?"

"You are in the driver's seat, Serena. Explore. Do whatever you want." He peeled off his remaining skintight glove. So many scars—across his knuckles, the backs of his hands. One of his thumbs was bent and crooked, a break that hadn't healed right. "Please yourself, love."

He was inviting her by issuing a command. With a moan, she took up his challenge. She rocked forward. Definitely good. She rocked back. Ouch! No, it felt rather good, too. She wriggled back and forth, then side to side. Her clit brushed his coarse curls—pleasure most delightful.

"Does that please you?" she asked.

"Sweetheart, every breath you take pleases me right now. I suspect that if you sat there and just read a book, I'd climax. What I want is for you to be in charge."

"Why?" But she bounced on him the way she thought he would like it.

Harder, faster, and harder, yes, harder. The bed cracked back against the wall. The bedposts racked. The mattress squeaked.

Drake moaned. Despite her weight on top, he thrust up his

hips. His neck strained with the effort. His bronzed, muscled, beautiful neck. She bent and licked him.

"Serena!"

He tasted of warmth and sweat and shaving soap. She suckled his neck. Against her tongue, his arteries pulsed. His blood would be hot and rich, thundering through him. Was this what drove vampires? The sensuality of this. The desire—

His hips rocked her on him; she found his rhythm and moved with him—she could barely ride a horse, but this—this was so wonderful, so perfect to do. Her hips collided with his crotch. Her bottom slapped him. Her tongue slid up and down his neck, reveling in the movement of his throat as he swallowed. Her lips felt his heartbeat—

Sweet, intense, a touch of the divine, her climax exploded inside her. His hands roamed over her—down along her spine, cupping her rear, roughly fondling her breasts. She sobbed into his neck—it was all she could do. Her entire body seemed to be coming apart.

Pleasure flooded endlessly, her cunny squeezed his cock tight. Her hips flailed on him, and he held her tight now.

His cry was strangled, tight, a harsh, rough sound. His hips surged up. His head thrashed against his greatcoat. "Oh yes—" then his cry of pleasure turned to a sharp yelp of pain.

Blood. Slippery, coppery, shocking. His blood was in her mouth, on her tongue. Rearing back, Serena saw the wounds on his neck.

She'd bitten his neck.

Serena lay on his greatcoat, taking deep, unsteady breaths. What had she done? Blinking, she sat up. Mr. Swift—Drake, or did she dare still call him that?—sat on the edge of the rumpled, sagging bed. He held his cravat to his wounded neck to stanch the blood flow.

"I am sorry. Dreadfully so." She was shaking. He had to

know what she was. In an instant he would drive a stake into her heart.

Drake half-turned, revealing lips cranked in a smile, eyes alight with mischief. "I made you come so hard, you bit me. No need to be sorry, sweeting."

Serena almost sobbed in relief. He thought it had been pleasure that made her bite him. He seemed to view his wounds as a badge of honor. It would be best to let him continue to think so.

She hadn't remembered biting him! The pleasure had ripped through her, and her mind had seemed to melt in her skull. Her teeth had grazed that delicious flesh. And then—

Her mouth had been full of blood and she'd been . . . coming.

Serena tried to fasten her pelisse, tried not to let Drake see her frantic breaths. Her dress clung to her sweaty skin and the buttons slipped from her fingers, which were damp and trembled. Would gloves help? Where had her gloves gone?

Drake drew the red-speckled fabric from his neck. "Stopped now, love. I told you, I'm not afraid of a little bite." He folded it, wound it around his collar. "We should go. Perhaps find a place for a drink. A spot of brandy would do you a world of good."

Why did he behave this way? He spoke not a word of what they'd done, as though that intimacy had been swept aside. They'd made love. It meant nothing to him.

Blast this button. How many mornings had she found herself hurried outside William Bridgewater's door, her wrapper clutched to her and a swirling lonely ache in her belly? Had a few stolen minutes of intimacy, of love, of pleasure and tenderness and belonging, been worth the coldness after? Worth the heartache that never went away?

Foolish to compare one man to another—but she knew she'd made the same mistake. She'd offered too much for a fleeting moment of intimacy. Had surrendered too much.

At least he didn't suspect she was a vampire.

After yanking his greatcoat off the bed, Drake swirled it around his back, sliding his arms in the sleeves in a fluid motion. To Serena's surprise, he crossed to her, then dropped down on one knee. He rested his chin on her knees, and he gazed up with a smile he must know could melt a heart.

"It was wonderful, love. The most perfect gift you could give me."

Serena blinked away the burning threat of tears.

"Now, I must offer marriage. You're owed marriage. I'm not a gentleman, love, not much of anything, but I'd take care of you well. Keep a roof over your head, and I promise I'd keep you happy in bed. So, it is to be marriage then?"

Serena gaped in shock. Even if she'd wanted marriage, she would never say yes to that! She pushed his hands from her knee and stood. "No."

"Sweetheart, we could have made a child."

In a small voice that made her wince, she said, "I don't expect marriage." She ran her fingers through her tumbled hair, trying to plait it.

Sighing, he paced around behind her. He straightened the pelisse on her shoulders. "Let me, Serena."

Her hair tugged lightly at her scalp as he brushed his fingers through it. "So long, so beautiful," he murmured.

She stood still and let him work, her eyes closed. He was taking great care, and the gentle intimacy of that made her heart ache.

Would he ask her again to marry him? Instead he stooped and gathered silver glints from the floor—some of her fallen pins. Coiling her hair bared her neck, and his fingers brushed there. "We'd better go, sweetheart—hunt Lukos down and protect you."

So she was reduced to damsel in distress, and he was distant from her. She snatched up her bonnet. "Then let us go from this place." Without looking back, she crammed the bonnet on, messing up her hair again, and she strode to the bedchamber door.

What was it with London and fog? It was the thickest stuff Serena had ever known—cold as sin, wet and dirty, too. It carried the soot of burning fires, and she knew her face would be black with it.

Serena wiped her glove across her cheek, saw the streaks of black on the dark blue satin. Fashionable clothes posed a nuisance. The modiste had wanted to use peacock blue for her dress. How did a woman creep about in the dark in brilliant blue?

A nervous giggle fought to get free. She swallowed hard. She was only thinking of such ridiculous things because she didn't want to think of what she'd done. She'd made love. Turned down an offer of marriage. Bitten an innocent man's neck.

Proved she was a vampire.

Her heart ached so harshly she didn't think the pain would go away. How could a vampiress marry a vampire slayer?

The rain had stopped, though puddles sat between the uneven cobbles. Skirting around a muddy mess that smelled of dung, Serena leaned against the rough wall for a moment and remembered. . . .

Bloody inconvenience, William had snapped. Why didn't you tell me it was your fertile time?

She'd been shaking, head bowed. Why hadn't she? Would he have stopped?

But this time . . . it was too soon after her courses. There couldn't be a child, could there?

There was a chance there could.

The silence made her look up.

There was no sign of a tall hat, broad shoulders, swirling gray coat.

Where had Drake gone? He hadn't paused, hadn't waited. He'd kept walking and now she was alone. Did he want so desperately to be rid of her now? Tension stiffened her limbs and she took awkward, jerky steps down the lane. Her neck felt icy cold, her heart pounded. He was in danger. She felt it.

Shadows fell upon shadows as she passed a narrow alley. Stifled, a male grunt reached her and she turned, hand at her throat. She shouldn't be able to see in the stinking gap between buildings—there was no light, just blackness—but she could. She saw a beaver hat, the tiers of an expensive coat, the gleam of boots, and the flash of an object as it was lifted to a man's mouth.

And she saw white-blond hair—the hint of it beneath his hat. Crossing her arms in front of her chest, Serena stalked into full view of the alley. "What is that? What did you just drink?"

"Nothing, love." Drake held the glass by his hip, and he paced toward her, his shoulders rolling easily, his legs taking long strides. There came the brief shatter of glass. He'd dropped the tiny flask to the ground, and it broke on cobbles.

Was it liquor? Just a gulp for courage or was he dependent on the stuff? Serena breathed in a sweet smell that wasn't alcohol, and Drake grimaced as though he'd just tasted poison. She knew nothing of drugs, but the change in Mr. Swift was immediate. His eyes dilated, turning an eerie, glassy green, his pupils pinpoints of black. His shoulders jerked, his arms twitched, even his hands seemed to move as though strings controlled them. Then he seemed to relax all over, and a lazy smile came to his lips.

"Opium? Is it opium?" she demanded.

He laughed at that. "No, love. Solange."

"Good heavens, you drank solange? But that—" Serena couldn't finish, horrified. Words leapt to her mind. *Solange lures even the noblest of men to behave with complete sexual aban-*

don . . . a mortal man will readily become its slave . . . Was that what had happened between them—the drug had made him desire her? "You must stop this," she insisted.

His leer sent chills to her heart. "I don't want to."

"It will destroy you." A foolish and stupid statement. He knew that, of course. Perhaps at first he hadn't cared. Now, she doubted he had any choice. "You will stop it—I will inform Lord Sommersby at once—"

Suddenly she found herself pressed against the wall. "And what do you think he'll do?" Drake rasped. "Try to save my sorry arse? He'll let me die. He wants me to die. Always has done. He'll see me turned out of the Society. He won't raise a finger to help me. Do you care about me, Serena? Don't you give a damn about me?"

You don't care about me. You gave me that terrible proposal—to scare me away. You didn't really want to marry me—I was just a mistake you had to take care of. She silenced the foolish thoughts. Swallowed hard. "I won't let you kill yourself."

"Sweetheart, I hunt vampires. Every night I commit suicide by stalking demons—only so far I haven't been successful."

"Stop it!"

"Blast it, Serena, I love you. But like this, what I am, I can't have you. I should be strung up for making love to you."

So much pain in his eyes. They opened so wide, and she had to look down because she couldn't look into those wild, drugged eyes. "You made love to me. You shouldn't die for that. You don't deserve to die."

"In your world, your class, you should be bound to me now. My bride, my wife, the one woman who will despise me for ruining her."

"You didn't ruin me."

His grip loosened and she took a breath. "Beautiful, beautiful, Serena. You can't understand—"

His mouth closed on hers—she tasted the horrid flavor of solange on his lips and pulled away. His fist came up and pounded into the brick beside her head. He'd punched the wall in rage.

It was enough. She broke free and scurried out of the alley. A door opened ahead and light poured out. She had to blink.

A man filled the laneway. Huge, well-dressed, eyes and hair black in the foggy gloom, but she knew him at once. Lord Sommersby.

He turned to the other man who followed him out the door.

Drake Swift caught hold of her skirt. "Serena, don't—"

Serena yanked her skirt free and ran toward Lord Sommersby.

Jonathon heard the slap of boots running over the cobbles and turned. Silhouetted against the light spilling into the lane, a woman hurried toward him, a slender but curvaceous woman with skirts flapping around her legs. She skidded on the wet stones. Chivalry drove him forward to catch her elbow, her outstretched hand. Her head tipped back and he saw glossy black curls, parted lips, and a streak of soot on her cheeks.

Miss Lark. An endearment almost slipped out of his mouth. Abruptly she brushed at the sagging rim of her bonnet. "What did you find out, my lord?"

Vivid pink flushed her cheeks, and the curls at the side of her face were tangled. Cold, bitter fury lashed Jonathon's heart. "Where did Swift take you?"

Miss Lark recoiled. Hell, he'd snapped at her.

"A brothel," she said. "We discovered two victims. Jades who might have been bitten by Lukos."

"A brothel?" The words erupted from him.

"Please, my lord, we don't need to waste time on false propriety. I've already been to a brothel—and it appears I shall have to do so often. Vampires frequent such places, just as gentlemen do."

A retort came to his tongue, but he bit it back. For all her prickly pretense, she was shaking. "Miss Lark—"

He stopped as a dervish raced out of the dark—a wild, possessed lunatic crashing through the fog, screaming at the top of her lungs.

"Help! Murder! 'E's killed 'er!"

The dark figure plowed into his side, rocking him on his feet. Spinning, Jonathon caught . . . a girl, a slim waif with tattered hair and tear-strained cheeks. "Easy, lass." He tried to soothe, but the girl swept her gaze up him. At the sight of his shoulders, his chest, she paled and stuttered helplessly, "N-n-no!"

"Where is she?"

She froze like a tiny rabbit.

"Let me help her, lass. Tell me where she is."

The girl scurried back from him. Damnation. He grabbed for her dress, caught it, but she spun, and the fabric ripped free.

A man emerged from an alley—Swift.

"Catch her!" Jonathon yelled.

But as Swift lunged for the girl, she lashed out. Silver flashed. A blade?

"Jesus bloody Christ." Swift reeled back, and the little creature drove forward, slicing toward his gut. His hand snaked out toward her wrist, but too damned slow.

"Bugger ye!" the girl screeched, and she ran, nimbly avoiding Swift's grasp.

Hell and perdition, Swift moved like a man in a trance. Jonathon knew he couldn't deny it anymore—either drink or drugs controlled Drake Swift.

Miss Lark grasped his arm. "It's Lukos—I'm certain of it. We must go after her."

Jonathon saw only determination and horror in Miss Lark's large, silvery eyes. But he couldn't shake off the feeling that this was a trap.

Still, sometimes a man had to walk into a trap, but with his eyes open and a crossbow in his hand.

Serena sank to the cold ground beside the young girl's body. The girl couldn't be older than fifteen. Her head lolled back, and her thin legs were splayed in the dirt. Torn open, her bodice revealed sharp collarbones, small grimy breasts, and bite marks. Small punctures scattered the fragile chest.

Lord Sommersby knelt and stripped off his glove. He put his bared fingers to the girl's neck. Serena felt the earl's breath, warm against her cheek. She knew she couldn't let herself trust Sommersby—so why did she draw such strength from having him close?

The poor sweet girl. She hadn't had a chance. Serena looked up. Swirling fog poured down the alley, and Drake Swift was out there, in the mist, a makeshift bandage wrapped around the knife wound in his side. He'd called it a "flea-bite," but it had bled through the first cloth Sommersby had wound around his waist.

Wild Drake had gone in search of the vampire, with Lord Denby and a few other men. She should have stopped him—he was under the control of solange. But what could she say in front of the others? Drake had caught her gaze, for just a moment, had lifted his brows, sent a silent message. *Don't tell him.*

Damn him—she wouldn't.

She didn't have that sense that Drake was in danger, not like she'd felt it before she found him with the solange.

Sommersby gave a quick nod. "A faint pulse." Startled, Serena glanced down as he pressed a folded cloth into her hand.

"She's alive?" She held the cloth to the wounds—even though they no longer bled.

Thank heaven, the poor thing lived. But the breathing was so feeble, and there was such a great pool of blood beneath her neck, shoulders, and head. Serena brushed at the dirt on the girl's cheeks.

Sommersby's lips thinned, his expression grim. "Barely." He stripped off his coat and laid it over the girl.

The girl's lids flickered up. Her eyes seemed almost black, pupils enormous. Her lips trembled. "Lukos." A hoarse sigh spilled out, the girl's lips rolled back from her teeth, and she stiffened. At once her limbs slackened.

Desperately, Serena touched the girl's neck, searching for a pulse. It was just a murmur, so slow and light, she wasn't sure if she truly felt it. She stepped back as Sommersby gathered the girl in his arms and stood.

Lukos had taken the girl's blood and carelessly tossed her away to die. She would drive the killing stake into Lukos's foul heart with pleasure.

Horror and rage entwined around her heart, ice cold and burning hot. Would she become a monster like that?

On shaky legs, Serena raced after the earl as he carried the girl to their carriage. "If Lukos wants me, couldn't I draw him out? Couldn't I act as . . . as bait?"

Sommersby bit out the answer. "Not on my blasted life, Miss Lark."

13

Attacked

The drapes lifted and furled open, the velvet whipping like a cape caught by a violent wind. Serena watched them float in the air, snap and dance, then settle down again. It should be impossible for them to move—the window was shut tight and locked.

She was . . . home, home with Althea, but she didn't feel safe. The candle flame wavered, and she glanced to the clock on the mantle. A quarter of five in the morning.

Althea had insisted she go to bed and had fussed over preparing her room. A maid had laid garlic flowers along the window's ledge, and Serena wore a cross around her neck. "Whatever you do, no matter what impulse drives you," Althea had warned, "do not open the window. Ring the bell for a servant, for me, for my husband. But if Lukos comes, don't let him into the house."

Again the window banged in its frame. Serena sat up, blankets spilling to her waist. Should she summon anyone? What if the men were still out hunting? What if Althea came alone? She really couldn't put Althea at risk.

Her feet wanted to slip down to the floor. Her legs demanded that she walk to the window. She wanted to touch the smoothness of the drapes and fling them wide.

Instead, she thought back to her carriage ride home with Lord Sommersby.

She had protested the moment the coach left the physician's home. "I do believe it is a perfectly logical plan."

His lordship had rested back against the seat opposite, swathed in shadow, eyes hidden. His pose reminded her of a slumbering lion—relaxed, majestic, and dangerous. "You are not going to arrange yourself as a pretty temptation for a monster."

"Well, I trust you to save me at the appropriate time."

His mouth had tightened, and that harsh, hungry look touched his features—the expression she'd seen in her erotic dreams.

"Do you pay the physician to treat all the victims you save?" she'd asked.

He had given a simple nod.

She had made love to Drake Swift, yet at that moment, wantonly, she was so aware of Sommersby, of this heroic man. This man who made it his duty to care about an injured street waif.

Dark stubble along his jaw had given him an enticingly roguish look, a sensual shadow that vanished into his white collar.

Do not look at his neck, she had warned herself.

And then the carriage had stopped at Althea's home, delivering her from temptation—from the temptation to kiss him. To seduce him. To put her lips to his delectable neck, the way she longed to with a desire that bordered on madness . . .

Serena.

An accented voice. A mere whisper. Not her imagination, she knew. Lukos was here.

Serena.

Her name sounded more beautiful and compelling in his voice than it ever had.

He wanted to lure her to the window.

She gazed at the drapes. Suddenly, before her eyes, she could see a bedroom like a scene painted on the fabric. The brothel's bedroom? She closed her eyes, but the vision followed her. She felt a tickling against her skin—like the brush of a man's soft hair. Her nipples puckered, her breasts tightened beneath her thick nightdress.

You suckle the right, Swift. The left is mine.

God, yes.

Wide awake now, she opened her eyes wide. The drapes stirred once more, but that haunting erotic image was gone. That had been Lord Sommersby's hoarse voice in her head, answered by Drake's throaty growl. The sultry memory of both voices sent a shiver of desire down her spine. Her heart thrummed, and heat flooded her skin.

For one exotic instant, she'd seen two breathtaking men bending to her breasts. Sommersby and Drake! They'd opened their mouths to take her nipples inside—

And then it had vanished. Why had she even had such a vision? Was it Lukos who had put it in her mind? Was this how vampires seduced their prey?

Anger flared at the memory of the young girl, so limp and small in Sommersby's arms.

Damn Lukos. Damn vampires. She didn't care if she was one of them—damn them all.

What if she went to the window suddenly, crossbow in hand? Could she destroy Lukos?

How could she not try?

Serena slid off the bed. Glowing embers in the fireplace gave a weak light, enough to let her see. Creeping around the bed, she winced at the icy touch of cold boards against her bare feet.

Then her fingers brushed the bedside table and slid over it to the taut string of the bow.

It would be so easy to try. She might succeed.

And if she failed, Lukos could come into the house. Althea was enceinte, and it was known that vampires liked to prey on women who were with child.

She couldn't take the risk. But Serena took up the crossbow, the sharp arrow. She crept out of her room and down the silent hallway. She had to go to Althea and tell her Lukos had come. He might try to gain entry elsewhere. They had to be ready.

A glow showed around the large library doors. Was Althea up and reading? Althea spent most of her time in this room, reading the books her father had left in England or writing in her own journals. Althea was documenting techniques of vampire hunting from a female perspective.

Serena gently pushed open the door. "Althea, I—"

She stopped dead in the doorway. Her hand gripped the knob tight. Her jaw dropped open.

A naked man's rump. That was the first thing she saw. A stunning male body—wide shoulders, bunched biceps, narrow hips. And the arse. Oh heavens. Solid muscle, hard, perfectly sculpted.

She was looking at Lord Brookshire's rump. He was pumping enthusiastically into Althea, who moaned in ecstasy and held tight to that gorgeous arse.

Althea's shapely naked leg entwined around Brookshire's. Long red hair spilled over his shoulders.

A burning flush raced from Serena's hair roots to her toes, and she took a step back. But she stopped. In the shadows, she glimpsed a long lean leg. Golden hair. For one mad moment she thought it was Drake Swift.

It was Bastien de Wynter. His leg rocked rhythmically. He groaned in unison with his brother. It appeared that—

It couldn't be.

A shocked gasp came from her lips—no one should hear it over the moans and grunts, but Bastien de Wynter looked up. His heavy-lidded gaze locked with hers.

Serena turned and raced from the library.

"It's at her window!" Jonathon shouted.

Moving out into the open for a better shot, he jammed a bolt in his crossbow and aimed at the shape at Serena's window. His finger slid to the trigger as the bat wheeled back, spun, and swooped down toward he and Swift.

The instant he fired the bolt, the bat darted and his missile flew wide. Damnation! The dark shape hurtled toward him as he struggled to reload.

Swift fired—his shot grazed the wide wings.

Bloody hell, it was as though the beast was protected from their shots. Wings spread, the bat aimed for their heads, soared low over them. Swift ducked, but stuck up his crossbow and fired blind. The bolt missed and the bat flew high, then vanished. Cursing, Jonathon loaded again, hoping the damned demon returned. Then he heard it—the beat of wings behind him. He didn't turn; he knew it would swoop again and as soon as it passed, he'd shoot.

The sound grew fainter.

Blast, the bat wasn't going to attack—it was climbing to escape. He spun around. Two bats swooped and rose, silhouetted against the moon. The first bat was the larger one and flew the highest. He had to bring down the closer one.

The twang of a bowstring, the whistle of an arrow filled the air. Swift had fired again. Jonathon let his arrow fly and grinned as he watched the result. Forced to bank to miss the first shot, the smaller bat flew into the path of the second arrow. Shrieking, the demon spun out of control, then plummeted to earth.

The ground trembled as the beast hit, only a yard from where Swift stood, the force jarring it back into human form.

Stake at the ready, Swift raced over, turning the body with his boot to expose the heart.

Jonathon saw the long black hair spilling over the sprawled naked body.

It was the vampire Roman.

"Hold him," Jonathon shouted.

A pleasure, Drake thought as he slammed his boot on the vampire's chest. "I could stake you now. Drive one of these through your heart, slice off your head, stuff your mouth with garlic. Or you could tell me where Lukos is."

"And in return, I am given freedom?" Roman croaked.

"In return, I give you a merciful death."

Roman spat, but Drake had expected it. He shifted to avoid the spray and drove the stake at Roman's heart. But he controlled his speed, and even as the point shoved into the vampire's chest and the vampire flinched, he stopped his swing. "Next time, I don't stop."

Sommersby stepped forward, holding a length of what looked like metal rope. Drake stared in surprise as his partner walked behind their prisoner, jerked the vampire's arms back, and trussed his hands together. He'd never seen this before.

"We take him alive." Sommersby pulled the rope tight. "I intend to learn how a man becomes a vampire."

"You're mad." Drake stared at his partner. "You're going to slice him up while he's alive?"

"Studying corpses has taught me nothing." Pacing around the vampire, Sommersby nodded. "I'm running out of time."

Roman spat at Sommersby, hissing through his fangs like a viper. He struggled against the ropes—Drake knew they wouldn't hold. "We have to stake him."

"G-god!"

The cry came from Roman. His face distorted in agony, and then his whole body twisted and writhed in pain. A red glow came from his mouth, his ears, his eyes, and he gave an unholy scream.

Drake jumped back. "What the bloody hell?"

Sommersby lunged forward—a silver collar in his hand. "Roman," he shouted. "Lukos is trying to destroy you. You have to pledge yourself to us. You have to let me put the collar on you, or you die."

"Yes, do it—" Roman's plea died on another scream.

Drake dropped to his knees beside the writhing vampire and roughly jerked up his head to give Sommersby access to the neck. His partner slid the controlling collar around Roman's neck but didn't fasten it.

This was a bluff. Only an innocent woman could capture a vampire this way. The collar would not work.

Sommersby paused. "Tell me where I can find Lukos, Roman.

"Covent Garden—"

The red glow consumed Roman's body. Within the circle of it, slices of bright red light crackled and forked like lightning. Sommersby jumped back and Drake took his cue—he leapt back just as a fireball engulfed Roman. Drake landed facedown in the dirt, gasping for air. Heat rushed over him, a fiery wave, and he could feel the agony of it even through his clothes.

Then it retreated. Rolling over, Drake saw his partner staggering to his feet. But where Roman had been, there was nothing but a large burned circle in the grass.

"Dead?"

"I would assume so," Sommersby growled.

"It's almost dawn. Better to hunt Lukos in daylight. I say we head to Covent Garden."

With a bleak emptiness in his eyes, his partner nodded.

Drake turned toward the house, and as Sommersby grabbed his arm, he snapped, "First I want to ensure the little lark is safe."

"She's safe with Brookshire and de Wynter. We have to hunt. Now."

Drake cocked a brow. "I know you're defying Ashcroft to hunt Lukos. He wanted me to keep him informed if you decided to disobey him."

Sommersby jerked around, eyes narrowed. "And have you?"

Drake grinned. "When the hell would I ever do what Ashcroft wants?"

Serena wrapped her arms around her knees. She perched on the edge of the Grecian chaise, surrounded by silken pillows and bolsters. The fire still burned in this room, but her blood ran ice cold.

Surely she hadn't seen Althea with two men. It must have been Lukos's work—somehow Lukos had planted the vision in her mind. Or she was going mad.

"Serena?" Soft, calm, impossibly normal, Althea's voice murmured to her from the door.

Shivering, she looked up to see Althea waiting in the doorway. This was Althea's palatial home, but she seemed to be waiting for an invitation to enter.

"Please, don't stand there." Had it been real? If it was only a vision, and she spoke of it, Althea would be horrified. Her friend would despise her.

"I should go back to my room—" Serena began. But was Lukos still at her window, determined to get in?

Silk rustled as her friend came to her.

"You're shivering." Althea draped a swath of silk around her—a throw from the chaise, trimmed with a foot-long fringe. Warmth surrounded her, the warmth of friendship, not fabric. "There is something I must explain to you."

Cheeks aflame, Serena let the silk slide down. "No. It was my fault. I should not have walked in." She glanced down at her feet. Lukos! She must warn Althea. But she couldn't force the name off her lips. She couldn't seem to speak.

Raw panic welled.

"Look at me, Serena."

Eyes wide, she did. "Vampire," she whispered. "He's here."

"Lukos?" Althea jumped to her feet. "At your window?" She grasped the bellpull.

"I think so." But as soon as she spoke his name, a sense of warmth rushed through her. Her body relaxed, leaving her with such a sense of exhaustion she almost collapsed. "No. He's gone. I feel it."

"Nonetheless, the men must look. And make sure." Althea tugged the tasseled pull. And sat again. "There are two things you must know, Serena."

"It's not necessary—"

"It most certainly is. You saw me in the library with Yannick and Bastien."

It had been real. Serena put her hands to her hot cheeks. "I didn't mean to walk in. I am so very sorry."

"You don't approve." Althea smiled gently. "Or do you?"

She couldn't think what to say. She . . . she wasn't sure how she felt.

"I have a very unusual marriage."

Blinking, Serena looked to her friend.

"You see, I am married to two men. The church records show only one, of course, for we had to ensure things were legal, done in the proper English manner. But I am actually mated with both Yannick and Bastien. They are both my lovers, my soulmates, my partners, and friends."

Clinging to her scattered wits, Serena looked down at Althea's belly. Then hated herself for making that telling glance.

But Althea merely smiled again. "The baby is the child of the three of us. Oh Serena, you look stunned. Horrified."

"I have no right to be. I've done worse." There, she had said it. Admitted it.

"What I have done—and I'm sure that what you have done—is not bad. Yannick, Bastien, and I have discovered that love is more powerful when we share it between the three of us. Our love has the power to save lives, to save souls, to give us unimaginable pleasure and joy."

"I had an affair with a gentleman in the house where I was raised," Serena blurted. "I lost the baby. He was infuriated that I had quickened. I was supposed to be happy to be saved from disaster, so I didn't cry. I never cried for the baby I lost. There—now you see that you don't have to explain anything to me."

"Dear Serena, you did nothing wrong. You must have been terrified to discover you were pregnant. And I do have to explain this to you. I believe you understand why."

She shook her head. "I don't."

"I had dreams, scandalous, forbidden dreams—dreams that were erotic premonitions. It is important that you understand it is not wrong, or bad, or impossible to love two men."

14

Brothers Share

"Why defy Ashcroft to hunt Lukos?"

Jonathon ignored the goading quality in Swift's voice. He tightened his grip on his crossbow and slipped into the shadows by the towering brick warehouse wall. Fog slithered up the alleyway. The dank, sooty mist clung to his greatcoat, his hat, condensed on his cold cheeks and chin, and dripped.

He was tired of creeping around in bloody fog.

"And why in hell doesn't he want you to hunt?"

Jonathon didn't answer. He scanned the impenetrable gray gloom ahead. If Lukos were in there, they'd never know it before he smelled their blood. Apprehension mingled with the pleasure of the hunt. His skin prickled and he flinched, as though he felt fingers grazing across his neck.

It was as though she were still out there in the night. Lilianne. His fiancée. Still watching him.

Why did he remember that night so vividly right now? The slash of a blade. The neat severing of the head from the neck. And then arranging her neatly in a coffin, covering that wound, pretending she was finally at peace.

Perhaps Lilianne was. He would never be.

"Sommersby—" A hand clasped down on his shoulder, and he jerked in shock. He spun to meet Swift's narrowed green gaze.

In Swift's free hand he held his crossbow, and he winced as he moved—the healing knife wound must still hurt. "It's not like you to charge into a trap—that's more my nature. What secrets are you hiding?"

"What secrets are you keeping from me, Swift?"

Those eyes narrowed into angry slits. Jonathon knew he should have no reason to fear Swift—he was larger, more muscular—but Swift was pure killer. Drake Swift was like random chemicals poured into a beaker—volatile, unpredictable, potentially explosive.

And Jonathon understood why. Trigger Swift's memories of his past and you unleashed his demons. Hell, how Jonathon understood that.

"If you're rescuing the delightful Miss Lark because you're in love with her," Swift said, "you're too late."

"What in hell are you talking about? What did you do to her?"

"She broke into your laboratory."

"Hell, you ravished her in my laboratory?" Rage gripped Jonathon so suddenly he almost shot off his bloody crossbow.

"Not in the way you're thinking, Sommersby. I feasted on her delicious cunny—until she exploded in the wildest, most wanton climax I've ever seen." Swift ran his tongue around his mouth, as though tasting Miss Lark's intimate flavors, and then he lowered his lids, looking bloody blissful. "It was heaven, Sommersby."

Jonathon felt his entire body shake. "Don't tempt me to shoot this bolt through the base of your bloody throat, Swift."

"So testy. I reined myself in that night. But last night, last night—I couldn't resist. I made love to her in the brothel last night."

"Christ Jesus." Jonathon's hand had fisted, had slammed into Swift's jaw before he realized what happened. His partner's head reeled. Blood sprayed.

Blood.

Swift clamped his hand to his nose, but he didn't throw a punch in return. Beneath his hand, he grinned as the blood leaked down to his lips.

"I offered marriage." His words came out distorted, through swelling lips.

In that stark moment, Jonathon knew he couldn't let Serena Lark marry Drake Swift. He couldn't let Drake have her.

"You bastard," he spat at Swift. "You took advantage of her. She was kidnapped only a few nights ago. She barely escaped with her life—and what do you do? Open your bloody breeches and rape her in a brothel."

"She was on top. And willing."

His left fist came up this time, catching Swift beneath the chin. But a tough-soled boot drove into his gut. Wind rushed out and he hit the wall behind him. Swift had driven his foot hard into his stomach. Bile rose, and Jonathon choked it down. Swift's left leg swung up. Jonathon rolled against the warehouse wall, but with no way of moving back, his hip took the brunt.

His entire spine hurt from the blow to his hip. "You want to kill me here? Now?"

"It's what your father wanted of me," Swift snapped. "The ability to kill without thought. Ironic if I tore his bloody son apart while hunting a vampire."

"My father—" Jonathon lunged forward and he fought the sudden weakness in his legs, the sensation of the world dropping away. Christ, Swift's kick had really injured him. But he could not show weakness.

"What in hell are you addicted to, Swift? It is opium?"

Swift rushed at him, holding the crossbow pointed at his face. Jonathon was pinned against the wall. He'd drawn back as far as he could, now had nowhere to retreat. All he could do was stand his ground as Swift caressed his face with the point of the arrow.

Swift grinned as he drew the arrow across Jonathon's lips. Jonathon kept them gripped together, fighting the invasion. If he parted them, would Swift shoot into his mouth? Was Swift that insane? Blood still welled from Swift's nose and dripped to his top lip. Their gazes locked. Jonathon saw the huff of their breath against the cold October air, between the wisps of fog.

He jerked up his leg, drove his boot into Swift's stomach, and sent him sprawling back. Swift fell, his limbs spread-eagled in the wet filth that stretched the length of the alley.

It had always been like this between them. Jonathon remembered the night he'd discovered Swift had seduced the girl he'd been in love with. *Brothers share,* Swift had laughed.

He could have ripped Swift's heart out and done it without any remorse. But Swift had saved his life that night while they hunted—Swift had taken the blow intended to kill Jonathon.

Staring down at Drake Swift, who lay in the filth on the ground, Jonathon remembered that night. He'd carried Swift home, helped his partner onto his father's flat wooden table and had stepped back to leave him to be sewn up by his father—

Swift's hand had shot out and grabbed his wrist. "If I can't walk, shoot me. Drop some of his poisons down me throat. Anything. Don't let me live as a cripple."

He'd pried Drake Swift's hand from his wrist. "You'll live as a cripple," he'd vowed. Anger had still raced in his veins. "If I have to live with humiliation, with a broken heart, you'll live as a bloody cripple. And I'll relish every moment of it."

"Ah, come on, lad," Swift had lain back, irises drifting back under his eyelids. "You didn't love her. You care more about being humiliated than about her."

His father had made restitution with the family, and the girl had married a fifty-five-year-old viscount who had a taste for fresh young ladies. *Better she marries him than Swift, his father had said. That man's a gentleman—Swift is an animal.*

His father's condemnation of Drake Swift had eased the pain of humiliation. Jonathon knew his father thought Swift was a more courageous hunter. He knew his father had always thought him a failure compared to Drake Swift. When he became engaged to Lilianne, he'd been terrified he'd lose her heart to Swift. And now he'd lost Serena Lark . . .

From the dirt, Swift's laugh broke into Jonathon's thoughts. "Clever move—" His voice broke abruptly. "Christ, rats."

Jonathon heard them then—the scuttling, the high-pitched squeal of them. Like a wave of black water they raced down the alley, filling it wall to wall.

Swift jumped to his feet in an instant. Lashing out with his leather boots, he tried to kick the rats back. Small black bodies flew into the onslaught. Then just as suddenly, as though they'd heard a silent command, they stopped. Turned and retreated.

"What in hell was that?" For the first time, Jonathon saw fear in Swift's eyes.

Then he heard it. Soft scurrying. But not rats. Likely the urchins that lived on the street—Swift had been one of those urchins before his father rescued him.

"Swift, we should move—"

Two small forms charged out of the black and rammed Jonathon's legs, knocking him off balance. One leapt on top of him, and he knew from the weight, the shape, even the smell, that this was a child.

Jonathon's hand gripped an arm. His other hand glanced off a rib cage barely shielded by thin clothes. This was a weak, starving child. But the boy wrenched free and slammed a fist into Jonathon's stomach. The force of the blow drove him back to the cold, rough ground, coughing.

The child had the strength of a soldier.

The second boy jumped at his head. A bare foot rammed

into his cheek and sent his head snapping to the side. Jonathon's jaw pounded against a cobblestone. He tasted blood. His crossbow—where in hell was it?

One of the boys let out a keening cry that echoed through Jonathon's skull as two small hands fastened on his exposed neck. Even battered, he should be able to fight off two malnourished children, but the grip on his throat was like that of a man twice his own size.

Where in Hades was Swift?

A pistol shot, and a human cry of pain was his answer.

Someone had shot Swift. Jonathon fought with the boys—kicking at them, flailing fists. But he was pinned, like the jawbones on the mounts in his laboratory.

Two lips pressed into his skin above his cravat. The lips parted, and he felt teeth scrape against his skin. The boy gave a laugh of pleasure, then plunged his teeth.

Jonathon punched, kicked, fought like a banshee, but struggling only sent his blood flowing faster from the wound to the vampire's teeth.

Hell, he was damned if he would die this way. He slipped his fingers into his coat to work a stake free.

Drake lay on his back in the muck, and all he could do was watch the wreaths of mist dance over his head. He couldn't move. Hell, he couldn't even blink his eyes.

Was he already dead?

Where in hell was Sommersby? Probably applauding in glee at finally being rid of the filthy, murderous, street scum his father had molded into a killer.

The bullet had ripped into his back. Just below his hat, right at the top of his spine. The front of his chest had exploded as the ball tore through him. He could smell the stench of his own blood, but he couldn't move his head to see the gory mess that was once his body.

The mist congealed in front of him. Swirling, it formed the shape of legs, arms, the thick torso of a man. And then it became a form as black as night. That form bent beside him, as though dropping to one knee. He couldn't turn to see it—he couldn't move his neck.

Long-fingered hands caressed his face. One fingertip traced an old scar, the one right under his eye. Drake saw only shadow above him, shadow hidden by fog. The finger stroked his cheekbone, ran feather-light across his lips. The way he'd traced Sommersby's mouth with the stake. Why had he done that? He knew—to irritate Sommersby, to show superiority.

The fingers lifted his chin. "You have lost much of your blood. You will die. It would be a pleasure to finish you."

Drake fought the dizziness. The effort seemed to suck the life from him. Why couldn't he move his bloody limbs?

"But it will be a greater pleasure to keep you."

Blearily, Drake saw fingers move to his lips. His eyes crossed; the pain almost drove him to pass out. Gently, lovingly, the fingers traced his lips. A bolt of sensual excitement sizzled through him, leaving him aroused, erect, and burning with fury. Something wet touched his cheek. Christ Jesus, a tongue.

But he couldn't wrench his head away.

"There are some who deserve to live forever," the demon continued.

Lukos. This had to be Lukos. Drake's heart pounded, and his constrained, rigid cock pulsed with each beat. He seemed to drift on a line between death and life, his senses fading, then becoming sharp and clear. But he couldn't speak. His tongue was frozen, and cold began to stiffen his fingertips, his toes. It spread, crackling like ice on a pond, claiming his arms and legs. He could feel his heartbeat slowing.

And the voice droned on, low, hoarse, against his ear. "It was amusing to give eternal life to discarded children left to die. It entertained me to give ultimate powers to the damned."

Drake's heart labored. He tried to keep breathing, tried to will his heart to pump. But it only sent blood pouring out his wound, soaking into the wet mud.

The tongue licked his ear. Drake almost vomited—his guts lurched and he couldn't sit up to fight it. He coughed, spluttered—would he choke to death first?

Lukos's pale hand settled on his chest—instantly the sensation of drowning in vomit passed. "I see your thoughts. You are damned, too. You belong with me."

"N-n-" Drake couldn't shake his head in refusal. His limbs were numb, his chest cold, his body racked by shudders.

"What would you do if you could never die? Never be killed? If you had the strength of an army and senses more acute than any predator? What would you do with such power?"

The demon's mouth touched his jawline. Cold lips slid along his neck, leaving a trail of pain and wet warmth. Lukos must be splitting his neck open with his fangs. Some vampires did—some almost bathed themselves in blood, to absorb its life-giving, youth-giving powers through the skin.

What would he do with ultimate power?

What could he not do?

Blinking, Drake wanted to scream. He couldn't see—there was a deep crimson ring around his field of vision, and everything within was shadowed and blurred. This was death, then. He thrashed, grunted, struggled, flung his body wildly, but didn't move an inch.

Something cold and hard, almost like iron, scraped his neck. Sudden, sharp pain flooded his body. The pain of teeth plunging into him, and he couldn't even fight.

He was giving up his bloody life without so much as a whimper.

Oddly, he felt fury, shame, but not fear.

As his life ebbed away, as the beast drank, contentment stole over him. Acceptance. Peace. What was beyond? Eternal darkness or eternal light?

In place of the will to survive, the drive to fight, a deep joy flooded through him.

Then desire began drumming hard through his arteries. The familiar tension of orgasm built in him. So this was death—one last shooting climax?

Drake couldn't feel his body at all, though he was aware of the intense, burning pleasure that seemed a part of his soul. But even this amazing pleasure was not as good as sex with Serena—nothing could compare to that exquisite night . . .

"Now my blood to you."

Instinctively, Drake opened his mouth as something brushed his lips. A drop of blood hit his tongue. One precious drop. His throat swallowed. God—

The orgasm roared through him, his balls seemed to explode, his cock bolted straight upright, and his seed launched out. A searing light filled his brain—

God, yes. Hell, no.

The hunt was over.

Someone shook him, abrupt but not rough. The motion sloshed Jonathon's brain inside his skull, but pain meant he was still alive to feel it.

Was he a vampire? He snapped open his eyes at the same moment he ran his tongue over his teeth. Normal, no fangs. A face hovered over him and he tried to swing at it.

"Sommersby!" Stern but filled with concern, a well-recognized voice sliced through his shock and snapped him back to reality. "It is I, Denby. What in the hell happened to you, sir?"

Jonathon tried to push up on aching arms, tried to struggle to sit. His stomach lurched, and he had to sink back to keep from vomiting. "Swift? Did you find Swift?"

"He was hunting with you? There's no sign of him."

Around him, the world tilted, and Denby's concerned face slipped out of focus. Jonathon turned his face to the side, expecting to vomit, but burning-hot bile sat low in his throat. He coughed, felt his shoulder sink into vile muck.

Jonathon shut his eyes. *If Swift had died, there would be a body. No body meant Swift had become a vampire.*

Pushing with his weakened right arm, he levered up onto his side.

"Sommersby, what in the blazes are you doing?" Denby demanded.

"Getting up on my damned feet."

Jonathon went to Serena—unwashed, covered in the stinking filth of the alley, and hovering between rage, despair, and exhaustion.

Lady Brookshire found him first—he'd collapsed on a settee in the drawing room, ruining the delicate ivory silk brocade. Then he heard Serena Lark's voice—rich, deep, a touch sleepy. Blearily, as though through a mist, he saw her, clutching a robe of apricot silk around her, rubbing her eyes.

"Is it truly Lord Sommersby, Althea? What has happened—?" Her voice rose to a strangled cry. Althea left him to catch Serena as she stumbled toward him.

"Swift. Did he come to you?" He tried to sit up—

Everything went black.

Jonathon cracked one eyelid open. The carved wooden arm of the settee no longer dug into the back of his neck, and heavenly softness supported his weak legs. Soft light played across a dark blue stretch over his head. A canopy with swaying tassels and painted frolicking nymphs on it—he was on a bed.

Soft fingertips grazed his chest, opening his shirt. Serena.

He craned his neck to see her, but lancing pain blurred his vision. He fought to stay conscious.

Her fingers worked again to ease the buttons of his waistcoat open, then set to work on his bloodstained shirt. Her touch sizzled through him, an electric charge against his skin.

"I suppose this is improper, but I don't care." She smoothly opened the falls of his trousers. "You need a bath, my lord."

"Jonathon," he groaned. "I want you to call me Jonathon. I had to see you, Serena, I had to tell you what happened."

"Was it D—Mr. Swift? Was he killed?"

He could barely focus on her face. He saw a blur of long black lashes, shining eyes, full lips. He heard the anguish behind the calm in her voice. She dropped the placket of his trousers and stood up suddenly.

"Serena—" He couldn't move more than lifting his arm to her. How could he still feel so drained, so dead? She needed warm arms around her; she needed a chest to cry against. "Did he come to you?"

"Come to me? How?"

Jonathon's heart tightened in pain. Serena Lark had loved Drake Swift. "He wasn't killed, Serena, he was turned."

15

Loss

Serena fought to stop tears. She'd soaked Lord Sommersby's—Jonathon's—chest, and her cheek slid in the warm, salty pool. Jonathon needed care and tending. That was her duty, and she must check her emotions.

"Did you love Swift so very much?" His chest rumbled with his deep voice. His hands gave warmth to her entire back—splayed wide, they almost covered her completely.

Love him? Confused, Serena lifted her head. Pale as marble, Jonathon's face was etched with pain. His dark eyes were completely black.

What did he know of what had happened between her and Drake Swift? Would Swift have told him? What should she say?

His hands released from her back, and she lurched up as soon as he freed her. With the back of her bare hands, Serena wiped her eyes. "Are you going to hunt him? Stake him?"

Jonathon's eyes, black as night, held on hers.

She thought of Drake Swift's dimpled smile, his wonderful lovemaking, his desire—for her—and her hands shook. Drake was a vampire now. He'd called himself an animal and a killer; now he'd become one.

"Where is he now? Did he escape dawn?"

"I don't know. I searched, Serena, searched even though I didn't know what the hell I was going to do if I found him. Lukos created him. When my fiancée was turned, her maker transformed her into a monster. If Drake is evil, I have to destroy him."

His admission, the aching pain in it, snapped Serena back to her senses. His hand reached out and caught hers. Her palm tingled at the gentle touch, as, large and strong, his fingers slid between hers. Her hand appeared miniature compared to his. Dried blood had crusted his palm.

"Not all vampires behave as soulless ghouls," he said. "Some are like humans—they possess mercy and the capacity to love."

He knew what she was. He was telling her that even though she was a vampire, she was not destined to be an evil predator.

"That's something I have never understood," she murmured. "Lord Ashcroft, the other hunters—all of them told me that no vampire can be trusted. That all immortals should ultimately be destroyed."

"I used to believe that, Serena. Now I understand that it isn't true."

She knew nothing about her parents, nothing about the vampire who had sired her. Was she destined to be evil?

"You could have been killed or turned, too." She spoke the way she would as a governess, kind but repressive. "You need to get into the bath. You need to rest and heal."

Getting to her feet, she took firm hold of his trousers. "These need to come off." Then she flushed, realizing what he must think.

"You can't strip me naked." He struggled until he was sitting upright. "I can handle a bath alone."

"We shall see." But her voice shook at the sight of him. Broad, hewn of solid muscle, his chest dwarfed her. Even on the enormous bed, he still seemed massive. Thick, dark brown, caked with mud and blood, his hair dangled over his eyes.

Shakily, he slid off the bed and gripped the bedpost for support. But he waved back her attempt to help him as he peeled his trousers down, revealing powerful legs. Black hairs dusted them, leading up his thighs . . . to his underclothes.

He paused with his trousers bunched at the tops of his boots and stared down at his long legs with a frustrated frown. "The boots," he said finally. "I'll need help with the boots."

"Of course," she said. She knew how boots were normally removed, but she was strong and had no need to turn her back and wriggle one off. She pulled hard. The boot resisted, then came off into her hands.

"How in blazes did you do that so easily?"

She removed the other before shrugging. "I'm strong."

Serena caught her breath as he casually kicked his trousers away, then moved forward to help him. She slid his arm over her shoulders and saw the marks on the proud line of his throat. Blood clung to his neck, a trail from the two puncture wounds, ragged and ripped.

"Serena, love, you can't help me to the bath. I weigh more than a dozen stone."

"I can," she assured.

He took an unsteady step and she followed, ready to grasp his arm.

The tub awaiting him was enormous and filled to the brim with hot water. The empty buckets stood at the side, and a fire roared in the grate.

The humid heat wrapped around her. Serena felt a flush spring to her cheeks. Her hair dampened at once, and her clothes began to cling. She touched her forehead and felt drops of water, like dew on leaves. It was dawn now and, in the country, there would be dew on leaves and sparkling in spiders' webs.

And Drake Swift would not see sunlight ever again.

He was a vampire, as she was.

Jonathon paused at the edge of the tub. Firelight glanced off his ridged abdomen, his solid thighs. "I know you were in my laboratory, Serena. What did you find there?"

The question rocked her. She hadn't expected that! "N-nothing," she stuttered.

"You found Drake Swift."

She turned away, straightening the towels piled on a chair. "Yes—but nothing else."

Behind her, Jonathon spoke softly. "My father called Swift a 'sewer rat.' He brought Swift to his home, brought him in as an apprentice because it enraged him that I . . . I hated to kill. My father thought it madness that I could be so big yet be so soft-hearted. He believed Swift was nothing but brutal and blood-thirsty—but he was wrong. He never saw Drake Swift as a human being."

She half-turned. Steam made his chest hair slick against his chiseled muscles. And steam, she realized, made his under-clothes almost transparent. Through the fine, white, damp fabric, she could see the abundant black nest of hair, the way his cock curled down to fit inside—

"Did you read my father's notes?"

She intended to lie; instead the truth came out. "Yes." How could she sound so calm? "Is that what you plan to do to me?"

"Of course not." His chest rumbled with his gravelly voice. "God, I could never—I want to find a way to stop your change."

She frowned. She had never considered that.

"My father made an astounding discovery," he continued. "A way to transform a vampire back to a mortal. But I don't know how he did it." He raked his damp hair back.

Her heart pounded erratically. "You think you can . . . save me?"

Jonathon's face was etched with pain. His eyes were completely black. "I swear I will find a way. I know you cared deeply for Swift, Serena, but I've desired you since I first saw you."

She had no idea what to say. Althea's words—*it is not wrong to love two men*—hammered in her head. "Thank . . . thank you. I must leave you now." She turned her back. Coward!

She tried not to think of Jonathon taking off the last piece of his clothing. She tried not to think of anything but walking briskly to the door.

"Serena."

She paused at the sound of her name.

"What did you want from the vampires' library? Why did you go? If there is a book that can help you, I need to know what it is."

He wanted to save her. He knew what she was and he desired her. He had always desired her.

She turned—Jonathon was immersed in the tub, his body slick and wet. Trembling, she shook her head. "I went to find Vlad Dracul's journal. I knew Ashcroft would want it, and I hoped to bargain with it for the truth."

As soon as she closed the bathing chamber door behind her, Serena ran for the safety of her own room. Once inside, she braced her back against her door and gulped down breaths. She felt tumbled inside. Hot, needy, fearful, hopeful. Completely confused.

Six hours, six wasted hours spent sleeping. Hell, he never slept more than an hour or two, and despite the rumors, he didn't take drugs to keep him awake. Jonathon let the cravat his valet had brought him flap around his neck as he strode down the hallway of Brookshire's home.

He found Serena in the library. A pot of coffee sat on one of the tables, the accompanying cup full but untouched. She had not breakfasted—he'd learned that from the footman as he had shoveled ham and eggs down his throat—he didn't have time to waste.

She hadn't heard him walk into the room.

Her back was to the door, her glossy hair drawn back in a chignon. Daylight spilled over her from tall windows, transforming her hair into a rich sable black. She shut the book with a bang. "There must be a way—a way to save a vampire."

Jonathon paused, a few strides from her.

Surprised, Serena twisted in her chair to face him. "My lord, you should be in bed."

So lovely, she took his breath away. To hear those words on her soft lips, to see the concern in her eyes— "Jonathon," he reminded her. "Call me Jonathon."

He saw one of the books in front of her. Newly published. The leather binding barely used, the pages crisp. Even from this distance he knew the book. *A Treatise on the Stake*. What vampire hunters would do to get published. What difference did it make how narrow was the point or what type of wood was used? Puncture the heart and the beast died.

Christ, how could he do that to Serena?

He had only a week to find a way to stop her becoming a vampire.

"Jonathon, you really should be resting." A soft flush touched her cheeks and she stood up from her chair. She advanced toward him. She moved like a vampire—almost as though her feet did not need to touch the ground. She moved like music, and his throat tightened.

He had to say something. He couldn't just stare at her like a cabbage head—his father's favorite term for him as he was growing up.

"Serena, I must go back to my laboratory."

"N-now? You are still weak." Her black brows drew together. "Thank you for this, for trying to save me. But you need time to regain your strength. To recover."

"I don't have the luxury of time."

Her lashes dipped. Of course, she didn't either. He cupped her face, her delicate chin, and she looked up, startled. Her lips parted, pink and tempting.

He slanted his mouth over hers, reveling in the hot beauty of her mouth on his, the lush pleasure of her in his arms. Her arms hooked around his neck and she kissed him.

Her mouth was warmth and heaven and salvation. He needed to hold her. Touch her. He needed to make her his. His hands clasped around her waist, his mouth slanted over hers.

But she had made love to Drake, she had cared for Drake—she must be in shock. Groaning, he broke away from the kiss.

Her gray eyes were half-closed and sultry, but they suddenly opened wide. "Are—are you going to hunt for Drake Swift tonight?"

Jonathon hesitated, but he owed her the truth. "Yes."

The window rattled. Instantly awake, Serena rolled over and kicked at the covers tangled around her legs. The drapes were wide, and moonlight poured into her room.

She slid the stake off her bedside table, trying to disguise the motion. Her gown had loose sleeves, and she slipped the sharpened wood in her right sleeve.

Don't fear, sweetheart. It's me.

Drake? Serena crept toward the window and let the stake drop into her waiting hand.

Serena. Come to me. I'm waiting for you. Outside. I will be in a carriage at the end of the mews. Please come to me now, my love. I must see you again.

It would be foolish to go, but he could not come to her unless she invited him into the house, and that she would not do.

Vampires lured their prey this way. They sent a command and the human obeyed. Only a ninnyhammer would trust a vampire, but she needed to see Drake.

If she took a crossbow and carried a stake . . . ? She would be alone; it would be madness to let herself be lured, but his deep, sensual voice called to her. The night called to her. She stood in front of the window and gazed out at the moonlit garden. From where she stood, the half moon was bright and beautiful, its mysterious other half a deep, shadowy blue.

Serena . . .

She wanted to go outside. She needed to feel the cool air ripple over her. She needed to be in the dark.

It took no time to slip on her pelisse—the simple gray one with the deep interior pockets. Hurrying to the shadowy corner, she turned an old iron key in the lock of a large, metal-bound trunk. She eased back the lid to display an arsenal of vampire-slaying weapons that still astonished her.

From the upper tray Serena took extra arrows for the crossbow and slipped them in a deep pocket. Pushing the tray back onto the opened lid, she drew out the smallest crossbow from the bottom. It would have to do; she couldn't carry the large ones.

She threw a deep blue silk shawl over the weapon, though she could still not carry it without looking conspicuous.

Juggling the wrapped crossbow, she went out into the hallway, turned the key in the lock of her bedchamber door, and pocketed it. She waited while a maid hurried by, then she turned and made for the servants' stairs. These were dark, narrow, and fortunately deserted.

But just as she reached the very bottom, the door flew open and a footman hurried in. He gave her a startled glance. She gave the young man—an attractive youth blessed with large dark eyes and full lips—a perfectly repressive governess stare. He flushed, averted his eyes, and moved past her.

The low-ceilinged basement felt cramped, imprisoning, and hellishly hot from the kitchens. Serena passed through the kitchen, only to find the cook snoring and two scullery maids hard at work on a mountain of pots.

And then, blessedly, she was outside in the cool, delicious, fall night air. Lord Brookshire and his brother entered often by the door in the back of the gardens, and she found it unlocked. The ripe scent of the mews assailed her; the vibrant sounds of the street echoed in the darkness here. This was a fashionable street, and lines of carriages traveled up and down.

Drake's carriage, black as the night sky, stood at the end of the mews, just as he had promised. She stopped, uneasy now that she faced it. A cloaked and shadowed figure sat up on the box, a figure that did not move as she took one more step closer. There was no trim on the polished carriage, nothing but shining wood to reflect the moonlight. Two ebony-black horses stood with unearthly stillness; they wore plain black harness.

She saw that the door of the carriage stood open, revealing the black maw of its interior. Then movement, and the moonlight glanced off silver-blond hair. Drake Swift stepped down from the carriage, his arm extended, his long-fingered, black-gloved hand waiting for her touch. Then he grinned—his teeth shone white, his eyes glowed. His eyes were silver—no longer green.

"Are you going to shoot me, Serena?"

"Only if you give me reason to—" Her voice died on his name. He looked just as Drake Swift had in life. But this was not Drake Swift, this was a demon.

"Do you mean, do I plan to bite you?" His lusty grin widened, his eyes burned. Just looking into his eyes took her breath away. "I won't. I would rather have you bite me again."

He was still a scandalous, cheeky wretch. She shook the crossbow so the shawl slid off it. His eyes widened as he saw it.

"You've been turned into a vampire. This is not the time to speak of—"

"Of sex?" he murmured in a forbidden tone that ignited a fire in her. "Of fucking, as we did in the brothel. Wanton, pleasurable fucking. Why shouldn't we speak of it? We both want to do it again."

He drew off one of his gloves. She gasped at the sight of his fingers—the nails were long, clawlike. With a flick of his fingers, he slashed his own neck. And smiled all the while he did it.

Blood welled instantly. Whose blood?

Mine, my love, he answered. *Touch my neck.*

"I know why you are speaking in my thoughts—but it won't work. You won't control my mind. And you aren't Drake Swift anymore."

I am. I don't feel any different than I did as a mortal, Serena.

She touched his neck, and a dab of his red blood smeared her fingertip. Just a trace, easy enough to wipe it away on her skirts.

Taste it, Drake urged. *A drop won't change you, but it will make you understand.*

She jerked her head up at that, and the blood dripped off her finger to her skirts. "What will it make me understand?"

Who you really are, Serena.

16

Rope Play

"How do you know who I really am?" The crossbow bumped against Serena's leg, and her finger ached from holding the trigger primed and ready to fire. Slowly, carefully, she let the string slacken. And she wiped her finger clean, afraid to taste it.

Drake gave a rueful grin—he licked his finger and ran it along his wound, which vanished. *I learned everything from the vampire who made me. If you have the courage to follow me, I can show you everything.* His deep, sensual voice murmured in her thoughts, startling her even as she quivered in arousal.

"From Lukos," she said coolly. "From the vampire who wants to possess me."

You have nothing to fear, angel.

She had a choice—she could find the courage to follow her heart and find the truth, or she could hide. The breeze caught Drake's cape and threw it up behind him, like great dark wings. His silvery-green eyes flashed in the moonlight, and he reached out to her.

Drake lifted her hand and brushed the most gentlemanly

kiss to her fingertips. *Do you know why you can hear my thoughts?*

"Because vampires do this to lure prey?"

No, sweetheart. You can hear my thoughts because I love you. Even as an immortal, I am yours. I belong to you. And I will always protect you, Serena.

He caught her hand in his and strode out of the mews. She had to trot to keep up with his long, determined strides. She was so wet, so lusty and wet. Drake was a beautiful man. A desirable man—but did she burn so intensely because he was a vampire and because she was?

"But don't you belong to Lukos now?" she asked.

A slave? I am no man's slave, little lark. Lukos believes I have become one of his disciples, but I have not.

"But what happened? How did you get away?"

Since he thinks that I serve him, he allowed me my freedom. Drake pushed open a wooden gate in a tall stone wall and led her through. Moonlight flitted through an elegant garden, reflecting off stone fountains and statues. Fallen rose petals covered the ground.

"Where are we?"

This home belongs to a countess—there is a small dinner party tonight, but the night is warm, and soon the gardens will be full of trysting lovers.

"Why are we here?" she whispered. She refused to speak only in her head.

To steal a few minutes of pleasure.

Suddenly he vanished from sight. Her skirts lifted! "What are you doing?" she gasped. "Aren't you horrified to have been transformed? Aren't you angry?"

No, little lark. I am not angry. Now, bend over—grasp onto that statue.

The statue was a nude woman, of course. A bounteous water

nymph, with large stone breasts and lovingly rendered nipples. Of course the only place for her to grip was on those breasts. Serena heard Drake's low chuckle as she clutched the plump stone bosom.

"Wait!" She cried the word through a whisper. "What of your change? Did it hurt? How exactly do you change?" But the wind was blowing up her skirt, the breeze naughty and erotic against her hot cunny. Wanton desire raged with propriety—she had wanted Jonathon this way, after making love with Drake. And now she was with Drake once more. She was wicked, utterly wicked, but she didn't care.

Warmth and wetness touched the back of her legs—Drake was licking her.

"The change—" She struggled to speak. If she knew how he'd changed, was it possible it could be reversed?

Was for the best. Do you know how strong I am now?

"But you are strong so you can prey on mortals."

I don't have to kill for blood. Vampires are superior to mortals. Vampires aren't evil—I've learned that in just the short time since I turned. Now hush and let me slide my tongue up your bottom.

She stilled. His hands wrapped around her legs to keep her steady, to keep her under his control. His tongue washed over the cheeks of her bottom, and her legs quivered. Like a mare in heat, she pushed her rump back toward him. Her legs parted wider, her hips swayed. She wanted him to mount her, to fill her from behind.

Play with your lovely breasts, he urged in her head. *Tug your nipples.*

He pushed her thighs farther apart, and she balanced on her toes to accommodate him. His tongue slid down the valley between her cheeks—damp with sweat—and she heard his groan of pleasure. To her shock, she realized he liked the scent, the taste. Her anus tightened as his tongue reached it, as his tongue pushed in against the snug puckered ring.

Relax for me.

She tried. She truly did. But her derriere resisted his tongue, and he pushed it harder against her. She gloried in the wetness, the heat, the sheer forbidden pleasure of it. This was most assuredly a naughty thing. But it felt so good.

Speak to me in your thoughts, he said in hers. *I will hear you.*

Balanced by gripping the statue's breasts, Serena tilted her bottom back toward him. The tip of his tongue breached her rear. Oh, the delicious delight! So wet. She let herself try to speak through her thoughts, but all she could say was *ooh!*

In her head, she heard Drake's deep chuckle.

Brilliant lights exploded before her eyes—the garden's fairy lights, the glowing windows of the mansion blurred.

Drake plunged his tongue deeply into her bottom. Serena remembered the girls of the vampire brothel—and the large rods they had taken into their derrieres. No wonder they did. It felt magical to be filled this way.

The statue's nipples jutted into her palms. She was gripping tight, rocking back to his thrusting tongue.

In front of her, far too close, bushes swayed.

Then she heard a muted voice nearby, a man's voice. "I say—did you hear that?"

She expected a woman's voice to answer; instead a deep, throaty voice groaned. "I can't concentrate on a thing but your hand down my breeches."

"There's someone out here."

"Probably a vampire. There's been tales of them stalking the gardens of Mayfair. Now drop your trousers, Beecham, and let me pound myself into that tight arse of yours." The deep voice held such hunger, such lust, that Serena's entire body heated.

She was eavesdropping—but what could she do? Drake's

tongue was driving her mad, filling her arse with pure, wet fire, and his fingers—his fingers toyed between her slick nether lips. He wouldn't stop to find somewhere more discreet.

One of the men grunted—a sharp, fierce grunt followed by a deep, soft moan of pure sensual pleasure.

Drake's tongue circled inside her anus, twisting, caressing. His fingers, wet and slick with her juices, rubbed over her clit. It was like releasing a crossbow. Her tightly strung body exploded. Her keening cry rose over the dead bushes, the stillness of the garden.

"Jesus bloody Christ!" one of the male lovers shouted.

A deep, hearty laugh startled her. She floated slowly back to earth, to reality, to find Drake on his haunches behind her, a wild grin on his face.

You are incorrigible! Serena scrambled to pull down her skirts. *Why did you come in here? To get caught?*

A little risk adds spice, my love.

He had heard her thoughts. It was so incredibly intimate to speak this way.

And I did think about sinking my fangs into the neck of one of the rutting gentlemen, Drake continued, *and giving him the most incredible orgasm.*

You wouldn't!

I would. His laugh rippled over her tingling skin. *Would you spank me, then, my love, since I am so naughty?*

If I threaten to do it, I will have to. With my charges, I quickly learned that one cannot make an empty threat. Even when I spoke in haste, in anger, in the heat of the moment, I had to follow through with what I said.

Bushes cracked, and she tensed. But the next twig that snapped was farther away. The men had given up their clandestine joining and were escaping back to the house. Unsatisfied, frustrated, and very likely terrified.

Serena refused to allow the chuckle that bubbled in her throat to escape. *Who was the vampire they spoke of? You?*

I've only been turned for two nights, love. Come with me and I will show you everything.

Tell me now. She truly wanted to flee the garden. She didn't want to be caught by anyone. How many couples had heard her scream? But she stood her ground, ignoring her mussed skirts, her pounding heart.

Drake tucked her arm in his and led her back toward the gate. Y*ou are a half vampire, Serena. You are the child of vampire and mortal. The only one ever to be born. And you, my dear, possess power beyond your wildest imagination.*

I have no objection if you want to spank me now, Drake teased as he tapped the ceiling and the carriage lurched off. Serena must have been stunned by the news, and he wanted to ease her shock a little.

I knew . . . I'd hoped that it wasn't true, but now I know it is. She had curled up on the seat opposite—he'd wrapped her cloak around her, for her hands felt like ice.

He frowned. *How did you know?*

Lord Ashcroft knew. He corresponded with the woman who raised me; he had her send weekly accounts of my progress, and she was to detail any signs that I might be a vampire. She tipped her head back against the squabs.

Drake's heart ached for her. She'd grown up with a woman who'd hated her—how he understood that. She looked so alone, so small and sweet and frightened, that he crossed over beside her, sat down, and wrapped his arms around her. He wanted to promise his eternal protection; instead he joked, *Now I know why you bit my neck while you fucked me.*

A fire burned, like molten silver, in her eyes. *You won't shock me with such language,* she admonished as she tipped up her nose to look prim. *I am well aware that it excites men to speak in such a base way.*

Does it? You understand men very well then. Drake grinned. *And it wasn't my intention to shock you. You are a vampiress. You have a strong sexual drive—a perfectly healthy sexual drive.*

She blushed, and he laughed gently. When she tried to act the prudish governess, it only aroused him more. As a mortal man, born in the stinking slums, he hadn't been worthy to even kiss her pretty hand. But as a vampire, he held power, immeasurable power.

He felt as though he'd finally found where he belonged.

Serena's hair was mussed from her fierce orgasm. He could taste her most intimate flavors on his tongue. Still rock hard, his cock throbbed against his linens. Since becoming vampire, Drake had found his erections harder, immensely larger, and more insistent.

"Lord Sommersby is trying to prevent my change. He wants to save me." She spoke aloud, plucking at his black wool cloak, and worried her lip with small, human teeth.

Blast, Sommersby. Drake heard the soft catch in her voice as she said his name. She cared for Sommersby. "Sweetheart," he reassured. "There is nothing to fear in becoming a vampire. I promise you."

"Tell me about my great power."

Sheepishly, he smiled again. "I do not know very much, love—only that you are supposed to have power equal to the strongest vampire queens."

"I read about them. Some can send mortals to different times, to unknown dimensions. Some can change weather and can unleash power that could destroy a city." She shuddered. "I am not certain I want that responsibility."

"Serena, you are a queen among vampires—don't be frightened of what you are."

"You admit you don't even know what I am. Yes, I am frightened." Large, beseeching, her eyes held on him. "Do you know who my parents were? Who my father was? Did he attack my mother? But he couldn't have killed her. I wouldn't have been born. Is there a chance she is still alive?"

"I do not know yet, Serena."

"Yet?"

"I'm trying to build Lukos's trust in me. To learn more about you from him. He destroyed his last disciple and he's not ready yet to believe in me."

"His last disciple? Do you mean Roman?"

Drake nodded.

"So he knew, then, that Roman was betraying him." Sadness touched her eyes. "I almost feel sorry for horrible Roman—his greed saved my life."

Drake brushed a kiss to the top of her head, to her gleaming black hair.

"What about Lukos?" she asked. "What do you know about him?"

"Lukos sat at the devil's right hand. He was a powerful demon, and he needs a mate. It is his intention to breed a stronger race. A race that could destroy both humans and vampires. He needs your power."

She ran her fingers through her hair, brutally tugging the strands. "Lukos thinks he can *breed* me? I don't believe it. This is all completely mad."

He cradled her close, stroking her back. "You are an admirable woman. Any other woman would have swooned. Or been hysterical."

"Give me some time," she muttered, "and I might provide you with both."

"You have nothing to fear, Serena. Lukos cannot touch you, and then you will change. After that, you will have incredible strength."

"*After* I change! You mean to turn me!"

"All Hallow's Eve, love. Your birthday."

"But that isn't—" A tear welled in her eye. "Ashcroft lied about my birthday, I suppose. He told me it was in late November. The rotten man even stole that from me. And I am going to change and there's nothing I can do about it!" Her voice rose. "They know everything about me? How?"

"I don't know. All I know is what I've told you." Gently, he brushed his knuckles along her bare neck. Serena gave a gasp. He lifted her fingers to his throat.

"Where are you taking me?"

My home. The rooms I now live in—where I pretend to be a mortal gentleman.

Drake groaned as she traced her fingers along his throat, as she ran her fingertips along his carotid artery. *You will start to feel the change as your birthday nears. Your transformation will be more intense than mine. I want to help you. Protect you.*

He gave a wicked grin. *And I want to indulge in a lot of raw, wild, sweaty, sticky sex.*

"And how will being tied up help me to discover who I really am? How do ropes and bindings free me to find the truth?" Serena could not resist crossing over to the enormous bed that dominated Drake's bedchamber. He had brought her back to the rooms he rented on St. James Street.

With her hand on the thick, gilded column, she peered down at the jumble of silken ropes. "I don't want to be tied up. I was bound once before—I did not like it."

From behind her, Drake's sensual baritone whispered through the warm, quiet bedchamber. "You trust me, little lark. In your soul, you know you can trust me." His fingers slid down the line of buttons that followed the curve of her spine. The buttons popped open. Down, down, toward the small of her back.

Her dress loosened, the sides dropped open. His soft breathing surrounded her.

Nervously, she asked, "If I am a vampiress, will I be attacking you in your sleep to steal your precious seed?"

"Is that a promise?" He laughed, and reminded, "We will hunt together, in the night."

She gulped. She didn't want to become a vampire! Not even for Drake. But could she escape her destiny?

"Not all vampires are demons, love," he murmured. "I've fed once already and gave only pleasure to the woman who offered her blood. She slept, awoke healthy, hearty, and very sated. When you change, there will be many handsome men who will clamor to have you drink from them."

Her heart gave a twinge as, madly, she thought of Jonathon.

"My turn to undress. Watch closely."

She did, but in a heartbeat his clothes simply tumbled to the floor. Empty. Blinking, Serena dropped to her knees in her gaping dress and grabbed at them. She lifted his empty shirt. He'd vanished before her eyes. She hadn't seen it happen.

A black shape swooped and circled tightly, taking care not to come near enough to collide. Only moonlight lit the room, and she strained to get a closer look before he glided into deeper shadow.

"Drake!" Serena called his name sternly, as a governess would. "I demand that you show yourself at once."

The bat hovered in front of her, and she watched carefully. She wanted to see how this could be done. One instant the bat beat its enormous wings, the next Drake Swift stood before her, his hair and eyes as silver as moonbeams. His arms crossed in front of his naked chest. Around him, on the floor, lay his discarded clothes.

She had never seen him completely . . . naked. He was absolutely perfect, and he winked.

"How do you shift shape?"

When it's time, you will learn. But feel free to touch me.

Need thrummed in her, controlled her. Her cunny ached for him. Her fingers itched to feel the rough and the smooth of his skin, itched to dally in the hollows of his sleek haunches, to stroke his belly, to curl around his cock. Unable to stop herself, she reached out. His hand met hers partway. He slid his fingers between hers and drew her into a kiss—into a lusty open-mouthed play of mouths, a duel of tongues. His tongue slid into her mouth, filling hers with his warmth, his taste.

He tasted of berries and sweetness, not blood. There was a trace of smokiness—a cheroot, perhaps. The tang of alcohol. It was like kissing an ordinary man—

No, there was nothing ordinary about kissing Drake Swift.

He broke the kiss, and her gown spilled to the floor—he'd pushed it down her hips. Drawing his fingers through her hair, he pulled the pins out. The weight of her hair fell down her back. *Now the corset,* he whispered. He yanked the knot free easily, expertly loosened the laces. *There is nothing more seductive than undressing a woman.*

His gaze slid down to her bared breasts, the nipples hardening before his eyes. Then he looked down to her wide curve of hips, to the black curls at her crotch, to her generous thighs. Her body was silver-white in the moonlight, her nether curls as blue-black as the night sky,

Exquisite. Beautiful, he said.

Mine.

He paced to the bed, and she watched, breathless, as he lifted a coil of rope from the bed. Drake let the length of it slither down from his palm. *The pleasure of rope work is in the anticipation.*

Serena glanced at the shadowed paintings on the wall, each depicting a young lady bound and aroused—and felt her eyes widen. What a choice for decor! The painted ladies' nipples jutted out and their heads tipped back in submissive pleasure.

This was different than being a captive. This was play, and it aroused her.

She stood with her hands over her breasts. She felt she needed some attempt at modesty, even though she wanted this. Her breath came in desperate pants as Drake lowered to his knees before her. The first rope brushed against her bare ankle—she'd grown up in a world where it was scandalous for a lady to show her ankle. She had to shut her eyes at the pure pleasure spiraling through her body—the ropes were fashioned from a material that was smooth but braided, which teased her skin.

Drake tied the end of the rope around her ankle with a sturdy knot. The rope bit lightly into her skin. Serena stiffened as he bent to her other leg. He would tie her ankles together, trapping her—

Instead, he picked up a second rope and slid this around her ankle the same way. Now two lengths of rope trailed from her legs across the floor. To the first leg, he wrapped a second rope around the loop of the first, and then he began entwining the ropes around her legs.

Oh, it excited her so—the brush of the rope, the pressure of the binding. It looked so erotic to see her legs crisscrossed by black ropes.

He looked up, smiled. She knew why—to reassure her, to share the moment of trust and intimacy.

Firelight reflected in his silvery eyes as he touched the rope to her wet nether lips. His eyes were like mirrors; she could see the shadowy shape of her face in them—she couldn't guess at his thoughts.

You are soaking the rope. He sawed it lightly between her legs. Oh! It pushed up between her nether lips, opening her. Her juices drenched her curls, her thighs.

Serena saw Drake wrap the ropes around his wrists and caught her breath. The black length wound and wound, imprisoning him as it pleasured her. He lifted—the rope rasped, ignited her clit like a lit fuse reaching a cannon's gunpowder.

Before she could even moan, the climax burst. Her legs went weak—the sawing rope held her up. It sparked another orgasm at the end of the first. Then another. She just kept coming—and she desperately grabbed the bedpost for support.

Drake unwound his wrists and let the rope drop from between her legs.

Oh! She gasped. *I didn't think I could come again without dying.*

Rich, throaty, his raw, masculine laugh shimmered through her. She'd spoken in his thoughts. He'd heard her.

He took the rope, sopping with her honey, and tied her wrists together. She was too weak with pleasure to resist. Holding the rope, he led her like a prize mare to the center of the room. He stretched, up on his toes, and threaded the rope through an eyelet hook. He was going to suspend her from the ceiling?

No!

Yes—you will enjoy.

Pulling the rope, he lifted her arms. He didn't lift her off her toes, thank heavens, but her arms were held up above her head. Her breasts were lifted, her reddened erect nipples pointing at him.

He brought more rope. Tying the new length to the knots that rode on her hips, he pulled two portions between her thighs. They parted her cunny lips again, ran up between her derriere cheeks—and if she rocked she could tease her clit against them.

Don't move. You aren't to come yet.

She was on the brink, though, and had to hold completely still. Just the slightest rasp to her throbbing, abraded clit and she would explode again.

At her belly, Drake threaded ropes between the two that slid between her thighs, tugged up, and she almost squealed. She fought not to come—suddenly understanding the maddening pleasure of trying to hold back. Was this was it was like for Drake? On the brink of orgasm, but fighting it hard? What exquisite torture it must be for men, when every thrust was a trigger to their release.

Drake paced around behind her, swinging a black rope. The end slapped her bottom, and Serena gasped in shock. It hadn't hit hard, but it had stunned her. He spanked again with the rope, slowly, then waited. She moaned in anticipation.

Without warning, his strokes came quickly. He lashed her with the rope. It stung a little but pleasured her intently. She was so close . . .

With a sudden, fierce motion, Drake slid the rope through the ones between her cheeks, and she hovered, fighting the climax. He tied a knot and pushed it lightly into the puckered entrance to her ass. Heavens, the pain of trying not to give in—

He moved swiftly—with a vampire's speed. The ropes encircled her waist. He wrapped her breasts in the ropes, making a figure eight, squeezing her sensitive bosom.

She licked her lips, ran her tongue over her teeth—she needed something to chew on. Smiling, he obliged her need without a word. He pressed a length of rope between her teeth, wound it around her head. It caught her hair and tugged, yet she loved the pressure. She dabbed at the rope with her tongue, but Drake pinched her nipples, and she bit hard in the rough strands.

She wanted him inside. Rocking her hips, she pushed back, pressing her rear against his groin. His cock nudged her steamy, moist cunny. She felt tiny, delicate, almost weightless, and she wanted to be filled. She didn't want him to be gentle.

Drake squeezed her bottom, his hips thrust up, and she was so drenched, so ready, that his cock slid easily inside. Up and up until her bottom squashed against his pelvis, and she was full, stretched, and sobbing in pleasure.

His fangs brushed the back of her neck, sending shock and

need rippling down her spine. He withdrew, right to the tip, until she whimpered. *Please.* He thrust back in, so hard their bodies collided, and she cried out with the sheer pleasure of pounding against him. *Yes! Mine!*

Serena, I want you. Even in her thoughts she sensed the anguish in his words.

I want to come . . . now . . . oh, it's going to happen! Why she had to tell him, she didn't know. Didn't care. Tears splattered her cheeks. She loved this—being bound, being impaled on his cock, being unforgivably naughty.

Serena pumped back, hard, grunting like an animal. He was huge, frighteningly huge, but she wanted it all, as deep as he could go.

She'd been wrong. If this was a vampire's world, she wanted it.

Thrust in me, she begged. *Do this to me.* Scenes from the forbidden Society's books flashed in her mind, scenes of muscular powerful demons with legs spread, impaling sweet ladies on their large cocks.

She cried out in her thoughts—*I'm coming! Coming now!*

Yes, she was coming. She bit down on the rope and let her body explode. It was so impossibly good. Her cunny clutched at him, and wave after wave of pure, head-spinning ecstasy took her.

God! God, my sweet, you're so scorching hot, so tight, so . . . good! His cock raged forward and she took it, loving it, coming again around it. He fell against her, gripping the rope above her head. His cock jammed hard against her womb and his body bucked as though beyond his control.

Suddenly, heat seared inside her quim, and he grew impossibly large. He stilled, tensed, and roared her name by her ear. *Serena!*

One last orgasm took her, and Serena hung off the ropes chafing her wrists, as though her muscles had melted into fluid.

You are mine! he cried. *Mine forever.*

17

Rule

I want to share my blood with you. As he spoke in Serena's mind, Drake tried to force his scattered wits to come together. He couldn't think, and that scared him. A cold numbness began to steal over him, and his fingers were stiff and icy as he untied the ropes that bound her.

Dawn was coming.

He wanted to be the one to turn Serena—to claim her as his soulmate, to ensure that Lukos could not have her—and he had to hurry.

The ropes slid off her body as he sliced through the knots with his fangs. She rubbed at her wrists—he saw the chafed skin, and his heart lurched. *Did I h-hurt you, love?* His thoughts were blurring, his words beginning to slur.

She shook her head. *I liked it.* She turned to face him, bathed in moonlight, rubbing her wrists, staring at them in surprise.

Drake understood. She was stunned to have enjoyed bondage games. The innocence in her eyes twisted his heart in a way that no pain he'd endured ever had. Exotic and midnight black, her silky hair spilled over her shoulders, covering her round, full breasts. His touch was tentative—a first for him—as he brushed her hair back from her neck.

Her eyes opened wide, and she pushed his arm away as she stepped back. *I—I am not ready to become a vampire. I don't want it—I thought I did, but I don't. Please—please don't turn me.*

I won't, he promised. Inside, raw panic sliced through his exhausted body. He needed to turn her as soon as possible—it was the only way to ensure he protected her from Lukos. He slid his arms around her, drew her into his embrace, held her tight. Her heart beat hard against his naked chest. Warm, supple, beautiful, her body molded to his. He kissed the top of her head, a tender gesture that made his heart ache. He'd never been tender with any other woman—except Mary, who had given birth to his child in the slums and died doing it. He hadn't been able to protect Mary.

In the vampire world, he was still a newborn, barely formed and with no knowledge of what he was capable of doing. But he would protect Serena.

I want to go home—to go back to Lady Brookshire's, I mean.

The longing in her eyes told him how much she wished she had a home. He could give that to her. They could soar together, rule the night together. *And I can't let you leave, sweeting.*

She struggled against his embrace. *I'm a prisoner?*

I need to keep you here for your own good. Lukos must claim you before you turn on your birthday—he will want to bond with you by changing you that night. That way, he can claim some of your power.

One sweep of his incredibly powerful arms and he lifted Serena off her feet. Her legs dangled over his arm, her hand splayed over his chest.

You cannot just sweep me up and force me to do as you wish, she protested.

I can try, sweet lark, because I love you.

He lifted his wrist to his mouth with his arm against Serena's back, supporting her. A quick pass of his arm across his fangs and he sliced open his flesh.

He held his bleeding wrist only a hairbreadth from her lips. He wouldn't force her. But the scent would speak to her nature. It would call to her.

Drake groaned in pleasure as Serena's tongue, warm and wet, licked the blood from his wrist.

"How could you let this happen?" The instant he shouted the words at Lady Brookshire, Jonathon hated himself. Althea was enceinte. Delicate. And Serena's disappearance was not her fault. Hell, if anyone should shoulder the blame, it should be he.

Rubbing his hand over the back of his collar, he groaned. "Blast . . . Althea, my apologies . . . in your condition . . . I mean . . ." His words died as he struggled to make a logical sentence. It was the thought of Serena at risk that stole the words from his mouth.

Althea kept her back to him and continued to rifle through Serena's wardrobe. "Since I stayed in England against the wishes of my husband only because I was worried about Serena, I assure you I had taken great care to protect her," she answered archly. "And I would say that she left willingly, wouldn't you?"

Jonathon strode around Serena's bedchamber for the fourth time. The window was shut, garlic flowers in place. The sheets, though tumbled on the bed, were not torn as they would be from a struggle.

"I believe I know who came for her," Althea said. "A man she trusted."

"Swift." He had reached the same conclusion. "I'll rip him apart." His gut clenched. The most logical reason Serena had not left a note? She did not want to be found.

"He might not mean to harm her." Althea placed her hand on his arm, and he jerked in surprise.

"He means to turn her," Jonathon barked, losing his grip on his temper again. "He means to make her undead!"

"Which she is meant to be," Althea pointed out, with a calm voice that reminded him of Serena's muted governess tones. He knew he'd insulted Althea, a vampiress herself.

"I found his lodgings tonight, but I didn't wait for him," he admitted. "Goddamn me for that stupid moment of weakness."

"Not weakness, Sommersby. Mercy. Love."

Jonathon forced a smile to his lips as Althea patted his arm. Like Ashcroft, his father had never accepted the idea of good vampires. His father had warned the Society about tolerance for a superior being. *We allow them to prosper, they will enslave us,* his father had warned.

But both Ashcroft and his father were killing not to protect or to save, but out of fear.

"I will have my husband and Bastien go with you—"

"No, it's too dangerous for them." Jonathon patted Althea's hand in turn, then left her to stand at the window, at the lightening night sky. "I can guess where Swift's taken her, but I fear I'm already too late." He hung his head. "If she becomes vampire, I've lost her.

"No," Althea said, gently. "You will never lose her."

It is not wrong, or bad, or impossible to love two men. I want you to understand that.

Serena remembered Althea's words once again as her tongue swirled over Drake's warm, tangy skin. As she licked his wounded wrist. Driven by a primal, powerful need, she ran her tongue along his wound, tasting his rich, hot, coppery blood. She didn't love the taste of blood, but once she took it in her mouth, she couldn't stop taking more. Tears pricked—she wanted to stop, but she couldn't pull away.

What was it like to be vampire? To want blood so much it was beyond control? To revel in the fierce moans of the victim as she drank?

Less blood flowed. Her tongue no longer slipped into the tear in his flesh; it skimmed over smooth tissue.

Thank you for healing me, Drake whispered in her thoughts.

She felt a burst of excitement, a sense of power, but also fear. *I don't think it was I. I think it was you.*

It's almost dawn.

Starting guiltily, Serena saw weariness in Drake's silvery-green eyes. She had to fight a yawn, too, as exhaustion stole over her. She'd been awake all night. But Drake would succumb to the daysleep, and that would give her a chance to escape . . .

When they'd been making love, she'd trusted Drake, but now she felt a sense of panic, a need to get away. To be alone, to think . . .

He hadn't asked her for her blood. Only given his. Why?

Drake held out his hand. *Sleep with me, Serena, love.*

The gravelly invitation had spoken to her heart. She heard the aching honesty in it. She felt so tired now. Drake's bare chest and his powerful arms looked so welcoming. He moved to the bed and fell back onto it, his arms spread open as though waiting to embrace her.

She had to make him believe she planned to sleep with him, so she went to his arms. She closed her eyes, trying to fight the contentment, the sense of belonging she felt as he held her. She had to keep to her plan and leave.

To go where? Back to Althea, so she could tell her only friend that she was a vampire's child? Back to the Royal Society, who were planning to cut her up for scientific study?

Or *did* she stay with Drake, who intended to turn her into the undead—because that was her destiny?

She had nowhere to go. Nowhere to consider her home. The thought weakened her, left her heart like ice, but she tried to fight the paralyzing pain. For her entire life, she'd never felt she had a home, never felt she'd belonged. She had always been unwanted, but she had endured.

Serena closed her eyes and mimicked the slow, steady breathing of sleep . . .

After a long time, Drake sat up; the bed groaned softly with his movement. Serena shut her eyes tight and struggled to keep her chest moving evenly. Was he watching? The bed creaked again, more loudly. He'd left it.

Why was he awake? With her lids open a crack, she watched him cross the room, his white-blond hair and naked skin lit by the dim glow of the low fire. He seemed weak—he stumbled. Serena heard the click of a lock, saw he'd passed through a narrow door, a different one than the one they'd entered.

Serena lay motionless. A clock ticked somewhere in the room. A log popped in the grate. She heard the creak of hinges, the thud of another door closing. Only then did she feel safe enough to slide off the bed.

Creeping quietly through shadow, she found her shift and corset. Her toes bumped the thick fabric of her gown. Groping, she touched the trim of her pelisse. Ignoring her corset, she pulled her thin shift over her head, then wiggled into her gown. She managed two buttons at the top of her neck, and her pelisse covered the rest. She didn't bother with stockings and crossed barefoot across the room, slippers in her hand.

Was it foolish to look where Drake had gone? Carefully she opened the narrow door, so slowly it didn't make a sound. It opened to complete darkness. She strained to see and caught a glimpse of something dark that gleamed. The fittings on a coffin's lid.

Drake was in *there*.

Heart pattering in her throat, Serena pulled the door closed and darted to the door that led out to the other rooms—that would get her out of Drake's house. Her slippers coasted quietly over the carpet. When she reached the door to the bedchamber's sitting room, she turned the doorknob as silently as she could.

Locked.

Damn and blast!

She withdrew her silver cross and chain from her pelisse pocket. Her cross wasn't only a cross, after all. She flicked open the hinged lid and slid out the slender lock pick Mr. de Wynter had given her.

What are you doing, sweetheart? Drake's seductive baritone sang through her mind.

Serena's hand jerked the cross so hard she broke the chain. The edges of the silver dug into her gripping fingers as she turned to face Drake and met his amused silvery-green eyes. She did not know what he would do to her. He was no longer the man who had captured her heart.

Trust me, little lark. He held out his hands.

She couldn't. She wasn't ready—

Starlight exploded in the room, a glimmering column of it that swirled around Drake, engulfing him as he cried out in surprise.

What was happening? *Never mind,* screamed a logical voice in her head, *unlock the door!*

In her shock, she'd dropped the lock pick, and she had to step closer to Drake to get it. Within the sparkling lights, his body glowed like pure gold, and he seemed transfixed—like a statue. She bent, and her fingers touched the metal pick when the lights vanished. Horrified, she saw Drake's eyes.

The silvery gleam was gone and they looked like deep, dark pits. Before her eyes, his face distorted—his jaw lurched wide, his fangs lengthened.

She jumped back in horror.

The bedchamber door flew open behind her and she spun around. Black shapes swooped inside, transforming the instant they crossed the threshold, and she faced Leonardo and the new vampires who served Lukos—the vampires who were now his loyal disciples.

A howl exploded from behind her, a sound like a soul being taken to hell. Drake! She turned back to him, dizzy on her feet. He hovered in the air, arms and legs wrenched back and pinned against the wall. His head was twisted back, throat exposed. His eyes were huge and still that horrible, soulless black.

Lukos! It must be Lukos who controlled Drake.

The window—if she could reach the draped window—

Leonardo launched across the room toward her. His lips, white and bloodless, curled back from long fangs.

Holy water! She had it in her pocket, but one vial used now would gain her nothing. She didn't even know if it would work.

She turned and ran, but Leonardo's hand snaked out and grabbed her wrist, yanking her back. She spun and kicked, but he swirled her so her back was to him and he wrenched her arms behind her.

An animal roar erupted from Drake, but Leonardo's grip tightened. He jerked her around to face the door.

Heart in her throat, Serena knew who would walk in.

She expected a horrific demon with horns, inhuman face, unearthly white skin, and vicious fangs. A hand slid around the door—a large hand in black leather gloves. Then he filled the doorway, massive and dark.

Lukos.

For the first time, Serena saw the vampire who wanted her. Black hair streaked with white was drawn back into a queue. A cape draped over his flawless gentleman's dress clothes. His face was that of a fallen angel. Eyes of silver that seemed to swirl with blue and violet mists. Sharp cheekbones, a harsh chin, long aristocratic nose.

He was beautiful.

His eyes glowed in the blue light that poured into the room. He leaned on a walking stick, and she met his gaze, refusing to show the fear that coursed through her. Her palms were soaked; her underarms smelled of her own desperate sweat. At her side, Leonardo bowed, and the other vampires followed with the same gesture of genuflection.

Lukos waved his hand, and magically the door slammed closed behind him. He threw a slow smile to Drake, who writhed against the invisible power holding him. "You have betrayed me, thrall, and you will be punished."

Serena had to struggle to force her head to turn away from Lukos—it was as though he controlled her muscles, as though he could will her to obey.

No. She had to fight this. Her fingers felt numb, her shoulders felt as though they'd snap apart, and she had to stop fighting against Leonardo's hold.

Look upon your lover for the last time.

Serena's head jerked to the side by its own volition—no, by Lukos's control. She shivered in emptiness the instant she snapped her horrified gaze to Drake. He gave a valiant struggle against the power holding him but slumped, exhausted, still pinned against the wall.

No—spare him! She willed the thought to Lukos, even as her skin crawled at the thought of speaking so intimately with a demon.

He needs to be punished.

Drake's head snapped back hard, over and over, pounding against the wall. Blood smeared the wallpaper and dripped down onto Drake's shoulders.

No—stop! She screamed it in her thoughts. *I will do anything you want if you spare him.*

How noble you are, my dearest Serena.

Lukos's voice echoed through her mind, rich and captivating. Gritting her teeth, Serena willed herself not to respond. She felt a warmth wrap around her heart—it was as though by imagining a shield over her heart and her soul, she could create one.

You think I am beautiful, do you not? Lukos asked.

"What are you?" She cried it aloud. She felt stronger. She felt in control of herself.

Doesn't hell possess the most beautiful amongst us? The fallen angels?

"You are not a fallen angel. You are merely a vampire. A carcass without a soul."

Brave words, Serena, for you are not yet vampire. I knew your mother. She is as old as recorded time, as powerful as a deity. I wanted her but could not possess her—but with you, I can rule the earth as it was intended. Between heaven and Hades is the paradise of the vampire—we will rule here. I will be the one to command the wind, the seas, the sun. And you will rule at my side.

"I most certainly will not rule at your side!" She forced calm into her voice, though her thoughts whirled. It was madness. Her mother had been a mortal, not a vampire—hadn't she? Her father had been the vampire—surely her mother had been an innocent?

Lukos laughed, and in the twist of his features, she saw the cold cruelty in the eyes. *You will spawn a race, Serena. You will rule the world.*

"Never."

Not even to save your lover, Swift? You can have him as your thrall, if you wish. But you must serve me.

She heard his command to his disciples. *Take her to the bed.*

Drake's howls of rage echoed in her ears as Leonardo began to drag her to the enormous bed. Tears stung at her eyes—stupid tears.

The holy water. It was her only hope. Serena prayed that Lukos did not want to bother with undressing her—

If she could get her hand free, she could throw the water at Lukos.

The next howl almost split her eardrums. An unearthly shriek of pain and fury that echoed so loud in the room it left her deafened.

Drake? She twisted in Leonardo's arms to see Drake drop to the floor. Lukos's power no longer held him.

Leonardo jerked her back, then his scream exploded beside her ear. He released her, and she stumbled forward, grabbing the bedpost to stop her fall. A cry of surprise wrenched from Serena's throat as Leonardo's body crashed to the floor beside her. A crossbow bolt protruded from his back.

Her hand sank into her pocket, fingers closing around the smooth glass of the vial as she saw Lukos. The demon slowly rose from the floor, his hand on the arrow that stuck out through his chest. A perfect shot, through his heart, but he was still alive.

Impossible.

Lukos roared and reared up onto his haunches. He held his hands out in front of him, palms flat. A stream of fiery white light seemed to shoot from his hands toward the door.

Where Jonathon stood, jamming another arrow into his weapon.

18

Truth

He smelled blood.

Drake tried to stand but his leg gave way, and he dropped back to his knees. Serena. He had to protect Serena. Rage ran through him like a hot river. From his position, half-crumpled on the floor a few feet from the door, he smelled the hunters as they poured into his room. He could smell their blood. His fangs lengthened, his body screamed to attack, but he was weak.

He had to fight both the vampires and the hunters to protect Serena.

Through blurred vision, Drake saw Sommersby. Bow sight held to his eye, Sommersby fired again. The arrow sailed and ripped through Lukos's heart, but the demon staggered to his feet and pulled both arrows out of his chest.

An arrow through the heart couldn't kill him?

Where was Serena? Drake saw her stumble toward Lukos holding a vial. No! He fought to stand as crossbow bolts shot across the room, missing Serena's head by inches. Were the bloody hunters trying to hit her?

Two hunters—Russex and Williams—jumped on Lukos,

slashing with stakes, but he threw them off with one twist of his body.

Serena!

Drake got his footing—just as she tossed the contents of the vial at Lukos.

"Aargh! Witch!" Lukos jumped back as the water splashed at him.

Drake stared in astonishment. A stake through the heart had done nothing, but he feared water blessed by the church?

Staggering, Drake launched across the room, making a wild backflip to land at his maker's side. Fangs bared, he went for Lukos's throat, the way he'd learned to kill with a dagger on the streets. Drive in and rip forward. Pull out the windpipe, the jugular, and destroy.

As his fangs punctured Lukos's flesh, the blood filled his mouth and flooded his senses. Lukos clawed his naked body, the sharp nails ripping easily into his chest and his belly, but his fangs were seated deep, and he held on.

Pleasure surged as he sucked down Lukos's blood. Then a searing stream of light and heat hit his chest and sent him sprawling back on his floor. His maker had hit him with magic.

Sommersby ran at Lukos, sliced with his drawn sword—

Lukos gripped it before it hit his throat. For a mortal, that blade would have sliced off fingers, or a hand. But Lukos, unhurt, easily wrenched the weapon from Sommersby's hand and lifted it. Drake stuck his foot out as Lukos charged at his partner. All the weapons in the room, the magic, and what saved Sommersby's life? That Lukos tripped over Drake's foot as he drove forward with the sword.

As the demon stumbled, Sommersby threw himself to the right, landing hard on the wood, grunting, rolling toward the bed.

The blade flashed. Drake launched up, without bloody well thinking, and he found himself face-to-face with his maker, who now brandished a sword that would slide through his neck like a silver knife through fresh butter.

I offer you the power you have always yearned for and you throw it away. You cannot claim Serena. You are not destined to father a superior race. You are garbage.

The blade swung. One of Lukos's vampires flew forward, shouting, and Drake saw Serena give a grim smile from behind. She'd used his trick of tripping an opponent, and before Drake could flash an answering smile, the golden-haired vampire fell against Lukos, who turned with a roar of fury. He moved to swat the vampire away, and the blade took off a hand. The disciple fell to the ground, clutching the wounded arm to his chest. Blood now bathed Lukos; his white clothes were soaked in it. With a cry of rage, Lukos kicked the wounded slave out of the way.

Drake leapt over the bed and grabbed a burning stick of kindling from the fireplace. The flame scorched his hand but was quenched by his grip until only the tip flamed like a small torch. But as he ran toward Lukos, something drove through his shoulder.

Stunned, he looked down at a protruding arrowhead. A hunter had shot him. He sprinted forward—it would take a few seconds for a reload.

He lifted the burning log and launched it toward Lukos's eyes. It twirled once in the air, flames streaming back. Lukos moved with impossible speed, and the burning wood struck the bed hangings. It lodged in the folds, and with a whoosh, flames spread through the gauzy fabric. As though blown by the breath of God, the fire roared instantly up the hangings and crossed the canopy.

He heard a sound behind him.

A damned hunter ready to shoot.

Drake spun around. Sommersby stood there, a crossbow

trained on him, aimed at his heart. There would be no way it would miss.

Serena raced forward, knowing she had only a second to stop Jonathon. Fire blazed across the canopy, and the hangings fell like flaming wicks to the sheets. Smoke raced along the ceiling in gray-white wisps and billowed through the room. She ran through it, screaming, "Jonathon, no!"

"You betrayed her, you bastard." But Jonathon hesitated, and she knew that meant his heart ruled his mind. She had a chance.

"Jonathon! Drake didn't betray me." She sputtered in the smoke. It wouldn't hurt the vampires, but in a few more breaths, she would collapse. So would Jonathon and the other hunters.

Jonathon swung around to face her, lifted the bow, and fired. Serena froze as the arrow whistled to her—in that blink of an eye, she trusted. She didn't move. A scream came from behind her, followed by the thud of a body—a vampire.

She screamed as someone grabbed her shoulders, then almost collapsed in relief as she saw it was Drake.

You have to get out.

She saw him glance toward the window and knew what he meant to do. He would shatter it so they could escape. But it must be dawn—Drake would be escaping into daylight.

Lukos blocked the doorway, and there was no other way but the window. The heat singed her face, the inside of her throat, with each breath. Her lungs felt as though a fire burned inside them.

"Look out!" Jonathon shouted.

Drake leapt back, pulling her with him, and she saw the bed canopy sway. Burning embers rained around them. Before her horrified eyes, the flaming canopy toppled inward, sending out billows of choking black smoke.

Tears poured from Serena's eyes, and it was agony to open

them. She realized Lukos was gone, leaving his disciples dead on the burning bedroom floor. But the fire now raged in front of the door—they couldn't get out that way.

She heard Jonathon order the hunters to escape, saw men shoulder the fallen and try to drag them to freedom. Jonathon was at her side. She was coughing now, as was he.

Drake shouted, "Take her out of here now!"

She tried to protest; she screamed in Drake's mind. *But what about you?*

Jonathon was at the window. The curtains were a line of fire, but Jonathon ripped them down, and the others stamped at the flames with their boots. Sunlight poured in.

She tried to find Drake in the smoke but couldn't see him. Had he ran through the wall of fire at the door? He wouldn't survive it.

Fear for Drake paralyzed her. She couldn't move. Then Jonathon kicked a hole through the windowpanes.

Serena turned helplessly back to the door—but Jonathon grabbed her wrist and pulled her to the shattered window. She leaned forward and desperately sucked in the cool night air. The air would feed the flames; the breeze would send it racing through the rest of the house. The smoke began pouring out of the window around her, and the ground below seemed to spin before her eyes.

They were the last house in the row, and a small clump of bushes lay below the window. She knew she could jump out a window! She'd jumped off Sommersby's balcony to escape Drake.

Jonathon grabbed her waist. "Serena, wait—"

There was no time for dawdling, for second thoughts. She pushed back Jonathon's hand and jumped. As she plunged down through the night air, she cried *Drake!*

* * *

Jonathon awoke to find himself in bed—in a borrowed nightshirt. Crisp white sheets tangled around his legs and hips, and sunlight peeked around closed drapes.

Where in hell—?

He was lying on his stomach, and as he flipped onto his back, he hissed with the pain. But he wasn't in hell now, he realized. Last night he'd been in hell—in the battle with Lukos, in the middle of a fire. Now he was safe. The sting of his bare skin reminded him his back was riddled with claw wounds. During the attack, one of the vampires had shredded his clothes while clawing his back. At least the wounds to his skin were superficial. Now he had bandages wrapped around his back and around the blistering on his neck where some burning fabric had landed.

Despite the grogginess in his head, Jonathon forced himself to sit up. He heard the click of the door's latch and glanced up in surprise. His throat dried. Serena stood in the doorway, dressed in a clinging ivory silk wrapper, with her raven hair tumbling free. His heart hammered as she walked into his room.

"Thank heavens you are still alive," she said, and she looked guilty.

He sat up abruptly. "I'm fine."

"You shouldn't have risked your life for me." She shook her head, dark curls dancing. "I went there with Drake Swift willingly."

Jonathon stared at her pale, strained face, not comprehending. Serena was angry he'd come to rescue her?

"You were in danger; I came to you." He growled the words out. Were they the right words? Or had he said the wrong thing again?

Silence stretched while she stared down, and he tried not to gape at her like a lovesick puppy. A faint shaft of sunlight touched a tear on her cheek.

The tear caused him more pain than any of his wounds. Serena loved Drake Swift, not him. She loved a demon; she preferred a vampire to him. She'd tried to stop him shooting an arrow through Swift's heart. But Jonathon knew he hadn't stopped for Serena. He'd stopped because he'd realized he wanted to murder Swift out of jealousy.

Wiping the back of her hand across her cheek, Serena paced to the curtains. She pulled them open with her back to him. "You came to rescue me because of her, didn't you? Because of your fiancée."

No. He'd gone to rescue her because he loved her, but it was pointless to tell her that. Once she learned what really happened with Lilianne, she'd despise him forever.

But he had to tell her.

On the bed, Jonathon groaned and rubbed his jaw. Stubble rasped his palm and, despite his bath, his hand came away streaked lightly with soot.

"I killed her," he said.

Serena turned, her hand on one of the drapes. Her dark brows drew together in a puzzled frown. "A vampire killed her. You tried to rescue her. You can't blame your—"

"Don't try to absolve me of guilt." He watched her walk over to him, moving cautiously as though she were approaching a mad dog. "I killed Lilianne, and it's the wretched truth."

"Tell me why you believe you killed her," she urged, softly, calmly, and she sat down on the bed at his side.

Jonathon breathed in the scent of her—rose soap, the tang of ashes still in her hair, the unique scent that was her skin, her breath, her life. A scent he couldn't define but knew he couldn't live without. A perfume that aroused him, that wrapped around his male senses, that spoke to his heart.

She was so near to him her skirts brushed against his borrowed nightshirt. Her hand covered his, smooth and warm.

She'd been through hell and she was strong enough to offer comfort to him.

He couldn't sit beside Serena and see her face as he told her the dark truth. He wasn't that courageous. He got up from the bed and paced the carpet. He fought to control the bitter rage that welled up, and he tried to simply tell his story.

"Lilianne was not killed by a vampire, she was turned. It was my fault, of course, for she had followed me. She was an impulsive woman. Impetuous. She always demanded my attention. As much as it would infuriate me, I wanted a woman to want me, to need me, to make demands of me. I believed it meant that she cared about me."

"And she did."

Jonathon glanced to Serena. He could read nothing in her gray eyes, in the flat line of her lips, in her guarded expression.

"I don't know if she loved me." He bowed his head. "I drove her mad—perhaps I was more a challenge than a true love. She wanted me to drive her about in Hyde Park, to pay her calls when I needed to do experiments in the day. She wanted me to bring her to balls at night, but I had to slay vampires. We had one thing in common. We both wanted a family—"

"Couldn't you have stopped hunting for her? Taken time away from your experiments?"

"No. Any day I didn't hunt, I allowed another innocent person to die. A child. A young woman with a whole life to live. Or a man who shouldered the responsibility of a family."

"You said that Lilianne followed you? Why?"

Jonathon closed his eyes. "We became engaged—I asked her only because I'd hoped she would be content with an engagement for a while. I wanted to keep her, but I wasn't willing to change for her. She wanted to force me to be passionate. She wanted to try to make me into the kind of man she wanted. She was falling in love with someone else, but she wanted to give me one last chance. She was desperate, and she acted without thinking."

"She found me in Hyde Park—" He remembered the furious way he'd snapped at Lilianne as she'd darted out of the bushes. Then, with tears streaming down at his impatient demand that she go home, she'd slapped him and raced away.

Softly, he admitted, "When I found her, she was lying on the grass, pale as a ghost, with the mark on her throat. I thought she was dead. I should have—I should have decapitated her, so she couldn't rise, but I couldn't bear to do it to her."

"And she was a vampire."

With his back to Serena, he nodded. "I spent weeks tracking her down, following the stories of child victims. Those who survived told me about a beautiful lady, with hair and eyes like moonbeams, who they could not resist."

He heard Serena's sharp gasp behind him. "You . . . you were the one to destroy her."

"I was the one who found her. The choice of whether she would live or die was mine. I went with my father and Ashcroft to her crypt. I told myself that she was no longer human . . ."

In his mind, he was back in that night . . .

He had walked past the other stone coffins, swinging the crowbar so it struck his legs. The rhythmic pain convinced him he was not dreaming. His lantern threw light into the gloom. Quick, relentless, his heart had hammered in his chest. He planted the edge of the iron bar at the join of the lid and coffin.

Stone scraped stone as the lid slid away. The crowbar struck the stone floor with a clang as he dropped it—a loud, endless sound that seared his brain and rang in his ears.

With his hands against the cold lid, Jonathon shoved on it, pushing it aside as much as he needed. The lantern threw golden light down into the box. Light that touched Lilianne's golden hair and pale lashes, that slanted across perfect lips, rich and red.

He'd held the stake to her chest, but she slumbered on. As his father and Ashcroft had walked forward, boots thudding the cold stone floor, Jonathon had pressed the point of the stake just below Lilianne's breast—into the pretty white dress she'd been buried in. He had lifted the hammer—

He couldn't bring it down.

Swallowing hard, Jonathon spoke again. "She looked at me. With sheer, mad terror at first. She knew who I was. I saw it in her eyes. I saw recognition. Then love. And hope—the certainty I had come to rescue her. In that instant I believed that vampires did not really lose their souls. Whatever happened to create them, they were still human inside. But I thought of what she would do because she could not help it. Of children who would be bitten. My father, Ashcroft, some of the other old men of the Society were waiting, the excitement of the kill in *their* souls. Sometimes afterward, I wondered who the real demons were."

He dropped to the bed by the pillows, far away from Serena. He let his head lower to his open hands. "I did it. God help me, I did it. I was looking down upon her and her eyes changed—they became red and demonic. I knew I had to kill her or she would kill me, and I drove the stake into her. I destroyed her out of fear. That's what I've hated myself for, all these years. That moment of fear, that moment when I lost courage. I will never let that happen again."

The bed creaked. Dimly, Jonathon saw the shimmer of Serena's wrapper as she crossed the room to the fireplace. "Is that what the Society wanted you to do to me? Were you supposed to kill me when I changed on my birthday?"

Hell and perdition, she knew. Jonathon couldn't deny that was what Ashcroft had planned to do to her, but he vowed, "I would never harm you; I will never let you be harmed. No one will hurt you, Serena. Not Lukos, not the Society, no one." He wanted to go to her, to touch her, but such pain radiated from her darkened gray eyes, he knew he didn't have the right.

"Does Althea know what I was?"

He hesitated. Finally he nodded. She was entitled to the truth. "Yes. It was Ashcroft's plan to bring you under the control of the Society."

Serena bit her lip. "So she was never my friend."

"Serena—" At a loss for words, he said, "I don't believe that."

She shrugged as though she didn't care, the way he would when he was deeply hurt. "And you know who my mother is."

"No, I do not know anything about your parents. Many of my father's journals are lost. I was not lying when I told you that."

She picked up the fireplace poker and jabbed the logs. Sparks flew up. "Did you know that my mother is the vampire? Did you know that much?"

The truth would drive the wedge further between them, but he could not bring himself to lie. He gave a grim nod. He didn't approach her; he leaned against the carved wood bedpost as she prodded the fire. "I wanted to find a way to keep you from changing."

She placed the poker back with deliberate care and turned to face him. "And have you found a way to keep me from changing?"

Damn, she would probably slap his face, but it was a risk he had to take. Three strides brought him in front of her, and he clasped her hand in his. His hands were huge compared to hers, but she possessed greater strength than anyone he had ever known. "No, love."

"So, on All Hallow's Eve, I will be a vampire." She pulled her hand from his, and Jonathon felt the crushing weight of failure.

He had vowed never to fall in love after Lilianne, but he'd fallen impossibly hard for Serena, and he was going to lose her.

Jonathon watched Serena run across his room. "Even if you change," he whispered as she disappeared out the door, "I will never stop loving you. I will do everything to protect you."

19

Prophecy

Serena stopped at the foot of the stairs and blinked back tears. Had Drake perished in the fire? If he hadn't, would he come for her tonight?

Moonlight spilled through the windows, scattering silver-blue squares over the gleaming hardwood floor. Serena felt the draw of the night. She walked over to the corridor window and pressed her palms to the cool panes of glass.

She was afraid. She hated to admit it, but she was. Afraid to face losing Drake. And too hurt to face Althea, now that she knew their friendship was a lie. She should have suspected it from the first. A countess wishing to be friends with her?

Turning from the window, she hurried down the corridor to the red drawing room as though pursued by demons. Smoothing her skirts, she pushed the gilt door open.

"There she is!" Althea cried. The countess relaxed on a chaise of red silk and gilt. "Bastien, please pour a sherry for Miss Lark."

Jonathon and Lord Brookshire were in a muted conversation by the fireplace, though both had offered quick bows when she walked in. She felt warmth on her neck and half-turned. Jonathon's intense dark gaze rested on her back. Was he speaking about her? Or just watching her?

Mr. de Wynter brought the sherry, exquisite in his evening dress. His naughty smiles full of secret promises and scandalous innuendoes were so like Drake's.

Shakily, Serena lifted the sherry to her lips, but she couldn't swallow. *Drake.* She called out to him in her thoughts.

As though in answer, the footman rapped, then opened the door. With the fixed gaze of the proper servant—directed at some point on the opposite wall—he announced, "Milord, milady, Lord Ashcroft."

Startled, Serena stepped back, and sherry splattered her pristine glove. Jonathon left the mantelpiece and prowled toward her, and a sense of safety washed over her as he stood by her side. She drank in his presence, his delicious masculine scent. Impulsively, she rested her hand on his forearm—formed of solid, steely muscle beneath the finest tailored coat—as elderly Lord Ashcroft entered.

She managed a curtsy and rose to Ashcroft's curt nod. "Miss Lark." Stooped and scrawny, the man who wished to kill her rested heavily on his cane. But his eyes—clear, blue, and bright as though they belonged to a young man—stayed on her a long time. Long enough that she caught her breath, that she glanced to Jonathon.

Then she stopped. Jonathon was a famous, noble vampire hunter. He risked his life every night to save the innocent. Lord Ashcroft had been like a father to him. Jonathon had hoped to find a way to stop her change. If he couldn't, would Jonathon truly turn his back on his calling to spare her?

Shuddering, Serena retreated from Jonathon and Ashcroft with a murmured apology. Her head was reeling. Holding her sherry, she fled to the bookshelf and pretended to study the titles. What did Ashcroft think of as he looked at her? Was he envisioning her laid out on a table, with her chest opened up, and her flesh pinned down?

Was Jonathon thinking that he would have to stake her when she transformed?

Could she survive this night—behave as though all was normal, have dinner with all of them, knowing they wanted her dead?

"Miss Lark."

She jerked around to face Ashcroft. Was he going to stake her here? She almost giggled at the absurdity—she doubted Lord Ashcroft could drive a stake in her heart without expiring himself. Instead of a stake, he held out a book. She realized he had carried it tucked beneath his arm. A thick volume, one that reminded her of the hundreds she'd read for the Society.

"This is for you, Miss Lark. It is imperative that you and Lady Brookshire try your hand at deciphering parts of this book."

"What is it, Ashcroft?" Confident, lush, Althea's voice rose from the chaise.

Serena felt a prickle along the back of her neck, and she glanced up. Jonathon had returned to stand near the fireplace, but he was listening, a brandy cradled in his palm, his dark brows drawn together. A predatory gleam touched his eye as he watched her.

Ashcroft bowed toward Althea. "A prophecy book."

Serena gaped. She had heard a rumor of such a thing from Mortimer, the curator of the Society's library, but they were kept under lock and key and she had never seen one. Prophecy books were written by monks, by ancient scientists—the volumes locked in the vault were those reputed to be true.

Why would Ashcroft offer her this book? Simply because he couldn't translate? His lordship must know she had gone willingly with Drake; he must know about the confrontation. She took the book warily.

Althea pushed up from her chair, back arched, belly thrust forward. Both Brookshire and his brother were at her side in a blink to help, but Althea waved them away. She slid over, one hand on her back.

Serena saw Jonathon push his glass onto the mantelpiece and begin to move toward her, but Ashcroft intercepted him. "Let the ladies review the book. They have the greater experience in that arena." She strained to hear as Ashcroft lowered his voice. "You and I have much to discuss, with All Hallow's Eve in only four days. You have refused to follow orders, Sommersby—"

"A few more days and I will find an answer," Jonathon broke in.

"Not in a few days, Sommersby."

Straining to hear Jonathon and Ashcroft, Serena let go of the prophecy book as Althea pried it from her fingers.

"I will find a way to stop this." Jonathon lowered his voice. The anguish in his controlled baritone made Serena shiver. "If I had my father's journals . . . I don't understand why he hid them . . . why he wouldn't give them to me . . ."

"Your father was a cautious man." Ashcroft accepted a drink from Lord Brookshire, who had strolled over to join the conversation.

"I wonder . . ."

"You didn't destroy Drake Swift. And you failed to slay Lukos." Ashcroft sipped his drink.

Serena saw Jonathon flinch. "Swift helped us escape. As for Lukos, I shot him directly through the heart with a crossbow, and it merely enraged him."

"Lukos is not a vampire. Not as you would know one to be."

Pure fury flashed in Jonathon's deep brown eyes, turning them the black of a thundercloud. "Then what in hell is he? I need to know to combat him."

"And you were not to hunt Lukos." Ashcroft laid a calming

hand on Jonathon's shoulder. "Your loyalties have become confused, Sommersby."

"My duty is to protect innocent people. That is exactly what I am doing. Now tell me what you know about Lukos, Ashcroft, or—"

Ashcroft swung his cane to collide sharply with Jonathon's boot. "We shouldn't distress our charming hostess with an argument. Let us move over there." He directed Jonathon to cross the room.

Damnation! How could she listen in now?

"Serena?" Althea's amber-lashed, green eyes narrowed. "Have you been listening to me? Lukos is mentioned, at least I believe it is this Lukos. The writing is Latin, but there are odd words that I don't recognize. Words I've never seen anywhere before."

Slowly, Serena turned to the woman she'd once thought was her friend. Althea, of course, did not know she knew the truth. She couldn't speak of it—it would be foolish to reveal that she knew the Royal Society planned to destroy her.

Althea carefully turned the brittle pages. "We should sit down with this."

Serena nodded. She took the book from Althea and offered her arm, like a good servant. Like a thoughtful friend. Yet she was alone, friendless, with nowhere to turn.

Once Althea settled on the chaise, she pulled Serena down to sit at her side. "Read this passage. I believe it speaks of Lukos's rise."

Serena tried to focus on the medieval text, the Latin words. Her life was at stake—it gave her the push to see the words. She translated quickly, reading in a soft voice. "A rend in the earth shall set him free. And signs shall be sent to his disciples, to those who serve him nobly, and they will know these signs. They will feast in blood in preparation to his rise, until the seventh day before Samhain, when they will fast in honor for the final ascension. Lukos must also fast—"

Althea clutched her arm. "He is supposed to deny himself blood. We can only hope that means he isn't hunting. Let us see if it speaks of his destruction . . . prophecy books always speak of destruction . . ." Althea smiled.

Serena returned it, though her stomach roiled and her lips wavered.

Althea read further. "It says that Lukos's aim will be to create an army but that he will bear one son, and that son will destroy him." She set the book down on her lap, and Serena turned away from her shocked gaze. "You must read this."

She moved the book to her lap. Althea rested her graceful hand on her shoulder, and Serena read. "It speaks of a woman bred to be his mate. Vampire, human, and descendent of a god—created to destroy our God's creation, man. Lukos will find her after a thousand years of imprisonment. That is to be me, of course. But how can I be a descendent of a god?"

She took a long, shaky breath, put the book on the chaise, and strode to the window. Street flares glowed beyond the stone walls surrounding the mansion. The sky was a deep blue-black now. Was Lukos denying himself blood or would he rise tonight and hunt?

She turned back to Althea. "Lukos will not give up, will he? He will come for me again." She managed a wry smile. "Perhaps I should show him the book."

"Do you believe that is your destiny? I don't. And Lukos, too, would refuse to believe that he could not outwit the writing in a book."

"I want him to come for me. That way I can destroy him."

"No. You need to be kept away from him. Let the men hunt. Trust me—"

Serena took a deep breath. "I cannot, my lady. I know that you only befriended me to lure me here for the Royal Society. You don't need to pretend anymore. I know exactly what I am—"

Althea pushed up from the chaise and rushed over to embrace her. "I have pretended nothing. You are my friend. There is something else you need to know about me. Come here."

You are my friend. Following the only woman who had ever shown her kindness, Serena struggled to believe. So many people had lied to her.

Althea stopped in the farthest corner of the drawing room, near doors that lead to a terrace. "I am a vampire."

Whatever Serena might have expected, it wasn't that. A hysterical giggle slipped from her lips. "No—you can't mean that."

Althea nodded, her elegantly styled red curls bouncing. "Yannick and Bastien are also vampires." Wearing a suddenly mischievous smile, she glanced back to the men. The four drank brandy and gesticulated together, oblivious. Althea parted her lips wide, revealing white fangs that lapped over her lower lip.

Serena gaped in astonishment.

Laughing, Althea drew her into a hug. "We share a kinship, you and I. It may be your destiny to be a vampire, but it is not your destiny to be a killer, or a vicious demon. I have never hurt anyone when I've fed. If you are good at heart, you can be a good vampire."

"A good vampire?" Serena couldn't believe it, but that was what Drake had told her. He hadn't hurt anyone. "You were certainly correct that I would love two men," she admitted.

"I had dreams about Yannick and Bastien," Althea explained. "Erotic dreams that opened my eyes to the pleasures and strength of that kind of love. They proved to be premonitions. Both Yannick and Bastien possess special powers. We were destined to be together, the three of us, because our combined love makes us stronger."

She felt Althea clasp her cool, shaky hands. "Let me explain to you the power of a love shared by three."

* * *

Drake woke to a parched mouth, shaking limbs, and stale darkness. Sweat drenched his body. His shoulders were jammed against the satin lining of a coffin. Where was he? How had he got here? He couldn't even force a groan through his swollen throat.

Thick, bloody, his tongue yearned for a familiar taste.

Not blood.

Solange.

Flames. He remembered flames engulfing his rooms. Using the greatcoat from a dead vampire to shield his body, he'd charged through the fire, rushed through the back kitchen, and run out into dawn.

Not knowing where to go, he'd shifted shape and flown above London as the first rays of the sun began to sear him. Close to death, he'd found a cemetery and, to his luck, a casket unearthed and discarded by resurrectionists. Drawing on the last of his strength, he'd pushed the coffin back in the grave, dropped in it, and closed the lid.

It had been a goddamned nightmare. He'd feared he would be buried alive. But it was that or burn with the rising sun—

Solange.

God, how he wanted it. But now that he was a vampire, to take solange again would destroy him.

He sent a message to Serena in his mind. *I'm alive, little lark.*

20

Soaring

Revulsion washed through Serena as she stood at the door of Jonathon's laboratory and thought of what her fate was supposed to be in this horrific place. Candlelight reflected along the rows of glass jars, and the discarded white fangs gleamed.

As though he knew her thoughts, Jonathon wrapped his arms around her and drew her against his chest. He cradled her close and stroked her hair. Serena's heart pounded so hard she knew he could feel it. She took a deep breath, letting her eyes close, letting her whole world become his wonderful smell of sandalwood and witch hazel and male skin.

As Jonathon splayed his hand over her back and held her tight, she remembered the worry in his dark eyes at dinner. How he'd leaned close, his breath warm by her ear. "I need to take you away from here. I can't leave you here tonight."

She'd been astonished. "You don't trust Althea?"

"Althea I trust. And Brookshire and his brother." His voice dropped until it was a mere murmur—a husky, compelling murmur. "But not the rest of the Society."

"What do you plan to do?" she'd whispered in return. She'd

pushed her food about on her plate, glancing down the table to Ashcroft, who appeared jovial yet watchful.

"Take you home with me."

And being Jonathon, he'd said not a word on the carriage ride home. He'd stared out into the dark. Rocking with the carriage, she had asked, "Have you learned anything at all about how vampires are made?"

He'd only grunted in response, and she knew the answer was "no."

And then she'd heard Drake's voice, weakly in her head. *I'm alive, little lark.*

She had touched Jonathon's arm, to tell him, and stopped as he turned. For Drake's safety, she couldn't tell Jonathon—she still was not certain he would not kill Drake.

They'd arrived at his elegant mansion and, for the first time, she walked in through the front door. There seemed to be no servants. Jonathon had taken off her pelisse, lost in a different world.

Now, she thought of Althea's words as she gazed into Jonathon's dark, beautiful eyes. *Make love to them both and the three of you will gain strength and power. And something even more precious.*

Was any of it truly possible? Were her dreams really erotic premonitions?

"I would never let any harm come to you," Jonathon promised. He cupped her chin to tip her face up, the touch of his fingers magical.

Drake was safe. And her cunny throbbed in time with her heart as Jonathon's fingers traced the line of her jaw. So delicately, as though he knew that the light touch ignited a flame of passion in its wake.

"You tempt me so much," he groaned. "You are so exquisite. So perfect."

She smiled shakily. "Hardly that."

"You are." His palm gently cradled her cheek. "You are unique."

"The first child of a vampire and mortal?" she asked ruefully.

"Yes, but also courageous, strong, intelligent . . . compassionate."

"But a demon."

"No, sweeting. You could never be a demon."

Hot, firm, sensual, his lips stroked against hers. Not a kiss, just a soft brush—a brush that sent desire arcing through her. Heat raced over her skin. Her lips parted on a gasp and his mouth captured hers, tasting of brandy and smoke and erotic heat. He shifted over her, pressing her gently back against the wall of the corridor, and she drowned in the sensation of such a large, warm, beautiful man holding her. Kissing her. Teasing her tongue with his.

Jonathon braced his hands on the wall on either side of her head. Serena felt pinned, yet she took a deep breath, savoring the sensation of surrendering control. She trusted him.

He was so tall, he had to bend over to kiss her, and his mouth was so luscious—wet and hot and demanding. He urged her lips to open more until they were locked together, devouring each other. He slid his right arm down to cup her waist, surrounding her slim body with his huge, powerful arm.

Yes. She locked her arms around his neck to hold him close. Beneath her hands, Jonathon's powerful muscles flexed. Did she feel the thrum of his blood?

She wouldn't think of *that*.

Think of his big chest pressing against you. Think of his hard, beautiful leg sliding between yours to spread them. Think of his cock, his hard, big cock pressing against your belly.

How she knew what he meant about temptation. His broad

shoulders beckoned, and she skimmed her hands down from his neck to touch them. So straight and wide and delectable. She loved the pronounced vee-shape of his back, the alluring taper to his narrow waist.

While he kissed her senseless, she explored his broad back, stroking the planes of hard muscle. He moaned into her mouth as she slid her hands lower, tracing the line of his spine, down, down, to the firm indent at the small of his back. His trousers followed the taut curve of his buttocks in an almost indecent way. Filled with daring, she trailed her fingers along the shape of his gorgeous arse, and her cunny clenched at the intimacy. Cupping a cheek with each hand, she squeezed.

She thought of holding his rear as he pumped into her, and her legs almost gave out.

He eased back from the kiss, his breathing harsh. "I will always protect you, love."

"I'm going to change," she whispered, her throat tight from her quick breaths. Her lips still sizzled from the caress of his hot, demanding mouth. "We have to face the truth. Four days in your laboratory will not unlock the secrets of vampires. You won't find a way to stop my transformation."

Like black curtains, his lashes swept down. He touched his mouth to her cheek, the gesture so intimate that her heart stuttered. "I don't know what else to do. I don't want to lose you."

"To Lukos, do you mean?"

"No, sweeting. I will destroy Lukos before he hurts you. I mean to the vampire world—to its dark, erotic allure. To Drake Swift."

She frowned. "He is safe. Did you know that?"

He shook his head. "Not for certain, but Swift can survive anything. How do you know he is safe? Did he communicate with you telepathically?"

She nodded and saw pain in his eyes. How could she convince a vampire hunter and a vampire it was their destiny to both make love to her? How could she even accept such a scandalous thing?

"I want to take you to bed," Serena whispered.

Jonathon chuckled. At those words on Serena's lush, lovely lips, his cock reared against his linens, weeping into the fabric. "Are you commanding me to your bed, sweeting?"

She pressed close, breasts plumped against his chest. "I want to make love to you," she murmured, a black-haired vixen with dazzling eyes that made him think of moonlight, the way it would sparkle if it could be caught in a bottle.

Her voice was rich with need, firm in its demand. "I want you now. Before you go out to hunt."

On a raw groan, he promised, "I'm not going out. I won't leave you alone."

With Serena, his size was an advantage. He scooped her into his arms, laughing at her startled look. He left his laboratory behind and carried her down the hallway.

"You do want me in your bed, even knowing what I am?"

"I don't intend to wait until we get to bed, sweeting."

Approval and astonishment warred in her eyes. "I want you now," she gasped. "I'm on fire."

"If that's so, draw up your skirts, angel." He stopped and balanced her with one hand while undoing the buttons of his falls. Was he mad? They were in the corridor. But his few servants rarely came here, and lovely Serena was tugging up her skirts, revealing shapely calves clad in gossamer-thin stockings, pretty knees, and the ivory skin of her thighs.

He tore open the placket and wrenched out his rock-hard cock. Her skirts were bunched up and spilling over her hips. She looked down.

"Good heavens. You're enormous."

Any other man would feel a burst of pride, but apprehension washed over Jonathon. What did she see? Some women thought he looked too much like a beast—too big, too intimidating—with the pelt of dark hair on his chest, his large muscles, and the club of a cock between his legs.

"I had no idea a man could be thus endowed. It's . . . amazing. Will it fit inside?"

His laugh rippled up from his tight throat. A jolt of pleasurable agony hit as he took his cock in hand, as he stroked the full head against her slick, welcoming lips.

No drawers. Just heat and wetness and texture—velvet lips, springy curls, creamy juices.

"It will, but it's too big to go in unless you are very, very wet."

"And I am," Serena breathed, and her sultry voice wrapped around him, as beautiful and tempting as her embrace.

"Not enough." He shared her smile. He stroked his cockhead to her vulva, searching for her clit. At her sharp cry, he knew he'd made contact. His leaking juice coated them both as he teased her clit, stroking, stroking. He loved to start this way, to bring her to orgasm once or twice, until she was drenched, until she was boneless in his arms, until she was so sensitive she would feel his every thrust in her soul.

"Yes, like that," she urged.

Devilishly, he stroked slowly, building her pleasure with torturous care. His hand was under her arse, and he supported her against the wall. Her head dropped back, her hair tumbling free. She ground against him, rubbing her clit to his cock. Her mouth opened on a soundless scream, and she came against him.

She rocked with it, bucked with it, her head back, her eyes shut. He waited until that moment when a blissful smile curved her lips. Teased her clit again.

"No . . . I'm much too sensitive . . ."

"Have courage, sweeting. I know you do . . . you have the courage to soar where you never have before."

"Oh, you are arrogant, my lord, aren't you?"

He laughed at that and bent to her lovely neck. Sweet perspiration coated her skin, and he licked it away.

A few long passes of his cock over her sweet little nub and she cried, "My lord!"

He was certain her voice had rung through every corner of his house, and he didn't care.

"You are so beautiful," he whispered in her ear as she came again. A lovely, languorous orgasm, and she clung to his shoulders afterward.

"I think I will die if I come once more. Feel my heart."

"I will, sweeting, but first, I want to fill you with my cock."

"I think you will find I am most satisfactorily wet."

How could she find the wits to tease? His were gone, burned to ash by desire.

He parted her sticky lips with his cock, and her honey flowed out. He thrust slowly forward, slowly, slowly, filling her inch by inch. Her cunny held him tight, opening for him, caressing him in wet fire.

God, yes.

He met her gaze as he thrust, stared in her luminous eyes as he withdrew to the tip and plunged deep.

"Ooh, your every stroke . . . caresses me inside . . . and oh, what it does to my clit—"

Sweat dripped down his forehead as his muscles strained to hold her, as his body yearned to pound hard.

She begged, "Harder, deeper . . . yes, just like that!"

Her climax triggered his, his come roaring through his cock like a ball through a cannon. His brain burst into flame, his lungs burned, and his last thought was to capture her mouth in a kiss—

He held her tight as his orgasm controlled him, and when the last spasms died away, he slumped his shoulder against the wall. But he still cradled Serena in his arms—his biceps twitched, his forearms felt numb. His climax had leeched his strength. Gasping for breath, he slid his cock out and lowered her feet to the floor.

"My legs are too weak to stand." She laughed and he swept her up again. Discretion was in order, so he pushed his cock back into his trousers.

"Do you think anyone will guess?" she asked. Her cheeks were flushed, her hair in disarray, and they both smelled of mingled juices, of pleasure.

"No, my sweet. Of course not."

"Liar. And I do believe I can walk now."

"Ah, but you do not have to." Though he risked stumbling on his shaky legs, Jonathon kissed Serena as he carried her to the stairs. As they reached the stairs, he couldn't stop kissing her, loving the taste of her mouth so much, until he glanced up and saw his servants. Reluctantly, he released her mouth, still tasting her on his lips.

He jogged down the stairs, with her in his arms, and quickly reached his bedchamber. She lay on his bed, delectably disheveled, and watched him as he peeled off his clothes.

"Much better than the theater," she teased.

As he yanked down his small clothes and his cock leapt upward, he swept a munificent bow. "At your service, my love."

Her eyes sparkled in response.

By the glow of the fire and one candle, he helped her undress. His large fingers struggled with the tiny buttons of her gown, but he slipped them free of their loops.

"Thank heavens!" She peeled the silk away from her. "I was about to expire from the heat."

He gave a playful frown. "But I intended to make you hotter."

"You want more?" She looked astonished, glanced down, and saw his cock rising. The sight of her in corset and shift had his desire burning once more. "I can promise you I am completely drenched." A wicked smile curved her mouth. "And what is your most devilish desire, my lord? What would you like to do most?"

"Serena—"

"The Royal Society possesses the most graphic and shocking books—it appears that authors and artists believe vampires have very inventive couplings."

"And proper young ladies should not look at those books."

A shadow touched her eyes, so he teased, "And what intrigued you the most?"

The return of her smile made his heart lurch. "No, Jonathon, I want to know what pleases you."

"You. With me. Now."

He had never known this light-hearted teasing, had never expected to mix sex and laughter with such explosive results.

"I want to know," she teased.

"Will you strap me if I don't divulge, Miss Lark?" He lay down on the bed at her side.

"Why would you want to be strapped, Lord Sommersby? Why do men like punishment?"

He levered up on his arm and teasingly tugged a raven curl. "Because our young governesses mete it out on us when we're impressionable boys."

She rolled onto her side, so casually naked with him it took his breath away.

"I should think your governesses must have had a terrible time."

He didn't want to tell her the truth—that his first had strapped him with abandon and his second had awoken in the night and gone down to find his father and he laying a cadaver on the drawing-room floor. She had run through the house screaming. There had been no third.

He reached out, gently pinched first her right nipple, then her left. A soft tug on her velvety nipple and she squealed for him. "Jonathon!"

Bending to her breast, he flicked his tongue over creamy skin, spiraling down toward the peak. He heard her breath hitch in anticipation.

He should be back in his laboratory, trying to save her life, trying to find his father's journals, trying to find a way to stop her transformation.

Flushed, panting, she rolled onto her back, and he followed, her sweet breast in his mouth. Braced on his arms, he moved over her. His senses filled with her—the luscious taste of her nipple, the throaty beauty of her moans, the scent of her sweat, her juices, her lovely skin.

He couldn't leave her now. Not now.

Jonathon skimmed his hand over the lush curve of her hip, his heart thrumming with a desire so strong he suspected it could kill him.

As his hand slid between her thighs, Serena parted her legs. She wanted him inside her again. She ached for him so much. All six-and-a-half glorious feet of him moved between her legs. She marveled at the sight of his huge muscles bunching, rippling beneath his lovely skin. No doubt he was grinning with such pride because he saw her look of rapture.

She touched his jaw, letting her palm skim the lean ridge, savoring the softness of his skin, the tickle of his stubble, and all the while he stirred the entrance of her quim with his cock. Desire had turned her mind to a puddle of candle wax, but she focused on one word. Hero. Jonathon, Lord Sommersby was most definitely a hero. He had saved a young girl, he had dedicated his life to rescuing the innocent, he had promised to save her.

Heart tight, aching, she wrapped her legs around his hips. Her heels rested on his tight buttocks.

She was so utterly soaked that his cock slid in on one thrust.

"Do you know what I really want?" he rasped on his first long, slow thrust.

Exquisite pleasure roared through her as her inner walls parted for him. He pumped deep into her, bumping her womb with each thrust.

"Harder," she gasped. She wanted him to pound into her. She wanted his groin striking hers, his cock driving impossibly deep—

Breathless, she gasped, "Your . . . answer . . . what . . . do . . . you . . . like?"

"I'm a man of privilege but I have simple tastes, love. And what I like is being deep inside you." He paused, buried deep within her, his lips an inch from hers. "And your legs around my neck."

"Yes," she gasped.

But as he eased her legs up, she was captured by him, completely at his mercy. Her legs were bent over, her quim tilted up in the air as though presented as a gift.

He linked his hands in hers and he thrust inside again. Oh, he could go deep this way, so deep he was touching her soul. Each expert thrust teased, each jolt of his hips hit her throbbing, stinging clit—

God, yes.

A demonic possession seemed to take her. She wanted him to be rough, to lose his control, to pound hard. And she wanted to come. She tried to thrust up to him; she wriggled to saw her clit against his shaft.

He pinned her hands and plunged in and out, over and over—

Ecstasy exploded like a fork of lightning, like a bolt of magic.

Her nails drove into his palms. She screamed his name, banged his shoulders with her heels, arched up to tear at his neck with her teeth.

Jonathon came too, his body ravaged by it. "Serena, sweet Serena—"

He collapsed on top of her, supported on his arms, and he bowed his head over her chest.

She fell back, panting. Shocked by what she'd done. How could she be sweet? She'd scraped her teeth viciously over his skin. He hadn't cared. He'd liked it.

He bent and kissed the tip of her nose. Gently nuzzled her lips. "It was the climax, Serena. When you come, you lose control—of inhibitions, of fears, of rules."

She shut her eyes. "I hurt your neck."

"You didn't. They were love nips. That's all," Jonathon reassured.

He hated to see her look so troubled, so shocked—even with her eyes closed and her long lashes brushing her cheeks, she was obviously appalled by what she'd done.

More pleasure was in order. To ease her fears, her worries.

"I can't make love again for a while, not yet," he murmured. "But you can enjoy as many climaxes as you can bear." With that, he buried his face between her thighs—he'd never done this, never devoured a woman afterward. Her taste and his exploded on his tongue, ripe and earthy. Their pleasure combined.

She trembled as he nuzzled her clit, so gently, with infinite care. He guessed how sensitive she must be—hell, he was in exquisite agony after a climax. Her toes brushed his shoulders, stroked. She was caressing him, touching him, any way she could.

He plunged his tongue deep into her cunny so his lips pressed against her nether ones—the most intimate kiss. And now to send her to ecstasy once more—

To his surprise, she jolted beneath him on the third lick of her engorged clit. Her hips arched, her hands clenched. She fell back, gave the softest, prettiest "oh" and a luxurious sigh. "I came again but it was so different—like a gentle wave washing through my body."

"Roll over," she whispered huskily. "I wish to taste you."

Roll over—?

She coaxed him onto his stomach and he obeyed. Exhausted, he splayed his arms out, and his weak legs were parted. Warmth and wetness touched his low back. He twisted around to be met by the most erotic, astonishing sight.

Serena held back her long curls as she licked the hollow of his low back. Her small, pink tongue danced over his skin. He forgot to breathe as she shifted to straddle him. She bent once more, and her hair poured over him like a wave. With her soft tongue, she traced his spine down to his tailbone. Pleasure vibrated through his head, combined with shock. What was she doing?

She glanced up and winked.

Winked.

Her tongue slid down between the cheeks of his arse. Shock had them clenched tight, and she tried to pry them apart.

"Serena—"

She shook her head, and he saw her eyes crinkle in a saucy smile. Christ Jesus.

A sweet sound of pleasure spilled from her as her tongue stroked the valley of his ass. He couldn't believe she was doing this. It felt so bloody good.

How could she know to do this? He'd never done it. He'd never even licked a woman's derriere. And her tongue touching his puckered anus was magical sin. Her tongue circled his rim, pushed into his ass.

Her tongue slicked against his sensitive walls. Slid deeper, deeper, in the most unbelievable caress. He was spent. Utterly sated. His cock half-limp. But he felt the rush of blood to that exhausted organ, felt the wash of pleasure.

She thrust her tongue

Lord!

Intense screaming sensations shot from his arse, through his ballocks, and a climax roared through him. He had nothing to shoot, but his brain still dissolved in ecstasy, his heart burst in his chest, and he tore his teeth into his pillow as he came.

Jonathon rolled over, intending to capture Serena in a kiss. He couldn't believed she had touched him that way. Dazed, he saw her drinking a glass of wine. She swirled it in her mouth and spit it into the basin. He felt a jolt of guilt, but she smiled. "You taste very intriguing."

"Come here, sweeting. Let me do that to you."

But she went to the window, pulled the curtains aside, and threw up the sash. The cool October wind spilled in, whispering through her hair, tossing the inky black strands against her pale neck.

"Close it, Serena. We can't give Lukos an entrance."

She took a long breath, her breasts lifting. "I need the night air, now. The moonlight," she admitted in a vulnerable whisper.

"I know." He watched her lean out the window, shut her eyes, and take a deep breath. It was dangerous, but he couldn't deny her the pleasure.

She drew back suddenly and Jonathon bolted upright. He grasped the stake from the bedside table and sprang off the bed.

Moonlight poured in and a shadow flew inside. Jonathon grabbed Serena's arm and pulled her back as the shadow transformed. Into Drake Swift, naked and illuminated by a wash of silver-blue light.

21

The Choice

"Who do you prefer, my love?"

Serena gasped at Drake's blunt question as he strolled nude, and utterly unconcerned, through Jonathon's bedchamber.

"I thought you'd be alive," Jonathon growled. He still held the stake, and her at his side. His arm wrapped possessively around her waist.

"And I thought you would poach on my preserve the first chance you got," Drake snapped.

She caught her breath as Drake walked up to her. He swept his gaze over her naked, flushed body and bowed over her hand.

She'd created a disaster. She must convince them to share a love between three, yet both Drake and Jonathon were furious to discover she had made love with them both. A polite veneer covered their anger, but she felt it simmering. Both were so skilled at control, they could posture like this—but at some point they would explode.

Just as in her dream, she had no idea what to say.

Drake leaned forward and kissed her, cupping her breast as he did. His tongue slid into her mouth, and he kissed with fierce possessiveness. At his flagrantly intimate gesture, her face flamed with embarrassment. Drake was determined to anger Jonathon. And she was at fault.

They had once been partners, they had once protected each other—surely they must care for each other. It was her destiny to bring them together, but she had no idea how to begin.

Drake straightened. His silvery gaze held hers. "Vampire or mortal?" he asked. "Or should the one who pleasures you best be the one to claim you?"

Dark and enigmatic, Jonathon's eyes flashed as Drake's hands slid down to her nether curls. Serena caught Drake's hands, drew them away. But she gasped as Jonathon calmly tossed aside the stake and pulled her back. Neither man would back down.

"I don't wish to choose." Her voice was a mere whisper, almost drowned by the crackle of the fire. "I want you both."

In front of her, Drake stilled, and she held her breath for dizzying heartbeats. She glanced to Jonathon—his jaw dropped open. Through the heat flaring across her skin, the intense ache at her nipples and her quim, she knew what she'd done. She had shocked them.

Drake spoke first, his voice husky and filled with the uncertainty that spoke to her heart. "Do you understand what you are inviting us to do?"

"I—I think so."

Jonathon frowned at her stutter of uncertainty.

Drake cupped her bottom and squeezed. Hot, wet juice pooled between her legs. "Tell me," he urged. "Tell us."

As a governess, as a secretary, she'd hidden in the shadows. As the woman standing between two seductive, aroused men, she was the center of attention. Was she truly ready for this?

Jonathon crossed his arms in front of his huge chest. His cock was half-erect, yet still astonishingly large, and it bobbed at Drake's words.

"Althea told me . . ." She stopped and began again. "I've dreamed of the two of you. Very naughty dreams . . ." Bother it. She would have to be blunt. She'd faced down vampires, why was she so unnerved by sex—by an act of joining, and love, and sharing?

Because she feared she'd hurt them both.

"I had erotic dreams where I made love to you both. Althea told me that the dreams are premonitions. That she and her husband and Mr. de Wynter live in a ménage. That we are destined to have one, too, and that will give us the power to defeat Lukos."

Drake moved close and caressed her cheek—this time Jonathon did not pull her back. Too shocked? Something bumped against her tummy—Drake's cock, leaving a sticky trail against her skin. Drake reached for her quim once more.

Sharp lines etched around Jonathon's mouth as he watched, as Drake's fingers opened her slick lips wide. It was so unbearably erotic to be touched and watched.

Swallowing hard, Serena reached out and stroked the firm ridge of Jonathon's hip, while wriggling against Drake's hard cock.

Drake slid two fingers inside, and her legs almost collapsed at the pleasure, at the way Jonathon's brows shot up at the slick sound. Drake must know she'd made love to Jonathon—but that must happen when they shared her.

Both men would go inside her. Their passion would be shared in every way . . .

Her legs almost dissolved beneath her, like spun sugar against her wet tongue.

Drake pressed the length of his cock against her quim as his fingers toyed there and sensation swamped her. He kissed her cheek. This must be a dream—but she pinched her thigh, where her hand rested, and the jolt of pain proved it was all so very real.

"I'm game," Drake groaned. "What about you, Sommersby?"

* * *

Jonathon strode forward, aware of his cock bouncing against his belly, heavy as lead again and insistent as hell. He could not do this. Premonitions could be damned. Shared love? Not even to destroy Hell itself could he share Serena.

Not with bloody Drake Swift—a man who could too easily steal her heart away.

Roughly, Jonathon jerked Swift's hands away from her cunny, releasing the scent that made his head swim, his cock pulse, his heart pound. White-hot arousal raced in his veins. He had to claim her, love her, make her come and want him and desire him. Only him.

Somehow he would stop her becoming a vampire. Somehow he could keep her.

"I want you for my own, Serena." He drew her away from Swift and kissed her, determined to recapture the magic of their intimacy. His mouth closed on hers and Serena shut her eyes, threaded her fingers in his hair and held him. She pressed her body to his, breasts to his chest, belly to his groin, and her hot skin surrounded his cock.

He kissed hard, his mouth coaxing hers open, and he kissed hungrily, as though he could touch her soul with his tongue and claim it for his own.

Swift touched his shoulder, and he flinched in fury. *Sommersby, she wants both of us to suck her nipples, both of us to lick her cunny and her arse. She wants both of us to worship her, both of us to fill her with our cocks. She will not be satisfied with only one.*

Jonathon pulled back from the kiss. How in Hades could he hear Swift's voice in his head? Because Swift was a bloody vampire, with the power to touch a person's mind, to coerce, to coax, to seduce.

Brilliantly silver in the moonlight, Serena's eyes shone at him. *Please, Jonathon. Can we try? We are destined for this.*

His heart thundered at the sound of her voice in his head. She, too, could speak in that most intimate way—shared thoughts. Could she hear him? *I can't believe I am destined to share you. Hell, I believe I am destined to save you.*

I love you, Jonathon. I'm so confused by loving both of you so powerfully. I'm almost afraid to try this . . . but I have to. It's the only way I can survive . . .

He could not believe they had spoken that way. And she sounded so vulnerable. So afraid.

Jonathon scooped Serena in his arms again to carry her to his bed. Huskily, he vowed, "I'll try. For you, I'll try."

He fell back on the bed, the mattress squeaked a loud protest, and Serena sprawled on top of him. Shimmering like black silk, her hair spilled over his chest.

Jonathon cradled her full rump. He kissed her mouth—tasting wine and sweetness—and he groaned. "If you really want this, Serena, if this is what you wish, I'll try anything you desire. But I want you to straddle my face."

She rose up, holding her curtain of raven hair back with one hand. Like a demure, blushing maiden, she shyly moved over him. He gripped her satiny thighs and pulled her dripping quim to his mouth. She tasted lush, salty, ripe—the intimate blend of them both—and he buried his face between her thighs and savored.

He knew no fancy tricks, he just loved the taste, the wetness, and the way Serena was moaning and squealing as he indulged. A lick of her clit, sweet and hard against his tongue, sent her thrashing against him. Her cries were ones of delight.

"Apparently she likes what you're doing."

Jonathon heard Swift's deep voice over Serena's gasps and cries. Heard the begrudging admiration in it. Yes, he damn well knew how to please the woman he craved. He brushed his teeth lightly over her clit, slid his tongue into her passage, delving into hot cream.

"Make love to him, Serena. Sit down on his cock."

Swift again, giving bloody directions. But Jonathon couldn't protest, not with Serena on his face. And as she lifted up and scrambled down along his body and he saw the agony in her eyes and heard her harsh panting, he knew he wanted this.

"Are you not too exhausted?" he asked.

"I want to make love to you both all night," she breathed, her words both wanton and sweet.

He had to remember this wasn't a contest between him and Swift. This was about Serena.

He gritted his teeth again as she held his cock upright. God, the tight feel of her gripping his cock once more—

"Do you like his large cock?" Swift murmured at her side, sounding like Lucifer.

She nodded, biting her lip. "I like you both."

"And you are so very skilled at dealing with naughty boys." Swift laughed.

Jonathon drew her down, kissed her, so she could no longer banter with his partner. But she drew back after devouring him with enthusiasm, looking as though he'd seduced her very breath away. Pride swelled, along with his cock.

She lowered herself on his shaft once more . . .

Serena braced her hands on Jonathon's broad chest as she worked, worked slowly, to take his cock inside. She bit her lip as it cleaved its way in. It was a beautiful beast—with a thick shaft, almost as thick as her wrist, and beautifully dusky brown. The head was velvet strained to the limit, and a drop of his fluid sparkled on the tip. The size of his balls startled her the most. A lush black nest surrounded his huge cock and ballocks, erotically masculine.

She giggled. Each cock reflected its owner. Jonathon's was handsome, large and broad, straight and dark; Drake's devilishly beautiful, long and golden, leaning rakishly to the side.

Jonathon's cock pressed against her womb. "Oh heavens."

She had to stop, and she still hadn't taken him all the way inside. Both times he had slid inside her, he'd controlled the depth, and she realized that he hadn't buried himself completely in her.

Jonathon's mouth was a tense slash, his eyes filled with concern. "Are you all right, love?"

She feared he'd try to rescue her by lifting her off. "Yes," she managed on a throaty moan. And she moved up and down, not caring about the rhythm, just wanting to make him slick, to make her wetter, to try to take him in . . .

Closing over her breasts, his hands supported her and he smiled at her, a lopsided loving grin that sent Serena's heart in a plunging spiral in her chest. She didn't dare close her eyes and spoil the moment. So, bravely, she held Jonathon's gaze and rose up. She moaned at the exact moment he did and shared his awed smile.

Oh, how she loved this. She couldn't resist . . . performing to entice Drake. She loved the thump of her bottom against Jonathon's groin. The teasing jiggle of her arse cheeks as they struck and the oh-so-harsh but wonderful pounding of her pelvis. Her breasts bounced madly. Perspiration beaded on her upper chest, ran down her nipples. Sensual sweat coated Jonathon's sculpted pectoral muscles, his beautifully ridged stomach, his forehead.

Yes, she was destined for this.

"Ride him." Drake was behind her. He lifted her hair, trailed his fingers over her shoulder. "I do like to see the agonized look on his face as you fuck him."

"He's . . . he's beautiful," she agreed, and she saw astonishment and pleasure in Jonathon's eyes. Did this mean Drake and Jonathon were connecting? Althea spoke of building magic—was this how? It felt like magic.

"You like fucking him, don't you? How many times did he make love to you tonight?"

"None of your business," Jonathon grunted, but the question inflamed her even as it shocked her.

"Many, many times," she breathed. She rode faster, gasping desperately for air. She pounded too hard, and screamed.

Jonathon squeezed her breasts gently. "Easy, sweeting, I'm big enough to hurt you." His hands grasped her hips, lifting her up slowly, lowering her gently, and she marveled at his strength. She had hurt herself but didn't care. She loved that taste of pain sweetened by pleasure.

Jonathon released her hips and she rode him fast. And hard.

Her clit demanded attention. She ground it against his groin with every stroke. She was climbing to the peak and she wanted to race toward it—

"Slow down," Drake urged. And then he began worshipping her bottom. With fingers, with just a little penetration, but heavenly. Then his tongue slid in, twirling around her tingling rim. She looked behind her, stunned by the sight of Drake's lean, powerful body sprawled over Jonathon's legs as he licked her bottom.

Drake rose up, looked deeply into her eyes. "What do you want now? You have the power to ask us to do whatever you want." But she knew he didn't truly mean that—he wanted to tempt her to ask for what he wanted. His finger slid into her wet puckered hole, but the pressure of Jonathon's cock fought his entrance.

"Gently . . ." Oh God—the richness of his voice wrapped around her and his finger thrust in . . .

Pressure. So much pressure. She whimpered, suddenly on the brink of "no." No, she was too afraid. No, she just wasn't able to—

Then pain vanished and pleasure flooded. She turned again and saw Drake's hand hidden between the ivory globes of her arse. "Two fingers, now," he murmured. "Now, my cock."

"No," Jonathon warned. "She's innocent, still, not yet ready—"

"She wants us both. Two cocks to give her unspeakable delight. Two cocks to fill her to the brim. Give the lady what she desires—"

"Bastard," Jonathon snapped to Swift, but he didn't stop thrusting into her.

"Gentlemen!" She wanted to feel the glorious, shocking sensation of their hands and mouths on her, their cocks in her, not mediate.

"We will behave," Drake promised. "But I want to be inside you, my special one."

My special one.

All she'd wanted was to be an ordinary young lady. But ordinary young ladies didn't agree to such scandalous proposals, didn't want two men making love to her so much it hurt. Serena did as Drake bid, leaning forward until her nipples touched Jonathon's chest. Drake's fingers thrust deeply into her bottom. Oh lord, the fullness . . .

Serena turned to watch. Strands of her hair fluttered across her nose, stuck to her lips.

Drake, one hand on his cock, dampened her bum with his juice. The head, perfectly shaped to invade, pushed in. Her first impulse? To scream. She let out a little cry, a strangled one, and swallowed the rest.

Althea had promised this would be exquisite. She wanted to believe.

"If you want to stop, we will stop," Jonathon promised. He held her hips, his hands strong and comforting.

Stop? She was about to climax! Drake worked slowly. He gained an impossible inch and her body fought, trying to push him and Jonathon out. She stayed completely still, until he urged, "Keep rocking, it will ease my entrance."

Eyes shut, she began riding like a wanton. Not caring if the men could stay inside, just driving herself, driving like a bolting team—

The little death. How she understood the words. Two men held her tight, their raw grunts like music, their cocks thrusting hard. They wanted to find that little death.

She shattered. Blankness swamped her brain, sheer delight burst inside.

Jonathon's eyes shut, raw vulnerability twisted his face, and he launched up. She felt the flood of his hot come fill her quim.

"You died first," Drake crowed in triumph to Jonathon, then he yelled and bucked against her. He was coming, too, and she was burning, drenched, soaked—completely loved.

"I'll summon a bath, Serena."

Jonathon's voice washed over Serena, waking her with a start. She lay on his bed, and crisp sheets covered her damp, naked body. She smelled of both he and Drake—their sweat, their skin, and the rich, pungent scent of their come. It was heady, erotic. She didn't want to wash it away.

She'd made love to them both. She wouldn't let shyness take over.

Jonathon slipped on a banjan. Drake's hand traced along her bare arm; she rolled over to see him and met his smile. He lay, uncovered; his muscles glistened and his cock slept. Jonathon left the bed, and Serena shivered as she felt the tension between the two men. After climaxing, they'd avoided looking at each other or speaking.

She didn't know what to say. Had they created magic?

Jonathan had heard her voice in his head, she knew he had, but was it because she was a vampire or because they had created an enchanted connection?

Serena concentrated on the bed canopy above her head. She tried to send a bolt of magic power to it. Her head throbbed with the effort, but nothing happened.

"You are the most special woman, little lark."

Pain settled around her heart. "You know I wasn't an innocent for our . . . our first time."

Drake touched her cheek. "It is of no consequence to me."

"It is to me." She was trembling.

"Tell me, then." His voice was soothing, a balm to the sudden pain in her heart.

The bed creaked as Drake shifted to move close to her.

"What did you say to her?" Jonathon's body loomed over her, anger in his voice.

Possessively, Drake's muscular arm slid around her. She stared down at it—the bulge of muscle, the golden hair, the seductive pattern of veins. His hand rested on the white sheet just beneath her breasts. Should she tell them of her past? Did it really signify to speak of it?

"Serena had another lover before me." How matter-of-factly Drake said it. She felt her cheeks burn.

Defiantly she stared into Jonathon's eyes, punishing herself by reading the emotions there. Surprise, then shock. "You loved another man?"

No censure, just a question, and open vulnerability in his dark brown eyes.

"There was going to be a ch-child." Like a fool, she stuttered on the word. "But . . . but I lost it . . ."

"You miscarried." Jonathon spoke bluntly, but his lashes dipped and the lines deepened around his tense mouth.

She managed to nod. "He was relieved, of course. I'd been a dreadful fool. And escaped by the skin of my teeth—"

"You lost a child, Serena," Drake said. "Someone broke your heart. Give me his name and I'll rip him apart."

"No, the mistake was mine. I was supposed to be strong enough to resist—"

"Rubbish." Jonathon sat down on her other side. With exquisite gentleness, the back of his hand caressed her cheek.

On her right, Drake's lips brushed her temple. He asked softly, "Who was he?"

"It truly doesn't matter." She remembered how Althea had insisted that she must find honesty with Jonathon and Drake. Althea's bond with Yannick and Bastien had required honesty to become strong.

Serena took a deep breath, because the name of the man didn't matter, but she sensed neither Jonathon nor Drake would give up until they knew it.

"William Bridgewater," she admitted. "The eldest son of the family who raised me. I wasn't in love. I realize that now. I just wanted to love and be loved."

"But he got you with child and didn't marry you." Anger, hot and harsh, resonated in Jonathon's question.

The power she held shocked her. At a word from her, would both men hunt down and punish William? But it wasn't what she wanted—she wanted to erase the past. She wanted to make all that had happened vanish, she wanted to make it not so, and that she could not do.

She wanted an ordinary life. And that she could not have either.

She glanced from Jonathon to Drake. Jonathon had been forced to stake his own fiancée. Drake had been born to the terrifying world of the stews. They shared pain between them.

"No. He was . . . happy when I lost the baby. It was a great relief. I was supposed to be relieved, too, but I was heartbroken. I realized then I didn't want to marry William—that I had made a terrible mistake."

"You risked your heart for a man who was not worthy of you." Jonathon bent and kissed her cheek. "You did nothing wrong. The mistake was that blackguard's."

"Indeed."

"But neither of you are to hurt him. Or call him out. Or kill him."

"Oh, but think of how terrified the coward would be when confronted by a big, bad vampire."

Despite the pain she felt at her memories, she had to giggle. "You mustn't."

"If that is your command, I will obey." Drake gave her a reassuring squeeze. "I feel sated and exhausted after our delicious lovemaking, but not more powerful. What about you, my love?"

Trust Drake to move to the topic of sex, to steer away from a painful discussion. Serena shook her head. "But Althea insisted it will give us the power to defeat Lukos."

Would you wish me to help you bathe? Drake asked. *Sommersby will prepare for Lukos.*

Serena cast a guilty glance toward Jonathon. What exactly was the etiquette of sharing two men? How did they both feel about this? If she made love to one man alone, was it like an infidelity?

"No. I can bathe alone." Suddenly embarrassed, Serena slipped out from under the sheet. She darted into the connected bathing room.

Soothed by the warm water, Serena finished drying herself with the last of the heated, soft towels. A light knock sounded on the door, and it opened.

Drake walked in, fully dressed. He laid her shift and gown over a straight-backed chair. *Do you want Jonathon to keep you from becoming vampire?*

"I don't know." She spoke aloud as she picked up her shift. When young, all she'd ever wanted to be was a proper, nice young lady and please Mrs. Bridgewater, who had raised her.

She turned her back to Drake, not knowing why she needed to, and slipped her shift over her head. She would never be ordinary. But what did she want to be? Mortal or vampire? The only mortal she could trust, the only mortal she cared about, was Jonathon.

I will help you dress, Drake offered.

A forbidden intimacy or not? Blast, blast, would she hurt Jonathon by accepting? But she couldn't dress herself—bother—so she nodded. She felt strangely relieved to keep her back to Drake as he fastened the gown.

Serena sat down on a velvet-covered chair and pulled on her slippers. "Jonathon won't be able to stop it happening. I know that."

And then you will be vampire, as I am.

He sounded delighted, and she understood. "You and Jonathon are battling over me. You cannot. We are supposed to share a love between three!"

Drake slipped his arms around her waist as she straightened her skirts. He brushed a kiss to the top of her head. "The shared lovemaking was delicious, and I will indulge your desire for it anytime, but I won't share your heart."

"It's our destiny, Drake," she whispered. But how could she convince them—

Bang!

Something big and hard had hit the window. Lukos!

Drake grabbed her hand and drew her back into the other room. Jonathon, fully dressed, had laid an arsenal on their rumpled bed. Stakes. Holy water. Three crossbows—

"They've just started to attack," Jonathon shouted as he grabbed up a crossbow. He tossed one to Drake.

The curtains were wide open. It was pitch black, the moonlight gone. A huge black shadow flew at the window—the glass bowed in the frame. It exploded inward. Instinct sent Serena's hands to her face as fragments of glass and painted wood rained inside.

Drake grabbed her and pulled her back. She stumbled, but

Drake held her as he retreated. Shadows poured inside and instantly transformed.

Jonathon fired, and a bolt streaked toward the seething mass of blackness coming inside. The bolt shot through them all, slicing through air, and flew out the window. The black shapes began to take form. They were like gargoyles, horribly shaped with hideous faces and long fangs that curved to below their jowls.

Drake moved from her. She saw him raise his palms—a stream of light shot from his hands and burst into the writhing black mass of demons.

She had no idea he had such power—he was not an ordinary vampire. It was because Lukos had made him—he had taken some of Lukos's power. This must be what Althea had meant.

Unearthly shrieks echoed through her head, and the demons exploded into such foul-smelling dust she almost choked on it. But more oozed in through the window.

Every arrow Jonathon fired passed through their black bodies. Drake threw another bolt of white light at them, and once again they vanished into stench and choking soot. But Drake dropped to his knees on the floor. *I don't have the strength!* he cried in Serena's thoughts.

They hadn't created enough magic!

"Where the hell are the hunters from the Society?" Jonathon shouted. He thrust a crossbow at her, and she grabbed it and took immediate aim.

She fired at the head of the nearest demon, and her heart sank as the bolt harmlessly passed through once more. Beside her, Jonathon flung the holy water at the beast, the droplets spraying the entire line of horrific demons. They evaporated, but more inky-black shadows amassed at the window.

"They're endless," Serena breathed. She grabbed the vial that Jonathon handed her and threw the water in an arc, hitting as many as she could.

"We have to run." Jonathon gripped her hand and thrust a crossbow at her. "They'll trap us in here. Swift is too inexperienced—doesn't have the power."

Drake shot a look of raw fury at Jonathon. "True, *milord*, but you'd be dead now if it weren't for me."

"Blister it, Swift. Get moving."

Lukos wants us to run—he wants to force us out.

Jonathon stopped so suddenly, Serena crashed into him. Turning, Jonathon pointed his weapon at Drake. "How do you know what Lukos wants? He was your maker—are you his servant?"

"Hell, the bastard wants to take the woman I love. I want to destroy him as much as you do."

"So what do you propose—that we stay in this room and wait for him?"

Footsteps, fast and heavy, stormed along the hallway outside the locked bedroom door. Serena bit back a cry of fury. Were these vampires? Were they trapped already?

"What the bloody hell—?" Jonathon spun and leveled his crossbow at the door.

Serena lifted hers to shoulder height, lining the sight with her eye.

Goddamn! Drake swung back around to the window and sent another bolt of astonishing magic from his hands to drive back the gargoyles. He howled in pain as he did it.

The door bent inward in an impossible arc, then the lock shattered, wood splintered, and it burst open. Serena saw crossbows, pointed at her. Her finger trembled on the trigger. Recognition clicked—the men were vampire hunters. Horror-struck, she recognized them—Mr. Smythe and Mr. Thomas.

"The arrows won't work!" Serena cried, but Smythe fired. It all moved so impossibly slowly. She saw the flick of Smythe's finger, the snapping inward of the taut string, the launch of the arrow. Bewildered, she saw it fly at Jonathon. She jumped and slammed into his side. The impact was like hitting a wall, but she sent him staggering. The arrow sliced between them along his shoulder, tearing his coat. She felt the gentle rush of air as it passed.

Jonathon yelled in fury, and in that sudden jerk his finger hit the sensitive trigger and his arrow hurtled toward Smythe. The arrowhead found its home in his forehead, dead center between his eyes.

Serena swallowed her scream as the next hunter, Thomas, took aim at Jonathon's heart. The Society wanted to kill them, not save them! Over her. Over her! They wanted her dead. They'd kill Jonathon to do it.

A stream of white light shot from beside her—Drake! The bolt hit Thomas in his chest, and the hunter sailed back at the door. His weapon released, but the arrow flew harmlessly to the ceiling, hit it, and rebounded to the floor. With a dull thud, Thomas's body hit the wall and slid down.

Serena felt Drake's hand close around hers. Jonathon grasped her other hand. She ran to keep up. Drake jumped over Thomas's body without a glance. A man he'd hunted with, but a man who'd betrayed him. She knew she had to be logical and hard-hearted, but she glanced down, needing to look one last time.

Come, Serena, we have to go, Jonathon urged.

Serena couldn't imagine where they could be safe. Where would be a haven from the Society? From vampires? Daylight would protect them from vampires, demons—but that was hours away. And Drake would have to be protected from the light—

My world, Drake shouted in her head. W*e must go to the stews. I know my way around there as no one does. The Society can't follow us there and the vampires will be stopped by the dawn.*

The stews. Drake thought of them as his world?

We need your carriage, Sommersby.

Jonathon nodded. "You know the hidden passages in this house, don't you? The Society won't know—unless you've told them."

Drake grinned, showing fangs. "Hell, no."

"Use the tunnel to get out of the house. Get to the stables. I am not leaving my innocent servants here to be slaughtered. But take Serena and get her away from here. I'll follow if I can."

She couldn't leave him alone. "Jonathon—"

Meet us in Covent Garden, Sommersby. I will guide you. Drake grabbed her hand and forced her to run down the hallway.

22

Craving

Drake hated to bring Serena here—to the filthy, stinking flash-house that had been the only thing he'd ever called a home. When Jonathon's father had taken him in to apprentice, he'd had a fine bed, but he knew that it wasn't home. He hadn't belonged.

Serena tried to hide the horror in her eyes as she saw the sort of room he'd lived in—tiny and dirty. Brown and yellow stains marked the walls, and the corners smelled of piss. He'd slept on the floor, with a tattered blanket when he could fight for one.

And some nights, he'd shared the blanket with Mary while his babe grew inside her.

Drake crossed his arms over his bare chest to hide his shaking. Damned solange. He still craved it, but he had none to take. A vial would slake the thirst he had for the stuff, but he didn't have even one damned drop.

"But what are you going to do?" The flicker of one penny-candle reflected off Serena's worried eyes. "Can you find somewhere to sleep in the daylight?"

He gave a rueful grin. *There's a cemetery near. I'm sure the occupants of one of the crypts won't object to a visitor.*

She shuddered for one instant before she stiffened her spine and gave him her impassive and prim governess face. Hell, even as a vampire, he had nothing to offer Serena. Many vampires were centuries old and had used their powers to amass great wealth. He had nothing to give. Not even a home.

Moans came through the flimsy walls—the moans of girls serving men. The men who'd paid them, those who owned them, or the boys who shared their beds. With a spike of regret, Drake remembered back to a scene from his youth—to lying on the blankets laid on the floor, his arms pillowed behind his head as he grinned in triumph and watched two girls pull off their dirty dresses for him. He'd felt like a king—a knife in the ribs had saved them from their "protector" and he'd claimed them as his.

What had happened to them? Were they still alive or dead?

He had power now, but was it enough power to right those wrongs? To help the damned?

A low rap sounded on the door. Drake moved to it with a vampire's speed and opened it a crack. He knew it was Sommersby—he'd guided his partner here through his thoughts only because he feared putting Serena at risk if he did not.

Drake knew his partner hated him. And he hated sharing Serena.

With a brief nod to him, Sommersby barged in and strode right to Serena. Possessively, Sommersby slipped his arm around her waist, kissed the arch of her neck. "You need to sleep, Serena. We need to find a way to stop Lukos—"

"We know the way," she insisted, stepping out of the earl's embrace. "Shared magic. But it will not work until you gentlemen accept it."

Sommersby shot a disgusted glance at the rough pallet and the two tattered blankets—a luxury in a place like this. In return, Drake snarled as the earl swung off his coat and dropped it on top of the blankets, the way he had done at Mrs. Bellamy's brothel. Did Serena appear any more impressed by Sommersby's chivalry than she had by his own? He couldn't tell.

"But not tonight, my love," Sommersby said. "Not here. You need to sleep."

Endearingly, Serena put her hand to her pretty mouth to stifle a yawn. Drake felt his muscles growing heavy and weak as the need for daysleep stole over him.

Damnation. Dawn was close—so close. And he had no choice but to leave Serena alone with Sommersby.

"Are you certain you can share?" Serena asked.

Tucking his coat over her, Jonathon paused. His mouth dried at the sight of her lying on the pallet. Her hair fanned out behind her, a shimmering raven-black halo about her breathtaking face. Lithe and sensual, her body relaxed on the meager bed as though she slept on the softest down. Even here, amid squalor, she was lovely, tempting, irresistible.

"It is not in my nature to share, sweeting." He lay down alongside her and wrapped his arm around her waist. Swift had left to seek refuge from the dawn, and he had her alone.

"I know. You are an earl."

He nodded. "The head of my household. I was raised to lead, to shoulder responsibility, to have my wishes met. I never expected to have to share the woman I adore."

"But Althea says—"

"Lady Brookshire fell in love with two vampires. How can it be the same for us? I am mortal, and so are you."

Frank honesty shone in her eyes. "I'm not mortal. I've realized I have to accept that."

Jonathon couldn't resist brushing a kiss to her temple, and he stroked her hair. "Did you like being shared?"

"Heavens, yes."

Definitely honest. He adored that about her. He understood in that instant how hard it must be for her to keep her secret. To believe her entire life was a lie because she had thought she was a normal girl, when all along she was someone quite different. Someone special. Powerful.

"Did you?" she asked. "You climaxed."

"I've never done anything like that in bed," he admitted. Even after all its exertion, his cock was rising again. His heart pounded like a thousand bat wings, and he wanted nothing more than to tumble back onto that rickety cot and have Serena ride him. He wanted to hold her hands, caress her breasts, and watch her lovely silvery eyes as he thrust up into her and she drove down hard on him. But she must be exhausted, and the gentlemanly thing was to let her sleep.

Her pink mouth curved in a shy smile. "It did feel . . . magical."

He bent his head, snuggling against her warmth. "I understand the power of it—listening to you and Swift finding pleasure. God, I can't explain it. All I could think of was giving you pleasure, and I wanted Swift to come. I wanted to see him explode." Christ, he didn't want to think about what it meant about him that he'd enjoyed another man's pleasure.

Serena held the top of his coat, pulling it up beneath her chin, and his heart broke. The more their intimacy grew, the more he knew he couldn't share her.

She gave another wide yawn, and even that told Jonathon how close they'd become.

"I wish Althea had told me more," she murmured. "She told me I must find out for myself exactly what my destiny is, how our love is to make us powerful . . ."

Jonathon pressed his hand against her silky cheek as her lids fluttered shut. He would give anything to protect her. But did that include sharing her with a vampire?

* * *

Drake soared over the rabbit warren of his world. Around him the sky deepened to the color of black pearls. He swooped down, marveling at the power, at the freedom.

With a beat of his wings, Drake propelled his transformed body faster. Thick soot hung in the air here, obscuring the waning moonlight.

Serena . . . just at the thought of her name, arousal shot through him—through his thoughts, but not his new form. He remembered taking Serena while Sommersby was inside her. The damned earl had a huge cock, and through the thin, delicate walls of Serena's snug arse, he'd felt his cock stroke against Sommersby's.

His blood has roared at the sensation. His fangs had shot out, his jaw screaming with the pain of it, and Serena's glistening neck had been so close . . .

But she'd come and he'd fought to hang on, to hold off long enough to see Sommersby give in to the explosive orgasm, before he succumbed to his own.

He'd never come so hard in his life—either alive or undead. He'd felt power surge through him. Instead of being weakened by his climax, he'd been slammed with a force that seemed to make his senses stronger.

Drake moved silently, slicing along a current of wind. First he would feed—he would find some brutal whoremonger filled with rich blood—then he would return to Serena . . .

Serena opened her eyes, surprised to find she was alone beneath Jonathon's coat. She sat up, and a sharp pain in her bottom made her cry out. She slapped her hand there—something pricked her finger. Her fingertip jabbed on a splinter from the pallet beneath her blanket. A long one, one that had poked through her shift.

Jonathon? Drake? Rubbing her sleep-filled eyes, Serena saw Drake, standing in the dark corner—the one that didn't stink—with his back to her. She caught her breath at the sight of his naked broad shoulders, the long line of his spine, the hard muscles of his rear.

It must be night. Still the same night, or had she slept through an entire day?

Drake? She asked again. They were alone in the room. Where was Jonathon? Why did Drake not seem to hear?

He had braced his hand against the wall as though he was too weak to stand, and she saw the glass vial in his hand.

He was still taking solange?

It would destroy him!

Without thought, she jumped up, the tattered blankets falling away, and she ran to him. She gripped his forearm. At first his arm jerked out, and she knew he meant to throw her off, but he hesitated. His eyes shone, reflecting the moonlight that slid in through streaks in the filthy window.

That pause gave her enough time—she grabbed the vial and tried to wrench it from his fingers. The slippery smoothness was her ally—as was his surprise. He couldn't hold it. But she'd pulled too hard, and the vial fell from her grasp. It bounced on the worn, dusty, plank floor without shattering. But as the vial lay still, the fluid dripped out onto the floor.

Beneath his brow, Drake leveled her with a look of fury that sent her scurrying back.

Serena fought for courage. "You are going to stop this. Now. Tonight."

Empty and desolate, his silvery-green eyes stayed on hers. "I want to stop. For you, I want to stop."

Jonathon eased out of the shadows as he felt a stirring of air by his face. A large shadow swooped by, and though he strained to watch the transformation, he found himself magically confronted by Sebastien de Wynter, nude, and leaning casually against the brick alehouse wall.

De Wynter arched a brow, crossing his arms across his chest. He seemed unconcerned by the cold air, by his vulnerable nakedness, by his dangling genitals, which Jonathon deliberately did not look at.

"What do you want to know, Sommersby?"

He remembered his note to de Wynter. *I know you don't trust the Royal Society. If there is anyone I can trust to give me the truth, it is you.*

However, he hadn't trusted even de Wynter enough to reveal Serena's location. So he'd chosen this filthy alley several blocks away.

Succinctly, while keeping watch down the alleyway for demons and for footpads, Jonathon explained the attack by the Society—by men he'd believed they could trust.

Grim horror etched de Wynter's face, and the silvery eyes dimmed. "You believe they wanted to capture Miss Lark?"

"What other explanation is there? Ashcroft doesn't want me to attempt to stop her change, he wants to study it. And Althea is at risk—"

"Goddamn it, I know that."

Staring into the swirling fog, Jonathon thought of the man who had been like a father to him. "Ashcroft wants to save humanity—it's distorted his view."

"His lordship wants to play God," de Wynter spat. "Althea has played along with Ashcroft's wishes, but she never trusted him. Now, however, she is afraid to leave Miss Lark; she wants to protect her. My wife believes that Serena must bring you and Drake Swift together to create the power to stop Lukos." De Wynter shook his head.

"How in Hades is that supposed to work?"

"I have no idea. All I know is that it does. Drake Swift was turned by Lukos—and Lukos was an apprentice to Lucifer."

"Lukos is a tenth apprentice?" Tension rippled down the back of Jonathon's neck. He knew the legends of the ten apprentices—men who would be allowed to enter a labyrinth of underground caves, which would take them to the realm of Lucifer. There they would make a pact with the devil to acquire occult knowledge—alchemy, magic spells, the secrets of nature and animals. Nine scholars would graduate, having undergone intense, bizarre, horrific ordeals. The tenth would be retained by Lucifer as payment and serve at the devil's side.

"Aye. Since Swift was made by Lukos, who was in turn changed by the devil, he should possess the powers passed on by Lucifer. I was created by Lucifer and given powers known only to Old Nick. Your science, Sommersby, can never explain what we are."

"There is no riddle that science cannot—"

De Wynter's mocking grin reminded Jonathon of Swift's. "Do you want to learn, my lord, or not?"

Grinding his back teeth, Jonathon nodded. "Continue."

"The demons that remained with Lucifer grew too powerful and broke free of his hold. They became determined to overpower the devil and rule earth and the Underworld in his place. Each one fights for power and, like Lukos, each one seeks to be master."

For the first time, true fear wrapped around Jonathon's heart. Lukos possessed untold power, the capability to carry out unimaginable evil. "But what are you, de Wynter? Do you understand how you have life when you should be dead? What happens within you when you create magic? How do you survive on blood—"

De Wynter held up his hand. "I don't know. How do *you* breathe? How does your heart beat? What is your soul?"

Jonathon fought to bring the answers to the tip of his tongue, but de Wynter grinned. "How are all those miracles created from a fuck, Sommersby? From seed and womb? You can explain it, but you can never understand how such a miracle came to be."

"I believe that I can," Jonathon insisted. "I have to believe that."

De Wynter's pitying look sent hot anger through his gut. The vampire was naked, unarmed, didn't even have a soul, but was more at peace that he'd ever been.

"I am forcing Althea to leave England tonight," de Wynter continued. "I know the Society has been lying to her. They want our child. They want to ensure she stays until the baby is born, then they want to rip it apart like the soulless beasts they are. They want to study it in the name of your blasted science!"

Hit by de Wynter's enraged words, Jonathon recoiled. He'd removed the hearts of children. He'd cut up men's brains. He had staked the woman who had loved and trusted him. Was he a soulless beast? Was de Wynter, the vampire who loved his wife and child, the one who truly possessed a soul?

"Listen to me, Sommersby—it took the combined magic of my brother and me to protect Althea from a powerful foe. Swift can't summon his full power yet. It doesn't work at his command. The love of an intense, committed, loving threesome would unleash his power, but even then you will not have the strength to stop Lukos."

Jonathon lifted his crossbow and leveled it at de Wynter's naked chest. "I don't believe you."

"No, Sommersby. Your problem is that you do."

"So I allow Lukos to take her?" Jonathon shouted.

"No. You become vampire. You let Swift change you, and you combine your strength with his."

Cold shock slid through Jonathon's veins. Become vampire?

He had destroyed Lilianne because vampires were evil—he couldn't become one.

Or could he? He grabbed for de Wynter's shoulder, trying to ignore the man's nudity. "When you changed—"

"Did it hurt?" De Wynter finished with a grin. His silvery green-blue eyes glinted with irritating mischief.

"No, I want to know why you aren't a ghoul driven by the need for blood."

"Indeed, I am not. I need blood, but I ensure that I kill no one. I have powers that a weaker vampire does not possess—that's why the Society has let us live."

"If I changed, would I be . . . be more than a mindless demon?"

"I have no bloody idea, Sommersby."

"So I take the chance of becoming a soulless killer to save Serena? There's no other way?" Jonathon raked his hand over his jaw. What an irony—would he finally understand how a vampire was born by making the ultimate experiment of himself? But could he let himself live as a vampire? Or could he transform, destroy Lukos, and then destroy himself?

Serena, a seductive internal voice whispered in his head. *Become a vampire and you can be with Serena for eternity—*

"My brother and I were twins," de Wynter said. "We were connected by a bond from our mother's womb. You and Drake Swift grew up together, hunted together. That bond may be as strong as that of brothers."

No, Jonathon reflected. He and Swift shared only one thing—loving Serena. They had never had a bond—only animosity, jealousy. He sure as hell didn't consider Drake Swift a brother. . . .

Could he really invite Drake Swift to suck his blood out of his neck? And trust Swift to transform him instead of letting him die—?

Grimly, Jonathon nodded. "Saving Serena is worth any price."

* * *

Stay with me. Let me stay with you.

Serena reached out to stroke Drake's forehead, to brush away the beads of sweat, but he grasped her waist and drew her to him. His long, erect cock betrayed his arousal. His muscular chest glistened.

Help me through this, love. The craving is so strong . . . But I will fight it, fight it for you.

Bright, hot, his eyes stared beseechingly into hers, yet his fangs were out, stark white against his beautiful lips. Serena felt her stomach flip over with nerves. Drake looked utterly innocent and helpless and needy, but at the same time he was a powerful vampire.

His eyes changed. The lashes lowered and a molten fire touched him. A wicked grin came to his lips, a grin reflecting the most lascivious thoughts.

I want you. You. Only you. I want you to want me.

His words were barely coherent, but the raw hunger stunned her. His palms tapped the underside of her breasts, covered by shift and gown and unsupported. Her nipples hardened, knowing his touch.

But it was the drug driving him, and she couldn't bear that. She pushed his hands away.

"I have nothing to give you, Serena, but you have my heart." He spoke aloud, weakly. His hoarse, angry laugh made her shiver. "Not worth bloody much."

"Why did you take the drug?"

"To feel like a king, love. Why else? And so I'd sleep a dreamless sleep." He ground his pelvis against her, rubbing his hard cock between their bodies.

Need and desire welled up. Need that swamped reason, that shattered rules. She burned underneath her gown, and her head pounded with the yearning to climb on top of Drake and take him deep inside. But she couldn't. She asked shakily, "What do you dream of?"

"Crying. Screaming. Holding a dead baby. I dreamed that a lot, but I'd held a lot of dead infants. Even my own, my son, and I lost Mary, his mother, while she was giving birth—"

"Oh God." Her heart ached for Drake—she understood his pain. "So the solange helped you escape. Helped you forget."

"I dreamed of when I was a pitiful infant and my mother tried to smother me. She told me when I was a boy—told me about how she'd pushed the blanket against my mouth and nose, muffling my cries, and thinking how it would be better if I were dead. She'd been drunk, and she'd watched my legs kick slower with tears streaming down her face. Someone stopped her—another whore in the flashhouse—who told my mother she'd burn in hell for killing me."

Serena bit back the tears, and when he reached out to her hand, she held his tight.

"My mother died when I was a boy. She choked on her vomit and I slept right through it. She hadn't made a sound . . ." Vividly green, his eyes held on hers. "I still want to forget, Serena, but you don't want me to take the stuff—"

"I can't force you to stop. And I can't imagine what it is like to be haunted by memories like that. But you have to want this." She realized that. "You have to find the strength within yourself."

Just as she had to—she had to find the strength within herself to face Lukos. To face the truth of what she was.

He cupped her cheek, drew her to him, and his mouth slanted over hers. Hot. He kissed like Jonathon—his kisses were raw and hungry, his mouth wide, his tongue demanding. His fingertips traced down her back, sending pleasure rushing over her skin in his wake—

Startled, Serena pushed at Drake's jaw, pushing him back

from the kiss. She lurched away from the pallet "No—I can't do this. It isn't right to make love to one of you alone."

Eyes glinting with lust, Drake laughed uproariously at that, and she felt her face burn. "So, you will only make love with the two of us? Then you'd better tie me down to this bed, Serena, because my body is craving sex with you, and I can't trust myself."

Shivering, Serena reached for the tattered blanket. With shaking hands she tore off a strip. "Are you certain?"

"Do it. It's the only way you can protect yourself."

23

Power

Drake began to thrash on the bed, but the bonds at his wrists and ankles held him fast. Sweat dripped down his forehead, his nose, rolled to his lips. His neck gleamed with it, tempting her to taste, and Serena had to look away as she rinsed the white washcloth in the basin.

His rigid cock lay along his belly, and his hips rocked and bucked. Deep, throaty groans came from his tense lips. His nipples stood hard.

Hiking up the skirt of her shift, Serena sat on the bed and bathed his face. She slid the cloth down to his gleaming neck, and then ran its coolness across his sweaty chest.

Solange. She remembered the sweet, cloying scent of it filling her nostrils as she awoke to find herself tied to a billiards table. Only days ago. *A lifetime ago.* All she'd wanted that night was the truth. Now she knew so much more . . . and nothing more.

The solange had not destroyed her.

Her mouth suddenly formed a startled "o." She'd forgotten about that entirely. She was half-vampire. The vampires had *known* that, of course, and had used the solange to subdue her—to give her that wool-headed, confused sensation. They had used it on her, but she had not been sent into a blank trance, the way a vampire should be.

What if she had some strength against the drug because she was half-mortal? She couldn't be certain, and it was easy to think of other reasons. Perhaps she simply hadn't ingested enough.

Shakily, she turned over her pale wrist. She needed something that would cut. Drake's fangs could penetrate, but he was beyond control—

She had nothing else. No knife or razor, and she was afraid to leave Drake long enough to find one.

Drake's fangs.

On her knees, she inched along the rough wooden bed, stroking her hand along Drake's chest. As she neared his shoulder, she bent and pressed her wrist to his fang. He jerked. The point of the canine sliced her flesh . . .

Hot pain radiated, but she forced herself to hold her arm steady. The coppery aroma of her blood crept into the air, and her heart raced.

With a shuffling grunt like an angered beast, Drake turned his head. His tongue lapped out, cleaning her blood from her pale, veined skin.

His fangs plunged in—she didn't have time to even scream—

The flick of his tongue teased her skin. Pleasure sizzled. He began to drink, suckling her blood into his mouth, and delight raged through her with each pulse.

Such intimacy . . . to have him taste her blood, to have his hot mouth on her delicate skin . . .

Serena splayed her hand on his chest, aching to reach down for his cock. His beautiful erect cock, with the foreskin pulled back from the massive head. She couldn't. Not when he was so vulnerable.

Oh, the sucking at her wrist felt so good! With only his mouth on her wrist, tension built insider her, the luxurious tension of orgasm. She began to rock her hips, to squeeze her thighs.

She couldn't stop. Only drive toward it. Tighten and relax. Over and over, bringing herself to brink, until—

She shattered, riding the orgasm, trying not to pull her wrist free. Restraining herself only made the pleasure more intense.

Threading her fingers through Drake's hair, Serena stroked his head. Her vampire. She grew dizzy as he slowly, gently drank. He was teasing her, giving a light suckle, then taking a long drink.

She felt the pleasure building again.

Would this work? Would her blood help him?

"What in blazes is he doing to you?"

Serena cried out in shock, then whipped around to find Jonathon standing in the doorway. Furious, he strode in. "He was drinking from you."

"It's solange. He was addicted to solange and he was still drinking it even though he's a vampire." Her words spilled out in a hurried mess. "It will kill him, so I—I convinced him to try to fight his addiction. But . . . but I don't know what to do . . ."

Serena found her legs still trembling from her orgasm. He must know she'd climaxed from letting Drake take her blood.

"Do you have any idea how much of a risk you took?" Jonathon was in front of her, his large hands on her shoulders, and she winced, expecting him to shake her. Instead he wrapped his arms around her. Kissed her—one breathless kiss on her lips. "He could have killed you."

"But he didn't."

"He can't survive this—not in this place. He needs a clean bed. And you—damnation, you need rest, and food. I have texts on solange. There might be something there. To help free Swift of its grip."

She struggled to follow his abrupt sentences. "Wouldn't it be dangerous to return to Sommersby House—that's where you want to go, isn't it? Is there anywhere else we can hide?" She didn't know London well. Althea had treated her to many of the pleasures—the museums, libraries, and shopping after dusk at special modistes. She knew the locations of cemeteries but had no idea where to run . . .

Then she shook her head and managed a grim smile. "I want to go back there. Lukos will come for me there, and I'm tired of being afraid. I want to face him."

Jonathon kissed her again, his eyes haunted. "No, Serena. Not yet."

Despite her brave words, Serena found the next hour to be one of the most harrowing of her life. Fear for Drake consumed her as Jonathon carried him down to the waiting hackney. Dirty blankets covered Drake like a shroud. She tried not to think of it. As a vampire, he had only been taking solange for days—it couldn't be long enough to kill him, or to have destroyed his mind, but what would withdrawing from the drug do?

For all her hours spent buried in vampire books, she had no idea. She hated this helpless feeling.

The night was clear, cold, and her breath puffed out into the dark. Shivering, Serena huddled beneath Jonathon's coat as he loaded Drake into the carriage. They could be driving into a trap, but suddenly she didn't care. She was swaying on her feet, her hand on the hackney's side. Giving the blood had left her weak, and her stomach ached with hunger.

Jonathon leapt down, and she saw horror in his eyes as he looked at her. "I just need to time to recover," she vowed, wanting to believe it herself.

"Did he give you his blood?"

She heard the fear in Jonathon's voice. "No, I didn't let him turn me."

Jonathon swept her into his arms and balanced her with one

hand as he pulled himself into the carriage. Summoning strength, she left Jonathon to sit beside Drake. To keep wiping the sweat from his forehead, to ensure he didn't fall in the rocking carriage.

But Jonathon moved her to the other seat and took her place. Serena's heart soared as she watched him tend to his partner. Was it possible they could accept sharing her?

Perhaps he and Drake did have a bond but they had tried to hide it.

The thought gave her the strength to stay awake and upright on the carriage ride. The shades were drawn, but the lamps were lit. Jonathon watched both Drake and her, and she smiled, to show she was fine. She was feeling stronger with every passing moment.

By the time they reached Sommersby House, she felt able to walk inside on her own—strong enough to creep through the dark tunnel that led from the stables to the house. She pushed open the carriage door, letting in the pungent air of the mews.

Suddenly, Jonathon leaned over and gave her a quick kiss that sizzled like an electric shock. He lifted Drake in his arms and slowly rose to his feet. "Stay by me," he instructed, "but run for the hackney if I'm attacked."

"I couldn't leave you and Drake—"

"You will have to, Serena."

Serena fell back into the plump, velvet-covered chair in the blue bedchamber of Sommersby House. Thank heaven she hadn't had to run for the hackney. The house was eerily deserted—Jonathon had sent his servants to safety, and that left only the three of them—her, Drake, and Jonathon—in the enormous mansion.

Jonathon was still in his laboratory, or the library, she wasn't sure. A clock ticked in the room; she heard the faint chime of another. Three chimes—three o'clock in the morning.

Drake had slept soundly. He hadn't moved since they'd put him in this bed. She felt both relief and sheer terror. Was he recovering or near death?

Serena, speak to me.

She jolted awake. Sitting bolt upright on the chair, she looked to Drake. Beneath the rich, clean, silken sheets, his chest rose and fell . . . slowly. He looked asleep.

Serena.

She froze, now fully alert. She recognized the voice—Lukos! She tried to shutter her thoughts, the way slayers were taught, but her name filtered through. *Serena.* And then she couldn't stop his voice; she didn't have the power to block out Lukos.

I will give you your mother's name, Serena. I will do that because you belong to me.

No—She stopped before she said anything more. She would not respond to him. She would not listen. But his power . . . his strength . . . it called to her. Heat and traitorous desire sizzled through her veins. Her body responded—her breasts aching for a touch, her quim became hot and bubbling and so desperate for pleasure . . .

No.

Your mother. Eve. She is Eve, beauteous creation of God. Speak with me and I will lead you to her.

Stop! Stop! I don't want to know.

But you do. I know that you do. Listen . . .

Drake blinked, opening his eyes. He tasted blood in his mouth, rich, coppery, and delectable. His head felt as though it had been sliced up for one of Sommersby's experiments. He was looking at the room around him—firelight in a huge hearth, blue paper on the walls, blue velvet hangings around the bed, but he couldn't understand what he was seeing.

He wasn't in the stews anymore.

Serena? He tried to speak in her mind, but he couldn't seem to connect.

Then, with a stab of dread, he remembered the white skin of her wrist, and lust and desire and sheer depravity pounding in his blood.

Had he drunk from Serena? He must have.

Hell and perdition, what had he done to her?

Drake struggled to sit up, but his body wouldn't obey. He couldn't hear anything but a low shushing noise. His nostrils flared—he scented her, the ripe scent of her pussy, the sweet tease of her soft skin, the flowery beauty of her hair. His throat was tight and sore, but it didn't burn.

Finally, his mind and his body seemed to reconnect. He pushed himself up.

Serena! She was curled up on a huge blue-velvet chair. Enveloped by its massive arms, she looked so small. Had he hurt her? As though she suddenly heard him, she looked at him and her face lit up with a beautiful smile. She slipped from the chair and crossed to the bed.

His heart lurched—a sensation he'd never known with anyone but her—as she sat on the edge of the bed, by his side. She looked pale and fragile, and she wore a filmy nightdress that gave her the look of a wraith.

Groaning, he reached out to her delicate forearm. She wrapped her fingers around his hand, with the reassuring touch that made his heart pang. No one but Serena had ever touched him in this way. She let her fingertips play over his knuckles, and blood rushed to his cock. He felt the soft weight begin to stiffen, felt the demanding awareness of swelling shaft and tightening balls.

Serena lifted his fingers to her mouth and kissed his knuckles. With lashes lowered, her eyes were unreadable, but her lips were puckered in a most inviting way.

Sensual, yet loving. He'd never known a loving touch before.

How do you feel, Drake?

He thought about the stuff. About solange. The thickness of it on his tongue, the burn of it, then the relief . . .

A frown creased his forehead, made his temples ache. *Serena. What in blazes did you do for me?* He should be mad with the craving, but he didn't care anymore. *Did you let me drink from you?*

She turned her wrist over, drew her fingertips along it. The head of his cock lifted from his belly, pushing up the sheets.

Yes.

Sweetheart, you let me have your blood? The blood coursing through him, rushing to his cock . . . was hers. *Did I hurt you in taking it?*

Her lips lifted in a wicked smile. *You gave me an orgasm.* A pretty flush rushed over her cheeks, and she lowered her gaze. *Since I am half-vampire, solange does not seem to harm me as it does most vampires. How do you feel?*

Tired. Humbled. Saved.

She laughed, and he loved the soft, infectious sound of it. He smiled, though it hurt to do it.

We don't know yet. The craving may just have abated . . . for a while. But we can break this. And save you.

Loose, her black hair tumbled over the smooth slope of her shoulders, like a cape thrown around her slim arms. Tendrils ringed her throat like ties. Her nightgown looked like the material of fairy wings—light and airy, clinging to her breasts, then falling from their crests. She'd pulled up the hem to sit, revealing a stretch of white thigh.

Drake couldn't resist rolling over. He caught a whiff of the delectable scent between her warm legs and laid his hand on her bared outer thigh. A jolt of pleasure shot through him at the softness of her warm skin.

She was shielding her thoughts. He realized that now. He

pushed deeply into her mind, sensing a shadow behind her gray eyes. For one instant he breached her defenses and caught the whispered name. *Lukos.*

What about Lukos, sweetheart? Did he come? Did he speak to you?

"Lukos called to me." She spoke out loud, a sweet tremor in her low, husky voice. "He wants to lead me to my mother."

He tried to force words out of his throat, but it was too swollen. *It's a trap, Serena.*

She nodded, her lashes lowered. "I know. But I have to face him. He is going to come for me anyway. He is going to want to turn me."

Drake forced himself to sit up, and he swung his heavy, reluctant legs around. "Where is Sommersby?"

"The laboratory, I think."

Jonathon threw the last book on the table. Nothing. He'd searched the entire laboratory and, once more, he'd found no trace of his father's journals. It had been a fruitless search—he'd already torn this room apart a dozen times.

He had four books on solange stacked on the worktable, but he'd wanted one last chance to try to find his father's work—to learn if his father had prevented a way to stop Serena's change. Or to undo it.

His father had boasted about a great discovery—he was convinced his father had found a way to reverse the process without killing the vampire. But he had no more time. He was going to have to invite his former partner to change him into the undead.

Damnation. Where would he hide the journals if he were his father?

Jonathon slumped back on the stool and stared at the table where he had watched his father dissect fallen vampires. Candlelight flickered over the scarred surface. Strange . . . it looked as though his father had carved the letter M into the side of the table. It was rough, but no accident. It was a distinct letter.

He'd never noticed it before.

Jonathon picked up the candle and crouched, holding the flame close to the letter. There were other gouges and scars beside it, but no more distinct letters.

An idle game of his father's or did it signify something? He traced the M, realized that the last leg wrapped underneath the table.

Dropping low, Jonathon peered at the underside of the thick wood slab and held the candle to it. More letters—faintly carved, so they were not obvious. They spelled out "morning room." Still crouched, Jonathon moved the length of the table, searching for more. But there was nothing.

He straightened, frowning. The morning room was his mother's domain, where she composed letters after her breakfast. Why would his father put his journals there?

To be close to his mother's memory? The thought rocked Jonathon back on his heels. He couldn't credit it. In fact, he had not even bothered to go into that room to search. Had his father chosen it because it would be the last place anyone would ever look?

Drake stared at Sommersby in astonishment. "You want me to do what?"

Illuminated only by the flame of the candle stub, Sommersby gave a grim smile. "Make me into a vampire. It's the only way we can be powerful enough to stop Lukos."

Drake frowned down at the books sitting on the late Lady Sommersby's escritoire. "That's what it says in those?"

"De Wynter told me—and from what I've read, I believe him."

"Your father hid his books here?" Folding his arms across

his chest, Drake looked around the morning room. He had never come in here. The late earl had never allowed Drake to go near his wife. Strangely he had almost been afraid to walk in the door—then he'd sauntered in, roguishly, and informed Sommersby that he believed Serena had cured him of his addiction.

Now, he flashed a cocky grin at his former partner. "You realize I will have to drain your blood first. Take you to the point of death."

"Just do it, Swift."

"Well, let us arrange you prettily for your seduction, my lord." Drake pointed to the ivory silk chaise. "Go lie down there and look fetching."

Sommersby shot him an angry look, but he stalked over to the day bed and awkwardly lay down on it. Treating it as a joke, Drake sauntered over. "Ooh, a muscular virgin for my delight."

"Jesus Christ, Swift," Sommersby snapped, but he broke off as Drake bared his fangs.

Drake bent to Sommersby's neck and drew in his scent. Male. Sweat. Serena was sleeping innocently. How would she react once she learned that Sommersby was willing to become what he despised to save her? How could she not love Sommersby more than him?

Drake brushed his mouth over Sommersby's neck. Damnation, his skin tasted good. The texture rough with stubble, not satiny soft like Serena's.

Drake remembered the aching cockstand he'd got when he turned. He'd reached for his own prick, even reached for Lukos's cock as the change took him, as maddening lust had gripped him. His first feed had been a bit clumsy—but the pretty prostitute hadn't complained.

But he knew what to do now. He took one last deep breath to drink in Sommersby's erotic smell. Then he bit into that delicious neck. A quick clamp of his jaw drove his fangs through earthy, salty flesh. Springy pressure—the wall of the artery—

but the snap of his jaw sent his fangs through. Blood flooded. He sucked down that first quick burst of blood, then he gulped down the thick, lush stream.

Weakly, Sommersby's hand grasped him. Tried to pull him away. But the fingers slipped off his shoulders as he drank. He drank quickly and Sommersby weakened fast.

Even as his former partner grew close to death, his blood was hot and rich, and Drake moaned at the sheer pleasure of it. Sommersby's large body began to relax, the boots rolling outward, the arms hanging heavily.

Drake's cock throbbed with each swallow. He brushed his knuckles along Sommersby's cheek, rasping along the dark whiskers. His eyes were almost closed; his lashes lay along his cheek, long and lush and curling at the end.

Beneath him, the earl struggled, though his hips began to thrust. Drake spoke through his thoughts. *Don't fight, but be ready to drink.*

Going to kill me . . . wanted to . . .

Yes, I'm going to kill you—I have to.

He heard it—the low whoosh of Sommersby's last breath leaving him. Drake ripped his own wrist open and put it to Sommersby's mouth. The blood poured in, giving a burst of strength to the victim. As the earl took the first drink, Drake couldn't resist—he stroked the long length of the other man's erection. As vampire, he had not yet fucked another man, but suddenly he was tempted.

His fingers tested the girth of Sommersby's massive prick, traced the head through the trousers. Sommersby bucked up against his fingers, sucking down his life-giving blood.

"Oh dear heaven!"

Drake jerked up and saw Serena standing in a pool of moonlight. Her gaze was fixed on his hand toying with Sommersby's big genitals. Her eyes were wide and silvery, her hand was at her throat, but he sensed her arousal.

And he was damned excited.

Come here, love, Drake urged. *He wanted this. He wanted to change for you. We both have to be vampires for the magic to work.*

Serena could barely stand. She'd thought Drake was killing Jonathon. And now she knew—Jonathon would live forever, as a vampire. He was doing this for her.

Despite the cool air in this unused room, she was sweating into her dress—it was damp against her back.

Come to me, sweetheart, Drake urged.

Just at the moment the light in Jonathon's eyes had faded, Drake had given his blood and the light shone again. And now, watching Jonathon drink, watching the sensual way the men touched each other, all the while scenting the blood, she burned with desire. It was like a live thing within her. She couldn't control the need.

On trembling legs she stood in front of Drake.

Lift your skirt, my love.

Cool air rushed up her skirt as she drew up the hem. She saw Jonathon flex his fingers, growing stronger. Regaining his life.

Come.

Did Drake mean move to him or climax? With his free hand, he cupped her bottom and pulled her to his mouth. Her hot, juicy quim pressed tight to his lusty, skilled mouth. His tongue flicked, pleasured, while Jonathon drank.

Jonathon's fingers gripped Drake's forearm, his hips working.

Sommersby will come, Drake promised in her thoughts. *He will have the best orgasm of his life. And then he will be vampire. And I, my sweet, will give you the most intense orgasm.*

Yes, you will! She cried it as the tension tightened and burst inside her—a wave flooding her.

Jonathon pulled his mouth from Drake's wrist and shouted, too. "Serena!"

Jonathon watched her come—and his eyes changed from dark and mysterious to silver and reflective.

A hoarse, raw groan filled her thoughts. Drake! She saw Drake's eyes shut, his mouth clench, as he joined them in ecstasy.

24

Turning

Jonathon woke to burning thirst. His arms were trapped and numb, his legs cramping. He shot up—tried to—but he couldn't rise, and his head felt clamped to the ground.

Christ, man, he warned himself. *Do not let panic grip you.*

His fingers brushed smooth fabric. Silk? No, the satin lining of a coffin. One of the coffins his father had kept in the house. A mad fear welled up again as he realized he had slept within it, and he struggled for control. Now that he was a vampire, what else had he expected?

With shaking fingers, Jonathon touched his neck. No holes. No oozing blood. No trace of a wound.

Thirst. He was so thirsty. The fire seemed to spread from his throat through his body. Slowly, inexorably, like flames licking across an open field on a still, hot day.

Sommersby, you need to drink. Come to the bed.

Jonathon bent forward. His pulse, slow and steady and healthy, thudded in his throat as he sat up in the coffin. They had moved two coffins into Serena's bedchamber—to stay by her side. But Serena wasn't in the room. Only Swift, and he sat on the edge of the bed. Nude. Drake caressed his own cock, in the slow rhythm of an aroused man trying to pleasure himself but not surrender to climax.

Jonathon vaulted out of the coffin, astonished at the strength he commanded, the supple grace of his movements. His entire life he'd been plagued by a large, clumsy body. Now he moved with a fluidity that amazed him.

As he landed lightly on his bare feet, he cast a glance down at his own cockstand. Tall and proud, his prick swung like a lead bar. He'd never been so aware of it—its weight, the sway of the shaft and of the swollen head as he slowly walked over to Drake.

What devil possessed him Jonathon didn't know, but he bent and kissed Swift hard on the mouth. Their lips joined. Their tongues touched. He felt the roughness of male skin under his fingers, so different from Serena's delicate face. And he felt the grip of a hand around his cock and reveled in the sensation. By some instinct, Jonathon reached for Swift's staff, wanting to pleasure the man he'd once wanted to strangle.

He began to jerk his fist up and down the length of Swift's thick shaft. In response, Swift squeezed his prick tight, just below the head, and he felt the knob swell to bursting. Swift's other hand grasped his ballocks and played with them with brutal tugs and twists. Damnation, the pain felt good. All the while, Jonathon devoured his partner's mouth, hungering for the wetness, the heat, the passion of the kiss. Their fangs collided. Swift's scratched his tongue.

Blood. So good.

Was he being unfaithful to Serena? He couldn't stop. This was foreplay to blood drinking, and he knew it.

You've got big fucking ballocks. Swift's voice, speaking in his head. *What do you want, Sommersby? To suck me while I suck you? Me to invade your arse? Or your cock held tight in mine?*

Jonathon had never had a taste for raw, gritty sex. The dark acts. But he wanted this. Now.

I'd like you to fuck my arse, but first I intend to pleasure yours, my initiate. Swift laughed.

Eyes closed, anticipation running hot through his veins, Jonathon lay on the bed. He moaned as Swift's teeth scraped the firm flesh of his rear. He tensed, his muscles rock hard, then relaxed as pleasure rippled up his spine. His ballocks drew up, his cock hardened and grew. He shut his eyes, felt Swift grip his rock-hard cock. Accepting the gesture, he reached back for Swift's member—to return the favor. He'd relied on this madman more than once to save his life—and he'd done the same. They did share a bond. The bond of growing up together, of facing hell together. Of falling in love with Serena together.

Serena.

Jonathon heard Swift calling to her. *Serena, come and join us in bed. Come and play.*

Have Serena walk in and catch Swift kissing his arse, rubbing his cock, and him in the throes of ecstasy over it? Never. But he couldn't throw his partner off—those few extra days as a vampire seemed to give Swift more strength. Swift kept him pinned.

Jonathon twisted beneath Swift, and he saw the door open. Serena walked in, fully dressed, carrying an open book. She had been awake, in his house, unprotected while he slept, and the now-familiar surge of panic rose again—a jolt through his body that left him unable to think. He fought it. She was safe. Obviously safe. And though faced with the impossible—his transformation, hers, imminent danger—she had her nose in a book.

He could barely think, and his breath came in harsh pants. He wanted sex, wanted release. Needed it. Needed the harsh pounding of his loins, the thrusting while he grunted and sweat and drove himself to heaven, and gained the reward of another's orgasm before finally, exquisitely, surrendering to his own.

Serena padded across the carpet, looking like a dark angel.

Her hair hung loose in black waves and spirals, bouncing softly as she walked.

Her eyes widened when she saw him and Drake—what did she see? Two naked men sprawled on a bed, one running his lips over the other's arse, each grappling with the other's prick?

This is the pleasure of being vampire, Swift said, his voice strained. Jonathon flinched as Swift braced his fists on either side of his shoulders. *Sensual freedom . . . the freedom to enjoy carnal pleasure without restraint. In whatever way you desire. As a vampire, you are free of mortal restrictions—everything is pleasure. There is no pain.*

This is your destiny, Serena, he continued. *And yours now, Sommersby.*

Jonathon's cock pulsed, trapped between his belly and the bed. Hot desire pounded in his head. Swift moved off him and he took the moment of freedom to roll over on the bed. Serena's shining gray gaze roamed his body. She licked her lips, the motion of her tongue slow and agonizingly seductive.

Swift's hand slid the length of his own cock.

The book fell forgotten from Serena's fingers, and Jonathon's chest tightened as she crawled onto the bed. She knelt between them.

Drake leaned back on his elbows, grinning. Hell, how could he be so blasted casual about having beautiful Serena eye to eye with his pole?

Jonathon knew he could never be like that—each moment with her was intense erotic pleasure, and he became so focused on her, on desire, on ecstasy, that he was knocked off his axis. The cold, lordly manner disguised a hot, primitive need.

His jawbone began to burn, to throb. He ran his tongue over his teeth—sharper, pointed. How? How could it have happened? He couldn't remember the change, couldn't remember the night before.

Jonathon stretched out on the bed and held up his cock—hell, they were like puppies clamoring for a mistress's attention, and he laughed.

Sharing the laugh, Serena chose him. She wrapped her fingers around his cock, and Jonathon's heart almost stopped. Her pretty hands looked so small on his thick vampire cock. Lips pursed, she bent to the head. She kissed the straining knob, her kiss sweet and unbearably erotic.

Swift gave a sharp, pained groan.

Interrupted by that hungry growl, Serena drew back, and Jonathon wanted to roar in frustration. He clenched his fists, fought the powerful urge to thread his fingers into her black tresses and drag her back to his weeping cock.

Drake knew he had to intervene before Serena tempted Sommersby beyond control. *You need to feed first, Jonathon.* He used Sommersby's Christian name, to show they were now, as vampires, true equals.

He saw the brief nod Jonathon gave. *From you, Swift?*

Yes. Bite me. He said it as a light-hearted command, but Drake caught his breath as Jonathon leaned toward his neck. Serena watched with large, beautiful eyes.

No hesitation. Plunge, Drake instructed. And laughed roughly at his words. When he'd been a boy, living in the flashhouse, he'd been raped by a man, but now he was no frightened boy, no vessel for some hulking perverted brute—he was a vampire, powerful and strong, and he wanted this.

Jonathon pushed his shoulders back, pinning him to the bed this time, and touched his mouth to Drake's neck. Instinct guided his pupil. Jonathon's fangs pushed out and pressed hard in his flesh.

Find the blood, he urged. *Bite down hard. A clean plunge.*

On a jolt of pain, sharp and incredible, Jonathon's fangs drove in. Drake's blood rushed like a river in spate and he climaxed, shooting his hot, thick seed across his belly.

Serena squealed and he gave her a wide grin. *Come here, sweet. Take off your dress for me.*

He saw her hesitation, but also the sexual longing in her eyes.

Come, he urged. Her ivory cheeks flushed.

As Serena undid her dress—her wrinkled silk dress that she'd worn since first fleeing this house—Drake found his strength flooding back, even as Jonathon drank his blood. Erotic power burned in him. Instantly his cock was hard again, curved like a drawn bow.

Jonathon bore a proud cockstand, too, one that swelled with each gulp of blood. Drake grasped his partner's shoulder. *Enough.* Gouging his fingers into Jonathon's flesh, he pulled him back and the fangs slid free.

Drake held out his hand to Serena. *Now we can play.*

But she was staring down, not meeting his gaze, and his heart, his strong and invincible heart, skipped a beat.

"You are both vampires," Serena said softly. "There's no longer any reason for me to be mortal."

Serena knew what she should do after such brave words. She should wind her hair and draw it away from her neck, and offer that vulnerable place to Drake's mouth, or Jonathon's. But for all the bravado in her words, she shivered—she was about to make an enormous step.

Was she right to choose this instead of waiting for fate and destiny and prophecy to make the decision for her?

Jonathon had had the courage to do it—for her.

I want to be the one to make you vampire, Serena. Drake's reflective eyes shone brilliantly gold in the firelight. They revealed nothing, but she knew that though Drake might not have an immortal soul, he had a strong heart and a powerful capacity to love.

He levered up on his arm, his silvery-blond hair in wild

waves. *I love you. I've never known love like this before. No one has ever cared about me.*

Jonathon kissed her hand with an elegant flourish. His reflective eyes held hers. *No, Serena, you should wait.*

But you didn't, she whispered. *You did this for me.*

Serena's thoughts whirled as she weighed her decision. Once she became vampire, she could never be the normal woman she had wanted to be. If she destroyed Lukos, she might never discover who her parents were.

But if she became vampire, she would be with Drake and Jonathon for eternity. She had never belonged anywhere—she wanted to belong with them.

Drake leaned forward, strummed her nipples with his thumbs through her snug gown, and she couldn't think. Jonathon's warm mouth touched her neck, sending shivers racing down her spine.

She loved Drake. She loved Jonathon. How could she choose one to give her eternity?

Drake moved around her, the bed creaking beneath him, as he positioned himself behind her. He pressed close. Her quim throbbed like a second heartbeat. She loved snuggling back against Drake, loved the push of his hard cock against her clothed rump, loved the soft murmur of his breath by her ear.

Jonathon cupped her chin, pressed his immense, powerful body against her.

Drake's lips played along her neck, sending shivers of pure pleasure down her spine. *Can I seduce you into choosing me, sweet? You made love to me first, didn't you? You fell in love with me first.*

Wait, she cried to Drake. To her amazement, he did stop, lifting his mouth from her neck.

Serena caught her breath as she looked to Jonathon. Fangs now lapped his wide, firm lower lip. His once dark eyes shone like silver disks.

Could they hear the desperate pounding of her heart?

Jonathon's dark brow arched, the question unspoken—she wanted to nod, she wanted to cry "I love you both." But Jonathon left the bed. Had she hurt him because she had made love to Drake first? She pushed aside Drake's hands—aware that now she'd hurt his feelings—and she watched Jonathon, watched as he moved into the shadows and returned with a stack of leather-bound books.

His reflective eyes met hers, bearing an expression she could not understand. Guilt? The burden of duty? Then she heard his deep baritone in her thoughts. *My father's books on your life, Serena. You should look at these first, before you decide if you want to become a vampire.*

Behind her, Serena heard Drake growl.

Jonathon quelled Swift's frustrated snarl with a glare of autocratic hauteur, then he spoke to his partner. *She needs to understand who she is before she makes this decision.*

Drake's answer drifted to him. *All right. I can't risk driving her away—losing her heart. I want her to want to become a vampire.*

Jonathon carried the six journals to the bed and placed them on the sheets before Serena. Hope shone in her eyes, but then she looked down and he glimpsed her fear.

There's nothing to be frightened of. Most of it you already know. I haven't read them thoroughly—I only leafed through them. You should be the first to read them.

Soft, tortured, her laugh filled the room. *I think I would have let you have the privilege—how ridiculous to think I'm afraid to face this.*

Jonathon stretched on the bed at her side. He slipped his arm around her waist to give comfort as she opened the first journal. Each had the date inscribed inside, beginning with this one, marked 1798, when Serena would have been very young.

Does this book talk about my mother? Serena asked.

Lukos is trying to lure Serena to him, Drake added. *Lukos was trying to tempt her with the promise he would reveal who her mother is.*

Jonathon saw Serena's gaze move over the words on the first page. He remembered the first lines in the first journal. *A child! It is a disaster. It heralds the end of mankind, the rise of unstoppable demons. The first child of vampire and mortal. Of a powerful vampiress and an ambitious man who is powerful, wealthy, and utterly evil. Ashcroft and I fear that the Society would want to destroy this child if they knew of its existence. I cannot permit such a valuable creature to be destroyed. Ashcroft has vowed to protect it until it reaches its time of transformation . . .*

Serena looked up. *Lukos said that my mother is Eve, a creation of God. How could she be a vampiress? I don't understand—*

Jonathon flinched at the raw pain, the horror in her gray eyes. *In the last book, my father complains that Ashcroft knew the identity of your mother but never told him. . . .*

A disaster . . . She repeated the words slowly. Her voice in his head was so soft, so vulnerable. *I herald the end of mankind?*

I can't believe that, Serena. And I believe Lukos is lying to you—trying to trick you. I doubt he knows who your mother is.

So then it's Ashcroft I must face. She closed the book and tossed it to the bed.

Jonathon selected the last one, flipped to the page he'd dog-eared, and gave it to her. She read with startling speed, turning the pages, eyes widening. She set it down in her lap, now knowing his father's most amazing discovery. "So you can stop me becoming a vampire? You can prevent me from changing on All Hallow's Eve?"

She spoke aloud, as though determined to remember she was a mortal.

Jonathon nodded. "It's risky, but I believe I could do it." It would require harnessing the incredible power that would flow into her on the night in question and redirecting it, draining her life away, and then attempting a dangerous transfusion of blood. But his father's theories appeared sound.

"You read this before you changed, didn't you?" Frank astonishment showed on her face as he nodded again.

"Then why—why did you change?"

"I changed to protect you. I can only protect you from Lukos if I have the strength and power of a vampire and combine that strength with Drake's. But if you wish, you can stay mortal. You don't have to become undead. You can live in sunlight, marry, have a happy life. It's risky, but now, as a vampire, with heightened abilities, I am certain I could do it."

She picked up the closed book, studied it. Drake stroked her shoulders. Jonathon waited, knowing he had to let Serena make her own choice.

She nibbled her lip. "And I cannot be changed back, if I become a vampire?"

"No. Neither can Swift or I. The procedure could only prevent transformation at the time of . . . of death."

She bowed her head. *I am sorry.* When she looked up, he saw tears shining. *You should not have sacrificed for me—*

I love you. You are worth any sacrifice.

She dropped her gown to the floor—she wore nothing but her shift and her slippers. In that scrap of lace-trimmed muslin, she looked ethereal. At once he understood her intent. She was preparing to change.

I don't want to spend eternity feeling pain because I cost you your mortal life, Jonathon said.

Enough! Drake cried.

Drake's angry shout sent Serena cowering. Rage flooded through Jonathon and he confronted his partner, who grabbed his shoulder and pushed him off the bed.

As Jonathon leapt to his feet, he almost collided with Drake, who had jumped off the bed.

You bloody arrogant sod! Drake shouted. *You have a bloody gift. Eternal life. Incredible power. And what do you do with it? Wallow in guilt!*

Jonathon blinked as Drake's fist exploded into his jaw. He reeled back. Lifted his own fists, ready to pummel Drake into the floor. But before he swung, he stopped. He realized what he'd done. He must have deeply hurt Serena. She had no choice but to be half-vampire, and she was not a demon or a predator. Was Drake correct—had he been given a gift?

Brookshire and his wife, and his brother—none of them were brutal and evil.

Jonathon realized that though he was a vampire, he still felt as a mortal man. He felt love, he had a conscience.

Drake was right. And in his thoughts, he admitted it.

Of course I am, Drake crowed.

Gentlemen, behave! Serena frowned. She put the book down once more. *My choice is very simple. I want to become a vampire. To be with you and Drake.*

To Jonathon's heart-wrenching delight, she bent over and kissed the head of his erect cock. Her tongue swirled the head, and pleasure knifed through him as she made the most ecstatic sounds, as though she loved the taste of him.

She lifted and gazed at both him and Drake with great seriousness. She pulled off her shift. "I want you to change me," she said. "It has to be both of you. That's my destiny. To be turned by you both, to love you both. The power of a love shared by three."

I want your change to be an act of pleasure, Jonathon promised. *Of love.*

This is how it should be, Drake agreed. *A beautiful woman with the two men who will pleasure her beyond her wildest dreams.*

Jonathon gently eased her onto her back, his arms around her. Drake planted his face between Serena's smooth thighs. With a laugh, Drake murmured, *Now what was I about to do before I was so rudely interrupted? Ah yes, devour this delicious cunny.*

Drake licked and suckled with slurping abandon, while Serena moaned and writhed. Lust surged through Jonathon at the playful scene, and he bent to kiss her. Once again, she delighted and astonished him with her natural sensuality, as she stroked between his arse cheeks and played with his anus.

Gently, her finger dipped in, her nail lightly scratching his puckered skin.

God, yes.

She groped his ballocks and teased his arse, laughing in delight at his hoarse groans, while Drake feasted on her. He could imagine the tastes teasing Drake's tongue—salty, sweet, delectably ripe.

We could fight to claim her, Drake suggested, then returned to her lush, wet quim.

Absolutely not! she cried.

Jonathon could barely think. *If we change her together, we will both be bonded to her—*

Swift's voice, deep and suddenly serious, came to him in his thoughts. *Are you willing to do that, Jonathon? Willing to commit to three in the bed?*

I'm willing to try anything you gentlemen are, Serena replied saucily.

Jonathon caught the wicked gleam in his partner's eye. He still wasn't certain he could share Serena with Drake for eternity, but he promised, *I'm willing to try.*

Well, then, Drake suggested, *let us begin by filling you with our hard cocks.*

* * *

Serena loved this—gripping two male derrieres. Squeezing, stroking, letting her fingers delve in the damp valleys between their tight cheeks. She loved the naughty scent. Their hoarse groans were so unbearably sexy, music she could hear forever. She loved to hold two enormous cocks. So different, but both designed to give exquisite pleasure.

Strange how it felt as natural as breathing to lie between Jonathon and Drake and toy with their cocks! She loved them both—loved them both so very much.

Jonathon pushed Drake's shoulder.

Bloody hell, Drake protested, and he pushed back.

Gentlemen! she cried again. *Will I forever be acting as peacemaker?*

Two deep, throaty male laughs surrounded her. Drake's hand slapped gently against Jonathon's rear. She caught her breath at sight of a large, undeniably masculine hand on another man's rump and moisture rushed to her cunny.

It's time, my love. Drake's voice was soft in her mind.

Serena shut her eyes, fisted her hands into the wrinkled sheets, and prepared for pain.

Sweetheart, there is no pain. Relax for me, Drake urged, but he grasped the neckline of her shift, tore it with one sudden motion that sent her heart hammering against her rib cage.

Swift— Jonathon spoke in their shared thoughts with impatience.

Drake grinned. *I didn't mean to destroy it. But I want to enjoy the treats within.*

Serena laughed as he opened the torn garment and exposed her. His blond head bent to her breast; his tongue lapped at her nipple. She loved the wet, swirling caress.

Jonathon bent to her other breast, and she cried out. Both men's cocks brushed her bared thighs as their fingers caressed her everywhere—stroking her cheeks, her jaw, gliding down her neck, teasing her breasts, then skimming her belly, making her quiver, as their hands coasted toward her quim.

She craned her neck to see—to watch their lips at her nipples, their hands sharing the hot space between her thighs. Drake's fingers slid down to her passage, to the heat and wetness, while Jonathon let his fingers toy with her clit. Oh!

You are completely loved, Serena, Drake assured.

But she felt strange. Uncertain. As though she were in a dream. And she let her eyes drift closed, the way she had in her first love affair. As though she was not quite taking part, even as she enjoyed every naughty pleasure.

I love you.

It was Jonathon's simple words that made her eyes open.

He was leaning over her, smiling, his eyes both tender and hot with desire. Serena turned to Drake. He grinned, his lips soft and beautiful, his fangs curved and deadly.

She closed her eyes again—she was born to be vampire but too afraid to watch the moment of the bite. Drake's hair feathered her cheek as he pressed his lips to her neck—

Jonathon kissed the base of her throat, slid his mouth around. Drake's fangs brushed her skin at the left, Jonathon on the right.

You will have to bring me to the point of death. She tried to sound courageous.

Ssh, Drake warned. *Carnal delights first.*

Cradling her hip, Drake rolled her onto her side, and she stretched her arm beneath her head, her hair spilling around her. Jonathon eased her torn shift down her arm. He gave a sexy, lopsided smile that melted her heart, and he kissed her bare shoulder.

Drake was skimming down her body—his tongue traced her spine from shoulders to the small of her back. She gasped as warmth and wetness dipped in the sensitive hollow and swirled there. Delicious tingles flew up her spine.

Make love to me, Serena urged, and she pressed her mouth to Jonathon's chest. Through the dark curls tickling her lips, she felt his steady heartbeat.

I never imagined I would have eternity to spend with you, he murmured.

Drake's arm slid around her waist, and he eased his hot body against hers so she was trapped between them both. She turned to share a nervous smile with Drake, but he winked and moved down her body, to her bottom.

His tongue dallied there, in her snug entrance. Ecstasy sang through her nerves. Serena tipped her head back, closed her eyes. Drake's cock nudged against her derriere, and Jonathon's wedged between her thighs.

Her body welcomed them both—her derriere was slack, ready for penetration, her cunny drenched with her fluids. She felt no fear, no uncertainty, just enjoyment of the sensuality of one man kissing her mouth, another kissing her neck. Of two men groaning as they buried deep in her—the two men she loved.

Her teeth sank into her lower lip.

Oh! It hurts a bit!

They both pulled back. Sent effusive apologies until she giggled and moaned. *Try again, I can't wait any longer—*

They penetrated her at exactly the same instant. Jonathon filled her cunny, and sensation roared through her as Drake's shaft slid into her tight derriere.

Too much! Too wonderful!

A climax took her, melting, marauding, wonderful. She shattered with it, clung to Jonathon's powerful arms. Tears wet her cheeks as she cried out. Oh, would she survive it?

Opening her eyes, she saw she'd frightened Jonathon. Turning, she saw deep concern in Drake's silvery-green eyes.

More—

And they gave her more. Endless thrusts. She came again—it

was so easy to come. Just a few deep thrusts and she was in the throes again. She came over and over, until on the last, she cried, *You must come! It's beginning to hurt!*

Anything to please a lady, Drake whispered. He bucked against her, the sounds of his groans so enticing that another climax rippled through her sated body. A heartbeat later, Jonathon joined him, and she floated in bliss between two climaxing men.

Drake's lips touched her neck.

Serena gathered courage. *Yes!*

And he bit. There was a jab of pain, thankfully quick, then the strangest pressure against her neck. Drake's fingers played in her cunny, teasing her slick clit. Both men had withdrawn, and she felt almost delirious from orgasms. And this—this was so different. She'd feared being bitten, but truly, it was . . . almost as wonderful as sex.

Then Jonathon bit. A quick prick through her tingling skin. Her hands clenched for one fearful moment in the sheets. Oh—so good! Their mouths were hot at her throat. Jonathon tweaked her aching nipples. Drake's fingers played magic between her thighs.

They took her easily to the brink, and she tumbled over, floating on air as the men drank. No pain . . . there was no pain . . .

Only a sense of soaring.

Jonathon and Drake had survived this. She must find the courage not to be afraid. This was what she was meant to be.

Darkness crept around her vision. She couldn't move her arms. Her hands grew numb.

Her lids flickered down, no matter how hard she fought to keep her eyes open. Sleep. She wanted to drift into wonderful sleep . . .

A finger touched her lip, leaving the sharp coppery flavor of blood. Her tongue licked her lip clean. It was all she could do to move her tongue. But the craving began.

Her mouth tingled. Her tongue pulsed. She wanted more.

First your wrist, Jonathon, then mine, Drake instructed.

With her eyes shut, Serena felt warm, delicious, damp skin press against her mouth. Jonathon's wrist. She licked with her tongue, tasting rivulets of salty, sweet blood. Then she drank.

25

Bitten

Vampires possessed unearthly stamina, Serena realized as she lay on the bed, giggling up to the canopy. Jonathon and Drake each claimed a breast and nuzzled her sore but aroused and needy nipples. She had made love, and drank, and loved for two glorious nights. If only she could hide in this bedchamber forever . . .

But tomorrow night was All Hallow's Eve. If Lukos believed his destiny was to claim her and rule the earth, he would come for her.

This might be her last night to be alive . . . well, undead. A tear drizzled down her cheek, but she didn't want to stop caressing her lovers' heads to brush it away.

Dawn was close . . . so very close.

"You need blood, Serena," Drake murmured as he suckled her pert nipple.

Blood. The word enraptured her. It even sounded erotic. She wanted it. Heat spiked through her jaw, followed by a sharp pain. One more wondrous than frightening. She probed with her tongue and touched her long canine teeth.

She was vampire. She had been born to be vampire. Now she

was to do what she had been created to do, and she could not think of it as wrong or right. Her body craved. Her body demanded.

"Your neck looks so utterly delectable," she whispered to Jonathon, for she loved the contrast of his silky dark brown hair against his golden skin.

"I would love to have you drink from me," he answered, and he arched his neck back, willingly exposing his throat—

"Ah, but you know where all my blood is now," Drake teased.

Startled, she met his silvery-green eyes. "You can't mean for me to bite you there?"

"I'm vampire. I like both biting and sex play. Combining them is an experience unsurpassed." Drake, unsubtle as ever, gently pressed down on her shoulder and wore a hopeful expression. He wanted her to sink to his knees, take him into her mouth.

"You must be mad." Jonathon laughed. "I doubt our cocks are completely invincible."

To tease, she wriggled down between both men. "Perhaps I will taste Jonathon first. But I won't bite."

Wickedly, she took Jonathon's huge cock into her mouth and reveled at his pained groan.

Her quim was presented to Drake from the rear. At the pressure of the large, blunt head of his cock against her nether lips, she moaned in pleasure around Jonathon's cock.

Drake chuckled. Low, intimate, the unique sound shared by a lover. "Men do enjoy sharing, sweet lark, because one man is certain to get a delectable sucking. And the other man gets to watch."

She'd never thought of that.

"Watching you, Serena, between my legs . . . watching my pole slide between your lips . . ." Jonathon let his head drop back as he moaned.

"And I like to watch her ass wiggle as she does it," Drake added roguishly.

She felt a blush touch her hollowed cheeks. She swirled her tongue around the swollen head of Jonathon's cock, then slid him deep into her mouth, savoring the ripe taste that teased her tongue. Her fangs brushed the rigid length, the velvety head, and he moaned—in pleasure or panic, she wasn't sure. Drake slid his cock into her drenched quim, gave two languorous thrusts, then gripped her hips and pounded against her, his hips banging her rear. Serena thrust eagerly back at him. He was wild. Untamed. She loved it.

Her mouth filled. Her cunny filled.

She came. Fierce. Intense. Light exploded before her eyes like a burst of cannon fire. Her destiny . . . magnificent vampire orgasms shared with two men . . . what a perfect destiny . . .

Jonathon's cock still filled her mouth—hard and rigid, and she was screaming around it. She didn't dare bite him, and as she drifted down from heaven, she knew neither man had come. How could they have such control? Sweat drenched her, her hair was a snarl—she was undead and she had never been more alive.

With gentlemanly nods of consent, they traded places. Drake slid his cock into her mouth and she lovingly suckled it. Huge, thick, Jonathon's prick splayed her cunny walls wide as he slid into her. As Drake had promised, lovemaking was different now that she was a vampire. Every sensation amplified, exquisite, so arousing, she found herself instantly in ecstasy. A long, slow climax welled and washed over her. Heavenly.

Bite me now, Drake urged in her thoughts.

His cock swelled against her fangs and she scented blood. So much of it filling him, making his cock taut and rigid and fat.

Drake thrust forward, apparently not caring that her teeth scraped him. His fevered moan rippled over her. He tasted so rich. So delicious. A thick, juicy delight just waiting for her to bite—

Her jaw clamped down. Serena swallowed her own gasp as blood spurted. So much and pumping hard. She saw Drake's head snap forward, saw the flash of pure agony. His hands fisted in her hair. *Yes, God, fuck, yes.*

The hands gripped tight, tugging her curls at their roots, the slight pain strangely exhilarating. Blood flooded, she drank.

"I'm coming!" Drake shouted.

Sour and creamy, his semen filled her mouth—she drank in his two most intimate flavors. And came once more doing it. Jonathon's large hands clamped tight on her hips and held her as he shoved forward and launched his seed deep inside her.

Drake withdrew from her mouth, his cock going slack, and collapsed. Fearfully, Serena watched him tumble back, his eyes shut. Had she drunk too much? Two wounds punctured the head of his poor cock.

Drake?

Jonathon slid his hands around her waist to embrace her, but guiltily, she gazed at Drake's cock. Oh, his poor sweet member. Two trickles of blood had dribbled down. Spots stained his ballocks—

Wonderful, Serena. Drake's voice. *Unbelievable. Thank you, little lark.*

I feared I'd killed you.

No, but for a moment, I did fear for my John Thomas.

A helpless giggle slipped out. Then Jonathon lifted her. *Now it is my turn to eat you.* But as he lowered to her throbbing, creamy cunny, a soft rap came from the door.

"You are the lord and master," Drake said. "Answer your door."

"Bloody hell." Jonathon threw on his banjan and left to answer, autocratic impatience radiating. Serena bit her lip to hold back a giggle. Any servant would quail when faced with that glower—and the footman on the other side was pale and trembling. "The messenger insisted it couldn't wait, milord."

Jonathon shut the door and frowned down at the missive. "It is for you, Serena."

Althea, perhaps? But surely Jonathon would have said so. Remaining taciturn and silent, he brought the letter to the bed as Drake helped her to sit up. Sharing a surprised look with both men, she tore the seal open, and read . . .

> *Serena,*
>
> *It is I, your mother. I have become aware that you still live. You must understand that I believed you did not. Come to me, so that I may make you understand who you truly are.*
>
> *Yours, your mother,*
> *Lady Draycott*

Serena read the address. Upper Brock Street. An address of nobility.

"A trap," Jonathon assessed. "You will not go."

She fluttered the letter in frustration. "Whyever not? Lukos will hunt me tomorrow—whether I confront him here or at my mother's home." She swept her arm toward the window. "It makes no difference."

Jonathon's lashes lowered over his pained eyes. "She might not be your mother."

"I have to know." But even as Serena slid off the bed, she couldn't understand why her heart hammered with the fear that she would not be able to go. Why did she want to know with such urgency? Jonathon and Drake had insisted her past didn't matter.

But without knowing her past, how could she understand her future?

She reached for her borrowed dressing gown.

"Where are you going?" Jonathon jumped off the bed, racing to her side.

She tied the belt. "To find your peerage."

With Jonathon at her side, holding the candle, she found the peerage book in the library. Jonathon cradled her waist, leaned over to read. "It's out of date," he noted grimly. "The only Lady Draycott mentioned died five years ago. Draycott must have taken a new wife."

"A vampire wife. So all I know about my mother is a name. Eve, Lady Draycott. And I don't know if the name Eve is true." She closed the book and realized Drake had joined them. "I will write back to her. If you men will not let me go to her, I will invite her here."

"Madness," Jonathon protested.

"She needs to know," Drake countered. "We can protect Serena. And she needs to have this."

"I will not allow it," Jonathon commanded. And he, of course, expected that would end the argument.

Serena solemnly shook her head. "You do not have that power, Jonathon." And she left them, even as Jonathon strode after her. She heard him stop at the doorway, felt his gaze on her back as she hurried away, and she didn't stop running until she reached the bedchamber to compose her letter.

The men, surprisingly, let her be. Her heart flip-flopped at that—they did understand how much it meant to her to know who her mother was.

An hour ticked by before she sat back in the chair at the escritoire. Crumpled pages surrounded her, but she finally had a brief note that satisfied her. But as she sanded it, a knock came at the door. Expecting Jonathon or Drake, she yanked it open.

The footman bowed. "The messenger came back, ma'am. He says he was instructed to return after one hour."

Frowning, Serena took the small, wrapped package and dismissed the footman. Was her mother mad as well as undead?

Fingers trembling, she opened the velvet pouch and tipped it upside down, and a locket slid out into her palm. Gold and delicate, with a heart-shaped fob—it meant nothing to her. It had no significance. With her thumbnail she pried it open. A small square of paper fell out.

She unfolded the tiny scrap, reading it as she smoothed it.

When I gave birth to you, I knew that you would change tomorrow night—your 25th birthday. Perhaps you have become vampire already, but what you do not know is that you will come into your power tomorrow night, at the stroke of midnight. Without my help, you will perish. You must know the secrets of allowing the power to come to you. I suspect you do not want to see me. You must. You must come to me, and together we will help you embrace your new life.

Lukos believes he has the secret—he believes he will be the one to help you claim your power. But there is much Lukos does not understand. He is one of the devil's apprentices and a man—both arrogant and foolish. I will not allow him to take you, Serena. But you must come to me.

Come to the village of Pemberton Hill. There is a mystical standing stone circle there. It is there that you will find your destiny.

It was not signed, but Serena saw at once the handwriting was Lady Draycott's—her mother's.

Jonathon and Drake would never consent to this . . .

But if they were to share love, she must tell them of this. Nervously, she tugged the bellpull, then sent the servant to fetch them.

"Pemberton Hill," she repeated as Jonathon reread the note. She'd read it aloud once, for Drake. "I've seen drawings, sketches, notations about Pemberton Hill in the Society's library. Pemberton Hill is near one of Lord Ashcroft's estates, is it not?"

Jonathon nodded. "Yes. Ashcroft has studied that ring of stones since he was a boy. I spent time there, with my father."

Drake laughed. A low, naughty laugh. "I heard that Ashcroft practiced sex rites there in his younger days. Hired buxom, talented prostitutes to perform perverse acts with him beneath the light of the moon."

Jonathon linked his hands behind his back, paced. "To go to Ashcroft's would be madness. He wants us destroyed. This is very likely a hoax."

"And if it's the truth, Serena could be in grave danger," Drake reminded.

Serena shivered but felt a surge of enveloping warmth as Drake came up behind her and hugged her.

"Still, I believe we have to go," Drake said.

"I want to go," Serena insisted. "I need to know."

Even as Drake hugged her, Jonathon walked up to her, rested his hands on her shoulders, and kissed the top of her head. "I know how much it means to you to know about your past. I promise I will be at your side to protect you, no matter what."

Aroused beyond compare, Althea twisted her wrists, trying to break free of the knots. Once again, Bastien had outdone himself. She was well and truly bound to the bed. Though she cast a glance down and had to bite back a giggle. With her ripe, round tummy, did she really present an erotic picture? Her breasts, full and plump, looked magnificent, though, and her nipples were now long and full and a seductive berry-brown.

Bastien tied the last knot to the bedpost, then slid off the bed, obviously admiring his handiwork. She giggled as the baby squirmed in her belly, then gasped as Bastien selected a long, slender dildo from her vanity and strolled toward her. He licked the tip of it, and she trembled in anticipation—

The door swung open, and Yannick marched in, running his fingers through his hair. *Bastien, you are supposed to be preparing to leave for the docks.*

Sorry, brother, I became distracted while helping Althea pack her erotic toys.

That was not at all the truth, but Bastien shared a wink as Yannick groaned in frustration.

Join me, brother, Bastien suggested, indicating her submissive position with a sweep of his hand. His golden hair hung around his shoulders. They were in the dark, only the soft shimmer of the moon painting his beautiful body.

Yannick, who should have been the voice of reason, shifted to his bat-form to shed his clothing. But he paused at the edge of the bed. "Althea, I have to be honest with you—"

A confession? What had he been up to? Cavorting with another vampiress? After all, she was the size of a carriage right now. Though she knew he and Bastien would never stray . . .

"We are not going to the Carpathians—though we will make it appear that is our destination. Instead, we are going to Italy. To a lovely home I have purchased near Venice."

She tugged on her knots. "But my father is expecting us—I wished to see him."

"It is not safe, love. Not now. Later, perhaps . . ."

She threw a desperate glance to Bastien, who nodded, the wretch, instead of coming to her rescue.

One last pull at her bonds only proved she was securely tied. *Oh! Bugger you both! You tied me up to tell me this, didn't you? It had nothing to do with sex! Cowards. I demand that you untie me.*

You do it, Bastien urged, clapping a hand on Yannick's shoulder.

But Yannick shook this head. *I'm the earl. I command you to do it.*

How could you lie to me about this? Althea roared. And she yanked so hard on the ropes that the bed shook and banged the floor. *How could you do this behind my back?*

To protect you. Yannick brushed the back of his hand against her cheek.

Althea took a deep breath and sighed as Yannick began to untie her feet. *I do not believe Serena would do me any harm—*

Bastien broke the rope at her left wrist with one fast tug. *No, but Ashcroft is a madman.*

Althea wiggled her feet. Goodness, her ankles were swollen. *Ashcroft was always kind to me when he visited the Carpathians. He brought me treats from England, treats I had long forgotten.*

She held up her hand as both men protested. *I know. I am a vampiress and everything has changed, but I want to be with my father. I have no intention of going to Italy.*

We are going. Tonight, Yannick vowed, arrogantly. *I am perfectly capable of kidnapping you if I feel it is for your own good, and the good of our baby.*

Althea fumed, rubbing her wrists. *Do it and I will never forgive you.*

26

Banished

It was All Hallow's Eve.

Serena clutched her bonnet as Jonathon's curricle raced along the road to Pemberton Hill. A brilliant whip, he urged his horses on a breakneck pace, deftly avoiding ruts in the road. Large, round, and silver, the moon hung over them. Another curricle raced ahead—Drake Swift, and he drove his team at mad speed.

"Do you think my mother exists?" She had to shout the question over the rattle of the wheels, the thunder of horses' hooves. And then she remembered—she didn't have to shout at all. *Do you think she truly did write to me?*

I don't know, love.

In the back of both his carriage and Swift's, trunks rattled. Trunks with crossbows, stakes, holy water . . . almost every weapon stored in Jonathon's house.

I am not naïve, she added, though her heart ached at what she would say. *Even if she is my mother, why would she want me now? After five and twenty years? It is because I am of some value to her, because of this magic power.* She sighed. *I don't feel as though I possess magical powers.*

You are magical, sweetheart. His smile warmed her to her toes, warding off the chill that seemed to run through her blood. His fangs flashed with the smile, reminding her of who they were.

Serena struggled to concentrate. Who was she really? Would her mother be there? Why lead them to Lord Ashcroft?

The moon followed as they charged onward. Jonathon kept a firm grip on the reins as he watched the road. Guilt nagged. Both he and Drake were here to protect her—what if they were attacked?

She couldn't think of that. What if she was truly destined to possess magical powers? If so, she could use the power to stop Ashcroft from destroying her. To protect Drake and Jonathon. Even to defeat Lukos.

Couldn't she?

They crested a rise, and the valley spread before them. Serena gasped at the sight of Ashcroft's mansion—it was below, the pale gray stone gleaming beneath the enormous white moon. The rippled surface of a lake sparkled, and patches of black woods spotted the rolling land. Moonlight slanted over, and she saw them, on a plateau halfway between their position and the house. The rings of stones.

There were vampire slayers who believed these sites to be the portals to hell.

Serena shivered and Jonathon slowed the horses. They caught up to Drake's carriage, already stopped on the first stretch of level ground, but Serena stared down at the ring of stones, trying to see in the center. A white-clad figure seemed to be moving inside. Ashcroft? Or Lukos?

Jonathon's arms slid around her. *Courage, Serena. I'd ask you to stay here, but I can't know you are safe unless I have you in my sight.* He drew out his pocket watch. *A quarter of eleven. We haven't much time.* He swung down from the curricle with one easy leap and jogged around to her side, gray greatcoat flapping around him.

Jump down to me, sweetheart.

As Jonathon lowered her, his powerful hands at her waist, Serena saw Drake striding toward them, carrying two crossbows. His coat billowed behind him like wings. He handed her a weapon with a wink. *I remember, Serena, that you are a perfect shot.*

She had proven that in Jonathon's bedchamber.

She stood between them both—Jonathon so tall and broad, Drake so wildly brave and strong—and being part of the three gave her courage. But she knew her greatest strength must come from inside.

With Drake flanking her left side, Jonathon at her right, Serena found a worn path that led from the road, between rocks, to the cleared plateau. They moved in silence to a stand of trees, where the path narrowed and disappeared into darkness.

Jonathon took the lead, and Serena blinked, letting her eyes adjust, as they plunged into shadow.

Serena.

Shock and surprise gripped her heart at the sound of the husky, beautiful woman's voice. She saw slight movements in the dark. The graceful wave of a slim hand. The ripple of a cloak tossed by the wind.

A woman stepped out from the shadows in front of Jonathon.

Her mother.

Jonathon pulled up short and stood with legs spread, crossbow resting at his side. She saw his obvious warning in the restrained power of his stance, in the way he was blocking the path between her mother and her.

Her mother held up her hand. *Do not go farther. Lukos waits there. He believes I am bringing you to him, but of course, that is not at all what I am going to do.*

She heard her mother's ethereal voice in her head, a sound as poignant and lovely as the song of a brook, the murmur of waves, the whisper of the breeze. From the abrupt way Jonathon straightened even more, the catch in Drake's breathing behind her, she knew both men could hear her mother too.

Her mother drew the hood back, revealing her pale oval face.

Serena froze in surprise. At first, it was as though she had found a mirror in the woods. Her mother looked the same age as she and possessed the same blue-black hair, the exact arched black brows, the identical nose. But her mother was far more beautiful than she was. The mouth was large and perfect. The eyes ice cold.

Jonathon took a step closer to her mother, and he lifted his crossbow. "Who are—"

With a wave of her hand, her mother sent a wave of air that pushed his bow back down. "Silence. I wish to speak to my daughter."

Serena felt Drake move close behind her, protectively.

Mother? Even as she spoke the word in thought, she looked at her mother's face and had no idea what more to say. She searched helplessly for words. This was wrong. There was no delight on her mother's face, no warmth, no happiness.

But . . . who are you? Serena asked, and even in her thoughts, her words sounded full of tears.

Lady Draycott, my dear. An English lady.

But you are also a vampire? I—I thought you were mortal. I thought my father was a vampire.

He was not. Her mother gave a wave of her hand, as though dismissing her father entirely.

Why—? Serena took a deep breath. *Why did you abandon me?* It must have been for her protection. She wanted to believe it was to protect her from the Society. To save her life.

A proper lady would never be so blunt, her mother admonished. A smirk touched her mother's lips. *And I excel at behaving like a proper lady. But we haven't time for decorum, have we? You wish to know why I discarded you.*

Discarded! The word was like a knife to the heart. At once Serena understood why she had been foolish to give the past so much power. But she was determined to be strong. *Yes, why did you discard me?*

Jonathon stepped back to stand at her side, and Drake came forward, and she saw pain flicker in her mother's shining eyes.

I had such power, her mother said in thought. *Finally the power I deserved. And then I became pregnant. It was madness. I am a demon. Demons do not bear children.*

You . . . you didn't want me?

Of course not. I made love to a man I believed was mortal. But he was not, and then I found I could not destroy you, not without bringing about my own death.

Drake glared at Lady Draycott, radiating hatred. He spoke aloud, his voice a growl. "Do not listen to her poison, Serena." He swung one arm up and pointed the crossbow at her mother's chest.

Jonathon reached over and lowered it. "The truth," he said with brutal calm. "Give your daughter the truth."

Lady Draycott, her mother, snarled and showed long and deadly fangs. *Silence. You men are insignificant. I could destroy you with a snap of my fingers.*

Serena darted forward. *No!*

Both Jonathon and Drake grasped her arms and pulled her back.

Lady Draycott sneered at Jonathon, then at Drake. *Men are so pitiable. As for you, Serena, I had no idea how important or how valuable you would be. You will be the most powerful vampiress. You wish to know who I am? I am as old as creation. I was fashioned by the hand of God, fashioned before the eyes of the man I was made for. And he was appalled by what he saw. He refused me—me, the gift of God! I was the first wife of Adam, and I was banished from Paradise.*

"Lilith?" Jonathon's deep voice broke the stillness.

You do not believe me. You think I am merely mad. I am not Lilith. I am Eve. The first Eve, the forgotten one. Adam saw me created from the earth, fashioned from dirt, and he was repulsed.

"And you lured Serena here to give her to Lukos. Why?"

I would never give my powerful child to that stupid, arrogant male. Lukos wishes to populate the world with vampires. I cannot allow him to gain so much control. We, the vampiresses, rule the world of the immortals. We cannot allow a monster like Lukos to possess such power.

Serena gripped a tree trunk. She was the daughter of Eve and would rule the world of immortals? That had not been in the Society's books—books that had, of course, been written by men—

Pain sliced suddenly through Serena's belly. Stunned by it, shaking in crippling agony, she almost sank to the ground. Jonathon caught her, and she saw his horror as nausea hit her stomach. Sparks shot before her eyes, and her vision blurred.

"It has begun," Lady Draycott said. "You must go to the standing stones, Serena."

"Lukos is there," Jonathon argued. He held her tight.

Serena clung to his shoulder. Hot pain raged through her, as though her blood were on fire. She wanted to claw her skin off; she wanted to let her burning blood pour out of her body. She wanted to die.

Drake shouted through thought, *What in blazes is happening to her? Stop it!*

Dimly, she heard her mother's voice in her mind. *There is no choice. It must happen at the stones. There is much to be done. First, we must destroy Lukos. We haven't much time before the power consumes her—*

Blackness closed in on her vision, and Serena fought to stay conscious. But her mother lifted her hand and a globe of violet light floated toward her. It surrounded her, enveloped her.

She tried to touch it, but it faded before her shaking fingertips made contact. Warmth coursed through her limbs, her heartbeat steadied, and she felt strong once more.

Through the dappled purple mist, she saw Jonathon. Jonathon running toward the standing stones, like a madman pursued by demons.

"Bloody lunatic." Drake hoisted her over his shoulder and followed.

Jonathon had acted like a madman, throwing aside logic to save her, Serena realized. Drake let her down just as Jonathon charged forward with stake raised—he'd thrown aside his useless crossbow. Standing in the middle of the circle, white robes dancing in the wind, Lukos lifted his hand.

Serena choked on a scream, but she could only watch, helpless, as Lukos smashed his hand at Jonathon like an angered bear. Jonathon's stake drove into Lukos's arm, blood spurted, and Lukos shoved him back. He tumbled head over heels and slammed into a stone.

But he was up in an instant.

Serena felt a warm hand in hers—her mother's. *Come back with me, Serena. Allow the foolish men to fight.*

She tried to wrench free from her mother's grip but couldn't, and her mother towed her to the edge of the circle. The touch of her mother's hand eased the pain racking her limbs and her heart, but her legs and arms were trembling uncontrollably. She didn't trust herself to fire the bow she still held. She could hit Drake or Jonathon.

From the periphery of the stone circle, Serena held her breath as Jonathon charged again and her heart pounded as she saw him leap aside to avoid the bolt of violet light shot at him. Drake attacked with a stake, but Lukos simply grabbed Drake's arms and threw him away. His body sailed back through the air, arms and legs splayed wide, and he smashed back against a stone altar. His back cracked, seemed to bend in half backward.

The fall must have broken Drake's back.

Fear roared through Serena's body, screamed in her skull. Could even a vampire survive that? Drake wasn't moving . . . dear heaven, he wasn't moving . . .

Fury raged then, and her pain vanished. Fingers shaking, she aimed her bow, fired immediately. But the bolt arced over Lukos's shoulder. Jonathon leapt to his feet again, and he fired a shot. His bolt slammed into Lukos's gut, and Lukos yanked it free.

Lukos lifted his hand, and Jonathon staggered back and fell in the dirt.

There had been no bolt of light, but the monster still had the power to drive Jonathon down.

It was hopeless. Only her mother had to the power to stop him—

No, Serena. I do not. Not alone. Her mother pulled her crossbow from her hand.

What are you doing—?

Lukos fixed his gaze on her. No! He took two steps to her, his fangs glinting as a grin of triumph came to his handsome face. She felt drawn to his strength. To his commanding smile and the allure in his gleaming eyes—golden eyes that burned like the sun.

The thought popped unbidden into her head—with Lukos, she could rule the world . . .

Serena, you are mine. Lukos's low, accented voice vibrated through her, and her nerves sizzled in response. No . . . she had to fight—

Serena bit back a cry as Jonathon appeared out of the mist once more and jumped at Lukos's back, his hand slicing toward the demon's chest. Lukos flung Jonathon over his head. The demon tossed Jonathon's enormous body as though it weighed nothing. His boot stomped down, and with his victim pinned, he reached for Jonathon's head. The monster's hands clamped Jonathon's jaw and twisted as though to break the neck—

Then heat engulfed Serena. Burning heat. It shot up her arm to her hand, and the skin of her palm screamed as though on fire. Her entire hand seemed to become molten, like malleable wax.

Even as she gasped in shock, a white force poured from her hand and became a shimmering light. It hit Lukos in the face. He released Jonathon and fell back.

"Your power!" her mother cried in delight.

Serena felt drained. She was shaking. She hadn't consciously done that. It had just happened.

Help me, Serena. We must banish him. You have the power now; your rage has brought it into you. Take my hands—otherwise the power will be too strong for you.

She must hold the hands of the mother who had hated her. She looked to Drake, fear in her heart. He had known this pain—his mother had wanted to kill him, and he had found the courage to survive. He was struggling to get up, his hand on his back. Groaning and in great pain, she guessed, but alive!

She reached out, slipped her hands into Lady Draycott's—into Eve's—and closed her eyes as power surged through her veins.

Say this word with me, Eve urged. *Paradise.*

Lukos charged forward and Serena's vision became his; suddenly she saw the world from his view, as though she were inside his head, looking through his eyes. She saw herself and her mother, their hair whipping in the wind. She saw their clasped hands and the white glow that surrounded their fingers.

Desperately she chanted the word in her head. *Paradise. Paradise. Paradise.*

Open your eyes, Serena!

A green glow seemed to come from her mother's eyes. It engulfed them and radiated out like ripples on still water.

Serena . . . no . . . you are mine! Serena! Lukos's last plea flooded her mind, but the green light flowed around Lukos like fog, silencing his voice. He punched at it, twisting and writhing within its grip. It swirled around him like a maelstrom, while he gave one last desperate scream.

Then, in a wink, the lights vanished, leaving her blinded as though a hundred candles had flared, then extinguished at once.

Drake! Jonathon!

"No. Damn you, Eve." A man charged out from behind a stone. A man with a crossbow. "You were to give her to me!" he shouted.

Ashcroft. Dear heaven, it was Ashcroft.

Serena watched, stunned, horrified, as Jonathon lunged at Ashcroft. Jerking wildly around, Ashcroft pointed the weapon at Jonathon's chest. "Sommersby! You betrayed me!"

No!

She jumped, springing across the ground like a lion, but she hit something—a force struck her and it felt as if she had smashed into a wall. Her chest seemed to crumple, as though a weight crushed it, as though her ribs had been broken like kindling. The fire came after, a fierce burning through her chest. Her heart exploded—the pain seared her.

She fell to the ground like a sack of stones. Blackness roared around her, swallowing her whole.

Serena! Jonathon ran forward. The bolt had ripped through her chest and sent her plunging to the ground. Ashcroft held a sword above his head as he raced toward Serena's fallen body. Decapitation. Sever the head from the body. The vampire would never rise.

No! Jonathon leapt, knowing he didn't have enough time—

Magic! He lifted his hand, praying he possessed enough

power. Scorching fire raced down his arm, and a miraculous circle of red fire grew in the palm of his hand. It streaked forward and hit Ashcroft's arm. The sword tumbled backward, and Ashcroft howled in pain.

Before he could fire again, Jonathon saw a bolt of white light streak toward Ashcroft—it struck him directly in the torso and exploded in concentric circles. Pure white, the light hit Jonathon's eyes, and the pain screeched back into his skull. It blinded him and knocked him back—he stumbled and fell onto the ground. His hip hit, his shoulder bounced, and agony shot through his body.

A scream burst from the center of the light, unearthly and high pitched. A shriek of agony. Hell, was that Ashcroft? A sound rose, as though the air were thick with bees, and the drone shut out the screams.

As Jonathon blinked and could begin to see, the sound stopped, and the light sucked in on itself, like a vortex, until it became a pinpoint. Then it vanished on a breath of wind.

Ashcroft was gone.

Jonathon forced himself to his feet and staggered to Serena's fallen body just as Drake reached her. Jonathon's breath rushed from his chest, and he sank to his knees at Serena's side. Ashcroft's shot had been perfect, piercing her below the left breast. It must have destroyed the heart.

"A crossbow bolt cannot destroy her," Eve said. "I who was fashioned from earth, piece by piece, know that. What is a wound but that which can be healed?"

Serena's mother pushed him aside, and Jonathon fell back to let her kneel by her daughter's wounded chest. Eve lifted a slim velvet rope from around her neck and opened the small pouch that dangled from it. "This is the soil of paradise. That from which life was created."

The pale hands rolled the dirt into a ball. It smelled of richness and earth. Jonathon's nostrils flared, and his body drew in the scent. Warmth rushed through him. Instinct begged him to touch the sacred earth that brought life—

Jonathon fought that urge, and he leaned forward. All he wanted to do was protect Serena, and goddamn, he didn't trust Eve. She had rejected Serena; why help her daughter now?

But he had to let Eve work. They couldn't waste precious seconds.

Eve pulled the crossbow bolt free, and Serena did not move. Fear and pain lanced his heart. His gaze wavered. Was it too late—?

Have faith.

He heard the word in Eve's lovely, enthralling tones. Could he have faith?

He glanced to where Ashcroft had been, but the blackguard had vanished completely. Ashcroft had paid the ultimate price, for what purpose? To destroy a woman he simply did not understand?

Eve pressed the ball of dirt into Serena's wound from the front, and Jonathon flinched. Dirt packed into a bleeding chest wound?

"And thus the dirt becomes a new heart," Eve whispered. "It beats with strength, and it allows life to endure. Life—the miracle, and the most precious gift. Life—the cross we bear to know the sweetest pleasure."

Eve bowed and held her hands together in front of her, as though praying. Uncertain, heart pounding, Jonathon did the same. From the corner of his eye, he saw Drake dip his head.

Eve dropped her hands. "Now you both must touch her, for it is love that gives the miracle. Life springs from love and pleasure. You—" Eve pointed at him, then pointed to Drake. "And you have given her both. You must touch the dirt and give it the power to become the heart."

Eve paused. "But—"

"But what?" Drake snapped at Eve, eyes narrowed in suspicion.

"You must love her absolutely and completely. It is the power and depth of your love that will save her."

Drake's hand already rested on the cool earth pushed into Serena's chest. Serena's face bore no expression, not even the contentment of sleep. Her lips were a simple line, her eyes shut, her lovely features relaxed.

Save her, Eve urged, *so that she may rule at my side. Rule as a queen of vampires.*

Jonathon placed his hand on top of Drake's, the man who had been his partner, who had made him vampire, whom he had trusted with his life. Could the power of a love shared among three save Serena's life? He prayed it could.

Was he saving her to lose her to Eve? Who would Serena choose? He and Drake, or the mother she had always longed to have?

He bent to her cheek and kissed her. *I love you, Serena.*

27

Between Three

Drake touched Serena's face, kept his hand pressed to her heart. *I love you.* His chest felt it as though it were trapped under stone, as if he were buried alive. Was love powerful enough? He'd never believed in love before finding Serena.

I love you.

Hell, was *his* love powerful enough? Was he worthy to save the life of the woman he adored? He had lost one woman and he had lost his child. He would give anything for Serena—if he had a soul he would gladly give it away to save her life.

His knees sinking in the grass and dirt, Drake bent to Serena's lips, as though he could revive her with a kiss—and he collided with Jonathon's head. *Bugger you, Sommersby,* he snarled, his possessiveness rising, but he moved back and let Jonathon kiss her first. A love shared between three . . . he had to accept it to save her.

Jonathon brushed a soft kiss to Serena's lips. Stunned, Drake saw a faint glimmer of a tear shining in the other man's eyes. He had seen hollow emptiness in Sommersby's eyes before—the night he had lost his fiancée, Lilianne, to a vampire—but Sommersby had not shed a tear that night. Not even after he had been forced to stake her. In that moment, Drake saw the depth of Jonathon's love for Serena.

Drake's own eyes burned. He fought not to cry as Jonathon sat back and gave him his chance to gently kiss Serena's soft, warm, motionless lips. Men—Christ Jesus, especially vampire males—should not give in to maudlin emotion.

He nuzzled the warm skin of her neck, inhaling sweetness. He'd lost his soul, but that was nothing compared to the heart-break of fearing he'd lost her—

Drake? Jonathon?

Drake jerked up and gazed at Serena as she blinked her eyes open. Her brows dipped as she looked up at him. *You're safe. Thank heavens! And Jonathon—?*

Safe also, my love. Ashcroft is gone. On her opposite side, Jonathon took her hand in his. *We saved her life together, Swift. We are committing to loving her together.*

Hell. Drake glanced back to Serena, to smile at her beautiful eyes; then he faced the man he'd once envied for being a gentle-man. *I'm willing.*

As am I, Jonathon answered.

Lift her. Drake fought the pain in his heart as he asked Jonathon to do what he wanted to do—pick up Serena and hold her to his heart. He had to prove he could share her.

Jonathon scooped Serena into his arms. Her torn pelisse and gown gaped open at her chest. There was no wound anymore, no sign of dirt, just healthy, soft pink skin. Her breast was ex-posed, soft and plump, the nipple puckered.

Assured Serena was safe, Drake spun to face her mother. He would cut the woman down before he would allow her to take Serena from him—

He stopped, hands raised. No, he wouldn't. It would hurt Serena too deeply. He would do what Serena wished, because he loved her so much.

But as he confronted the beautiful vampiress who looked so much like Serena, Drake reeled back in astonishment.

A tear raced down Eve's cheek—legend had it that vampire queens had no emotions at all—but Eve glowed with love as she smiled at her daughter, still nestled in Jonathon's arms.

"You have love, my daughter," she murmured. "Something I have never known. These men have proved their worth. I wanted you to help me, to help me deliver vengeance upon men, but I cannot demand that of you when you have known true love. I do not have the power to take you from such a strong bond. Your magic will be stronger than mine, with strength born of love."

"What do you mean?" Serena asked from against Jonathon's big chest. The sound of her voice, growing stronger, sent warmth and hope and joy through Drake. But deep hurt showed in Serena's eyes. "You wanted me only for my power? To use me for vengeance? And what of Ashcroft, were you going to give me to him?"

Eve shook her head, defiance in her silvery gaze. "A lie believed by an arrogant man. He wanted immortality."

"You killed him."

"Oh no, Serena. I have given him immortality—in banishment. A man should be careful what he wishes for."

But Eve, to Drake's surprise, hung her head in humility. "I made a mistake, Serena," she said. "A mistake when you were born. I wanted only to be free of you. You, of course, can never forgive me. Let me embrace you. Let me help you welcome the rest of your power."

Jonathon lowered Serena to her feet, kept his arm around her. Drake moved to her side.

"Trust me," Eve urged.

Serena nodded, but Drake held her hand as Eve came to her, as Eve embraced her and chanted mystical words. "Retreat, gentlemen," she commanded. Drake refused, as did Jonathon, until the golden glow surrounding the women forced them to. The huge, monolithic stones shook; the ground undulated. The trees around them whipped, and birds screeched as they flew to the sky. Drake gripped the stone beside him and hung on for his life. He saw Jonathon plastered against another, hanging on. Would the earth open and swallow them both up?

The forces stopped so suddenly Drake clung to stone to avoid falling. Eve released Serena. "You have embraced your power, daughter. I will leave you now—"

"Mother, no." Impulsively, Serena reached out. "Stay. I can understand the fear of having a child—I have experienced it. I don't . . . I don't want to lose you again."

Drake was touched to his heart by Serena's capacity to forgive and to love.

Eve stepped back, into the shadows cast by the standing stones. "I must leave, Serena. Dawn is coming, and there is one more task your men must complete to ensure you heal completely. They must make love to you tonight. For the mystical power of sex will mend you. I will come to you again—in time. You will need to learn to control your power; you will be summoned to take lessons from me and the other vampiresses. They have bid me to help you . . . and I thank them for allowing us to be together."

Drake's heart ached as he saw Serena's mother smile lovingly at her daughter. *I thought you would hate me,* she admitted.

Gently, Serena shook her head, and Eve embraced her once more. "You, my child, are unique amongst vampires. That is why Lukos desired you—for you were born of the first union of angel and vampire." She released Serena and stepped back.

"Angel and vampire? Wait!" Serena cried.

But Eve vanished.

Drake slid her arm around Serena's waist, and Jonathon let him have his turn to hold her close.

"I don't understand," she murmured. "I was fathered by an angel. I cannot believe it."

"I've always known you are an angel, little lark," Drake said.

Large, luminous, Serena's eyes met his. Drake's heart soared as she reached for his hand. She also slipped her hand into Jonathon's. "Now, shouldn't we make love?"

Above her, the moon winked from behind a blue wisp of cloud and Serena winked back as she lay back on the altar stone. Jonathon and Drake's greatcoats provided comfort from the hard, smooth stone. How did one pose to look like a most willing sacrifice for exotic sexual rites?

Wantonly, she parted her legs, hitching up her skirt. Then she laughed. She was a true vampiress now, capable of the most amazing feats. She was free of Lukos, safe from Ashcroft, and she now had a mother.

Serena shut her eyes. She thought of the night sky, rich and black. She thought of air, of soaring, of wings open wide to embrace the wind—

Drake. Jonathon. She saw them both. Saw them change, and then return to human form, naked and beautiful beneath the moonlight. In the blink of her eye, she joined them, and her clothes fell to the ground. One instant she was a bat, spreading her wings in the fresh, cool midnight air, the next she reclined on the altar, determined to spread her wings in another way.

She let her hands cover her nether curls and her breasts, and suggested shyly, *I know that both of you men care deeply for each other. And I know you lust for each other—vampires do.*

Jonathon immediately reddened, but his cock betrayed him—it jolted upward, his juices glistening on the tip.

Drake's grin widened. He stood in an intimidating stance, legs spread, erection pointing at the night sky. *What are you suggesting, my love?*

"I want you to play together. To pleasure each other," Serena whispered. "No pleasure should be barred to us."

"You won't be hurt?" Jonathon asked.

She smiled at his frown. "I want this. It would be... erotic." Though it was also humorous to watch the men awkwardly face each other. Their hands collided, and they parried around each other like clumsy dance partners. But, bathed in moonlight, their bodies sculpted into planes of blue-silver and dark shadow, they were beautiful. Then Drake planted a hot, sensuous kiss on Jonathon's wide, hard mouth, their cocks bumped, and Serena was lost. Lost in erotic need.

Their pricks rubbed together, each dampening the other. They drew apart from the kiss, linked by a silver trail of saliva between their mouths and a glistening bridge of juice between their cocks.

Serena slid her fingers to her aching cunny, down through her wet curls. The men stroked each other, Drake's hands coasting down Jonathon's hard stomach and Jonathon caressing the silvery curls on Drake's chest. Serena tweaked her clit as four male hands grappled with two pricks and four dangling balls. When they joined for another kiss, they ground their cocks together, merging pale curls with dark.

And then, like true men, they wrestled. Drake began, trying to force Jonathon to turn. Drake wanted Jonathon's arse. A river of juice soaked Serena's hand as she played with her cunny—mesmerized. But Jonathon rebelled, fought back, and both men tumbled to the ground. They snapped with fangs, jerked cocks—their own, each other's—and clutched each other's arse. They panted and grunted but didn't speak.

She perched on the edge of the altar, pinching her left nipple and languorously rubbing her clit. How she ached to come . . . but she wanted to last . . . to build her pleasure.

Jonathon flipped Drake onto his back, the slimmer man landing heavily into the dirt, arms wide and legs spread. Leaping on top, Jonathon ruthlessly thrust his cock at Drake's closed mouth. His own mouth wide, he lunged to Drake's rod.

Serena's heart ceased to beat and she hovered on the brink of climax. Would he bite—the way she had?

Heavens, no. He licked. Long, glistening, pink, Jonathon's tongue slicked along Drake's shaft. Drake opened his lips and let Jonathon's cock sink in. The whole long, thick length of it disappeared. Jonathon thrust slowly, lifting to watch his cock vanish into Drake's mouth. It must be going all the way down his throat, for Drake's lips now touched Jonathon's coarse pubic curls.

Take me deep, Sommersby, Drake urged.

I want to fuck your face, Swift, Jonathon answered, and he gobbled up Drake's member. The slurping of their fierce suckling filled Serena's thoughts. Her body tensed, her clit was aching and swollen, and she wanted to come.

Enough! Jonathon released Drake and rolled off his partner.

Laughing, Drake levered up on his elbow, and he wrapped his hand around his thick, heavily veined shaft. He clutched tight so the head swelled and reddened, like a large, juicy plum. *Join us, Serena, love.*

Shakily, she jumped down from the altar stone and padded across damp, cool grass. All around bare branches creaked and clattered in the breeze. She should be freezing, but aching desire kept her skin hot.

She felt safe. Safe and free.

Drake got to his feet first, drew her to him, and captured her mouth. His fingers delved into her quim, stirring, stretching. *You are so wet, so ready for us. Tonight, on this special night,* Drake whispered in her thoughts, *we should do something very naughty.*

Anticipation whirled through her like a maelstrom. *What could be naughtier than what we've already done?*

Jonathon, lying on his back on the rich earth, gave her a

shrug. *I cannot imagine, Serena, love.* His large hands slicked his juices and Drake's saliva along his thick shaft, over the prominent veins, up to the swollen head. His heavy balls dangled between his muscled thighs.

She was molten between her legs, barely able to stand. As Drake slid his finger into her quim, she locked her gaze with Jonathon's hungry, intense stare. Oh, this was magic indeed.

Drake's finger drew out, with a suction sound that made her blush. Gently, he fingered the bridge of skin between her quim and her anus. His naked cock poked her bottom.

He helped her lay down in the velvety soft grass, and Jonathon rolled to her right side. Drake lay down at her left. Under partly closed lids, she saw Jonathon's large, elegant fingers trail down to her black nether curls.

Jonathon rested his hand on her mound, palm hard against her clit so her surprised squirming gave her jolts of toe-curling pleasure. Two of his large fingers slid into her soaking passage, thrusting lazily in and out. Then Jonathon slid his finger out, and Drake's finger slid in so quickly she caught her breath.

Do you want us both in your sweet pussy at once? Drake murmured. *It would be the most intense pleasure.*

A rush of crazed need washed over her. She'd never dreamed of two cocks in the same place. Could it be possible? The idea was forbidden, naughty . . . and she wanted it. Wanted to try. She couldn't begin to imagine what it would feel like . . . whether she even could take them both . . .

"Yes," she breathed aloud.

Drake entered her from behind, and such a river of juices flowed from her that he slid in instantly to the hilt. As Drake thrust, Jonathon kissed her deeply, capturing her tongue, sucking at it. He began to work his cock at the edge of her drenched passage, beside Drake's. She took deep breaths against his mouth. Relax . . . it was . . . alarming but good . . . and she must relax . . .

She was a vampiress. Anything was possible . . . and everything was delicious . . .

She felt a tug as Drake held her intimate lips open to let Jonathon inside. Jonathon groaned as his cock skittered to one side.

"You have such a sweet, tight cunny," Jonathon whispered.

She couldn't speak as Jonathon kissed her deeply again before releasing her to grip his cock, to lead it back. By a miracle, his cock pushed in a little beside Drake's, stretching her entrance impossibly wide. The pressure on her walls . . . it was heaven.

Drake moaned in unison with her, teasing her hard nipples with his fingers.

"What does it feel like, Drake?" she whispered naughtily. She turned so her cheek rested against his. "Having Jonathon's cock rubbing yours?"

Drake licked inside her ear. "Angel, I would much rather hear about how good it feels to take two thick poles inside."

Jonathon groaned. He kissed her again, the roughness of his jaw teasing her. "Are you certain, sweetheart?"

Her quim throbbed, and she felt as though she was soaring to a pinnacle. How she loved the teasing pushes of Jonathon's cock combined with Drake's slow, deep thrusts. Then Jonathon filled her completely, right to her womb, and she gasped at the pleasure, the twinge of pain that suddenly melted in ecstasy.

She tightened her hands, drove her nails into Drake's hip, Jonathon's arm.

"There, we're both in." Drake gave a raw laugh. "I can tell because she's clawing us."

"Does it hurt?" Jonathon whispered. She felt his entire body tense.

"Oh . . . no . . . it's so intense, though . . . oh!" They both began to thrust, filling her, giving her pleasure—

She clutched both men, screaming her pleasure up to the moon. Then, like a bolt of power from the heavens, the climax seared through her. *I'm coming!* Her body came apart, like rose petals in a fierce wind, and her senses scattered to the sky.

Drake bucked against her, mouth straining, his breath in rasps. And Jonathon joined him, shuddering with his climax.

Serena gave a heady, joyful laugh. There could be no greater magic than an orgasm shared between three.

They slumped onto the soft grass, still joined. She was drenched with their seed and her juices. She giggled.

"And what is so funny, my love?" Drake asked.

"All I ever dreamed of being was an ordinary Englishwoman." She closed her eyes and gave a sigh of pure delight. "I am so happy I am not!"

As both men's softened cocks slid out, Drake kissed her lips. "You are my salvation."

"My light," Jonathon vowed.

"My heart."

"My soul." Still lying on the ground, Jonathon crossed his arms in front of his chest.

"My universe." Drake drawled, fixing Jonathon with an equally belligerent glare.

"Your peacemaker," she laughed, aware of the ripe, primal scent of both men marking her. She belonged to them. And they most definitely needed her.

Jonathon lifted her hand to his lips. "I love you, dear wife."

"Wife?" Serena gasped at the word as she sat up. Jonathon embraced her, then released her to let Drake nuzzle her neck.

"Yes, love," Drake whispered. "We want to marry you. Both of us."

Serena thought of Althea's unconventional marriage and laughed. She wiped at one tear but knew it was no longer foolish to weep in joy.

"You are proposing marriage?"

Both dropped to one knee in front of her. Vulnerability showed in Drake's silvery-green eyes and in Jonathon's shining, darkly silver ones. Both men glowed with hope.

Serena blinked away tears. "Then yes, Jonathon. Yes, Drake. I want you both to be my husbands."

Jonathon embraced her, and Drake joined in. "We have a few hours until dawn," Drake suggested. "And I do like making love in the countryside."

"So do I," Jonathon agreed.

Serena drew each man's hand to her bare breasts. Laughing, she gave herself to her destiny—to the utter completeness of love.

Epilogue

"I had hoped to find Vlad Dracul's journals before we left." Serena backed down the ladder and gazed at the towering shelves of the Royal Society's library.

Drake grinned. "I wish I could help, my love."

"Soon you can." Serena smiled. Drake was an enthusiastic pupil at his reading lessons, but perhaps the true allure was carnal pleasures. Lessons always goaded him into seduction, and seduction led to imaginative sex. She even fondly stroked the ladder as she stepped back to the floor. Two gentleman, a lady, and a ladder . . .

Defying danger and death made sex all the more enticing . . .

Of course, she was a vampire, and falling off a ladder couldn't hurt her. But still . . .

"I am pleased that Lord Denby has taken over the Society in Ashcroft's place. He is a very good man, Denby."

Drake nodded, but his perceptive gaze smoldered. "And you miss Althea, don't you?" He patted the straight-backed chair beside him. A memory flared—of her legs spread wide on that proper, uncomfortable chair with both Drake and Jonathon lapping at her pussy . . .

She felt a telltale flush of desire wash over her cheeks. "It is close to Althea's time. I *am* worried. At least she has forgiven Brookshire and Bastien for kidnapping her and taking her to Italy."

Drake grinned and leaned back, his long legs stretched out. "I suspect the 'kidnapping' sparked many sexual fantasies."

"Well, there is something freeing about being bound—" And her words died as she remembered Drake promising that very same thing. How true it was. She had trusted Drake, trusted Jonathon, and found exquisite love.

"In her last letter, Althea wrote that her father had joined them in Italy and loves the warm climate—"

Serena gazed up at the rows of books, hundreds and hundreds of books on the history of vampires. There was so much she wished to learn, but she, too, would be leaving England with the men she loved. In a few months, she would also be in Venice, basking in the warm Mediterranean breezes, having sweaty lovemaking on sultry nights.

"I wish I had found books about my mother. Or my father—"

Drake broke off her lament with a soft kiss. "You will see your mother in Italy, and you will learn all about your past then."

She nodded, wrapping her arms around his warm, strong neck. "But I do know that my future is what is truly important. My future with you, with Jonathon, and—"

She broke off as the door creaked open. Immaculately dressed, breathtakingly handsome, Jonathon strode in. Serena frowned—she knew when Jonathon was nervous, and she stood, curious. He held out a letter. "It is in Althea's handwriting. I hope that means all is well."

Serena tore it open as Jonathon and Drake joined her. She didn't truly need candlelight to read, but instinctively she moved to the light. Relief and joy flowed from her heart as she read. "Thank heavens! Althea has had a baby girl—both she and her daughter are well." She read further . . .

"Oh dear!" She clapped her hand to her mouth. "Both Brookshire and Mr. de Wynter attended at the birth, and now they insist that Althea is the most magnificent woman in the history of England. Which she is, of course."

Serena lowered the letter and smiled, first at Jonathon and then at Drake. "She is going to call her daughter Serena." Her lips trembled as Drake reached out and gently brushed a tear from her cheek.

"She is named for an angel," Jonathon murmured by her ear.

Serena stroked her still-flat stomach. *There is something that you both must know. . . .* She knew it was time to share it with them both, and she wished to do it in the most intimate way.

Jonathon's dark brown brows drew together, and she knew he hadn't guessed. Surprise dawned in Drake's reflective green eyes. Then delight lit up his face.

Serena nodded, bursting with happiness at Drake's joy. *I believe it might be twins. I am not certain, but I suspect it. And vampiresses have a certain sense.*

Jonathon blinked. *Twins? You are . . . enceinte?*

She nodded. *Our family of three is going to become five.*

Serena, this is the most wonderful gift you could give us. Drake lifted her, swirled her around with her feet off the floor.

She heard such joy in Jonathon's laugh as he cut in on Drake and proceeded to twirl her dizzy around the room. It was so wonderful to be happy about this. And to know her husbands were every bit as delighted.

"We do have time before the ship sails," Drake broke in

aloud. "Time for magic." Great seriousness touched his eyes. "As long as it will not hurt the babies."

"Oh no, vampiresses are strong. Althea assures that all should go well. We have much time for magic," Serena promised, breathless.

"Yes," Jonathon agreed. "We have eternity."

Don't miss this peek at Sharon Page's
BLACK SILK . . .

He caught her staring and gave her a most wicked grin. Enticing lines bracketed his firm, wide mouth, and adorable dimples shadowed his cheeks. "You came in here to seduce me, didn't you?"

With a crook of his fingers, he motioned her to move toward him.

Maryanne stayed at the door. "N—no."

The Oriental motif had not ventured past the door. This was an Englishman's study, resplendent with wood and leather, comfortable yet austere.

Both settings suited Lord Swansborough.

"Who are you?" he asked, and he tipped the decanter—the entire decanter—to his lips and took a swallow. He quaffed the drink—likely brandy—the way men in the country drank ale. Some spilled down his chiseled jaw, and he lowered the lovely glass thing and wiped at his beautiful mouth with his shirt-sleeves.

His lordship was the first man here who was interested in her name. And she floundered helplessly—she had a creative mind but all she could do was stare in astonishment.

He settled himself on the back of a chair, one booted foot dirtying the arm. The position displayed the long, lean muscular power of his legs.

"Your name, puss," he prompted.

Maryanne knew men used that name to describe a woman's quim, and she knew she must suggest another name. But what did she want to suggest? Availability or the truth—that she was not allowed to touch a man like he? "Verity."

Truth. Why had she thought of that?

He saluted her with the decanter. "Imaginative. Where is your partner, Verity?"

"I don't have one." Which was, at least, the truth.

"I see." Amusement, chilling amusement, showed in his rakish grin. "If I ravish you and make you explode in the most intense climax, will you give me my next clue?"

A jolt of shock raced, cold and startling, through her veins.

Lord Swansborough thought she was a courtesan, employed to work in this bizarre scavenger hunt. She'd heard couples speaking of clues and hunting in the salon. "I came here to find a friend."

The brandy decanter was almost empty. Had he truly drank that much? How could he still be conscious if he had? Her two glasses of champagne and that sickly drink had left her disorientated, and the giddy feeling was now a pounding inside her skull.

"Did you indeed?" he asked. His tone spoke ominously of a man's awareness that he had a trapped female in his possession. But there was a teasing note underneath, and she knew she would much rather be trapped in this study with Swansborough, than out in the rest of the house with the other scavenger hunters.

Tearstains itched on her cheeks and she was certain she looked disheveled. How much did her mask obscure?

"Come here, Verity." His voice had sobered and it rumbled with bewitching erotic promise.

Verity. Which sounded like her sister's name, Venetia. Had she thought of the name because her sister Venetia had had adventures, and she had yearned for her own?

But Venetia had told her that Swansborough was exactly like the men who had surrounded her. And he was drunk, therefore dangerous. Logic told her that, but her heart skittered at the gentleness in his black eyes. They were hazy with drink, but not wild with lust.

"Come."

A confident, autocratic command. She knew the other meaning of the word and a shiver of anticipation, hot, electric, weakening, shot down her spine.

Her feet obeyed, and she closed the distance between them, and with each step, her heart tightened. Sweat trickled down her bodice and her throat felt aflame. She felt exactly the way she did when reading erotic manuscripts.

She stopped—a little more than a sword's thrust away—and he grinned. "Who is the friend you came to find, sweetheart?"

He was Marcus's good friend—he had seen her perhaps a half dozen times. She was so close, she feared he would know who she was. That he could see behind her simple white mask and guess the truth of her soul. That she was Maryanne Hamilton, ordinary virgin, here in Hades to find a courtesan.

"Georgiana," she admitted, softly.

His black brow lifted. "Do you belong to her, sweeting?"

Mystified, she asked, "How do you mean that, my lord?"

"Do you know who I am?"

"A viscount. And you expect me to answer your questions, but you will not answer mine." She smiled and dipped her head. Heavens, had she just said that? "You are Lord Swansborough." Surely that was safe enough to admit. He would think her a jade who knew him from brothels and Cyprian balls.

She still wasn't certain what role she should play. Should she pretend to be experienced? Should she admit she was an innocent in trouble?

"But I hardly expected to find you in here, alone in the dark."

"But I often drink alone, sweet. There's no pleasure in drinking alone in the middle of a crowd."

He was foxed. Absolutely, "But why—?"

"I encountered a man. He spoke of a tragic incident that happened a long time ago. It is something I like to forget. And I needed a way to help me do that." His lordship lowered the decanter, let it drop the last inches to the table, where it rattled. "You are lovely, Verity. But then, the truth is always beautiful. Dangerous but beautiful."

"I am hardly dangerous, my lord."

He reached out his hand—bare of gloves. A perfect, long-fingered gentleman's hand. She had never touched the naked hand of a gentleman. He meant to kiss her fingers. Uncertain, she moved forward, for good breeding dictated it, and let him sweep her hand to his lips.

Lovely lips. Firm and delectable and brushing her gloved knuckles. The champagne inside her bubbled up once more at his hot, seductive touch, at the caress of his full lower lip over satin.

He drew her closer, his hand casually holding her fingers. She took one look into his dark eyes, at the sculpted curve of cheekbones, the autocratic nose, and lost her breath.

Shadowed by dark stubble gracing his jaw, a dimple teased. She looked closer. Beneath his thick, black lashes, his eyes focused in two different directions.

"In you, sweeting, would I find truth?"

In her?

Before she could even gasp, his mouth slanted down over hers, and his broad back blotted out the light. She fell into black shadow and reached out to him. She should not allow this, but she was here, and he expected it and—

No. She was Verity. Truth. She wanted to kiss him.

His lips pressed to hers, his tongue parted her lips and slid inside her mouth. She tasted him—delicious was too mild a word!

She tasted brandy, too much brandy, and the warm flavor of him that was so erotically male. His hand cupped her breast. He must know her nipples were indecently erect.

His large body surrounded her, his scent—brandy and shaving soap and witch hazel and the earthy hint of his sweat—washed over her, yet all she wanted was to kiss him deeper. Beneath her fingertips, his shoulders were solid lines of muscle and bone. Daringly, she trailed her fingers toward his neck. She left the almost-propriety of his shirt and touched his bare flesh.

And moaned wantonly into his mouth.

His tongue teased hers, and he toyed with her, letting his tongue thrust lazily in a promise that made her heart hammer and her quim turn to liquid honey.

She went rigid, suddenly uncertain.

He eased back from the kiss, bending forward to feather kisses to her nose, her right cheek, her chin. "Do you want to give me what I want?"

Oh yes, he was drunk. She tried to make sense of his words "W—what is it that you want?"

He stepped back and yanked his shirt out of his trousers. Before the hem could settle around his hips, he pulled his shirt off, over his head.